The Knuckl.

"*Knucklehead* is a great eye-opening read. Vachon weaves a story that is both impossible to believe and impossible to ignore—it is ridiculously funny and frighteningly real.

Be prepared to learn, to laugh and yes, to worry about what's happening behind the cyber world curtain."

—**Rick Roth,** Former Global CEO, Ogilvy Action

"This novel's topic is so important: We stand in the middle of a storm—not just a geopolitical one, but a cyberpolitical one. It feels as if no one trusts anyone anymore, and suspicion and confusion reign across our delicate cyberworld. Which way do we turn?"

—**Eugene Kaspersky,** Hacker-hunter and Chairman of Kaspersky Labs

"Craig Vachon has created a thoroughly entertaining international spy thriller that travels the globe with political intrigue in the current hot spots. He discusses the challenges and opportunities behind some of the newest high-tech advances and gives a behind-the-scenes look into the investment world of Silicon Valley. The author's deep knowledge of places and situations makes you wonder if the book really is fiction as the author claims. Ralph is a loveable character who I felt connected with from the first chapter of the book. *Knucklehead* is a fun, exciting, moving, and thought-provoking ride that literally had me laughing out loud at some points."

—**Greg Post,** Former Regional President of Sprint

"It's all too rare to find a fun, seat-of-your-pants, literary romp like this. I got wonderfully lost with Ralph in the many cultures as he travels around the planet. And kudos for the author in the entertaining explanation of how investors examine entrepreneurial ventures for investment. As an investor myself, a lot of the anecdotes and stories resonated with me...wonderful reading."

—**Raz Zia,** Former MD at Goldman Sachs and MD at Aldrich Capital

"*Knucklehead* is like being shot out of an Ethernet cable lined with exotic travel and baroque paintings and landing on a sea of electricity."

—**Peterson Conway,** PayPal Mafia

"A wonderfully exciting and comedic tale of Ralph, a venture capitalist and unlikely spy that leads us through an international tale of intrigue while unlocking the secrets of Silicon Valley. Fascinating and an absolute joy to read!"

—**Tim Martin,** CEO of LifePrint

"A terrific yarn with characters just absurd enough that they might be fictional, but not quite so absurd that the reader is left wondering who they really are or who they were based on—and that maybe she/he ought to be paying more attention to the promise and perils of technology. A fun and funny fictional look behind the Silicon Valley curtain at a world or misfits, schemers, brilliant visionaries, and accidental heroes."

—**Peter Loge,** Associate Professor, School of Media and Public Affairs at The George Washington University; Director, Project on Ethics in Political Communication; Author, *Soccer Thinking for Management Success;* Former senior staffer in the House, Senate, and Obama administration

"If a major amusement park ever wanted to build the ultimate spy adventure ride with mystery, suspense, white-knuckle twists and turns, comedy, and romance, *The Knucklehead of Silicon Valley* would be the perfect blueprint. Not only did I love the ride, but as with all great adventures, I learned a hell of a lot. I thought I knew what went on in the mythological land of Silicon Valley, but I had no idea how insane it truly is."

—**Bill Glasser,** Former Supervisor and Producer at Fox Television's "America's Most Wanted."

"Fans of Neal Stephenson's opus, *Cryptonomicon,* will thrill to Craig Vachon's new exposé of the wild west of our digital era. As Stephenson introduced us to the beginnings of this era, Vachon's adventure recounts peak Silicon Valley. Vachon's protagonist, Ralph, glides into and out of a series of fantastic predicaments that might be less fictitious than we think.

"This adventure is a good one, and you'll enjoy every minute of it."

—**Michael Gilligan,** President of Seek Common Ground

"A modern day 'Being There' – if Peter Sellers' Chauncey were a Silicon Valley tech investor! You will not only be thoroughly entertained but thoroughly educated as to the insanity that is the world of IPOs, internet privacy, and the potential of high-tech's misuse."

—**Brian Frazer,** Author of *Cartoons With my Dad: How Art Drew Us Together*

"This thriller takes us through an insider's view of high-tech Silicon Valley culture, authentically capturing its brilliance and ambition, as well as its silliness and hubris. Smart and captivating, it follows the protagonist who is at times ham-fisted and dim, other times deft and clever, through a fascinating journey of intrigue along the cutting edge of tech. Filled with humor, suspense, whimsy, wit, and moments of pure heart, this read is fascinating, educational, and a heck of a lot of fun."

—**Jordy Berson,** Former Head/CEO, BitTorrent

"Don't let the title fool you. *Knucklehead* is as smart as its seemingly befuddled hero is sly—a fast-moving, globe-hopping yarn woven from big money, killer tech, and an "Is he or isn't he?" spy whose formidable friends and powerful enemies make this highly-original story tick with the precision of a Philippe Patek watch."

—**Scott Stiffler,** Editor in Chief at Chelsea Community News, *ChelseaCommunityNews.com*

"An exciting look at the worlds of cybersecurity and international espionage. The author takes you on a wild ride through the underworld of technology as you jump from country to country meeting fascinating characters. A must read if you are into spy novels or just interested in how technology can impact our lives."

—**Anthony Gioeli,** Silicon Valley Entrepreneur and author of *International Business Expansion*

"If 'Tech/Spy/Finance/Comedy' wasn't a genre before, it is now! *Knucklehead* is a page-turning misadventure full of tech investors, shameless karaoke, and seemingly endless air miles.

"It is a delight to follow Ralph Gibson (who may or may not be a spy) in his globe-trotting tale of Silicon Valley financing, where 'billions' and 'international security' are daily issues and Ralph seems to know what he's doing, but clearly doesn't.

"*Knucklehead* is not a travelog, it's not a spy story, it's not a tech thriller... or is it? Ralph's just this guy, who happens to travel the world, is involved in billion-dollar investments... and may or may not be a spy.

"Loved it! You don't expect this book. A spy story without guns, explosions, or poison? A tech thriller where karaoke plays a central role? A comedy with the fate of the world in its hands? A hero who has no idea who he works for? Count me in!"

—**Brett Dewey,** Former Writer and Producer for "Saved By The Bell"

The Knucklehead of Silicon Valley

A Novel

G. Craig Vachon

Los Angeles   California

Published by:
New Galleon, an imprint of Genius Book Publishing
31858 Castaic Road, #154
Castaic, CA 91384
GeniusBookPublishing.com/newgalleon

ISBN: 978-1-947521-13-1

190912

*Dedicated to my lovely wife Rhonda and our ongoing
pursuit of learning and laughter.*

The Knucklehead
of Silicon Valley

Epilogue v.2.0
Very Early This Morning

" - Matt & I need ur for this meet in 15 mins in the private bar at the top of Wynn. Can U join us right now? Worth ur . Big "

"Faaaak," he grumbled as his suite was only 36 floors higher than his present position and he knew he'd be asleep in 10 minutes if given the opportunity. Ralph had seventeen 30-45 minute meetings that day including eleven coffees. He had wanted to head to his hotel bed about five hours earlier, but had gotten a few invites to stop into parties and be seen. Two-thirds of Silicon Valley was in attendance that week, and everyone was looking to cut deals. He was in the lobby of the Bellagio when his phone buzzed with that last SMS.

It was the week of the Consumer Electronics Show, and like every hotel bar on the Strip in Las Vegas, the geeks, nerds, wonks and wannabes were crammed into the space like bubbles in a champagne bottle even though it was nearing 2.30 AM.

The $5,000 per-night working girls didn't even notice Ralph now that he was past fifty years of age. They were only focusing on catching the attention of young hipster men rich from their stock option grants who used wax in their beards.

He punched in a request for an Uber and got lucky. A driver was just dropping off at the hotel. Ralph was in a car in less than ninety seconds.

When he got to the entrance of the private bar at the top of the Wynn, the huge bouncer shook his head "no." Ralph understood, as he was not what the bouncer of an ultra-hip club was trained to admit into the hallowed halls. "Lumpy," "goofy," "buffoon" and "teddy-bear" were all the kind-words used to describe Ralph's looks. And this bar was so cool, it didn't even have a name. Ralph was sorely tempted to blow off this meeting, but he owed this friend a favor as the last time they met he had made a decidedly poor impression. Adam owned a number of small start-ups and had built a few private social networks for some mega-celebrities. On a night when Ralph hadn't been paying much attention, he asked someone named Lady Gaga if she'd be kind enough to grab him an iced tea from the bar. The encounter didn't go over well for all involved.

Adam rescued him from the bouncer's glare. "Sorry, he's with me." The house-sized bouncer actually bowed as Adam pulled Ralph through the gateway.

"Okay, the meeting is going down in about five minutes. Matt needs us to look relaxed, but serious and tough, like we're his money men."

"Do I need to know anything else? Like who we are talking to?"

"Some Bitcoin dude." Adam nodded like Ralph should know the type. "Matt wants us to look relaxed."

"But serious and tough—got it."

Ralph got the bro-hug from Matt and was given a seat next to him on the couch. Matt was the former president of a unicorn now valued in the hundreds of billions. They had known each other for fifteen years, but Matt could pass for being in his thirties, and Ralph could not. There were two bottles on the table: an unopened premium vodka that looked like a crystal skull and a bottle of $400 Fillico water.

Only thirty seconds later, the expected guests arrived. Ralph took a mental picture. Dark hoodies and jeans. Forced-casual nonchalance. Some bro-hugs, some fist bumps. The waitress poured some of the expensive water. Not the vodka. The visiting CEO slouched deeply in his overstuffed chair. He kept his hands on his thighs, as when he lifted them, they had a slight shake. Ralph did his best to look both relaxed and tough.

There was some idle chatter, but that stopped abruptly when Matt spoke. "Well, I am thinking … five."

If there were blood pressure cuffs on everyone within listening distance, Ralph was sure that they would have all alarmed at the spikes. One of the visiting lieutenants inadvertently sucked in a lungful of processed casino air through his teeth. He swore under his breath, staring hard at Ralph. Sweat glistened on foreheads. Nearly every eye turned to the slouching CEO. He was looking only in his lap.

After sixty time-bending seconds where Ralph was sure no one within a hundred meters had even dared to breathe, the thirty-something-year-old CEO looked up and said, "No." His voice squeaked only slightly.

Matt nodded solemnly while staring hard at his opposite.

The visiting CEO did likewise. He took one deep breath and pushed out of his chair. His team followed. There were muttered swear words and threats from the team that was walking away. In thirty more seconds, the bar ratcheted back up to its normal hubbub and people were already trying to get to the chairs that had been vacated.

Matt and Adam exchanged a discouraged look. Matt signaled the waitress and asked her to charge the bill to his room.

"Hey, I am going to head up to my room and start the lawyers on the paperwork. Ralph, you were fucking huge. Seriously, I owe you. Thanks so much," Matt said while giving him a bro-hug.

"Matt, you want us to mess with them some? Ralph and I could organize some chaos. Shut the site down for a few hours maybe? StuxNet his ass," Adam suggested.

"Nah, thanks gents. Just gonna go hang in my room and lick my wounds. Let's let them go—for now."

Matt walked off to the elevators after another set of bro-hugs. Adam grabbed Ralph and asked him to follow him to the men's room.

Adam was still shaking, the adrenaline only just starting to wear off. "Dude, I probably should have given you more of a head's up."

"Should I ask what just happened?"

"Well, you'll probably notice that that meeting will be on the front page of the Wall Street Journal in the morning. And the reporter who was over your left shoulder may mention that you were there."

"What did we just see?"

"Standard shotgun negotiation. Matt owns about 30% of that Bitcoin wallet site. He had the option to buy the whole thing. He had to value the company and bid the price he'd be willing to pay. If he bid sufficiently, he'd pay the other investors for their 70% share. But Matt bid $5 billion and the CEO said 'no.' So now the CEO and his pals have seven days to pay Matt $1.5 billion for his 30%."

"Holy shit." Ralph shook his head as they were in adjoining urinals and Adam fiercely broke wind. "$1.5 billion? With a 'B'? And Matt's disappointed? What did he invest?"

"Not sure. I think he invested a couple of million about a year and a half ago. But he thinks it'll be worth five or ten times the amount he bid within the next twelve months."

"And what was I doing there?"

"You and your gray hair were the potential money, man."

"That's insane. I am not able to write a check like that."

"Yeah, but people know you and Matt and they think you might be the kind of people that could raise that kind of money."

Ralph shook his head to clear it. "And why did you tell Matt we could mess with the Bitcoin site? Those cryptocurrency dudes use serious defensive measures."

"Because you're the bigger badass. Your mojo is strong."

"Dude, I'm a minor-league social hacker with some interesting tech friends. That's all."

"That might be what you want everyone to believe. Sure. And I'll keep your secrets, but only if you can teach me how to do your 'tough face.' That's so on point."

Ralph rolled his eyes and glared at Adam.

"That's it. Fucking awesome. How do I do that thing with your eyes?"

Adam was mimicking Ralph's tough face in the bathroom mirror when Ralph left the men's room heading for the Wynn's lobby while requesting another Uber pick up.

Remarkably, the Uber was just pulling up as he got to the portico. He opened the door, said hello, and jumped into the passenger seat without even glancing at the driver. The driver smiled, took off her ball cap and sunglasses. Her near-fluid blue-black hair slipped to her shoulders.

"Sweetheart, you're the shittiest spy I know. Are you by chance busy tonight?" asked one of China's foremost intelligence agents as she held a micro-needle pen to his jugular.

1974

"Ralph, have you decided what you want to be when you grow up?"

"An honest, brave, compassionate human being, like my mom. Who also skis really often."

"No ... I mean, how do you want to sell your labor?"

"I don't understand."

Chapter 1
Winter 2016

And their eyes just glazed over, Ralph thought for the umpteenth time this week. *Authoritarian regimes inevitably believed they could utilize technology for their own whim. And more often than not, their whim involved attempting to control their populace—or better yet, their neighbors' populace.*

He was speaking with the telecommunications minster's top aide. The minister was also in the room but was three chairs away and feigning deep thought. He was probably catching a quick nap. The aide was young and probably thought he was being sly—with this obviously dim-witted, bloated, unkept, sockless American.

"The imaging of these micro-satellites can be aimed anywhere we want?" the aide asked. "Even to places that may not want us to aim them—places like, say, Iran?"

Ralph was pleased this particular question finally came to light. It was his opinion that this guy had been laser-focused on this one question from the start. And many of the times when Ralph made this same pitch, the "key" questions took hours to appear.

"Sure. But with that said, this is an open marketplace. The bidder willing to pay the highest price will get to control where these six hundred micro-satellites are focused."

"And you're absolutely certain that we can focus these satellites *any*where we want. *Any*where? And no one can block you?" The aide was almost giddy in his excitement.

The minister cleared his throat. For the first time, he addressed Ralph directly. "What will it cost to ensure that our neighbors do not have the opportunity to see into our sovereign nation?"

"Minister, of course our neighbors will never be allowed to …" The obviousness of his objection suddenly hit him. The aide angrily turned toward Ralph.

The minster continued. "Excuse my naive co-worker. In our culture, nepotism is expected. But this one spends all his time spending his father's money on Italian cars and sheesha, and not enough time actually thinking."

"Uncle!" The nephew-slash-aide was visibly hurt and surprised.

"Why are you really here, Mr. Gibsen? I assume it wasn't for the rude groping you received while entering the building? Although there are some who find that enjoyable."

Ralph had been stripped and body cavity-searched prior to being allowed entry into this facility. All of Ralph's electrical kit was currently plugged—and disgorging their data—into various devious-looking machines at the security checkpoint.

Ralph was a small investor and board of director member of this micro-satellite company. The company didn't have a single "bird in the sky" yet, but the plan was to launch hundreds of low-cost, off-the-shelf component-enabled, 3D-printed micro-satellites in the next few months. The satellite imaging industry was about to be disrupted with this new Silicon Valley approach. Over the last thirty years, large companies would hire retired NASA engineers to build huge satellites with triple redundancies and diamond-coated bespoke integrated circuits at a cost of six hundred million dollars. These decades-old designs were slow and had computing processing power from the Reagan administration. Ralph's investment was buying ICs and all the electrical/optical components off Amazon.com and 3D printing the micro-satellite containers. These shoe-box-sized satellites could do all the imaging, processing, and analytics of the bigger satellites, but cost $250,000 apiece and were software upgradeable, like an iPhone. So while the big companies could afford putting a new satellite in orbit every four or five years—at more than $600M/unit—Ralph's team could put up 600 satellites over the next six months, for 25% of the price of a single dinosaur satellite. And now Elon Musk's SpaceX, the Russians, Indians, Chinese, New Zealanders, and others were putting these micro-payloads into orbit about every seven days, on average. Ralph's company had even set up a website where people could bid on the location and time they wanted to capture their real-time imagery. Want to see what the frost damage is in the Florida citrus groves? As a commodity trader, you might. And as long as you were the high bidder, you could get 31cm resolution to know if you were buying or selling orange juice futures.

"I'm here because I wanted to be sure to show you this opportunity. To judge your interest," Ralph said. He was in the geographic region to show a half-dozen oil-rich ministers this same opportunity. "As you probably surmised, some of your neighbors are interested in buying this imagery service in bulk. There's also the possibility of silent investment."

The nephew-aide was keen to redeem himself. "And if we invest, do we get to determine where these damn things are pointed? Or better yet, do we get a back door to see where others want to look?"

"No." Ralph stared into the young man's eyes.

"No? Do you realize …?" The aide snarled menacingly. "Do you realize the punishment for sedition under Sharia law is death?"

"I am not aware of all aspects of Sharia law. But I am aware that technology is amoral. A kitchen knife is most useful in preparing a family's dinner. And it can also be used in harming another human being. But the knife itself is without morality. This satellite imagery is the same."

As the young aide huffed and geared up to tear Ralph a new hole, the minister raised his hand.

"Of course we are interested in pre-purchasing bulk imagery, as well as perhaps investment. My aide will arrange to collect your paperwork and begin the payment process."

The nephew-aide was aghast. "But sir, won't we demand our own paperwork and terms. This is how we always do business with Western companies …"

The Minister didn't respond. He stared at Ralph and apologized. "My nephew still doesn't understand. You won't be allowing for negotiations, I imagine. At least, that's what my counterpart from Jordan told me last night over sheesha. Isn't that so?"

"I have the commercial paperwork for you to sign. We'd appreciate a purchase order from you within the next forty-eight hours. I also have the investment documents for you to review. We will take discussion and your guidance. But please be aware, these investment terms have already earned a bid from another sovereign wealth fund in the region. So unless your offer is better, we will not want to waste your time."

The aide switched to Arabic, pleading to his uncle. "This camel fucker is too stupid to be a real threat to us,

Uncle. Shouldn't we investigate if this company is for real? He isn't even wearing stockings."

Ralph tried to hide a smile.

"*Muqiat al jamal.*" The minister smiled, shaking his head. "Our sock-less guest understands Arabic, and probably a dozen other languages."

Ralph realized they were talking only to each other, as if he wasn't in the room.

"I really don't speak dozens of languages," he admitted. "I understand only a few. I recognized '*mugiat al jamal*' because, well, it seems I get called that many times when I visit the region. It's not a very nice thing to say."

"No it is not." The minister started to laugh, and his laughing grew heartier. Soon Ralph joined him. The aide remained red-faced.

"Mr. Ralph, would you care to join me for some tea? My nephew can't join us."

The aide looked confused.

"Or, if you have some free time this evening, I'd love to have you over for dinner and meet my son. He wants to work in Venture Capital in the Bay area. Perhaps he can bend your ear and ask you a few questions …?"

"I'd be delighted to join you for dinner. Will you have a car pick me up from my hotel?"

"Of course. At 8 PM."

They stood and walked toward the elevators.

"If you will allow me to excuse myself, my aide will take you downstairs and return your electronic equipment. And we'll see you tonight."

The minister started to wander off, then abruptly turned back. "And if it isn't too much to ask, I'd like you to send me your Offering Memorandum for your Clam Pie Growth Fund. I think I'd like to invest in your venture capital fund. If you'd accept my investment."

"Let's talk about it tonight."

The aide corralled Ralph into the elevator. He was still red-faced and perturbed, and he wouldn't meet Ralph's eyes.

Ralph extended the olive branch. "Your uncle was pretty tough on you in there."

The aide didn't acknowledge Ralph's comment. When the elevator opened, he quickly walked to the security desk. He made certain Ralph could see an elaborate show of checking the plug-ins of Ralph's computer and iPhone. In Arabic he said to the desk staff, "Make sure we get everything we can off this asshole's stuff."

Ralph waited patiently. After a few moments, his driver approached him and explained that there were men in suits and badges disassembling the hotel's SUV, looking for something. Ralph merely nodded.

"Is there a coffee shop nearby?" Ralph asked politely.

The aide looked up with disdain.

"Seriously. When you eventually crack that computer and phone's Rijndael Asynchronous 256-bit encryption, you're going to learn that I bought the two items off eBay last week specifically for this moment. I created and adhered my company's inventory sticker onto the computer, so you'd waste your time and energies. The contact list on the phone is for a fifteen-year-old girl in Wilmington, Delaware. She obviously has a crush on an older sophomore boy named Anil. Her poetry is embarrassing. The MacBook computer was used by an Art History major at BU who thought Matisse took hallucinogens to create his masterpieces. So if you persist, you're going to spend an enormous amount of your team's effort, resources, and morale to discover that the teenage girl's Pokémon collection wasn't that inspiring. And when that's all you learn about 'me and my organization' from your … search, what's your uncle going to tell you? And if there isn't a nearby coffee shop, can I ask that you please go fetch me a cup of strong espresso?"

Ralph's storytelling skills were apparently convincing. Muttering something in Arabic, the aide pushed the computer and phone across the desk. Ralph collected his electronics and went outside to the armored limousine, where he helped his driver put the disassembled seats back as they were. Then they quietly drove back to the hotel. On the steering wheel, the driver's hands never stopped shaking.

Chapter 2

On Twitter, Ralph wrote a quick note to Elon Musk, CEO of SpaceX (and Tesla and The Boring Company). "We have faith in you @SpaceX and @ElonMusk—learn, adapt and make the next one awesome. #StartupLessons." Elon Musk might or might not remember meeting Ralph on a few occasions, but to Ralph this show of support in Silicon Valley was important. SpaceX's rocket had just detonated en route to the International Space Station (ISS). The note was retweeted a few hundred times.

Many, many people asked Ralph about working in Silicon Valley and why the "magic" couldn't be replicated elsewhere. It was well known that forty percent of the world's Gross Domestic Product was from companies that didn't exist before the year 2000, and Silicon Valley was a big part of that.

Was Silicon Valley born from the freewheeling, anything-goes hippies? Maybe. Did California attract folks with a different risk profile? Sure. But Silicon Valley was unique because it brought together like-minded people who had a desire to make the world a better place, a higher tolerance for risk—failure was a rite of passage—and where everyone was playing for equity. There was a guy in Palo Alto who would leave his flyer on every expensive car windshield offering to detail the car for $0 cash and twenty shares/options of the company they worked for—any company.

Ralph's small investment company was born when he was given a job with a modest cellular start-up company after returning to the U.S. from Japan. Over the following few years, Ralph said "yes" to many different challenges and locations. In ten years, he had lived in twelve cities throughout the world, and one day the little start-up got sold to AT&T for $24 billion. While Ralph's role never exceeded a lieutenant's, or maybe a captain's, the learning and rewards were sufficient. After AT&T bought the company, Ralph was offered other innovative roles—with equity—and soon found himself back in Japan, as well as India, the UK, China, and finally Silicon Valley. Ralph was never accused of being the smartest person in the room, but he was persistent and occasionally creative. His questions often made people think harder than they might normally. And he said "yes" often. Especially if it meant jumping on a plane at a moment's notice, foregoing all else.

Over the years, his peers, friends, and mentors often asked Ralph for advice on some small potential angel investments. And over time, Ralph had built up a very modest war chest to make some of his own investments. And thus, without any fanfare, he launched "Clam Pie Growth Fund."

Clam Pie made small investments in tech companies that tried to make the world a better place. Ralph was often asked how he came up with the name for his investment firm. He told people the truth. Other VC firms choose grandiose names like Accel, Sequoia, True, Atlas, Endeavor, Intel, Velocity, and A-to-Z. To Ralph, each sounded like they were trying too hard. With Clam Pie, he went with the anti-hubris approach—under-promise and over-deliver. (Plus, his mom's clam pie was his favorite comfort food.) Most people rolled their eyes when Ralph handed them a business card, but a few were willing to listen and learn if there was anything more behind the irreverent name.

These investments are called angel or seed investment because typically they are the first money into a start-up business. These raw, new companies have typically progressed beyond merely having an idea for a new product or service. The founders have recruited teams, completed some or most of the product, and have some customer acceptance. Traditional VCs typically only invest when the (uniquely differentiated) product has launched, there is a full team working on building the company, and there is some demonstrable customer traction/revenue. Ralph's specialty was finding three entrepreneurs working in a spare bedroom or garage who were trying to right a wrong that impacted at least a billion people. Some called these folks "social entrepreneurs." Ralph didn't. He just knew he liked to hang out with these types.

Over time, almost all of Ralph's investments started with him earning trust with these inspired entrepreneurs. He listened well. He asked decent questions. He occasionally pushed hard to understand what truly motivated these builders. What Ralph never did was offer advice without first being asked for it. He thought that the quickest way to lose someone's trust was to tell smart people "You should …"

And at some point, entrepreneurs did ask him for advice. And instead of answering them with words, Ralph answered them with actions. When working with entrepreneurs, his two most common phrases were "What can I help you with?" and "Let's …" It implied—and promised—that Ralph was willing to get his hands dirty.

One such entrepreneur sat in front of him today. They were in Ralph's favorite coffee shop. The founder wanted to use piezo ceramics strips to harvest the tides along the coasts. The idea was interesting, but Ralph knew of a few other groups working on a similar solution. Ralph knew within the first ninety seconds that he wasn't going to be able to help this entrepreneur. Sometimes startups were a wrong fit for what Ralph was trying to achieve. Ralph listened carefully, took notes, and asked clarifying questions. At the end of the forty-minute presentation, Ralph broke the news to the entrepreneur.

"Most VCs look for the same five criteria when considering investments: 1) Team 2) TAM 3) Sustainable differentiation 4) Scale and 5) Problem being solved. I'm just the same when I evaluate if I can help efforts like yours."

The entrepreneur nodded but was clearly confused.

"Can I spend a few minutes telling you what we look for in detail when we evaluate investment opportunities like yours?"

"That'd be great."

"First and foremost, we look for very strong teams currently working on the effort. This is by far and away the most important criteria to determine if a start-up might succeed. Most VCs like myself try to find great teams of entrepreneurs that have already worked together to some success—and some failure—in their histories. I say this because most people tend to learn much more from failures than from successes. We like to invest in the type of person that learns—and is also persistent. We like diversity and teams that have balance—too many detail-oriented or visionaries is never a good thing. Having a team that was self-actualized is really important."

"I have to have funding before I can put together a core team," the entrepreneur explained.

"I understand your thought process, but as venture investors, we want a leader who has already convinced a core group of business and functional leaders to work on the problem to be solved. The leader of the effort needs to have created a team based on the merits of the problem and solution."

"That's really difficult. The people I want to recruit all have bills to pay. They can't work for nothing."

"Yeah. I understand what you're saying, but the team members can work in their spare time. They can find consulting gigs where they can earn a living while also working on creating and building the new company."

"That's asking a lot."

"Yes, but an entrepreneur is asking for someone to invest hundreds of thousands or millions of dollars. The risks are huge. And no one who has been successful will ever tell you it was easy."

The founder nodded dejectedly.

"And just so I am crystal clear, before you approach another angel or VC investor, I'd strongly suggest you find your team and start working on your solution."

"Are all investors so inclined?"

"Pretty much—especially regarding teams. Bringing a cool idea to investors twenty or thirty years ago had a slim, but possible chance of being funded. Today, that's impossible."

"Hence, if I bring a full team to you, will you fund us?"

"Well, let's talk about the other investment aspects we consider. Total addressable market or TAM is a critical item, because the larger the TAM, the larger the upside in terms of revenue and company valuation potential. Many entrepreneurial endeavors often miss the mark on their first product. 'Pivots,' or radically changing business models, are common occurrences when start-ups miss the mark with their first efforts. If an entrepreneurial team starts with a huge TAM as its focus/audience, it can pivot to a subset. If it starts with a small TAM, then it's nearly impossible to create a business that can succeed by focusing on an even smaller subset. From my perspective, you need to take your idea to a few potential customers to learn if they'll pay for the electricity you generate. If you build these shoreline plants, and no one wants to purchase the electricity, the effort will fail."

"That's not realistic. If we tell people about our plans, they may try to steal them."

"Well, that's a great segue into the third aspect. 'Sustainable Differentiation' is the concept that you can protect your nascent business from large companies copying your idea. This is a tried and true problem/occurrence in Silicon Valley. In fact, there are Venture Capitalists today that make their bread by copying successful start-ups. This is because the second and third players into a burgeoning space are often the first to get acquired quickly by larger, more well-established public companies, who are often eager to optically enter into new product space and, just as often, appreciate the opportunity to acquire a young 'hip' team. So in my opinion—and remember, I am often wrong—your idea needs to be something you can protect, either through intellectual property, like a patent, or via some other method. So that's something else you'll need to work on."

The entrepreneur was questioning if this visit with Ralph was such a good idea. "What else should I know?"

"Scale is about building something once and selling it a billion times. I personally don't fund companies that provide services, because the day the team takes a day off, the company/investment isn't making money. As Warren Buffet is apt to say, 'If you can't find a way to make money while you sleep, you will work until you die.' And your concept is terrific with its opportunity to scale. The ocean's tides are forever. So long as your team can manufacture the solution efficiently with strong resiliency, I believe your company is fund-able with regard to this aspect."

The entrepreneur face gained a little color.

"And finally, start-ups must solve a significant re-al-world problem. One that people are willing to pay re-peatedly to solve. There are Silicon Valley companies that made boat-loads of money selling 'virtual cows' in smart-phone games, but I'm not one to invest in those compa-nies or those teams. With that said, I can say unequivocal-ly that your nascent company solves a real-world problem. Humans need electrical power. And as long as your team can produce power cheaper than the solar or wind com-petitors, I think your concept passes this aspect as well."

The entrepreneur left Ralph's office and wasn't thrilled with the fact that they had a boat-load more work to do to earn investment. But he was somewhat comforted in knowing what specific items he had to accomplish to be considered in the future. Ralph thought that this specific entrepreneur had a less than ten percent chance of accom-plishing the tasks Ralph had suggested, but he was often pleasantly surprised when he was wrong.

More often than not, founders came to Ralph for men-torship and investment, and he had to turn them away because they didn't meet his criteria. But because he was nice about it and would spend time explaining his strate-gies, they often became his friends, and a few became successful entrepreneurs. And occasionally they—and often their friends—would later invest in Clam Pie. Without much effort, and too often without knowing very much at all about his investors, Clam Pie became an entity that delivered, in Ralph's mind, "modest"—and occasionally exceptional—returns. And over time, these investors became part of the sourcing mechanism of new deals for Ralph and Clam Pie. It was a self-propelling system.

ↄↄ

As usual, Ralph was running late to the airport. It was raining hard in São Paulo and the streets were flooded. Ralph's Uber driver was laughing maniacally as he drove quickly through the foot-deep puddles.

Ralph had spent three days working with a potential partner, convincing them to try a new type of leather. One of his portfolio companies had created a cultured leather. This product started as a Petri dish soup of a combination of stem cells and DNA from cows, and then arranged via a CAD CAM file and a 3D printer. The investment was based on the premise that if the bovine population grew at the same vector as the human population, the human race would all be dead of methane poisoning within the next fifteen to twenty years. The cultured leather was true leather in both form and function but didn't harm a cow. The new leather also didn't require land, water, feed, a vet, waste management, transportation, a slaughterhouse, or a process to handle wastage—because you only printed the exact amount of leather you need.

Most of Ralph's meetings with potential partners or customers were predominantly spent convincing his audience of the viability of the product. And inevitably, the potential partner or customer would have a designated naysayer in the meeting, whose job was to shoot holes in

Ralph's pitch. Ralph loved naysayers. Without them, his presentation would be remarkably dull.

One of the first things he did in his pitch was to set a trap for the naysayer. It was important for Ralph to know who had that role. So Ralph would very often plant a known mistake on the top of page two. A naysayer often gets off on finding mistakes and pointing them out to the assembled masses, usually to show their boss how they are paying attention and are the smartest person in the room.

Ralph would apologize profusely for his knuckleheadedness, and then try to place the rest of the players in the room. Who did the boss trust in terms of their opinions? Who was asking the important questions? Who was an influencer and who was a champion? Who had something to gain or lose with this pitch? Who respected their co-workers and who didn't? Ralph believed he could read the room's interpersonal relationships and use this information to better his pitch. Aristotle's maxim of understanding your audience and adapting your message to meet their needs in order to be persuasive was never far from Ralph's mind.

∾

Ralph was really lame when it came to details regarding things he didn't care much about. In an airport recently, the check-in counter asked if he had a frequent flyer number with their—less-frequented—airline. He pulled out his phone, checked his contacts, and learned he did. He gave the check-in specialist the number. She gulped and told him he could use the first-class check-in area. In the lounge, with two hours to spare, he decided to look up the details of his account. He wasn't able to log in, because he needed to provide the last-known address he used with the account. He attempted five or six addresses, which would have taken him back eight or ten years. Nothing worked. He then employed the customer care rep in the lounge. She needed the same info. Ralph couldn't remember the last time he accessed the account. The agent knew his frequent flyer number but couldn't let him know or access any of the data until he could validate he was who he said he was. Ralph thought that was pretty silly but refrained from telling her so.

"Are there any other methods of validating the account?" Ralph asked.

"Well, can you tell me the last four trips you've taken on the network?"

Ralph dug deep into his calendar and, with some effort, provided her the details she needed.

When Ralph was finally granted access to the account, he learned he had 1.47 million miles, and had last made changes to his address on the account nearly thirty-five years earlier.

వ⁊

Ralph was typically the first person in line for breakfast at every hotel. He spent about 150-180 nights a year in international hotels. And jet lag was an old and dear friend. Rather than fight it, Ralph embraced it. He'd wake as soon as the first gray light on the horizon appeared. In a new city, the area immediately surrounding his hotel was always of curiosity. Where were the coffee shops, the subway entrances, the taxi stands, the convenience stores? Was there a park or museum or library close by? A pharmacy? A laundry?

Being first in line for breakfast meant he got to know the hotel team and waitstaff. He made extra effort to make them feel his appreciation for their contributions. He'd ask everyone their name. He'd ask questions about their favorite restaurants and hangouts. He'd learn their passions and hobbies. He'd compliment their English skills, and learn how to say a few simple phrases in their home language. On more than a few occasions, Ralph would ingratiate himself to the extent that he earned invitations to join in home cooked meals and funky parties. And he partook of these adventures as often as he could.

☙

When asked what his favorite automobile was, the great humanist and occasional philosopher Richard Petty quipped, not-so whimsically, "rental."

Ralph's commuter convertible was in the shop for slight repairs. When he picked up a rental car, the young agent smartly suggested he "take care."

Within three miles from the rental agency, Ralph watched three hubcaps depart the car. He believed strongly in his driving skills, and was never caught in the slow lane—unless he was passing someone dawdling in the fast lane. After about twenty minutes, his "OnStar" was buzzing. The young agent who had wished him "care" was advising Ralph the car had a tracker, and that the vehicle was self-reporting speeds at greater than 85 MPH. Ralph advised the agent that the car or their system was being hacked.

"Probably the Russians, or Chinese."

The agent told Ralph this was not possible.

Ralph assured the young agent that hacking must, in fact, be the case.

Later when he got to his office, Ralph spent $25 on Freelancer.com, hiring a favorite Russian Black Hat hacker. The hacker spent a few minutes coordinating a very simple and automated DDOS, shutting the local car rental agency down to all internet traffic for the forty-eight hours.

When Ralph returned the rental car the next day, the manager and the young agent apologized profusely for the confusion and alarm they had caused via their On-Star communication. "Our security vendor told us it was a major attack on our system, probably from the Russian military forces."

Ralph was able to nod and keep a straight face, until the manager examined the returning vehicle.

"Where are the hubcaps?"

Ralph explained that the hubcaps were not present when he picked up the car the previous day. "Remember—we discussed this? You noted the missing hubcaps on your office tablet. Just check your computer records."

Chapter 3
Summer 2012

"It's actually pretty simple being a secret agent," he thought for the hundredth time. Hollywood's version of everything, especially espionage, was considerably more naïve than the real world.

His task today was picking up a series of very specific sales receipts, documentable experiences—often ticket stubs and/or digital photos—and various sundries for the Agency. The Agency—it was excruciatingly secret, its actual name had never been spoken to him—employed Ralph in a housekeeping role. Ralph considered himself to be an important part of the espionage process, but fully realized his particular role was decidedly unsexy. No movies would ever be made about Ralph's adventures.

Today for example, Monday, he'd pick up a lunch receipt for two people eating Sashimi in central Singapore—and take a digital picture of the meal in order that someone far more secret/important than him could post the picture as cover onto their social media site. He was also tasked with wearing a blue—Ralph was color-blind so all his clothes were acquired/paired with other clothes picked by his wife—Brooks Brothers V-neck cotton sweater and getting some Shanghai Tang Spring Jasmine perfume on the neck of the it. (He was planning to walk through the Raffles Mall to the fragrance counters to meet this particular task.) Tonight, he'd fly to Kuala Lumpur, Malaysia, for the Agency and deliver a coded message in the form of a PowerPoint Presentation to a team of telecom professionals. His perfumed sweater—including various receipts and business cards—would go to the hotel's laundry and they'd somehow return a brand-new, identical sweater to him. And his work would be done.

At least that's what Ralph wanted to believe. In truth, he wasn't exactly sure he was a secret agent. His imagination was over-large, and even though he did get some strange requests from seemingly bizarre sources, no one had ever told him he worked for the government—for the greater good, he imagined. In fact, Ralph's secret agent life-story was only in Ralph's head, as it allowed him to intellectually accept the good fortune that seemingly followed his every move.

❧

This had been a long business trip. Three weeks on the road. He had started at his home base of Northern California, and then flew to DC, then Beijing, then Delhi, and then Singapore. Tonight and tomorrow he'd do his job in KL and then fly back to Singapore to get a direct flight back to San Francisco. After seven different hotel rooms, and four nights spent on a plane, he was looking forward to getting home to his oh-so-lovely wife, big goofy dogs, and warm cushy bed.

And so too were the three disparate teams of four professionals who were tasked with following Ralph. No one knew exactly why, but it was their mission to capture every moment of Ralph's trip while also ensuring Ralph and each team remained unaware of the next. It was a ballet of Bolshoi proportions.

Chapter 4

When he got stateside, Ralph would have to check into his real job. All this spy stuff was cool but making the world safer really didn't pay the bills.

Luckily, the Agency (at least probably it was the Agency) enabled him, with small but appropriate funding—or the investments were more likely laundered through other investors—to set up a modest angel investment firm that allowed him to pursue his "real" job of assisting small, mission-driven tech founders and their companies to become larger companies. As an angel or seed investor, Ralph had carte blanche to be curious about technology and the world. In addition, curiosity was the basis of a good spy, he rationalized. In moments of truth, Ralph understood that he wasn't really smart enough to be a real operative. Nor was he smart enough to be a real venture capitalist. Those gals/guys had to be very sharp. They were all trained exceedingly well. And it would sure have helped to be damn good looking (e.g., Roger Moore).

Ralph wasn't really any of those things. His training for the Agency—the imaginary name of the imaginary organization that Ralph worked for solely in his imagination—had been a three-day hands-on course when he was twenty-four years old. The class was led by an unassuming sixty-year-old salary-man wearing a thirty-year-old grey polyester suit in a worn-out onsen hotel on the outskirts of Tokyo—Warabi, Saitama prefecture—in 1988. Ralph had never been given a weapon or trained how to use one. He knew of no interrogation, withstanding-torture, or message-passing techniques. His seduction skills were completely lacking, as his close friends and many past girlfriends could perfectly attest. Everything about being an entrepreneur, angel investor, and VC he'd learned via his own mistakes. (And some of those mistakes/lessons had been huge.) After the training, he'd never again seen his instructor, nor either of his two classmates.

But upon reflection, there were actually five classmates when he first arrived in Warabi. They'd seen each other only very briefly. After a very long flight, they arrived to the center individually, had been awoken at sunrise and escorted to breakfast. They sat on old tatami mats and breakfast was served on trays.

Later, Ralph's mother asked him about the training. As the first woman to ever run a YMCA in the 1960s and as the creator of a leadership academy herself—one that was later folded into an Ivy League school—she was naturally curious. Ralph understood.

"We all were seated on the rice mats facing our instructor," he told her. "The room smelled of old wood and polish and was heavily incensed. I remember being so tired. I didn't focus well on that initial encounter. And yet, as our first breakfast, it was memorable. There was no coffee and breakfast wasn't a bowl of Muesli or cereal. It was a live and flopping six-inch black sunfish served on top of a bowl of very hot steaming rice."

Ralph remembered staring at that fish's big eye. It stared back at him. He watched his instructor—who never once introduced himself—stab the fish with his hashi and pick the fish apart. Instinctually, Ralph followed his lead. "I was starving. And I figured if the old man could eat the fish, it probably wouldn't kill me. We were told not to speak. Not to look at each other. No questions were allowed for the entire weekend. When I thanked my breakfast server, I was given the stink eye. But only three of us tried to eat the fish and rice. Two grumbled and asked to be excused. The moderately attractive woman—of course I snuck a peek—with a New York accent explained she was a vegetarian and could never eat this food. The other said something self-important about their past academic career as justification for wanting only 'cooked food.' These two were dismissed from the room with a scowl. The three of us who remained sat in silence for four more hours. I think the instructor was napping, with his head bowed forward. At noon, the server came back in the room with lunch. This is when I first noticed she was blind, and that she used her tongue as a sonar tool. She'd repeatedly cluck her tongue, and could somehow navigate the room with remarkable grace."

He told his Mom, "Lunch was sushi. I'm twenty-four years old, from Boston, and prior to this trip—as you know—I had traveled to the UK only once. I had only tried Japanese food once—a California roll in college—basically in an attempt to impress a girl with my worldliness. I watched our instructor—in my mind, I was calling him Miyagi-san, as it was 1988—grin at our server and devour the first piece. But there was some funky shit on that plate. Nothing I'd ever seen, nothing I could recognize, and nothing that even resembled a California roll. So, I started with some harmless vegetable-looking-minced stuff that was on the side of the wood block/plate. In retrospect, it was wasabi, and as I had placed all of it in my mouth at the onset, I thought I was going to die. My sinuses burned. My nose ran. Tears flowed. Sweat spewed out of my every pore. I had already swallowed the death mixture, and I was aggressively salivating like I was about to puke. I'm sure I turned the same color as the wasabi. But I didn't move. I sat there with my head bowed, and decided to overcome.

"Miyagi yelled at me in Japanese. I had learned only a handful of Japanese phrases on the plane ride from Boston to Japan, so I could only answer that I was sorry. '*Gomen nasai,*' I kept repeating. His tone was condescending, and that kind of pissed me off. He berated me repeatedly. At one point, after what seemed like more than ten minutes, he told me in English to leave. But for whatever reason, I decided not to. Probably because he sounded like your former husband—my father—I decided I no longer felt like I needed to please him. Two men wearing black pajamas and cloth masks came into the room and tried to move me. But I remained—and as you are well aware, when I am anxious, I get sweaty. And with my large-ish ass, the slight Japanese men were not going to move me, unless I let them. After even more Miyagi berating and awkward pushing/pulling from the ninjas, my stomach settled, and I ate a piece of sushi. And, oh my fucking god, it was delicious. Like a warm piece of salted butter without the guilt. So I quickly had another. And then, much to my surprise, the blind server started to laugh. And she laughed hard. She fell/sat down next to me and we all started to laugh. Everyone, even the ninjas, was laughing.

"And then she spoke quietly and urgently, and the two ninjas and Mr. Miyagi-san quickly left the room with heads-bowed deeply repeating, '*Gomen nasai.*'"

❧

For the next two and a half days, Mrs. Miyagi, the blind server, spoke to Ralph and his colleagues in a quiet but urgent voice. She found pillows to sit on, and they all got close enough to sit knee to knee. She smelled of a grandmother's soap and fresh baked cookies. She laughed and cried at her own recounting of stories. She shared her accomplishments and failures. Her loves and mistakes. She imparted wisdom and we were rapt. Ralph later told everyone who would listen that he had fallen in love with a woman fifty years his senior.

Ralph tried to transcribe the first Mrs. Miyagi lecture immediately following the wasabi incident. It went something like this:

"None of us really knows anything. We humans are at best confused bumblers. We bumble about, bouncing from one thing to another. Those humans that try to control the confusion and bumbling get frustrated and angry. They rarely accomplish anything. On the other hand, there is much to be learned from people who can know what direction or outcome they want to travel or achieve, but do not need to know each and every step of the way. Letting go of the desire to control is often rewarded.

"Plans are only worthwhile if they state the desired result, and the many potential ways to achieve that result. But when the unpredictability of unintended consequences happens, even the finest and most well-planned plans devolve into mayhem, confusion, and despair. Never follow a person who thinks they can control the bumble. They follow false gods and are very poor leaders. And they aren't much fun at parties either."

Ralph thought this was wonderful advice, especially under the influence of many evening beers and a few sakes. He slept soundly that first night, warm with the new wisdom and a comfortable buzz. When he awoke in the middle of the night to pee, he watched the ninjas removing two body bags from the facility. He walked drunkenly back to his room and passed out quickly. In the morning, he remembered this very fuzzy scene and convinced himself it could have only been a dream.

そ

It was strange, but Ralph never asked what he was doing there at that onsen near Tokyo. Not once to his recollection had anyone ever mentioned he was training to be a spy. He went to Japan because a large marketing company—the largest in the world—had offered to acquire his first fledgling company about three months earlier, and to employ him in the process. Since Ralph had never had a "real" job, this was an intriguing offer. He had spent the thirty months post grad school attempting to get his tiny speech-writing/advertising/PR/marketing company off the ground, to very little success. In fact, his success was so modest, he had to beg former professors to allow him to teach night courses at any colleges in Boston to keep grocery money flowing. Most only agreed, Ralph figured, because they were willingly a part of his mother's expansive fabric.

It was at one of these institutions that one of his former professors, Ned Hollingsworth, approached him about selling his company. It was a strange encounter, because at this particular university—Harvard—the preponderance of the students were very much smarter than Ralph. And Ralph was certain that his former professor was simply trying to get him to leave the teaching gig because Ralph might have been sleeping with a few of his students.

The discussion went something like this:

"Please don't knock up any of your students, Ralph. It would be embarrassing for me to have that discussion with the Dean. And my daughter is absolutely 100% off limits."

"But…. Understood and agreed, sir."

Hollingsworth's daughter was smoking hot.

"Would you ever consider selling your company and going to work for a large multinational company?"

"Never contemplated it, sir."

"Well, I want you to have lunch with these guys tomorrow. Most of them are former DARPA or MITRE employees and they have some interesting ideas about you and your company. Plus, I think it's time for you to do something new. And by the way, go buy a pair of socks and a pair of leather shoes. Wear them tomorrow."

"Will do, sir."

"And I am serious about my daughter. Dead serious."

Ralph had never heard of either of those organizations and hence had agreed wholeheartedly to a free lunch at a swanky club. The lunch the following day was at the Commonwealth Club, and the three guys who spoke with him were remarkably unmemorable, as was the discussion itself. Ned would have been disappointed, as Ralph didn't own socks or non-canvas shoes and had conveniently forgotten this part of his mentor's advice.

But three weeks later, with no further discussion, his fax machine lit up with an offer to acquire his small company, and for him to join a much larger company in Tokyo. The acquisition price was exceedingly modest, but the salary was a whopping $36,000 per year, plus an apartment. Ralph was over the moon excited, dreaming and planning of his newfound wealth. He said "yes" and soon found himself at the onsen hotel in Tokyo.

☙

On the third and last day of the training, Mrs. Miyagi offered the following synopsis for her students. They were taught the "ALLT" maxim:

a. Adapt (because none of us really knows anything)

b. Learn by being curious and pay attention

c. Laugh (because this will make everything else better)

d. Try to share

She ended the class with "We'll be in touch," and strolled out of the room. The three students and Mrs. Miyagi went separate ways. No one ever knew anyone else's real name. There was no fraternizing. Upon their departure, Ralph picked up a package and learned he would not report to the large marketing company that had purchased his smaller marketing company. The large marketing company had seconded him to Sony Corporation—at the time, the largest technology company in the world. On Monday morning, he would start working at Sony in Gotanda-ku Tokyo.

☙

At no time during this period was Ralph told he had just been recruited into the world of espionage. Ralph's first day at Sony Corp was remarkable only in that he'd been given a fifty-pound luggable computer—the precursor to a laptop—and a desk. But no one spoke even a word to him. He received no instructions. As far as Ralph could tell, he was the only English speaker in the huge office. No one offered him tea, a cigarette—in 1988, everyone in Japan smoked at their desks—or lunch. At dinnertime, Ralph left the office for his new apartment. After spending approximately $75 on Ritz crackers, peanut butter and jelly, and a large beer, he began to grasp that his perceived newfound wealth would be insufficient for life in Tokyo.

On the second day, Ralph found a health club membership card on his desk—he was perpetually forty pounds over his optimal weight, but ideal for a 6'3" lumberjack's frame—and some "Learn to Speak and Read Japanese" software on his computer.

"*Ohio gassai masssoo*," he read out loud. The entire office erupted with a hearty, "*Ohai o gosai masu*," in response, and then en masse returned to their work, without a second glance in Ralph's direction. The second day ended much as the first, but Ralph had finally spoken aloud. It was something of a minor triumph.

On the third day, Ralph decided to start the morning at the gym. He found it confusing, as there were places that allowed shoes and places that didn't allow shoes. And it wasn't entirely intuitive. Ralph had to pay attention. Fortunately, a fellow *gaijin*, Tom Warn, quickly and firmly took Ralph under his wing. Tom was British, a little older than Ralph, and had lived in Japan a few years. He also worked in the same industry.

"Ralph-san, buy some indoor trainers and keep them spotless. You are disturbing the '*wa*' of the gym by wearing your outdoor trainers into the building. And you'll find that the little '*oba-chans*' will non-verbally signal when you misstep," advised Tom.

"*Oba-chans*? And what is *wa*?"

He laughed at his own joke.

"*Oba-chans*—I think the direct translation is 'Grandmothers who like to act like children.' And *wa* is the most important thing in all Japan—it is 'harmony.'"

Ralph did some cardio and lifted a few weights—he was surprised that the weights looked similar to the ones at home in terms of their size/shape, but were lighter than he was expecting. He filed that away for future examination. He felt many sets of eyes followed his every move.

His new friend Tom offered to buy him lunch over the weekend. He suggested they play squash on Saturday morning and then spend the afternoon drinking beer, visiting the communal hot tubs, and discussing the concept of *wa*.

When Ralph got to the office the third morning, he greeted his co-workers with his best though mangled "*o hi o gosaimasu*" and they responded heartily. Then every single employee determinedly looked down and focused on their work. But by this point, Ralph was terribly curious not only what his job was, but also what his office mate's roles were. Curious and skeptical. Ralph watched his co-workers carefully, and was growing suspicious that they spent 90% of their twelve-hour days studying paperwork that seemed to pass from one worker to another. Ralph spent another day writing notes he faxed home to his mother and some friends, describing how he bought items at the grocery store that he wasn't sure he could afford, and wasn't sure any of it was even edible.

"I wish my camera could fit easily in my pocket," he thought, "so I could snap a quick picture of these groceries, develop an instant picture, and then send/share the photo with my friends and family." Maybe they might be able to help him decipher what this unknown food was. But, of course there was no such camera, or way to share like that. Ralph had many far-fetched ideas.

That evening, it was clear that the folks in Ralph's section were planning to do something together. Many whispers, nods of agreement, and then back to their studious demeanor. Ralph was slightly jealous that he wasn't being included in the plans. He was the last to leave the office that evening, and used the opportunity to satisfy his curiosity. While he couldn't read a character of kanji, he was pretty sure that the most recent document that was being passed around and studied was a restaurant menu.

On the fourth day, Ralph again visited the gym, and spent much of the morning watching his first aerobics class—in truth, he was checking out the age-appropriate aerobic teacher in her 1980s bright-colored leotard. She flashed a half-smile at Ralph, but he was absolutely certain she was out of his league. Hiromi was her name. And Hiromi-san was stunning. Ralph didn't consider himself much of a lady's man. In fact, his ego in this regard was extremely modest. It wasn't that Ralph hadn't had many dates with beautiful women—he had. It was that these first dates with attractive/smart/funny women didn't often lead to a second date. Part of the reason was that Ralph was deliberately, ostentatiously unkempt. His idea of fashion was raiding the second-hand store and buying four pair of identical khakis and blue button-down oxfords and wearing them so long he'd wear-through the knees and elbows. Ralph's social skills with beautiful women were also and equally lacking.

And yet, he somehow managed to approach Hiromi after the class and ask her, in his terrible Japanese, if she would like to have coffee sometime. And, remarkably, she laughed and said yes.

Euphoric due to a potential coffee date, Ralph noticed that many of his co-workers were looking slightly worse for the wear. Elbows on the desk, heads forward, and hands grasping heads. By late afternoon, the outgassing of stale booze from nearly everyone was evident. His coworkers didn't even pretend to study documents that day. Ralph tucked this away for further thought and examination.

That evening, Ralph decided he needed a beer. He had noticed a small bar as he walked home each night from his train station. Actually, he hoped it was a bar, but wasn't sure. It smelled of teriyaki chicken, but there was a vintage neon sign that might have been for beer.

He stood before the door that evening and realized that the "bar" probably wasn't. First of all, it was tiny—no more than twelve people would be able to sit in such a small space. Secondly, there was no apparent door. Ralph gently pushed on the area where he thought he'd have designed a door, and it only moved marginally. He could hear voices, but the wood was ancient, and the top half of the area was made of some sort of thick cream paper that let much of the room's light through. He pushed once more, harder, and the wood shifted slightly more. Then a small woman slid the door to the side.

"*Irashaimase!*" boomed voices in unison from inside the small shed-like building. Spooked, Ralph nearly closed the sliding door. But then he took a deep breath and entered the little warm room.

There was only one empty seat in the restaurant, and it was farthest from the door, at the end of a row of chairs facing the bar. The other chairs were occupied with impeccably groomed men, dressed in dark leather and with lots of visible tattoos. Ralph thought it best to walk around these scowling men and not disturb their dinner. But Ralph was not a graceful person, and his large gym bag and grocery bags inadvertently bumped into a number of the men he was trying to slide past. Ralph bowed his apologies and made his way to the empty chair. By the time he was seated, he was the recipient of several harsh stares.

As was often the case in Japan, the gaijin was the center of attention. Not only was he the only non-Japanese in the small yakitori restaurant, he was the only non-Japanese person to ever visit this modest eatery. Every eye was on him, and he felt uncomfortable. Only the gentleman behind the bar steadfastly refused to look at Ralph.

"May I have a beer please?" Ralph asked in his most modest voice.

One of the cultural lessons Ralph would learn later during his life in Japan was that Japanese often prized "wa," harmony. Everything that stood out needed to be pounded down. The ultimate schoolyard insult was: "You're not like the rest of us."

The man behind the bar simply ignored Ralph. It was easier that way. Ralph decided to try his luck in Japanese. He pulled out his "quick phrases" notebook.

"*Beeru ona gashi-masu.*"

The oldest man in the room started to laugh. He was covered in tattoos from head-to-toe. He wore a black leather vest and pants. And was missing a few fingers.

"The owner won't respond to you until I tell him it is okay to do so. Have you any sense at all? You've just walked into a restaurant full of bad-ass Yakuzas and didn't have the common sense to leave when you had the chance."

The laughing man's English was quite good.

Ralph rose to leave. "I am sorry," he said. "*Go men nasai.* I was just looking for a cold draft beer and maybe a quick dinner."

"You're crazy, man. Sit back down. What's in your bag?"

"Just some sweaty gym clothes."

More laughing. "The other bag."

"Well, it was to be my dinner before I stopped off here." Ralph reached into the bag and everyone jumped up. Suddenly there were seven handguns and a machine pistol pointing at his head. Ralph held out an orange roll of Ritz crackers.

The Yakuza boss barked something and, just as suddenly, all the guns disappeared.

"Crackers? You were going to have a dinner of crackers?"

Ralph was still in shock. "Well, I've also got some peanut butter and jelly for the crackers."

More laughter. The English-speaking head Yakuza asked his buddies a question in Japanese. Everyone shook their heads.

"Could you make us a few of those special crackers? My friends have never tasted peanut butter."

Ralph did what any person would do in similar circumstances. He broke out the Ritz crackers, spread ample peanut butter and a little bit of jelly, and started passing them out to everyone at the restaurant. Suddenly there was a large cold draft beer in front of him, followed by a large plate of chicken yakitori. In less than ten minutes, the entire sleeve of crackers was consumed.

"What the fuck?" Tomi-san asked when he learned there were no more Ritz crackers. Somewhere in the sharing of peanut butter and jelly crackers, he had introduced himself. He grumbled something, and two men suddenly rushed from their seats and out of the restaurant.

"Lalf-san, do you need another beer?"

The chicken yakitori was brilliant. The beer perfect. Ralph was beginning to relax and attempted to join in the discussion as best he could. He laughed even when he clearly didn't understand. Tomi-san did his best to warn *Lalf* away from any of the women in the room. "They all have clabs …" he laughed heartily.

The women, who realized they were the brunt of his attention, asked for a translation. When they got it, they all threw spent yakitori skewers at Tomi. There was even more laughter when the two men returned with a case of Ritz crackers, six jars of peanut butter, and six jars of jam. It was 1 AM when Ralph walked/carried a few of the smaller men to their big American Cadillacs. Ralph could hold his beer, and the Yakuza had been impressed.

"We're heading to Nagano for the next few weeks, Lalf-san. When we get back, we need to do this again," yelled Tomi-san. He was still laughing as he smoked the rear tires.

The next morning at the gym, Tom asked, "Are you okay? I think I need to teach you a new Japanese word. *Futsukayoi*. The literal translation is 'second day drunk.' Can I get you anything? Dealing with hangovers is one of Japan's favorite national sports. There are dozens of tools to help."

Ralph was green, but he was young, and after a good sweat he was ready for work. In the locker room after the workout, Tom asked him how he earned his hangover. Ralph relayed the story of the Yakuza and the Ritz crackers. Tom was amazed.

"Ralph, those are some really tough guys. Where did you say they were going?"

"They said they were going to Nagano. Where's Nagano?"

"It's in the mountains to the north. Ralph, you're amazing at this work. Just keep listening."

Ralph had no idea what Tom meant. He wrote it off as perhaps he really was *futsukayoi*.

༄

Back at work on Monday of his third week, Ralph was feeling more comfortable in his role. He still had no idea what was expected of him, but he was given free reign and was starting to look at some of the Sony marketing that was left around the office. Some of it was great. Some of it less so. Ralph used a few notes cards taped to the collateral to remind himself to ask questions about some of the marketing—when/if he found someone to answer those questions.

These were the days of the Japanese economic bubble. The country was basking in enormous property wealth. Sony enjoyed being the number one consumer electronic company in the world. Sony's philosophy was to vigorously innovate, build with top-quality, and assume the customers will come. There was no need to follow the standards of the day… hence they chose Beta vs. VHS. The collective confidence of the Japanese was palpable. Occasionally, the hubris was as well.

Ralph was still unsure of who his boss was. He assumed it was one of the guys near the window. They tended to be older, and his co-workers were deferential to them. Most of the time Ralph simply tried to look busy. He was pretty sure that's what everyone else was doing.

One Tuesday morning, a small older man walked into Ralph's workspace. Everyone leapt from their chairs and bowed deeply. On reflex, Ralph did the same, albeit slightly slower.

"Hi, Ralph. Nice to meet you. How is everything going?" asked the small man in one breath.

"Ah"—longish awkward pause—"fine?"

"I'm sorry it's taken me so long before I could come visit with you. Do you have everything you need?"

"Ah"—another squeamishly long pause—"yes?"

"And your team is working out all right? Your apartment? How are you adapting to Japan?"

"Uhh"—deep breath—"okay."

"That's great, Ralph. I expect many great things from you and the team. Let's meet in two weeks and you can give me a detailed progress update, okay?"

"Hmmm. Sure, but …?"

"Ralph, do you have any questions?" The older, unassuming man had a very kind face and seemed quite genuine.

"Ah, yes. Yes. I do." At that moment, Ralph fought back the flight response and tried to be brave for the next twenty seconds. "Who are you? Are you my boss or might you know who is my boss?" He looked around the room. "And do you know what I'm supposed to be doing here?" These three questions came out as a rushed plea.

"*Ii tone*? What the heck, Ralph? Has no one explained, well, anything to you yet?"

"Uhhhm, no."

The unassuming man began to laugh. A real laugh. A reach for your belly and bend at the waist laugh. Tears streamed down his face.

"So you've been in this office for two and a half weeks and you still don't know what you're doing for work?"

"Well, Mrs. Miyagi told me I needed to be patient and very observant. So I am trying to be patient—waiting for someone to talk to."

"Patience is good, Ralph. But who's Mrs. Miyagi?"

"That's probably not her real name. She never told us her real name. That's just what I decided to call her in my head. She was very wise and I wanted to follow her instructions…."

"Ralph, I have no idea who you're talking about, but let's start at the top. My name is Akio. Akio Morita. I am the CEO of Sony and you work for me. All of these people sitting around you, they work for you."

Ralph was absorbed in the discussion. He hadn't until that moment realized that everyone in the room was glued to Morita-san's every word.

"But I only speak English. Does everyone here understand English?"

"Yes, Ralph. Almost all of them have advanced degrees from the best U.S. colleges. And they've all been sitting here for two and a half weeks waiting for you to give them purpose. These are my hand-selected, special team of intrepreneurs. With you, we have recruited Kaisen engineers, designers, planners, statisticians, and artists. So what do you want to accomplish at Sony?"

"Well, how can I be most helpful?"

"Yes, good. A difficult question. A very thoughtful question. Yes. Your reputation has been well earned. Can you help me understand women?" Morita-san laughed at his own joke. Everyone snickered.

"Ah, no."

"Maybe something less challenging then. Ralph, you understand that Sony spends a trillion yen each year in marketing expense. And when I ask my experts and executives what I get for a trillion yen, everyone says they really can't tell me exactly. I'd like you to tell me exactly what I get for my investment."

"Okay, wow." Ralph shifted seamlessly into brainstorming mode. "Wouldn't it be awesome if you spent 40,000 yen on a press release, or print advertisement, or even a brochure, and you knew exactly what the Return on Investment was on that 40,000 yen?"

"If you like, that's your project, Ralph. Figure that out, and when you do, we'll find something else for you to do."

Chapter 5
2016

Three weeks on the road had taken its toll. D.C., Dubai, Abu Dhabi, London, Oslo, Boston, and the dreaded NYC. Ralph admitted to himself that he was a little depressed. He missed his wife and her wonderful laugh. He missed his big goofy dogs and the comfy over-sized bed and perfect pillows. To add another layer of challenge, the Friday afternoon Uber from The Capitol Grill to JFK airport had taken three hours. The traffic was absurd.

The day started when Ralph was picked up in a new, extra-large black BMW. The driver spoke little to no English, but he was visibly uncomfortable when Ralph requested to sit in the passenger seat, rather than in the back—in the so-called throne chair.

It was the same in every taxi, Uber, or black car that Ralph rode. No matter how culturally awkward it was, Ralph tried to ride up front. A psychologist might say that Ralph suffered from "Imposter Syndrome." Imposter Syndrome is a diagnosis where the "high-achiever" has an inability to accept their achievement, and is persistently concerned they'll be exposed for being less than deserving. Ralph would have bridled at that diagnosis, arguing he wasn't really successful enough to even "feel like" an imposter. In his mind, he didn't really belong in the same company as successful people. And as he was a natural introvert who had to spend a huge amount of his time pretending to be an extrovert, he learned that using excessive amounts of bluff and bluster as cover occasionally worked. But the bluff and bluster only reinforced his feelings of inadequacy. And even though Ralph didn't spend much time thinking about it, when he did he felt it was only a matter of time before he was found out.

This feeling of inadequacy was occasionally well earned. And because he often felt such well-earned inadequacy, Ralph was apt to amplify a story to make himself more interesting. On more than one occasion, he'd been humiliated when the embellishment was exposed.

The first time this had happened was when he was twenty-three years old and had launched his first business. A local newspaper reporter interviewed Ralph and asked him—while looking over her cheaters—what experience allowed him to lead a marketing firm at such a young age.

"Well, along with teaching at the grad school of a prestigious university"—this was technically true, but he had fallen into the job when the school lost its previous teacher to an emergency family issue in a far-off place; Ralph had said "yes" to the teaching role with less than six hours before the first class was to start—"I also have worked with … with some of the top national politicians, helping them with national policy speeches, on a national level."

The truth was much more modest. Ralph had written a few speeches for local and statewide politicians, and had been to the White House as the junior-most assistant to the assistant speechwriter. He had even signed a significant non-disclosure agreement regarding his role.

"Like who?" asked the skeptical reporter. A wry grin formed across her face. She smelled the fear.

Ralph paused, and then said the wrong thing. Before the words were out of his mouth, there was a sheen of sweat on his forehead. The amygdala in Ralph's tiny brain was overly active, trying to decide if this was a fight or flight situation.

A few years later, Mrs. Miyagi would have advised a retreat and an apology. But Ralph hadn't yet met her and learned her wisdom. She would have told him that the awkwardness could be embraced. Taking the long view, moments of awkwardness are momentary.

When the newspaper article came out, the story was not about Ralph's company, as he and his teammates had hoped. Instead, the story was about Ralph's lie. The reporter had done what every good reporter would do. She followed up with the politician, and the politician disavowed any knowledge of Ralph and his claims.

The disappointment in himself, and ongoing embarrassment, stayed with Ralph for many years. But he never fully learned this lesson. At one point in his career, a former boss didn't corroborate some of the accomplishments Ralph had claimed in a job interview. Ralph still got the job because he was able to find another person to corroborate his claims, but the process was ugly and ruined a friendship. On another occasion, a date, Ralph embellished a number of facts about his belief system. When the lovely young lady learned the truth, she was so disappointed that she walked out on their date and never returned any of Ralph's calls.

Each time this happened, Ralph made himself sick with self-loathing. Repeatedly, he vowed to never let it happen again. When it inevitably did, he promised himself he'd never again make such a mistake. And yet, via his own appraisal, Ralph often skated way-too close to public disgrace.

Over time, whenever his peers stepped forward into the spotlight, he took a step back. Yet, because of his debate team experience, Ralph had garnered a reputation for being a gifted speaker, and was often sought out to give talks about the entrepreneurial world—particularly about his pet project of the "importance of privacy."

As a professional, and as a human being, Ralph walked a fine line.

And at this particular moment, Ralph needed to make a scene. He detested having to "OJ" through an airport to make his flight, but he had to do what he had to do. It was messy, with many "so sorry" utterances, but with 10 seconds to spare until they closed the plane's door, he made his flight.

On this flight from nasty New York to the lovely Bay area, he found himself next to an equally road-weary woman of his approximate age. They were both using the warm towels to mop up the sweat. The etiquette in B class flying is a quick nod of acknowledgment and then studied, concentrated silence. If someone wants to talk, they can offer up a question. If the seatmate also wants to talk, they respond to the proffered question and then ask a question of their own. If there is no follow-up question, then no further communication is allowed. These road rules were well established among those who got a good amount of seat time. And don't get Ralph started on rookie B class flyers and their ignorance of protocol.

The woman looked at Ralph, slightly shook her head, and laughed quietly.

"I'm going to guess three or possibly four weeks. And somewhere north of 25 MPH. Am I right?"

Ralph was caught off guard. The question was well within the rules of etiquette, but her question was going to force Ralph into answering with a question, which would in turn allow for further and much undesired discussion. And perhaps more concerning to Ralph's pride was the realization that this stranger may be a very rare, sky-blue unicorn.

"Ah, yeah. About three weeks, including the Middle East. And I'm not sure I understand your comment about 'north of 25 MPH.'"

Ralph was proud of his quick thinking—he hadn't had to phrase his response as a question.

Road warriors have a never-discussed Bushido code of sizing up their seatmates. And unlike that lame Clooney movie, everyone knows that only poseurs focus on airline status. Because any one-year-out-of-B-school-rookie can spend a few months at a big four accountancy and get Global Service status—United Airlines' highest rank. Global Service is based on how much money a flyer spends in a year. And lawyers, consultants, and accountants don't spend their own money when they fly. Flights and hotels are always billed to the client at the highest rate possible— so their 15-20% markup of expenses is always more impactful to their own fees/profit. Experienced flyers focus on only one factor when sizing up their fellow warriors: miles. Ralph had 7.3 million miles flown on his primary airline, and probably had another 2M spread over a few others. He couldn't be sure, but he suspected his current seatmate may out-rank him.

"I just heard of this concept myself only last week. It's new measurement that people like you and I might find of value. And it's simple. Divide the number of miles you've flown and driven since the beginning of the year by the number of hours. That's your average miles per hour. I look at you and I'm guessing north of 25 MPH average. Do the math. It's been about 180 days. That's 4320 hours."

Ralph looked at a few of his airline apps and calculated he had traveled about 120,000 miles in the first half of 2016. "So my iPhone calculator tells me that 120,000 divided by 4320 hours equals 27.77. That's my average MPH?"

"I'm right. You are north of 25. That means that over the last 180 days, you've averaged 27.77 MPH, no matter what you've been doing. Sleeping, eating, showering, meetings in shitty conference rooms. You're averaging 28 MPH. Not bad."

And as much as he could guess the answer, he just had to ask: "You—what's your average?"

"Just north of you." She grinned. "But of course, I've averaged 30 MPH while wearing an underwire bra and pantyhose. So, don't mess with me. I'm badass." With that, she smiled and established the pecking order, flipped on her headphones, reclined her seat, and pretended to sleep.

❧

Ralph sat on planes often enough he had seen every movie, including the international ones. To bide his time, after answering work emails, he'd often give himself creative tasks to make life more interesting: Today's task was to create names for fantastical yoga moves. The first he wrote after visiting the plane's toilet.

1) "The Collapsible Crane:" Peeing in a plane's toilet when you are too tall to get close enough to the toilet. Knees bent and splayed, head hard-angled to the left or right.

The unicorn next to him was now awake, and she laughed out-loud when she saw what he was doing. "Can

I try my hand at some of these?" she asked. Together, they came up with:

2) "Leaping Sleeping Tigers:" On hour nine, trying to get over a sleeping person on the aisle in a lay-flat business-class chair on a long international flight (while keeping one's head held below the baggage racks).

3) "Smashed Origami:" Being taller than 5'5" and attempting to get into or out of a Tesla Roadster.

4) "Beatle on a Frying Pan:" Squeezing past the all-too-handsy uncle/aunt/older cousin who has a just left a long-term bad marriage.

5) "Scoosh Caboose:" Sliding across the compact car's backseat when the Uber arrives and the boss doesn't want to venture into traffic to get to the far-side seat.

6) "Angry Injured Bear:" The three steps after bloodying a stubbed toe when in a strange hotel room and forgetting where the bathroom is in the middle of the night.

7) "Sly De-Creepers:" When boxers or panties ride up too high on an uncomfortable conference room chair, and trying to rearrange without anyone noticing.

8) "Orbital Inhale:" A rare group-yoga move when three or more men over thirty years old all suck in their bellies while smoothing their shirt fronts—to optically lessen the visual presence of their overweighted-ness—when the twenty-six-year-old administrative assistant in a tight skirt walks into the conference room.

9) "Leaky Faucet:" In a bathroom without a mirror, checking your pants for any dribbles after your pee stream went extra innings when you were busy tucking it into the front of your pants, without showing everyone in the bathroom that you might have let a dribble down the front of your khakis.

10) "Kinky Owl:" Pretending to stretch your neck while in a restaurant booth in order to watch the cute waiter/waitress walk away with your order.

At the end of the flight, the two B class warriors were giggling. By the end of the flight, they had connected via LinkedIn and promised to keep in touch.

Chapter 6
2016

The Tool

Ralph was neither a famous investor nor entrepreneur. But he went to many events and met people who were decent investors and capable entrepreneurs. As such, he often got off-the-record requests from people he saw at these events—the tech press. Two London journalists, who had grown bored of the TED Talk format, had suggested that Ralph join them at a FiRe (Future in Review) conference.

The FiRe conference had been established a few years earlier when another journalist, a futurist, and a few science fiction writers were wondering how they could best improve TED Talks. They determined that the limitation of a TED Talk was that there was often little for the audience to "do" with the information provided. They thought that the ability to contribute was the next step in the evolution of the genre. So, FiRe was created for solving big problems, utilizing non-experts to bring alternative points of views and skills to the area of challenge. Ralph attended a few of these events, became intrigued, and made a few friends. The first project that Ralph was asked to participate in was one on making education more effective and efficient.

The premise was straightforward: In "Control Theory," a closed-loop feedback model is the most efficient and effective process there is. That's because the model adjusts its performance to meet a desired output response. Sadly, a human student isn't a great sensor in a closed-loop feedback process because they don't always perform exactly as they ought. As we all know, some people take "standardized tests" very well, and others do not. So over the last few years researchers have learned that an fMRI could uniquely identify when a single and unique new memory is captured by the human brain. "*Voila!*" yelled the researchers. The new sensor (fMRI machine) could discern the precise moment when a student actually learned something. Hence, an opportunity for a closed-loop feedback mechanism.

The concept was not without some significant challenges. Today, the cost of a new fMRI machine is about $1 million. It is the size of a large room, is ungodly loud (generating 110-118 decibels of noise when it's at work, which is about the same noise level as a rock concert or a steel mill), and needs the patient/student not to move or wear any metal. Putting such a machine into every classroom in the U.S.—and then the world—is simply unfeasible. But as every VC and entrepreneur knows in their optimistic little hearts, "unfeasible" is just a few short years of a smart team's efforts and resources away from "unlikely." And in Silicon Valley, "unlikely" is solved four or five times a week.

Ralph had even invested in a similar concept based on the principle that 60-70% of a doctor's patients never took their prescriptions as directed. A small company called Proteus decided to incorporate an IC into each pill so that every prescription/pill could be tracked by doctors, patients, families, and insurance companies. These self-powered ICs worked with the acids in the patient's digestive tract, reacting to zinc and copper electrodes, like a potato-battery. The pill's efficacy was read by a patch worn on the skin, like an oversized BAND-AID, and the data was displayed on your/your doctor's Smartphone and insurance company's network.

Closed-loop feedback companies are poised to make solving large, world-wide problems significantly more efficient. And efficiency makes start-up companies more valuable, and investors rich.

In order to "see" the memory being learned/implanted within each student's brain, the team at FiRe was exploring two important prongs: 1) How to dramatically shrink the machine so it could fit in a lunch box-sized apparatus to sit in every classroom and cost less than $10,000. And 2) For the creation of a curriculum to work in conjunction with the fMRI to heuristically study how each unique student best learns and provide each student with the most-appropriate (laptop-driven) teaching method and lesson plan—based on the quotation from Ignacio Estrada, "If a child can't learn the way we teach, maybe we should teach the way they learn."

It was an audacious plan, but the FiRe team had found a few investors to potentially fund a Z-Prize. Unlike traditional Venture Capital, the Z-Prize awards a single, large, lump sum to the contestants who complete the near-impossible feat.

And without fully understanding how or why, Ralph was invited to become part of the ongoing Z-Prize team and the attempt to define and bring the project to fruition. Ralph hoped his invitation was due to his keen mind, but in reality it was probably because he didn't miss many meetings—they needed warm bodies in the chairs—and/or maybe because he asked some decent questions every once in a while. He also suspected, quite rightly, it later turned out, that the engineering leadership wanted to explore the use of the augmented intelligence software being developed by another of Ralph's portfolio companies, and thus needed him as a member. If that was the case, it was okay. He was fine with being used in such a manner.

Much of the EdTech Z-Prize earliest meetings and discussions were regarding how to give the contestants the flexibility to meet the desired state. Ralph had no expertise in either the hardware or the proposed curriculum. During a break from the formal meeting, a famous VC named Roger Phillips, who had made a few billion in Facebook and Baidu, asked Ralph, "What are you hoping to add to the proceedings?"

Ralph was caught off guard. "Ahhh, I'm interested in how these companies will handle two things?" Ralph had learned this stalling technique years ago as a college debater. By telling the audience/judge that you were going to present two items for their consideration, you gave yourself a few extra seconds to think of an appropriate answer. "One, I'm concerned that the result will be difficult to quantify without circular reasoning."

"I was just telling Bill that same thing, just a few minutes earlier," Phillips said, pointing at another committee member sitting across the crowded conference room.

"And two, I want to think hard about how this could potentially be misused by …"

"Advertisers. Oh, and Facebook and Google. Wait— you were probably going to bring up FERPA, weren't you?"

Ralph made a wobbly, non-committal nod that he had learned in India.

"Right." Phillips obviously thought Ralph was affirming. "Ho-ly Shit. No one has said word one about privacy and FERPA. And kids!" Roger said in disbelief.

Ralph made a mental note to Google FERPA the moment he got a chance.

"So now I know why you haven't said more than thirty words in the first six meetings—big brains only need speak when they have something monumental to say."

Ralph wasn't sure this man was serious, but his fellow committee members seemingly thought so.

"Tell us what you're thinking … Ralph."

Ralph caught the man looking at his name badge.

"Well, simply put, Facebook and Google follow us everywhere online, to know all the things we like and dislike. If they also know how we best learn, could they or their advertisers become persuaders of superhero proportions? Or perhaps even something more nefarious?"

Silence. Ralph wasn't sure if he said something smart or had displayed his abundant ignorance.

"Ho-ly Shit! Do you have a business card? I think we should put Ralph in charge of this thing."

The members of the group shifted uncomfortably. A number mumbled their agreement or concern. More than a few whispered that they had had similar comments or thoughts. The herd mentality in Silicon Valley is a real phenome.

Thereafter, Ralph became the de facto conscience of the team. As the specifications of the Statement of Work were written, Ralph was given a gatekeeper role, where he applied his privacy concerns to the proposals. He was soon promoted to the smaller steering committee. He became, in essence, the face of the Z-Team and the EdTech tool project. At least to the outside world. But because Roger Phillips elevated him in that position and was still setting the agenda and success metrics, often behind the scenes, as it were, it was Phillips who was truly in charge.

☙

One of the roles Ralph enjoyed was asking the right question. Not that he was skilled at this task, but he wasn't afraid to ask questions and listen carefully.

"So why aren't we looking at other potential alternatives to the fMRI?"

"Because the fMRI is the right solution."

"It's a sacred cow then?" Ralph didn't like sacred cows.

"What?"

"The proverbial sacred cow. No one wants to kill or even question the sacred cow."

"We've done extensive research and already made this decision. Phillips has made it clear we are going to use the fMRI."

"Okay, humor me. Why is the fMRI, with its ridiculous form factor, noise, and inability to work with humans that move or wear metal zippers better than a BCI device?"

Forty-eight hours earlier, Ralph didn't have the slightest idea what a BCI was. But he had Googled various Human-Machine Interface or HMI methods, and BCI had been at the top of the list. He wanted to understand why this group wasn't willing to look at alternatives. In a rapidly evolving world, understanding and being willing to accept alternatives and course correct was a necessary attribute of every startup endeavor.

"But this has already been decided."

Ralph sighed. "And let me guess, 'We've always done it this way.' Right?"

The team member who'd been assigned to the technology selection gathered himself.

"Well, we can't keep searching for solutions. At some point—and the point has passed—we pick something we think will work and we move forward."

"So give me the rationale for why a fMRI was chosen over say something like the bidirectional BCI? Or the optogenetics approach?"

"Wait. I've never even heard of optogenetics."

"It's bleeding edge. Some team at UC Santa Cruz has observed that by using various forms and intensities of light against the retina, small clusters of neurons in the brain can be triggered. This in turn allows researchers to affect or implant specific aspects into the subject's memory. Or, with different light, reverse the memory. While not exactly what we're trying to do, I have to believe it's a simple algorithm tweak in order to measure the memory or lesson being learned versus implanting or reversing a memory." Ralph had a slight jump on this new technique, as he'd seen the researchers looking for investment only a week before.

"What's the delivery mechanism for the light?"

"It could be an OLED or LCD screen, I think. The student might be using the computer screen to consume the lesson/content, and the sensors on the panel are measuring in real-time if the student is definitively learning the lesson."

"What type/amount and intensity of luminous flux would we need to affect the neurons in such a manner?"

Ralph laughed at himself. He was already well over his head. "I have no idea, but I can introduce you to the researchers at UCSC where you can ask them these types of questions. Cool?" In any given conversation, Ralph often reached his intellectual capabilities quickly.

"Well, it's a bit of stretch, since we've already done all this work on the fMRI."

"Well, pivoting is part of our craft." Ralph had little empathy for people who followed a flawed plan simply because they had already made an investment.

❧

Over the following months, the committee would explore the merits of each of the techniques. The fMRI had challenges with subject movement and costs, but it had the greatest resolution, which made it best for accuracy of the memory. The BBCI (Bidirectional Brain-Computer Interface) technique, which can both stimulate and record from the nervous system, was best for using existing equipment, as it could use scalp-based EEG (electroencephalography or the measurement of electricity the brain produces in specific areas) recordings (hence could be accomplished for relatively low-cost), but the resolution was more challenging for anything more than crude measurements. For example, did Bobby learn that he liked Sally's slightly exposed bra strap, or did he learn the differential equation he was supposed to be studying? BBCI lacked the resolution to discern between the two "learnings." "Supplantments" were also explored, but the surgical process of inserting a small silicon chip—the size of a grain of rice—into the student's nervous system was deemed politically improbable.

The biggest challenge with each of these techniques was the process of trying to "read" minds, as our brains are structured in an extremely complex manner. We know that each neuron and all of its millions of connected neighbors form an unimaginably large and ever-changing network. Furthermore, this network is malleable and unique to each human. Imagine you're trying to understand a conversation between a big group of friends about a complicated subject, but you're allowed to listen to only a single person. You might be able to figure out the very rough topic of what the conversation is about, but definitely not all the details and nuances of the entire discussion. Even the best techniques only allow scientists to "listen to" or "read" a few small areas of the brain at any given time.

Researchers are making some impressive strides, but are nowhere near understanding the full conversation.

There are also communication input-output limits. Neurons communicate with each other through a complex interaction of electrical, chemical, and harmonic interactions. This native electro-chemical-harmonic language can be interpreted with various means, such as the techniques being explored by the Z-Prize (mostly some sort of electrical circuit), but it's not simple or straightforward. Similarly, when scientists attempt to "speak" back to the brain using electrical stimulation, it is with a heavy electrical "accent." This makes it difficult for neurons to understand what the stimulation is trying to convey in the midst of all the other ongoing neural activity. In other words, it's really messy in there.

As the project progressed, the smart money backed the optogenetics approach that Ralph had first asked questions about and, hence, Ralph became more and more credible in the committee. More gravitas than he thought he deserved. But this kind of questionably-earned-credibility often happened with Ralph. He had grown to accept this serendipity as part of his lot in life.

Chapter 7
2009

Everyone knew that Ralph had the emotional maturity of a fourteen-year old boy. He snickered when he saw the large, fancy cloth banners hanging off the lampposts along Taipei's main boulevard proclaiming: "TITS: Feel the Quality."

Only later did Ralph learn that TITS was the acronym for the "Taipei International Textile Symposium," an event with a forty-year history in the city.

On a Saturday afternoon in Taipei, one week into a two-week business trip, Ralph decided—after looking in the mirror—that he was in need of a haircut. It was certainly not the first time he'd taken a quick cut in Asia. For the most part, Asian barbers are similar to barbers in any country. They cut hair.

Ralph usually looked for the oldest, most traditional haircutter he could find. The two rationales were: 1) anyone messing around with sharp objects next to his head should have been around the block more than twice; and 2) old male barbers have stronger hands to give you the best head and shoulders rubdown—a real treat in Asia.

A few doors down the street from Ralph's business-oriented hotel was an elegant haircutting establishment. Ralph wasn't sure why he decided to frequent this place, but he thought maybe he had received a stray email advising of the spot. And it simply looked the right kind of place. Trimmed in blond wood and tan granite, Ralph saw six empty chairs and, staring forlornly at the floor, an attractive young woman in a short skirt. Ralph, being a deep-set cheap bastard, checked out the price list on the outer window to ensure he wouldn't pay more than his standard eight bucks for a haircut.

When he walked in, the young woman looked up and gave a small gasp of surprise. "Gweilos"—Mandarin for Foreign Devils; the literal translation is "ghostly man"—aren't rare in Taipei, but they tend to stay on the beaten path. Ralph was trolling a perhaps path-less-taken section of town. Ralph asked the girl if she would cut his hair.

"Tommy!?!" the girl called out. She looked perplexed and slightly anxious.

"No, no, my name is Ralph," he said slowly, with his best enunciation.

"Tommy!!"

From somewhere in the back, a five-foot, 105 pound man entered the salon with as much drama as he could possibly muster. He was wearing ridiculously oversized baggy jeans, with chrome chains dangling to and from each pocket. There was a very large construction utility belt around his waist. He wore a white blouse with excessively pouffed sleeves. His tan was deep orange. Tommy had the worst hairstyle imaginable. He was predominately bald, with just a two-inch diameter tuft of long, permed hair plugs too low on his forehead. He wore very dark sunglasses with frames that looked chunky in their faux solid gold.

"You heel for Tommy?" he asked very loudly. His entourage of four lovely women followed him into the room. No one walked—they glided.

"Ah, well, I am here for a haircut, please."

"YES, you heel for Tommy." The girls giggled and bowed on cue. Tommy bowed low and dramatically, as if he had just performed the lead role in a Broadway play to a boisterous standing ovation.

Tommy clapped twice. "Shampoo!!" And all of the girls scurried to their appointed tasks.

It has been mentioned that Ralph is a rather large lummox. The chair and shampoo sink was obviously designed for the local clientele—people of more refined size and grace. Embarrassingly for all involved, Ralph's enormous derrière did not fit in the seat. In addition, when Ralph leaned back to put his head into the area of the sink, it quickly became clear that he was too long. Only his shoulders were anywhere near the actual sink. His head was completely over the sink's faucets. Not to be stymied, Ralph used some advanced yoga moves, and bridged his body to rest his shoulders and upper back on the front edge of the sink. Two of the girls grabbed Ralph by his belt to ensure he did not topple.

The young women did not disappoint when it came to the shampooing and giving a head and shoulder massage. Many whisperings and much giggling made Ralph rather self-conscious. But he smiled, enjoying the many hands on his body. After a brisk towel dry and a great deal more giggling, Ralph moved to the throne closest to the floor-to-ceiling glass windows.

Ralph was quick to learn that Tommy was something of a known entertainer, as a group of passersby stopped in the street and watched the show through the window.

As mentioned, Tommy was vertically challenged. In order to see the top of Ralph's head, which was above

Tommy's, even when Ralph was seated in a very low chair, Tommy positioned Ralph with only his lower back and shoulders in the cutting throne. After many attempts to get Ralph low enough, Tommy broke down and demanded one of his admirer-helpers fetch him a stool.

Now a foot taller, Tommy combed and brushed every individual hair on Ralph's head. Before he began any actual cutting, he spent twenty minutes studying the hair and using more than a dozen hair clips, getting it all in just the perfect place. All the while, the four young attractive women would gasp in awe at the bold and dramatic moves Tommy made with the large pink comb.

"What rong?" asked the young lady who had adeptly applied the shampoo. Her English skills were obviously deemed to be the best among the team. Ralph tried his best charades to show her he wanted his hair short on the sides and back, but longer on the top.

"NO!" shouted Tommy. "You heel for Tommy!" It became clear that Ralph was going to have little say in his hairstyle that day.

Ralph tried again. "Please—short." He held his index finger from his thumb at about half an inch at the side of his head. "And Loooong." He held his finger from his thumb at about two inches at the top of his head.

"No!" was Tommy's only reply. He turned his back away from Ralph and pouted like a three-year-old girl. A standoff ensued. Tommy stomped his feet to the back room to find some refreshments.

Luckily, a fifth woman, who must have been one of Tommy's older assistants, appeared from the back of the salon.

Her English was stilted, but better than Ralph's Mandarin. Together, with the woman running between the two rooms, they forged a détente with the mercurial Tommy.

Tommy came back into the front room with swagger. He immediately retook his place on the stool, and resumed placing clips in Ralph's hair, tossing the few non-bound hairs about.

And then, with a great flourish, Tommy raised the velvet-wrapped shears from his industrial utility belt to a position as high above his head as possible. Tommy loudly invoked Buddha in prayer to assist him with this Herculean task ahead of him. The women's heads were all bowed and faces in the deepest concentration.

Tommy delicately unwrapped the scissors from the velvet sheath, and with just a hint of a shaky hand, made the first ceremonious cut. There was a palpable sigh from the room. Tommy exhaled, then jumped off the stool and posed. With the back of his right hand on his forehead, elbow high, left leg extended behind him, everyone knew Tommy was channeling Vivian Leigh. The small crowd at the window gave a golf clap for the performance thus far.

While Ralph had overfilled many coach-class plane seats in his time, he occasionally still felt anxious, without appropriate language skills in an awkward situation. And as many large people do, Ralph sweated when he was nervous. And Ralph's sweat wasn't a pleasant little sheen. It flowed aggressively and without abatement. This unstylish sweat was obviously distracting poor Tommy. He called out for some assistance. Several women laid several towels on Ralph's brow and mopped him up.

The next snip of the scissors came after sixty seconds of deep reflection. There was still a visible shake to Tommy's hands, but he was clearly becoming more confident.

Ralph was blind without his glasses, thus after the third snip he shut his eyes. This seemed to make everything go much better for all concerned. After another five or six snips, one of the girls gasped. Ralph's eyes shot open, and Tommy jumped off the stool, double pounded his chest, pointed at the sky, and began to dance like MC Hammer. After more than twenty seconds of doing the Hammer, Tommy resumed his Vivian Leigh pose, remaining that way for more than a minute. The crowd at the window joined the entourage in their hearty applause. This time, the girls mopped Ralph, and then Tommy's brow. The excitement was electric.

As this drama was playing out, the crowd outside had spilled over into the salon. The five empty chairs quickly became occupied. Tommy's attention became split between Ralph's hair and the new patrons' needs.

Ralph sat in Tommy's salon for more than three hours. Tommy would cut a small section of his hair, strike a pose, or dance about once every ten minutes. Ralph saw a jig, a variation from *Swan Lake*, something from Kylie Minogue, a number of dance steps blatantly lifted from Justin Timberlake, a couple of Keith Richard's guitar solos, and a signature Michael Jackson moonwalk. Often after the "move," as Ralph began to think of it, Tommy would take a break and spend time with other customers. Ralph got his hair shampooed a total of eight times in Tommy's salon. The young ladies in charge of massaging the shampoo into his scalp started to enjoy themselves and quit the nervous giggling. The fifth woman translated questions from the four assistants as necessary. At some point, one of the girls asked where Ralph was from.

"I grew up on Cape Cod, but now I live in California."

After the translation, Tommy and the four beauties all started talking and laughing at once. Tommy asked to have his words translated. The fifth beauty translated from Mandarin into English.

"Give our very best regards to Bubsy for all of us. Tell her we miss her, but we will take care of you while you are here."

"Bubsy? My mother? You can't know my mother. I don't think she's ever been to Asia."

Suddenly Tommy's English was okay. "Sure, sure. No problem. Sure."

"I think we're talking about some other person named Bubsy, right?"

"Must be. Sure, sure. So sorry. No problem." And then Tommy struck perhaps his most dramatic pose of the evening, raising cheers from the women and all bystanders. The moment was lost—but for Ralph, the questions remained.

When it finally came time for Ralph to walk away from Tommy's salon, he was given an autographed Tommy business card, and a promise that anyone of his assistants would be willing to show Ralph around Taipei that same evening. Ralph smiled and declined. He spent $21 on that haircut, and was calculated that on a per-hour—and certainly per-laugh basis—Tommy was a much better deal than his local $8 twenty-minute Supercuts.

So how did the haircut and styling look? In the end, Ralph would never be confused with George Clooney, and hence resumed his normal styling-via-a-towel the morning thereafter.

Chapter 8
2016

"Do you want me to stain your deck chairs?"

"Mom, you just told me this might be the last time we'll ever see each other—that we'll have to say our final goodbyes today." Ralph was trying his best not to cry.

Bubsy was busy staining her own deck chairs. With her advanced Parkinson's disease, the stain was flying everywhere. Bubsy never thought much of perfection. Even the dog wore signs of her staining efforts.

"I'm not leaving today. I might even have a few more days. And I like staining furniture. When you're done, it's like having something brand new."

Ralph admired her work and grabbed a paper towel to get some of the stain off of the dog. Nugget snagged the towel and ran with it, wanting Ralph to chase her.

"Does it hurt?"

"Dying?"

He nodded.

"Not much. Maybe some. My eyes are always too dry—they feel like sandpaper. My chest sometimes hurts. I can't swallow worth a damn. And I can't poop."

"Other than that, you feel great."

They both smiled. He'd stolen her joke. For thirteen years, she had been battling Parkinson's, heart disease, and diabetes. She couldn't have the necessary bypass surgery because it'd trigger the Parkinson's and she'd be bedridden for the remainder of her remarkable life. She'd told everyone that was not how she want to go. For thirteen years, she'd been answering his standard question of "How are you, Bubsy?" with "I feel great."

"It was perfect that you were able to visit two weeks ago with Jen and everyone else."

"It was perfect."

Ralph's mom had been in the hospital. Her doctors had told her she didn't have long. So, she called her people and everyone had gathered to spend two great weeks with her in the spring sunshine of Cape Cod. They shared breakfast and had dinner every evening with friends and family. Each was aware they'd never have this same chance again to share this laughter, to recount these same familiar stories.

"I'm not afraid," Bubsy said matter-of-factly.

"The next great adventure?"

She smiled. "I taught you that fear isn't productive. Right?"

"I'm going to miss you terribly."

"But I'll be around."

"But no phone calls to tell you of my latest adventures." For thirty years Ralph had called her every weekend to share all of the details. The first question she'd ask him would be: "What new adventures?" Or: "What have you learned this week?" Or: "What has made you laugh?"

"No. Probably not," she agreed.

"If you get a chance, send me a message to tell me you're okay. You'll figure out how."

"All right. That shouldn't be too hard."

Ralph wiped more stain off the puppy. Bubsy's muu-muu had dozens of spills.

"Have you decided what you're going to say at my party?"

"Bubs, it won't be a party unless you show up."

"Well, maybe I will," she teased.

"What do you want me to say?"

She paused for only a second or two. "I lived without regrets. That I loved to laugh and dance and swim and sing. That I cherished the life I led."

Ralph wiped away a few tears with the same stained paper towel that had recently been in the dog's mouth. His heart ached. Meanwhile, his role model hadn't once stopped staining the wooden chairs.

"Tell that story about the three fish," she said with a sad smile.

"Isn't the water glorious," they both said simultaneously, jumping to the punch line. They laughed.

She took a sip of her Tawny port wine, with the requisite four cubes of ice.

"I'm worried about your brother and stepfather. They don't do change very well. And they're going to bear the brunt of this change. Neither of them really knows my system."

Ralph smiled. "No one can know the unknowable, Bubsy." He'd been teasing her about "her system" of filing—little piles—for years. She maintained the household office, and no one has been able to figure out her special management magic.

"Speaking of which, since this is probably our final discussion, you're going to need to continue to work on your tolerance."

"I will." This has been her wise counsel for years. Something Ralph had been focused on, but never near perfecting.

"People read you easily. They know when you're judging them, and it turns them off. Laughter and learning are the only two worthy pursuits we have. Those can only be achieved when you allow people to share with you. Let them in."

Ralph took a deep breath before answering, "I will."

"And there will be a whole lot of people that will come to you, if you let them. You'll be in charge after I'm gone. Let them in."

Ralph was trying hard not to sob, all he could do was nod. Even though he wasn't quite sure what she meant by "be in charge."

They sat for a while in her beautiful garden. Quiet, except for the tolling of the massive wind chime. It smelled of just-mown grass, stain, and something sweet. Then something occurred to Ralph.

"Mom, I have a really weird question. But did you ever know a man named Tommy in Taiwan?"

She smiled and laughed. "The best damn dancing hairstylist I've ever seen."

"But, you've never been to Taiwan, how ...?"

"Oh Ralph, let an old woman have her secrets."

She smiled, put down her staining brush, and sat next to him. She leaned her head on his shoulder and grasped his arm. They sat that way for ten minutes, just listening to the world.

"Now you have to kiss your mother goodbye. And travel safe tomorrow."

He was on a 6:00 AM flight from Logan to Dubai.

"Happy Mother's Day, Mom."

Chapter 9

As the flight attendant brought Ralph's fourth ginger ale and cranberry juice, he was finishing an article about advocacy methods. The article that most intrigued Ralph was on a methodology called Deep Canvassing. The methodology—via significant in-field research done by a group called *Seek Common Ground*—determined the key to changing people's minds is to be curious about what those people think. Changing minds was never because someone berated the other into intellectual submission. It didn't depend on the most logical research. The biggest tool used to change someone's mind is a supportive environment that lets them think about their own experiences and how those experiences affect their opinions on the contended issue. And with the right training, the data showed the methodology works.

As he deplaned, Ralph realized that Deep Canvassing wasn't terribly different than Aristotle's maxim on persuasion—meld your message to meet the needs of the audience. But Ralph was absolutely certain that neither of these methodologies would be sufficient to convince Jen to allow him to purchase another old European sports car.

Once through the airport, he was soon in the front passenger seat of a clean Lexus.

"What business are you in, if I may ask?"

Uber drivers were always polite and inquisitive.

"Some days, it feels like I sit in airline lounges for a living," Ralph said. He wasn't in the best of moods. He got emotionally low after spending sixteen hours in an aluminum can—or in this instance, an Airbus A380 with 560 other souls. The flight to the Middle East was direct from Logan, but that was both a blessing and a curse. But by now he was used to it. Ralph thought about the life of an Uber driver. It really wasn't much different than his own life. Someone tells you where you should go, and you go. Simple.

But because Ralph had much time on his hands, his mind wandered. "What haven't I shared with an Uber driver or the Uber App?"

Ralph had designed, funded, and built many apps in his day. He knew what they were capable of. Each app had the ability to utilize all of the attributes of a modern smartphone. GPS for location, clock, accelerometer for minute movements, microphone, camera, video, data transmission and capture.

If I designed the Uber App for maximum data capture, what would I do? Well, first, I'd store and index all the personal information for the customer, including their financial details/credit cards. Then I'd know where they live and where they travel. I'd mine their calendar and contacts—their social media posts. I'd know the user's beliefs, their favorite hotels, restaurants, and their every meeting location. I could turn on the microphone when the user was en route to his destination to listen to his conversations and take video to see their emotions and their guests—facial recognition could give me the names of the guests, and the relationship could be established quickly in the cloud to determine the importance of the event.

In his imagination, the Uber App would be a perfect tool for the Intelligence Community. But most apps, he realized, would make excellent Intelligence tools. More than two billion people already use Facebook or similar social media apps to document and opine about their every move. And smartphone users almost never read the small print when they download these apps. Most apps ask for permission to do ridiculous actions in exchange for offering free usage. Ralph had once set up a Pineapple to spoof a "Free Wi-Fi Site" at a major convention in a top-five EU city and asked users to agree to Ralph's terms of use. These legal terms included Ralph having the "right to the first-born child, the deeds to all owned physical property, the right to discover and record all the information on the smartphone, and free ice cream for life." Ralph had more than 31,000 conference attendees sign-in to his spoof site and agree to his legally-binding terms. He was certain not a single person ever read the legal Terms of Use of a typical app.

"Excuse me, sir. Are you sure the address you want to go is correct?" The driver had his finger in his ear. Seemingly, he was listening to someone beyond Ralph.

"Yes, wait. What?" Ralph was caught off-guard by his driver's question.

"Are you certain?"

"Am I certain of what?"

"I am sorry," his hand in his ear again. "But, are you certain of the address you put in the app? Which company are you wanting to visit please?"

Since this was the most important meeting of the nineteen-day, nine-airport, circumnavigating-the-globe trip, instead of being weirded-out by the question, Ralph had second thoughts. His assistant had also questioned him about the location. He pulled out his smartphone and looked at his calendar app.

"We want to go to Addax Tower near Media City," Ralph told the driver. "Just like I inputted into the destination field of your app."

"But Sir, I am told that you are visiting Puma Mobile Security, and they have moved since your last visit. If you look at your recent email, you have been sent a new address. Please check for us," pleaded the driver.

"How are you getting your information about my email …?" But Ralph was suddenly concerned. He did remember a recent email that had mentioned an office move. "Hold on," he said, momentarily forgetting his concerns about his driver's question and access to his servers.

"Oh, shit." Ralph found the most-recent email.

"I am now driving to Puma's new office in the Landmark building near Sheikh Khalifah Mosque, correct?"

Ralph triple-checked, and then he agreed with his driver. In a city the size of Abu Dhabi, driving to the wrong destination would have been a huge mistake. The lateness of his arrival to this key meeting may have caused it to be postponed or scrubbed all together.

After his heart rate approached normal, and the sweat on his brow dried, Ralph thought about what had just transpired. "Excuse me. How does your app have access to my emails?"

"Sir, I am not sure, but we want to provide the best service we can to our riders."

౷

After the meeting, on the mind-numbing two-hour drive back to his Dubai hotel, Ralph thought deeply about the combination of an app like Uber with the Z-Prize tool and some sort of proven advocacy methodology. Not only would the app have access to the user's beliefs, likes, and dislikes, they'd also have all of the data from the sensors: the multiple cameras, audio, GPS, and the life-impacting data in all of the apps. Plus, it'd also have the necessary attention of the user, where the Brain-Computer Interface via the retina of the eye he had introduced to the Z-Prize researchers could be utilized to put forth a new closed-loop method to persuade. Combine all this with the Deep Canvassing interaction model that the advocacy team at *Seek Common Ground* had honed for effectively reversing long-held personal beliefs, and you could have a near-un-stoppable weapon that'd persuade even the most die-hard believer.

Ralph wondered, was this what Roger Phillips really wanted? And if so, why?

Chapter 10
Fall 2010

The three middle-aged men sat on the rooftop deck of Ralph's quiet Cape Cod post and beam vacation home, which he called The Barn. They drank copious amounts of red wine, admired the clear starlit night sky over the tidal salt marsh and told each other absurd stories—tales crafted of half-truths, embellishments, and flights of fancy. As they had known each other since they were in their early twenties, many of the stories seemed familiar but were often salted with secrets, things only they knew, or thought they knew, about each other. The men hadn't seen each other in years. Each had gone their own way. They had sporadically kept in touch, mostly via social media, but the face-to-face reminiscing was great fun. Each was relaxed and shared comfortable smiles—or as relaxed as McKenna could be, which in truth, wasn't very much. As the night wore on, one thing became increasingly clear: one of them, Peterson Conway, was probably insane.

"Do you remember when we were hanging out at your Plum Island beach house and we all took peyote and crashed Elane's Saab into that sand dune?"

"Why did she let you have her Saab on her year abroad?"

"I was the responsible one."

"But weren't you dating her?" he asked the other man.

"Yes, but Ralph was the responsible one."

"And 'the responsible one' was the person who was driving when we crashed into the sand dune," recalled McKenna.

The front-wheel drive Saab had been buried to its front axle in the soft sand about thirty feet off the roadway. The boys were in search of cheap beer and drunk women. They tried mightily—all three were large men—to wrest the car from the sand with little progress. Level 42's "There's Something About You" blared in the car's tape deck.

"Should we call someone?"

"Do you see a phone booth anywhere near here? And who would we call?"

"We could walk home."

"But we don't have any beer." Peterson was clear on this point.

"Did you see that?" Ralph asked.

"Dude, you're hallucinating," Peterson opined with great authority.

"Man, I swear I saw some blue lights from over that sand dune—maybe a fucking UFO."

The burly police officer said, "Son, do you mind putting your clothes back on?"

Peterson had worked himself into a lather trying to free the car from the silica and had tried to cool himself off by removing every stitch of clothing. He had then fallen down in the sand, and the sweat and sand had combined and clung to his athlete's body. The two others hadn't noticed up until this moment.

"I don't remember how we got out of that jam," Peterson recalled, back on the tree-top deck of Ralph's vacation home.

In truth, they all remembered vividly how McKenna had approached the officer, pulled him aside—out of earshot from the others—and removed something from his wallet.

"The cop was very cool to take us to the strip club—wasn't it the Golden Banana in Saugus—and then wait for us before driving us home," Peterson reminded his fellow wine drinkers.

"It must have been three hours. And how cool was it that the Saab was waiting for us in the driveway when we got back to the house?" Ralph and McKenna sat quietly.

They all agreed via a nod that outcome was pretty cool.

"What do you do now, McKenna?" Peterson asked. "Your Facebook page has links to a college in Boston and some very funny videos of you singing Southern Rock with your undergrad band."

They had just finished dinner, consuming a couple of pounds of fresh pasta and five bottles of red wine. The post and beam home held the smells of tomato sauce and garlic. There was a salad served, but not much of it had been eaten. The three pounds of homemade meatballs were gone. Ralph decanted another bottle of red wine, and wondered if he should ask his guests whether they enjoyed the wine—he was a partial owner of this particular vineyard. He decided to conceal his hubris at this time. Besides, Peterson had earned his Master Sommelier certificate in Paris twenty years earlier and may not like this young California Blend.

"I only put those videos on Facebook to annoy my kids." McKenna was a single dad with three girls, two in high school and one in college. Absentmindedly, he adjusted the shoulder holster under his suit coat. He had a concealed weapons permit and was not known to ever travel with less than two handguns. "And you know I can't talk about my job."

❧

McKenna had a rich and diverse past. He grew up in Woburn, MA, a horrible little Boston suburb most widely known for its residents winning a large class-action cancer lawsuit against the largest employer, a printing mill. His parents were well educated, but his dad died from an aneurism when McKenna was very young. Much like Peterson and Ralph, he had attended a small private prep school, paid for by his father's partners at his insurance agency. At the Upstate New York college, McKenna joined a popular fraternity, played in a well-liked Southern Rock cover band, and was recruited to join the CIA. Because of his penchant for high-powered weapons and his lax-ethical boundaries, McKenna was easily funneled into the "wet-ops" group at Langley.

McKenna traveled the globe for nearly three years, before the staff psychologist labeled him as "broken." McKenna was given the option of a three-week crash re-indoctrination to the "real-world" and enough money for grad school—or some "extended-rest" hospital time.

He chose grad school, and that's where he met Ralph.

In Boston, McKenna quickly learned that recreational drugs quieted the noise caused by his previous career. Like Ralph, he had earned a teaching aid role to further offset tuition and rent. Because no one else wanted the role, McKenna was assigned to the brilliant, albeit massively-flawed, Dr. Harold Lawson. Dr. Lawson (Doc) was the preeminent debate coach in the country. He personally had won the national championship three of his four years in college—only failing to win in the finals his senior year, due to excessive amphetamine intake, which caused him to deliver a fulsome six-minute rebuttal in ninety-five seconds—and then coached five (different) college teams to national championships.

Doc was also broken. Doc's IQ was 189. He had more degrees than he had fingers on his left hand, and smoked a pipe like a chimney. He had been tenured at four of his last five colleges, but had been fired over infractions as varied as showing up for lectures in drag, to defecating in the Dean's new Mercedes convertible, to offering to share some heroin and his wife with a nineteen-year-old co-ed. Doc was an active swinger and a person who would consume a 1.75 litre of Wild Turkey Bourbon and a bottle of Pepsi every single Saturday of his adult life.

In McKenna, Doc found his protégé.

McKenna had the brilliant idea of hiring erotic dancers from the Golden Banana in Saugus, MA to attract freshman to sign up for the forensics/debate team during the first week of school. The dancers were told to dress like sexy librarians. Ralph was all-to-willing to join the team—even when the giggling young lady asked him if he was a "master debater." Peterson fell into the same snare.

Ralph fell in quickly with the slightly older McKenna. When McKenna was drunk/stoned/high, which was often, he'd tell partial stories of his near past when he'd been with the Agency—Ralph assumed it was the CIA, but couldn't be sure. The stories fascinated Ralph, but whenever he asked for more details, McKenna would shut down. McKenna's car was a former Agency vehicle—he had bought it surplus, he claimed—with assorted flashing lights, a siren, and back doors with inoperable thick windows. When open or closed, the doors felt weighted like they were made of lead.

McKenna was adventure, and Ralph was drawn to it. As was Peterson. Doc was raw intelligence, and Ralph was drawn to it. So too Peterson. The college's debate team was one of the best in the nation, and Ralph and Peterson were drawn to the nerdy glamour. In the end, they had both found a home.

Debate tournaments were typically every weekend, at a different college somewhere on the Eastern seaboard. The team would load up a twelve-person rented van for a multi-hour ride to exotic places like Towson, Maryland and Ypsilanti, Michigan and stay at the cheapest hotels available. For twenty to twenty-five weekends a year, Ralph's team traveled on Fridays and returned on Sundays. Ralph wasn't the most natural debater, but he loved the challenge of the real-time argumentation. He wasn't the strongest researcher, but his on-his-feet analysis was solid and often unique.

It was an open secret among the debate community that intelligence agencies often scoured forensic and debate tournaments, as participants often make solid analysts and occasionally operatives—debaters often rely on quick thinking and verbal jousting to succeed. Plus, they are often unremarkably plain, and often nerdy—perfect for intelligence work. Not many supermodels went out for the debate team. Ralph remembered a certain discussion after one of these tournaments, but he was typically too drunk or stoned to remember much.

"That guy you were just speaking with ... what did he want?" McKenna had asked.

"Not really sure," Ralph said.

"He looks like a spook recruiter to me," McKenna said.

"Don't talk to those guys, Ralph," counseled Doc Lawson. "They just want to make you sit in a conference room all day and stare at research. Dull folks."

Which was just enough for Ralph to purposefully avoid them. Dull was never something Ralph wanted to pursue.

☙

"What about you, Peterson?" Now it was McKenna's turn to ask.

Both he and Ralph knew that Peterson's adopted parents had died early in his life and had left him a boatload of money, but they hadn't heard the ensuing story from the source.

"I tried a number of careers, but just couldn't find my groove. Zelda and I had a few kids. I love those kids, but we weren't always the best parents. Who is?"

Both men nodded their understanding, hoping Peterson would just continue to unload.

"The kids are both in decent schools and grew up fine. Sometimes, I think, in spite of our efforts. But most embarrassingly, in the last thirty, I—this is hard to say, but I spent the last twenty plus years thinking that I ... I might have been a spy. For Israel. But now I'm not sure if I was. Or am. Or—I don't know."

McKenna and Ralph each raised a pair of eyebrows.

"It is a terribly involved story, which I've never shared with anyone, but I'd like to share with you both. And it kind of explains where I've been in this life.…"

After grad school, Peterson was traveling in Tel Aviv to visit relatives when he was first approached by someone claiming to be from the Mossad needing help. Over a few months, he was asked to do simple tasks. "Go drop this off" and "go collect that." It was explained to Peterson that he was helping to build the back stories for multiple agents in the field. As an American Jew, Peterson felt that his help was contributing to the greater good. Over the next few months, his tasks became more involved. Over the years, he was asked to do more and more. When these tasks took him away from his life responsibilities, he tended to focus on the tasks, romanticizing that he was a necessary element of something larger than himself.

Ralph was swallowing hard. The story was too familiar. Ralph wasn't sure if Peterson knew that McKenna was a former—or maybe current—member of the Intelligence Community.

"Were you trained?" McKenna asked. "Did you have a handler?"

"Not much, and yes. And I fell in love with her immediately. Like a sad le Carré novel. And soon my marriage to Zelda was finished and I couldn't be bothered to remember my kids' birthdays."

They all sat quietly for a moment or two.

"This lasted seventeen years. Near the end, I was asking for something to acknowledge that I had done something good for the world. But I got nothing. Due to this, my relationship with my handler went sideways. And then one day, I was caught by the FBI with an expensive camera full of candid photos of important people from all over the country. The memory cards I carried had even more photos and even some video. People I had been asked to follow for fifteen or twenty years. And while there was no hard link to any crimes, there were plenty of awkward circumstances. I was given the option of placing myself in a mental facility for a good long time, or standing trial for conspiracy to treason."

"Wow." Ralph was too amped to keep his mouth shut.

"Yep. So—I've missed you guys. Two weeks ago, I got transferred to a hybrid program—five nights per week at the center, and two nights on my own."

"We've all missed hanging out with each other," Ralph said, attempting to sound as supportive as he could. "It's really cool that you reached out to us."

"A year ago, I saw her—my handler. She was being lauded on a website for her philanthropic efforts. She's the extremely popular wife of a very successful venture capitalist in Silicon Valley. You might even know her, Ralph. And it seems like she was just messing with me—some kind of weird power-play. For fifteen years...."

The room was quiet. After thirty seconds, Peterson continued, "The lead psychologist at the center where I stay reached out to her, at my insistence. She denied we knew each other. And I couldn't prove otherwise. Each and every communication we had had over nearly twenty years was via a burner phone or email account."

"Wow," was all Ralph could think to say.

"Do you know how hard it is to look back at a major portion of your adult life and think you were being used? It ruins you, man. Ruins you."

Chapter 11

Not all business class chairs are created equal, Ralph thought to himself. On a flight back from Tel Aviv, for instance, the KLM B class chair is merely one-and-a-half coach-class chairs, and without audio-visual distractions. On the opposite end of the spectrum, the Emirates B class chair is like a small luxury pied–á-terre in the Georges V neighborhood of Paris. The Emirates cabin has three screens for your information, communications, and entertainment. A shower and a lounge were available and in constant use. While sitting on his uncomfortable KLM chair, Ralph was replaying the last few days in his mind.

It had been a whirlwind. First there was the dinner with Peterson and McKenna. Ralph couldn't shake his anxious thoughts about Peterson's spy disclosure. It was potentially too close to his own thoughts or maybe the right word was fantasies. And more, he had started the week with a Monday meeting in Moscow. After seeing his business partners there, he took the 7PM flight that evening to Tel Aviv. After three and half hours of sleeping in a comfortable boutique hotel room, utilizing too many designer beveled mirrors, he attended the first of sixteen half-hour meetings from 7AM to 6PM, with sixteen different Israeli teams, all of which the Israeli Economic Development Ministry had meticulously arranged. After these meetings had concluded, Ralph took an Uber back to his hotel and had a couple of Stroopwafels for his dinner—his outbound flight to Moscow was via Amsterdam, where he picked them up—and was asleep by 8:15PM.

Ralph woke in a start. It was still dark out. But he was certain he had heard someone cough. Taking his head not more than an inch off the pillow, Ralph quickly glanced around the boutique hotel room. He swore, readjusted the pillow, and chalked it up to a dream.

Another cough. Louder this time.

"Excuse me—ah, Mr. Ralph. Sorry to bother you at this time. But you did mention that I could be in touch."

Ralph sat straight up. "Holy shit! How the hell did you get in my room? Who are you?"

"We met earlier today. Remember, it is me—Amir Cohen. We talked about my SDK company potentially working with your company to provide measurement analysis of the API's performance. Remember?"

"I have a few hundred dollars in my wallet. Please take it."

Ralph was still disoriented from abruptly waking from his very restful sleep.

"You misunderstand, Ralph. I need you to get a message to your people. It is most urgent."

"My people? You want to talk with my technical team about your API tool? Couldn't you just send me an email—in the morning?"

"Ralph, please stop with the stupid jokes. Your people. The people. It is most urgent. Agents' lives are at risk."

"Amir? Was it Amir?"

Amir nodded urgently.

"Amir, I have no idea what the fuck you're talking about."

What was the bit about agents? Ralph thought. He checked to make sure this wasn't a dream, because he had been reading two or three paragraphs of a spy thriller before he fell asleep. "What people?"

"Mr. Ralph, please be serious. I need you to contact your team most urgently and tell them that we have been exposed—either a mole, or potentially a Russian or Chinese hacker. Either way, we need help—right NOW. I need to pull my agents out. The Chinese delegation from Huawei at our meeting today knew things about our software that no one could ever know."

Ralph's head was starting to clear. Even in the dark, it was obvious that Amir was very anxious. Ralph could even see he was sweating. The previous day's meeting had been a speed-dating exercise for start-up companies and strategic investors. Ralph had thought his invitation was SPAM or a fluke, but the Israeli organizers had been very persistent. They offered to pay for Ralph's travel and expenses, just for him to listen to Israeli start-ups.

Amir continued. "Tomorrow you will be approached by the young pretty woman from Huawei. She calls herself Eva. She claims she works in the corporate development department. As you have been briefed, we are funded and managed by both your DoD and the IMoD. After listening to my pitch—the same pitch I gave to you—she offered me a $50 million 'grant' if I let her people get the HTTPS data feed from our tool. But Ralph, as you know, no one but your people and my very small team are aware of the feed we created. Not the U.S. DoD. Not the IMoD. This API we created for your people is transparent even to a Kaspersky security audit. We've passed a Black Duck and

Veracode source code security audit. This is my greatest work. It is my Sistine Chapel."

Amir was very close to tears. The words were flowing quickly from his lips.

"Okay, I have to pee. Give me a second, okay?"

"Mr. Ralph?"

"I have got to use the little skier's room. Hold on." Getting out of bed, Ralph wondered why James Bond never needed a quick bathroom break.

"Please hurry, Ralph. I need to leave."

"One second." Ralph shut the door. When he was washing his hands, he wondered if Amir would still be in his room. Why did Amir think Ralph could help him? And what "people"?

By now Ralph had learned that when he was confused, which was fairly often, it was always best to shut up and listen.

Amir was still in the room, but had his hand on the doorknob. Ralph had purposefully left the bathroom light on, in order to spill some light into the large hotel room.

"You've dribbled on yourself." Amir was pointing at Ralph's crotch.

Ralph looked down at his boxers. Yes, he had dribbled.

"Well, that's embarrassing. But not my largest concern at this very moment. Tell me exactly what you want me to communicate, and to whom, and I'll see if I can potentially help you. Okay?"

"Ralph—what is this? You have an obligation to protect my team. Your organization made assurances."

Ralph shrugged awkwardly. He waited because his mind was aflutter.

"Your people need to know that the Chinese know we have built this dynamic and untraceable backdoor into the API for your tool. Tell Koch or Phillips at SI that the

Chinese must have reconstructed the binaries or used a side-scanned electron microscope on the chips to find this transparent API. If the Chinese or the Russians know it exists, then they may be able to figure out how to block it. Do you have this?"

Ralph shook his head without much confidence.

"Ralph, I know your cover is to be a bumbling idiot American VC investor, but sometimes you play the role too well. Let's stop fucking around, okay? It is most un-professional. We have my team to protect."

And with that, Amir was out the door and gone.

✧

Ralph spent the next few hours trying to piece together what he had just experienced with Amir. There was no going back to sleep. The anxiousness emanating from Amir was contagious. Ralph decided to capture notes in his Evernote App. He opened a new personal file, titled it "Tel Aviv," and tried to write down every word that they had spoken. Ralph read it over twice, and edited his first draft by clarifying a few ambiguous pronouns.

Then he started a list of his most pressing questions:

- Who was Amir? And who did he really work for?

- Should I help Amir? (He certainly sounded like he needed help. But what if Amir was a bad dude? Building trap and backdoors into networks and software was at best unethical and almost certain to lead to trouble.)

- Who did Amir want me to relay this message to? Who is "Koch or Phillips at SI"? The only people I know at SI named Bill Koch is one of the largest funders of the Z-Prize efforts. He's not on the tools committee. (Double-check that!) Koch's reputation is that of an eighty-something-year-old industrialist with a penchant for funding hard-right wing politics in any number of countries. Koch's many businesses aren't often seen working with high-tech projects. When I initially saw Koch's name on the funders role, he didn't seem to fit the typical funder. Why would this particular person want to be far out of their comfort zone? Need to get to know him better—but vehemently avoid all discussions about politics. Phillips is a prominent and sometimes arrogant VC and sits on the committee with me. Are they connected somehow?

- And perhaps the most pressing question was: 'Why did Amir assume or believe I knew what the heck was going on?'

Ralph thought hardest about the last question. He was certain that everything Amir told him in the hotel room had nothing to do with what they had discussed at the conference. But what was he talking about? And why did Amir think Ralph could or would possibly help?

The deep thinking was caught short when Ralph realized he had only a few minutes to get to the bus for the day's meetings. Ralph showered quickly, used the wet towel to remove some muddy footprints, took a slow Uber to the meeting point, and was the last on the mini-bus. The only seat available was in the back row. The bus was heading to Jerusalem from Tel Aviv, about an hour's journey.

Within minutes of the bus getting on the highway, Ralph nodded off. He awoke with a start as a very tall and very attractive Chinese woman nudged Ralph's splayed legs to get into the empty seat next to him. Ralph wiped some saliva off his lower lip with his sleeve. Eva introduced herself as part of the Huawei delegation. Ralph was so doggedly tired that when he did finally make the connection to the late-night discussion, she had already looked away to scan the bus's other riders.

"You weren't at the party last night. I was looking for you," Eva cooed with her exotic accent.

"You … ah, were, umh, looking for me?" Ralph wasn't particularly adroit when a pretty woman latched onto him.

"Of course. Didn't you see me staring at you during the meeting?"

"Ah, no. I was pretty focused on the sixteen different one-on-one meetings with the Israeli companies presenting their tech to us."

"Oh." Eva didn't even pretend to hide her disappointment. She played with her hair and adjusted her skirt slightly higher. "Well, I was looking at you."

"Well, ah." Will Smith's character Hitch would have refunded his instructional fee immediately, as Ralph was a lost cause.

"Do you like younger women? I like older men because they are experienced. No games. Do you like my skirt?" she asked, managing to hitch it up just a little more.

"Erm, well, it is kind of, well, okay."

"Ralph, do you like me?"

"Ah, well, it's not …"

"Because I want to spend the night with you and—"

"Wait."

A few people on the bus turned their heads toward Ralph. He had interrupted more loudly than he intended.

In a softer voice he said, "I am an older, slightly-fat, mixed-race guy with wiry gray hairs sprouting indiscriminately from my nose and ears. I have no great wealth and nothing of value to offer you." Ralph took a deep breath and continued. "You are an attractive woman who could be a runway model if you didn't have an over-sized IQ. Because I am sleep-deprived and grumpy, can we cut to the chase? Right now, this feels like a bad trope. What do you want from me?"

"What are you saying Ralph? You are very …"

Ralph glared at this tall, blue-black-haired goddess with legs about four inches longer than his own, and then leaned back and shut his eyes.

There was a long pause. She poked him with her elbow. Ralph did not move or open his eyes. "They warned me you didn't always play by the rules," she whispered. Her accent had disappeared.

Ralph heart was racing, but he kept his eyes closed and tried hard not to react.

"I'd rather not do this here, but if you insist, I will comply. But before I do, let me just say that you are indeed too old and fat for me. I know you are straight because you immediately started to glisten on your forehead when I showed just a bit of thigh. Unbelievable. Are you a fifteen-year-old boy? And just so you know, we were prepared for other contingencies."

Ralph opened his eyes and saw an effeminate man in the row ahead turn, smile, and finger-wave.

"I might have slept with you anyways. For giggles. To torment you and your wife. But, for this particular discussion, we ask that you not raise your voice, as my people are only about two-thirds of those on this bus, and I wouldn't want to have to silence you here, if you decide you must misbehave."

Ralph was dumbstruck. He kept his eyes closed and listened.

"As you pretend to be oh-so-cool, I'll be trite and use the Hollywood idiom, 'We can do this the easy way, or the hard way.' Which do you prefer?"

Ralph decided to open a single eye. He was still mulling over her comments. And he started to get just a little pissed off.

"So, which is it?" she demanded.

Ralph said, just a little too loudly, "Which do I prefer? I don't know. I do know that you are kind of a joke. You've pretending to come on to me, and you're cute, but you've got no curves. Your body is like a twelve-year-old boy's. And you aren't even a little seductive. I wouldn't have slept with you."

Everyone on the bus turned around. Ralph was anxious and miffed. And the adrenaline was taking over. The finger-waver two rows ahead laughed.

"And just so we are clear, my wife is *hot*. And she'd kick your long skinny ass all over this bus."

Eva was glowing red.

"And for the record, I have no idea what the fuck you're talking about. Okay? No idea. Unless you want to start at the beginning, and explain a few things that have been happening to me over the last few months, I got nothing for you."

Embarrassment set. Eva fidgeted. The finger-waver caught her eye and motioned her to move forward to her previous seat at the front of the bus.

Ralph realized what had just happened. "I'm sorry. I'm tired and hungry and being a jerk. I'm sorry I said that stuff …" He trailed off into a very quiet mumble as she walked down the aisle of the bus.

Mr. Finger-waver stood up and sat down next to Ralph. "She's just one mission out of training. You've probably set her back by months. Hard to build confidence in such new recruits."

Ralph laughed without knowing why. He was giddy tired.

"You laugh at my misfortune, but Eva had an ampoule of Sodium Pentothal, and she didn't hesitate to use it on her first mission. Of course, on her first mission, she got her mark to talk and killed him within the first nine minutes of their encounter. Maybe the first time out was too easy for her."

"You know I have no idea what you're talking about."

"We can play this any way you want, Ralph." He paused. "But I am certain Amir visited your hotel room last night and told you what he thought he knew about our plans. And I need to know if you've told anyone else about that visit."

"I'm sorry, but I don't think I know who you are. My name is Ralph and I am here representing one of my portfolio companies called AnchorFree. We make the world's most popular internet freedom apps. We help more than six hundred fifty million people circumvent censorship each month. What do you do?"

"Amir is dead. Everyone on his team is dead, too. Very early this morning, I found them huddled in their safe house. Their bodies are now on a fishing trawler, being used as bait."

"What was your name? You're from Huawei, right?"

"The only reason I haven't killed you yet is because I need to know what you know, and who you have shared that information with."

"I don't mean to be rude, Mr. Huawei, but I'm certain you've got the wrong person. I'm a small venture capitalist looking for partnerships for some of my portfolio companies while visiting Israel. I assume you're joking with me when you say that some people are dead and being used as fish bait, as that'd be terribly illegal—and I'm sure the Mossad would find your admission to be compelling."

"Tell me what you know and who you shared it with and maybe we won't torture you."

"Cut the bullshit. I'm hungry and tired. I didn't get breakfast. My blood sugar is probably low. This isn't funny anymore. And I have no idea what types of games you people are playing. Furthermore, I don't know anything about what you are asking. I met a number of men named Amir yesterday—it's a popular name in Israel. You met the same people I did. Some are even on this bus. Why don't you ask them for the information you need?"

Mr. Huawei quickly studied the people on the bus. "You brought reinforcements with you? That's crafty Ralph. My people told me you were a lone wolf, so we didn't anticipate you'd have anyone to help you. I bet it is the two guys from Ericsson, am I right?" He smiled.

"This is getting silly. The joke is over, all right? As soon as we're off this bus, I will need a protein bar, some coffee and a two-hour nap. Then you can tell me why I'm the center of this ridiculous and bluntly kind of scary practical joke, okay?"

With that, Ralph leaned back and shut his eyes. He felt Huawei study him for a few minutes, then heard him stand up and walk back to his seat. When Ralph awoke, he was being nudged by the driver. Everyone else was off the bus and walking toward an office building, where the government had set up further meetings. Ralph wiped some more drool from his lower lip and shuffled off to catch up with the rest of the delegation.

⁓

Back in his KLM chair and a half, Ralph tried to make sense of what he had just experienced in Israel. He didn't think it was a practical joke. He did believe that Amir might be dead, and that he needed to figure out what all this meant as quickly as humanly possible. There were quite a few people who thought he knew more than he did. Ralph wasn't a spy—he didn't have "a team of people," and didn't know who to talk with about this situation. He was, in fact, afraid to tell anyone about it. He was perplexed, to say the least. But he gathered that whatever was going on somehow seemed to center on the Z-Prize tool.

Chapter 12
1992

Her infectious and unrestrained laugh abruptly stopped. "Are you Ralph Gibsen?"

Ralph was filling his coffee mug. He looked up and saw a gorgeous woman with a blonde ponytail. She was athletic and wearing what looked to be a unique hand-made scarf. He would have loved to say it was love at first sight. But as the other people in the breakroom would attest, the woman was sneering at Ralph like he had just forced her to swallow a bug. A rather large hairy bug.

Ralph overfilled his coffee, spilling it onto the counter and his pants. Then he said something suave, like, "Fuck." He grabbed a paper towel for his pants. "Yeah, I'm Ralph."

The young woman said, "Right." She spun and walked quickly from the breakroom, along with a three or four of the cool/smart women from the office. They giggled en masse as they rounded the corner, looking back at Ralph and the hot coffee dripping down the front of his pants.

After hurriedly cleaning up his mess, Ralph jogged to his office and dialed the office's "go-to gossip girl."

"Beth. What's going on?"

"Ralph, to what do I owe this pleasure?"

Beth ran PR and was the social queen and bon vivant of the office. They were working at the country's first nation-wide cellular provider, and they were much too young and inexperienced for their responsibilities.

"Well, just a quick check in regarding the press release for new 'voice activated-411' service."

"Ralph, why do you bore me with this? I've got everything handled. What did you think of the tickets I got you for *Cats*?"

"I uh, I didn't go. I guess I forgot."

"I know you didn't go, Ralph. Do you know why I know you didn't go? Because your ticket was right next to mine. And all I found when I got to my seat was your empty seat. Do you have any idea how hard it was to get those tickets?"

"Bethie, come on. We spend a boatload of money with every media outlet in town. People throw tickets at you."

"Not for *Cats*. This musical is hot. And I looked silly sitting there alone. Especially because I could have had an assortment of handsome men sitting next to me."

"Look, I'm sorry B. I just got busy at work. There's a ton to get done around here."

Ralph was in charge of new products. He was often the guy that pushed the entire team hard.

"Fine. Apology accepted. Now why did you really call me? I've never once let you down with my work," Beth remarked pointedly. "What's this call really about?"

"So ... I was wondering if ... they're these new people in the office today. Do you know who any of them are?"

"Ah ... someone caught your eye? Now I know why you really called. But my eleven o'clock appointment just showed up, so I'll need to get back to you soon. Ta ta."

"B—hold on, just wanted to know ..." But the phone was already back at dial tone.

Ralph was never easily dissuaded. He dialed four other women friends in the office. Each was skeptical of the social nature of the call.

"What's up, Ralph? You never call unless you're needing something yesterday. This is awkward."

Ralph rang off with each of them and had gained no new information. On the very next call, immediately after the social niceties, the young woman snapped, "She has a boyfriend and she isn't interested in you."

"Maggie, what are you talking about? I haven't even asked you ..."

"No, but you were going to—just like you asked Cass, Beth, Laurie, Cheryl, and now me. You've got no subtlety. Gotta go." And she rang off.

Damn, thought Ralph. He decided he needed to go for a walk-about.

The office had welcomed the new employees with banners and flowers. *It should be easy to find out who this new person is*, thought Ralph. But he walked around the few hundred-person office twice and didn't see the attractive woman from the breakroom. Instead, many women followed him with their eyes, unsuccessfully trying not to grin.

Ralph got back to his desk and was soon enveloped in his work. At 7:45 PM, just as he was thinking about heading out for dinner, Beth stopped by his office.

"Are we going to launch next Monday?"

"If billing and customer care can get their shit together, we will," Ralph snarled. He was perpetually at war with his billing and customer care team. In his opinion, they never had the flexibility and speed he needed. The tension between Ralph's team and the Care team was renowned.

Beth laughed. "Good to know. Well, goodnight."

"Hey, before you go, do you know anything about a new employee—I kind of caught some attitude this morning in the breakroom."

"New employee? Nope. Most start on Mondays."

"But she was definitely new. At least I've never seen her before."

"I am quite proud of you, Ralph. You made it thirty-one seconds before your restraint fell away. That's a new record for you."

"What do you mean?"

"You've been pestering everyone you know, pacing the office, and have spent more time in the breakroom today than you have cumulatively for the entire month."

"Well, see—this was a rather non-typical day. Usually if people openly dislike me, it's because I've done something dumb to deserve it. But this person, who I've never seen in my entire life, for some unknown reason, she spits out my name like—like its poison. And then she walks away in a group of people, and they all look back and laugh. And they weren't laughing with me. They were laughing at me. And did I mention that she was really, really hot?"

"Now we're getting somewhere."

"B, you know everyone. Who is she, and why doesn't she like me?"

"Well, my friend, her name is Jen Johnson. And you've worked with her for a number of years now. She's on the billing team."

"Shit."

"Yes, Ralph. She's one of the people you've been loudly calling 'the Naysayers.' You've sat on dozens of phone calls with her. She's been relocated from Santa Cruz to lead the billing team here. So, you'll be getting to know her while she tries to bend our nightmarish billing system to meet your outlandish whims and desires."

"But I'm just doing my job," Ralph stated defensively.

"The pot and kettle are both black, Ralph. And you haven't always been nice to that team. In fact, you've been mean and insulting." She giggled to herself. "I'm afraid you're going to learn that calling someone a 'naysayer' or any other name may have ramifications beyond just our silly billing system."

"Someday soon, our industry and many others will use billing adaptability and speed as a strategic advantage."

"You sound like a broken record. We've all heard you say that a dozen times. Start your own billing company."

"I just might. But I can't imagine it being a very exciting company. And it isn't like I'd be saving the planet or anything."

"Well, the reason Jen has been promoted and relocated to HQ is because she's adopted your thoughts on billing and will be leading the charge to make billing more responsive to the needs of the company."

"Why didn't anyone tell me?"

"And make you ego larger than it already is? No thank you! And just because she's adopted your rationale as her own, doesn't mean she likes you. She doesn't. She thinks you're an ass."

"But she doesn't even know me. She only knows my voice on conference calls. I can win her over, don't you think?"

"It's doubtful. You're not that good looking, and you're a horrible date. She's way out of your league. Smart as they come, and she has some sort of mysterious boyfriend."

"Why do you say mysterious?"

"Because no one has ever met him and she won't share any details. Zero. Someone told me they thought he was some sort of spy."

"Right." Ralph rolled his eyes.

"Anyway, if you really are interested in her, you'll need to play the long game. And you'll really want to unleash that awesome charm that occasionally flashes to the surface when no one else is looking. Not just to her, but everyone."

"What's with her laugh? It's like music."

"Oh, Ralph. See? Use that line. It'll earn you lunch, at least. For that I'm certain."

And Ralph took Beth's advice and attempted to be more thoughtful with his co-workers. He let down his guard and lessened the demands. And while his boss wasn't terribly impressed—she liked to call him her "hatchet man"—he got as much accomplished as he normally did. But with a kinder, gentler approach. And whenever he saw Jen in the office, he tried gallantly not to smile like the love-struck doofus he was.

About a month after their incident in the breakroom, Jen stayed late after a big meeting. Ralph was the only one left in the room.

"Thanks for helping prioritize things for us," Jen said without preamble. "Sometimes we only see a laundry list of things that needs to get done and my team gets inundated."

"Well, then we should do that at the end of every meeting. If it helps?"

"Sounds like a good plan. And, Ralph, if you have questions about me, perhaps you should ask me yourself, and not make a fool of yourself by asking all our mutual friends." She yawned. "It's kind of annoying being the new person in the office and having our mutual friends checking up on me. And it's awkward."

"Yeah, I'm sorry about that," Ralph said while thinking to himself what amazing green eyes she has. "I need to find more discrete friends."

She laughed. Ralph decided again that he loved her laugh.

As she was walking out the door she said, "You and me both."

Months passed, and as much as Ralph could recollect, he didn't remember a specific turning point. But he and Jen ended up becoming close friends. They often got invited to the same parties. They both arrived early to work and stayed late. And because of the work they did, they often traveled to the same cities for new product launches—she to coach the local customer care teams, and he to take the marketing and sales teams out for pre-new product launch drinks.

After six more months, the odd pair somehow became inseparable. All their friends accused them of dating, but the truth was they just really enjoyed each other's company. And Ralph was too afraid of making a move that would ruin their friendship. So he never did.

And then it all changed. During a quick business trip to Seattle. There was too much wine consumed at candle-lit dinner, one thing led to another, and suddenly they were a couple.

Six months later and Ralph got a job offer running a start-up telephone company in Tokyo. On a ferry bound for Hyannis, he proposed to Jen as they rounded the point at the Nantucket lighthouse. Both sets of parents were present. Ralph's proposal was meandering, but he managed to say the important stuff. "I can't imagine living without your magical laugh in my life for the rest of my days."

Even after a fancy wedding in San Francisco, in order that all their friends and family didn't need to travel to Tokyo, Ralph never learned much about Jen's previous life. The one point of immense comfort was that Ralph's mom—who had been civil but cool to a half-dozen of Ralph's previous girlfriends—treated Jen like an old, best friend.

In fact, Bubsy had quickly taken Ralph's new wife under her wing. It was no time before they planned vacations together. Jen soon became more well-known among Bubsy's friends than had Ralph. When the phone rang, Bubsy often wanted to speak with Jen directly, and Ralph was left asking how his mother was doing. Jen had even given credit to Bubsy for the idea of leaving the communications industry and starting her own international relocation business for busy executives.

❧

Ralph called Jen his girlfriend as he thought it was more romantic than wife. Very quickly Ralph learned that Jennifer could not sleep if the tags on the bed sheets were not in the lower left corner of the bed. If Ralph wanted to drive her absolutely mad, he wore his T-shirt inside out. She couldn't wink with her left eye, but she often tried. It made her look like she'd just swallowed a salty plum.

❧

But Ralph's girlfriend/wife/boss understood the rigors of being married to an entrepreneur. She adapted, even when running her own business. She was always receiving visitors from Russia, China, the Middle East; wealthy couples looking for vacation homes on either coast. Like Ralph, she'd also have to pop away at a moment's notice to meet clients and show them various properties. So, on one Saturday, when she would much rather be at the farmers market with her people, she jumped into the car with her husband because he had a meeting with a Chinese executive who could only meet at NASA's Moffett Field on the Saturday afternoon just before Golden Week. It was the only time they would spend together that week.

When Jen dropped Ralph off at his meeting, his host asked him who the woman was. Ralph said she was an Uber driver. He then confided to his host that she was the prettiest Uber driver he'd ever seen.

ℂℂ

The phone rang at 7AM. He answered with, "Hey, everyone quiet down. You—get off the chandelier! And get the donkey out of the kitchen. Quiet!"—pause—"Good morning, Sweetness."

Ralph liked to make his girlfriend think he was a wild party animal when she was away visiting her parents. The truth was he was in bed by 9PM, after watching the Patriots spank another lame New York team.

Jen's first question was, "Why is there always a donkey in the kitchen at Ralph's imaginary all-night parties?"

Sigh. How do explain to your girlfriend that any *great* party always involves farm animals? Hadn't she ever seen *Animal House*?

Chapter 13

Ralph thought about that awkward moment of asking the concierge to recommend a massage place that didn't offer "happy endings." Sex means very different things to different people. In much of the world, sex was nothing more than a biological function—like having to move your bowels as soon as you wake. In the last week alone, Ralph had been on several fourteen-hour flights, and needed a massage—an actual massage—for his occasional creakiness.

Around 1997, Ralph moved to Tokyo for the second time—but this time was with Jen. Mrs. Sato-san, their landlady, reminded Ralph of Mrs. Miyagi of fifteen-years earlier, but Ralph knew that couldn't be—this woman wasn't blind, and by then Mrs. Miyagi would have been more than ninety years old, maybe even a hundred. Mrs. Sato-san and her husband were a wealthy older couple who owned the entire apartment building, with a dozen flats, in Takanawa-ku, one of the most upscale Tokyo neighborhoods. Apparently, the couple was of old money—so much so, her grandfather's etching graced the 10,000 Yen note.

Being new in a foreign city, Jen became fast friends with Mrs. Sato-san, who showed her the wonders of Tokyo and Japan. Mr. Sato was a retired bookshop owner and was content to read his books, enjoy his afternoon cocktail, and let his wife lead his social calendar.

About six weeks after they had first met, Mrs. Sato-san had Jen and Ralph over to dinner. Earlier in the day, Jen and Mrs. Sato-san had taken an art class together. Much of the discussion centered on the art teacher, and whether she was gay. Mr. Sato-san quietly joked that he found the sensei quite attractive, and that if she were in fact gay, it would give him something to think about later in the evening.

"You've become such an old *sukebe*," Mrs. Sato-san sneered playfully. Ralph later learned this was not a nice term—roughly translated to "lecher."

"I am old, but a Japanese man never loses his need for the love of attractive women."

"It sounds to me like you're really just leading this conversation toward asking permission to take young Ralph to Soap-lando."

"It isn't a bad idea. Why thank you, my dear. Might you have some pocket money for us to spend after this dinner?"

Ralph blanched and reached for more wine.

As always, Jen was attuned to Ralph's many interpersonal cues. "What's Soap-lando?"

Mrs. Sato-san looked to Ralph. "Surely you have explained Soapland to your soon-to-be-bride?"

"Ah, no. I must confess, I only know it as an urban legend. When I lived here before—more than ten years ago—I had a girlfriend. And Soapland is terribly expensive, isn't it?"

Mr. Sato-san chuckled at Ralph's discomfort. "I always forget how prude young men from the USA are. Soapland is one of Japan's treasures."

Mrs. Sato-san chimed in, "Yes, look at him blush."

Now everyone in the room was staring at Ralph's discomfort.

"And I must hear the story of how you broke Miss Hiromi Shiseido's heart someday. People still gossip about you as a couple. Have you spoken to her since your return?"

"Ah, no." An awkward pause. "This beef is delicious. Tell me about it again please?"

Jen was persistent. "What's Soapland? And though I am aware of this former girlfriend, I had no idea that they were the talk of the town." She smiled at him. "I can't wait to learn more."

The sweat was accumulating on Ralph's brow.

"Isn't Ralph charming when he's uncomfortable?" Mrs. Sato-san playfully quipped. "Jen-san, Soapland is a series of establishments in Kawasaki-ku—just a few stops south of here—where men go as sort of a spa day."

"That sounds nice." Jen turned to Ralph. "Why are you uncomfortable?"

"Ralph's a good boy. He is uncomfortable because this spa focuses on meeting all of men's carnal needs." Mrs. Sato-san went into great detail. "First the gentlemen enter the facility and a group of young attractive women serve them a nice bowl of Miso soup, and then maybe a bottle of sake or whiskey." She looked over at her husband, "How does the pairing happen?"

"Most naturally, of course," claimed Mr. Sato-san.

"Of course!" Mrs. Sato-san chided. "Young beautiful women are *naturally* attracted to your old skinny limp potato."

Ralph knew that potato was the Japanese euphemism for penis.

Jen suddenly had a stern look around her eyes.

Mrs. Sato continued. "The woman takes the man back to a warm private room that has a raised stone or wood slab. She disrobes him. She lays him down and makes certain he is comfortable. Then she disrobes herself and turns on the handheld shower wands. The woman uses fragrant soaps and oils to bring a lather to her entire body. Without ever using her hands, she then applies her body to the man's body to ensure he is clean. Every square centimeter is clean. Isn't that correct, dear?"

Mr. Sato-san nodded affirmatively. Ralph and Mr. Sato each adjusted their pants and reached for more wine. The shine on Ralph's forehead was again in need of a wipe.

"Once the man has climaxed, he is further cleaned. Then perhaps a quick snuggle?"

"For those of us gentlemen, yes. For those of rougher repute, they might demand a further message of the head and shoulders." Mr. Sato-san was obviously proud of his snuggling.

"And then dinner and whiskey is served. The men smoke, play Go, tell lies, and come home five or six hours later. The best part is, they sleep soundly."

By this point in the conversation, the lasers streaming out of Jen's eyes were melting Ralph's skull.

The evening proceeded pleasantly. Ralph and Jen were invited to dinner again. Ralph promised he'd tell the story of how he broke Miss Shiseido's heart. Many thanks were given, and Jen and Ralph went home at a respectable hour. Mr. Sato-san ended the night at Soapland with his friends, and Ralph spent the remainder of the night using hot oils to massage Jen's feet.

To everyone's pleasant surprise, dinners with the Satos quickly became a weekly affair.

૨૭

This concierge didn't understand Ralph's request. A massage *without* a happy ending? To some modest extent, Ralph understood both Cantonese and Mandarin, but he couldn't speak either worth a damn. He WeChat-ed Eric Koh, his China right-hand man.

"Can you tell this guy I need to find a good masseuse? A high-quality back and neck massage, with or without oils—but without a hand job finish?"

"I've never seen my job description, boss, but I'm pretty sure this kind of request isn't on it. 'Protect the boss from getting hand jobs from nice Chinese girls.' Nope, not on my job description."

"Please Eric?"

"All right, pass your phone to him."

Ralph was soon assured that a trained and accredited masseuse would be at a local spa in an hour. "Or she can come to your room, boss?"

"No—doesn't feel right. The spa is better."

"Jen's not within 7000 miles, boss."

"But she would know."

Eric was sixty-something years old, tall, gangly, and unconventional for his Chinese ancestry. He had long hair and wore the latest youth-oriented fashions. He had six wives and multiple girlfriends. When Ralph first hired Eric, he noticed that Eric never submitted receipts for hotel stays in China. He learned later that Eric had set up his wives in apartments in the major cities and stayed with them when he traveled. He expensed a per diem that was less than a standard hotel rate, hence, Ralph never had cause for concern.

Over the years, Ralph had met most of the wives. Eric's first wife was in Singapore, his hometown. With his first wife, he had a child who was now older than a few of his girlfriends. His second wife was in Hong Kong. She was originally from Mongolia and was only fifteen years his junior. Wife three was in Beijing and was thirty years younger. She had used her stipend from Eric to get a college degree and then an MBA. She now worked in Private Equity and didn't rely on Eric's monthly stipend for her needs. Wife four lived in Shanghai, and was the most volatile. She'd threaten to leave Eric a few times a month, but always stuck around. Wife five was in Shenzhen and was about forty years younger. Still in her mid-twenties, she was very pretty, but uninteresting. Her only goals were acquiring things. Eric had recently paid for her driving lessons and was now expected to buy her a small car. Wife six was also in Shenzhen, but was more of a business partner, with various physical benefits. She was the only wife who knew about each of the other five.

Hence, the cultural chasm was large, and it was no small feat for Eric to understand Ralph's cultural mores and his desire not to have a massage with a happy ending. Eric acquiesced to Ralph's request because he saw firsthand how uncomfortable Ralph was around questions regarding his monogamy with Jen. Ten or twelve years previously, Ralph had infamously walked out of a major Samsung celebration party when a dozen women entered the private dining room and began to perform fellatio on the dozen men who were celebrating the culmination of this important business deal. This so-called Blow Job Party made Ralph run for the exit, embarrassing all involved. In the end, the deal was almost thwarted due to Ralph's poor behavior and inability to adapt to the situation.

Company representatives in Asia often tested Western partners with outrageous food stuffs and compromising situations to determine the potential partner's adaptability. And in this instance, Ralph simply failed. In the ensuing years, Ralph had consumed whale, dog, live man-of-war, and an assortment of brains. But he had trained Eric to protect him from any and all non-monogamy-inducing situations.

Chapter 14

On Saturday, as Ralph was walking between exhibits in the Chengdu Panda Park, the skies opened, and the rain fell like a freight train. Ralph didn't have an umbrella and went scrambling for cover. Unfortunately, everyone else did as well. There was no space left in the shelters, and Ralph was quickly getting sopping wet. Seemingly out of nowhere, two young women appeared—one on each side—and used their two umbrellas to keep the three of them mostly dry. Ralph was considerably taller than them, they had to hold their umbrellas with their arms fully extended.

Neither of the two women spoke much English, but Ralph thanked them profusely in what little Chinese he could speak. They quickly scanned each other's phones with the WeChat app, and were able to utilize the translation feature for instant messaging. The conversation was slightly awkward, as it was still raining aggressively, and one-handed texting is never easy. But Ralph learned they were childhood friends and fellow tourists from the town of Xi'an.

After more than twenty minutes of this downpour, Ralph realized that the young women's arms must be getting tired. He took over both umbrellas, to the new team's great relief. The rain muted itself to a gentle roar, and the threesome explored the various exhibits. There were approximately 3000 people for every exhibit. The scrum to get to the viewing area was a full-contact sport. But the young women were adept with a well-placed elbow, and they often got within a few feet of the enclosures. Pandas sleep often, especially after breakfast, and as the day passed the plethora of sleeping panda got rather monotonous. The rain lessened even more, but the heat increased, and the smell of thousands of wet humans in a steam room prevailed. Tea was suggested. But the line for tea was ginormous, so the three new friends found a DiDi taxi and went to the People's Park in central Chengdu.

The entrance to the park was pleasant, with considerable Communist statuary exhorting the people's successes in war and industry. Once inside the ample grounds, there were numerous teahouses to choose from, and the three new friends wandered around looking for the best. As they walked through the bonsai section of the park, there were dozens of laminated hand-written notes spread out on the ground, and just as many nervous older women hovering by. The two young women giggled and although many old women prodded them to look at the laminated sheets, the two girls took pictures of a few of them, spoke a few curt words to the pleading older women, and pushed Ralph along. When they found the teashop of their liking, they sat down and were given a menu that offered dozens of different teas. The two women ordered a few different teas, and a few sweet soybean dumpling treats. Ralph asked via WeChat about the laminated sheets. The women's body language demonstrated some uncomfortableness. Ralph switched topics and learned that one of them was a dance instructor for kindergarteners, and the other an art teacher for college students. They were both twenty-six years old, single, and loved to travel in China. After the tea, everyone was beginning to assertively fade due to the fierce humidity, and the fact that the young women had spent the previous night on a ten-hour train ride from their hometown of Xi'an to Chengdu.

Ralph didn't have any meetings that evening, so he offered to take them to a nice restaurant for dinner. They agreed to meet three hours later, and parted. When they arrived at the hotel that evening, the two teachers were more formally dressed than Ralph, but that was almost assured—Ralph usually dressed like he was heading for the beach. The grandeur of the hotel and its restaurant seemed to intimidate Ralph's new friends. He did his best to lighten the mood with a couple of funny questions about the food, and a few glasses of wine.

"Ralph, how did you meet your wife?" one asked.

Ralph gave them the full story. The conversation was a mix of English, Chinese, and WeChat for translation of the tricky bits. The two young women seemed to revel in the part of the story where Ralph told them of the difficulty he faced in attempting to woo his love. The women were rapt with attention, and they used the translation tool for almost every word that could be ambiguous. They had many detailed and nuanced questions. Ralph speculated this was their way of avoiding an awkward moment later in the evening, if Ralph was a cad and tried to proposition either or both. Or perhaps they were, in fact, spies? Wouldn't that explain why they were trying to find out more about Jen, who perhaps also might be a spy? *No, no,* Ralph told himself, *that's crazy Peterson thinking. They're just probably worried about my intentions.* Ralph took the necessary step—he hoped—to ensure they understood he was not a threat, especially as he was closer to their fathers' age than their own. This did not seem to give them comfort. The women had a question they wanted to ask, but Ralph felt they were holding back.

Over dessert, the question they most wanted to ask eventually came. "Ralph, if your wife went on a date, or went on several dates with a few different men before she married you, would you have married her, or would you think she was a prostitute?" The girls were looking at their wine glasses, avoiding Ralph's eyes.

Ralph took a moment to gather his thoughts. "I would still have married her regardless of her dating a few different men. I am certain my wife had a few boyfriends before I met her when we were in our early thirties." Ralph had never met one of Jen's ex-boyfriends, but he assumed she had broken a few hearts along the way.

"But what if … she had been paid to go on those dates, by the men?"

The women were now fiercely concentrated, their eyes looking directly into Ralph's.

Ralph suddenly had no idea where this conversation was going. But he was certain his answer was very important to them. "I would have married Jen no matter what her past."

The relief was palpable. But Ralph was still confused. "Can I ask why you wanted to ask me this question? Is there more I should know?"

They looked at each other and, after a moment, nodded. The young women admitted that they had come to Chengdu not for the purposes of being tourists, but of being escorts to some men that they had met online. Because of China's one-child policy, many families had chosen to abort female fetuses, and only accept male babies into their family. Over decades, this had produced a disproportionate number of males. In urban parts of China, the ratio of males to females of a certain age group was as high as 3:2. This "statistically abnormality," as the government referred to it, made for many desperate males—and their families—who desired nice healthy wives to produce sufficient progeny. One of the teachers explained that the laminated sheets of paper Ralph had seen in the park earlier in the day were made by anxious mothers looking for brides for their sons.

The two young women from Xi'an had taken a ten-hour train ride to Chengdu to be the pretend girlfriends of two thirty-four-year-old guys who wanted to show their families they were well enough to find women to date. Ralph learned that the men from Chengdu had paid the two women from Xi'an the equivalent of three month's teacher's salary, plus train and hotel fare, to pose as their long-term girlfriends.

The women quickly presented the ground rules to Ralph, which they had agreed to for this date. The gentlemen would be allowed unlimited handholding, a quick full-body hug, and a kiss on the lips—for no more than three seconds—upon departing. The men asked the women to study their histories and assorted business accomplishments, and to subtlety brag about their good fortune. The women also promised to appear to be traditional Chinese girls, by being deferential and polite to the family at all times.

The two women sitting with Ralph were having significant second thoughts about their agreement. Via some online research, they were certain their dates were probably gay and therefore not a physical threat. But they were afraid of how this would look to their future husbands and their families. They were asking Ralph for advice. At that moment, Ralph wished Jen were 7000 miles closer.

Ralph slowly typed into WeChat: "I cannot pretend to know your situation and the way things are changing in your culture today. But I also cannot imagine an appropriate future husband being upset over a three-second kiss and some handholding."

The women were relieved when they read the WeChat message. There was considerable discussion between the two teachers, but in the end, they decided to proceed. Ralph made them promise to send him a message the following evening after their dates were over.

The following evening, while at a business dinner, Ralph received notification that both women were safely back in their hotel. Both were pleasantly surprised that their experiences of being a fake girlfriend wasn't the least bit unpleasant.

In that last WeChat communication, they also apologized that they hadn't been entirely honest. They revealed that they had taken a payment from Huawei to report on their dates, including spending the previous day and dinner with Ralph. Then they added a last text: "Eva says hi and C U soon ;-)"

Chapter 15

Ralph could show you how to get to the so-called Dark Web, but felt the whole experience was overrated. Yes, you could find a pimply-faced teenager to troll your nemesis's Twitter feed or plan a DDOS attack on a small local merchant, but there was very little recourse on the Dark Web, and hence, at least half of the time, he felt like he received poor value for his Bitcoin payments.

Hacking isn't very sexy, no matter what Hollywood sells. In fact, it's a pretty dull endeavor. Ralph likened it to walking around any one of the massive hotels in Las Vegas and checking if any of the doors were unlocked. It is a boring, tedious process that is only achievable if it can be automated. But many hacks are successful because software has many "doors."

When Ralph really needed to get something done in the digital world, he turned to Fiverr.com and Freelancer.com. These sites were legit commerce. Need a new logo? Fifty dollars and you'd get three to choose from and two requests for revisions. Need a new website? No problem. Someone would give you a professional quality modern site for $25, if you wrote the copy. He especially liked that these for-hire sites awarded credibility points for those providing services whose work was well done. And since he had been an avid user for more than a dozen years, he had built a reputation as someone who paid promptly and offered strong endorsements.

The way these sites worked was two-fold: 1) You could browse digital services offered by 20,000 suppliers from all over the planet; or 2) You could post your digital needs, in the form of a specification document, and get suppliers to bid to do the work. Ralph typically employed the latter. He'd write up what he wanted to accomplish, and people/ developers would bid on their time and costs to be the supplier. This often allowed Ralph to test new business ideas. He'd build a website, offer some sort of service, and see how many people signed up. If lots of people signed up, he'd invest and develop the product to launch. This allowed him to efficiently understand and potentially mit- igate the market risks of any idea that popped into his head. And instead of investing hundreds of thousands or millions of dollars in an actual product, he'd spend only a few hundred dollars and learn if the idea had real merit.

But Ralph also used these sites for less honorable tasks. At one point in his career, these "less honorable tasks" in- cluded "forcing market adoption" of his software on his targets. And at the moment, he decided he needed to get the passwords for the shared Dropbox account used by some of the other members of his team working on the tool. He needed to better understand if there were people, or teams, working on the tool who had alternate agen- das. And as the aphorism goes, script kiddies hacked code. Pros hacked people.

Ralph hoarded lists. He had created a very large spread- sheet many years previously, and any time he ran across a digital list of people, he'd save the list in his spreadsheet. Sometimes a person would send an email with all of the recipients names exposed, instead of using the bcc option, or Fast Company would publish a list of the top 100 Most Creative/Efficient/Productive/Lopsided People—he collected them all. If the list had emails, then even better, but it was ridiculously simple to create a script—a simple technique to use a burner email account and check if, for example, Abe Lincoln can be reached via Abe@WH.gov, Abraham@WH.gov, ALincoln@WH.gov, Abe.Lincoln@WH.gov, Abe_Lincoln@WH.gov, or AL@WH.gov. If you sent a test email to all of these email addresses to the recipient you are trying to find, the email server will almost immediately send you back a note that will tell you which email addresses didn't work—they bounced. If one address didn't bounce, then by process of elimination, you'd know which email works. Ralph saved that information systematically. And later, when he learned the basics of hacking, he'd append the spreadsheet with further data that he'd gather via LinkedIn, Twitter, or Facebook. And later still, he'd add the data he'd garner via his social hacking endeavors.

In Ralph's eyes, the most successful and most interesting form of hacking was social hacking. Social hacking differed from normal hacking because it was akin to having someone open the door for you. It was often as simple as sending the "target" an email warning them that there has been inappropriate activity on their Facebook/Microsoft/Google page and the account would soon be closed to prevent further fraudulent activity. In the email, the target is directed to a page (that the hacker controls) that would appear to be a sign-in page—many browsers allow a person (hacker) to copy the HTML code of a legitimate sign-in page, and modify the code to suit their needs, by pointing to a hacker's database, opposed to Facebook/Microsoft/Google's. By setting up a fake sign-in page from Facebook/Microsoft/Google, the target attempts to enter their email and password, but fails each time. And now a hacker has captured all of the target's email and password combinations.

Once the target had entered every email-password combination they could think of (most people have an average of no more than seven login combinations), Ralph would have his software thank (or scold) the target and close the browser tab, and insert these combinations into his database. The entire "spear-fishing" process had been automated—via a $320 exercise on Freelancer.com—via anonymous Russian servers tied discretely to Ralph's social media interactors lists. Due to the fact that more than twenty thousand people followed Ralph on LinkedIn and Twitter, he most often didn't even know who his past targets were.

With this in mind, Ralph wasn't very surprised when he queried his database and learned that he already had the login credentials of nearly all of his fellow committee members. Only his primary target had not been tapped, the boisterous guy named Philips who had inadvertently revealed—via Ralph's Pineapple WiFi sniffing tool—that there existed a group of silent investors with a non-acknowledged purpose.

Armed with the login credentials, he did a quick search of his peers' Dropbox accounts and was surprised that they were all nearly identical to his own. The only divergence was in three of the accounts, where there was a single password-protected file that was inaccessible. Ralph tried every password he had in his database and then ran an ad hoc password generator he had built—again using Freelancer—that mined a target's Facebook account. To find any way in, the password generator would run for hours, testing 2000 passwords a second.

For the big fish that hadn't been landed yet, he decided he'd need to bring out the big rods. His favorite social hack was what he called the "two-factor spoof." Two-factor authentication was a tried and true security technique that made geeks and wonks feel more comfortable that their identity and security was assured. Two-factor authentication is based on sending you an alternative login query to an alternative trusted device. So Ralph sent his target an SMS from an anonymous Skype account—with the words Dropbox Admin as the handle—portraying that someone was attempting to get into the target's Dropbox account. "Is that OK?" Inevitably, the target responds, "No." At the same instant of the negative-response SMS, Ralph sends an email—looking like it is from Dropbox—suggesting the target create a new password, with a link to do the same. This linked-form is identical—including a very similar URL string—to an actual Dropbox form. The form asks for the target's old password and for them to create a new password. The form congratulates the user for creating a new password and closes the browser tab. Ralph now has the password that opens the account. He opens the target's Dropbox account, copies the contents to his hard drive, and then—to ensure there are no questions—changes the account's password to the target's new selection. The target now receives an SMS from Dropbox saying that the password has been changed.

All of this happened within seconds. Ralph pursued the bounty he'd scored, and soon he found the rogue file he saw in the three members' accounts, but didn't have in his Dropbox. He opened the file, and suddenly all hell broke loose. His computer was issuing all sorts of warnings. Someone was trying to breach his system. This was remarkable, since Ralph had used two different VPNs to

mask his IP, location, and identity. Someone with tre-
mendously sophisticated hacking tools—possibly only a
state-actor like the NSA or the Mossad had these "big-
iron" tools—was trying to break into Ralph's system.
Ralph moved IP addresses a few times, but he couldn't
shake them. His systems were wailing alarms and faltering.
In a moment, he realized his external hard drive was being
over-driven—he could hear it spin unnaturally quickly.
Before it fried, he unplugged it from his computer. Once
the hard drive was unplugged, the onslaught fell away. The
incoming hack disappeared as quickly as it came on.

The timing of the cyberattack, very close to his own
Dropbox hack, had Ralph ultra-anxious. Ralph ran to his
closet and grabbed an old laptop that he had air gapped—
it had no means to connect to the internet. He plugged
in the external hard drive and opened the rogue file. He
perused a few of the most recent documents. They were all
old-fashioned memos, looking like they'd been dictated,
including To: and From: headers. His three peers figured
prominently in the memos. They were mostly assigned
to finding answers to certain questions. There were a few
themes, the most prominent being an ongoing question
of whether or not the testing was still seeing 99.8% efficacy. The other prominent themes were if the "dark pattern
algorithms" were correlating correctly and if the delivery
mechanism could be improved and made to last longer
than a few hours. Ralph had discerned these themes in less
than five minutes and had more questions than answers.

The phone rang. Ralph rarely answered the home
phone, as he was married to the most beautiful and most
popular woman in their little beach community. The only
people who called the house—including his mother—
wanted to speak to his wife. And Jen was out walking the
dogs. So he let the call go to the machine. He certainly

didn't want to get into a conversation about Jen's social calendar with one of her well-meaning friends. The phone stopped ringing and immediately started again. This was Jen's signal for him to pick up the phone.

"Sweetness. What's going on? Everything okay?"

"Sorry. I know you're busy, but I'm worried about our boy."

Ralph and Jen had forgotten to have children. Their "boy" was their German Shepherd rescue, whom Jen doted after. In truth, the dog and his mother were inseparable.

"Well, I am deep into something important. But what's going on with Enzo?"

"He's got a gimp. And I've checked his toes and there are no stickers in between. There's no blood, but maybe he stepped on an urchin or something."

Without children, Jen treated her two dogs with near reverence and excessive protection.

"Can you make it home, or do you need me to come pick you up?"

"We're all the way down at Hidden Beach. Could you take a quick break and drive down and get us? You'd be back at your project in like five minutes, tops. I promise."

"Ah. Sure." Ralph had been married long enough to know Jen wasn't really making a request. "Can I just get a minute to close out a few things?"

"Really? You'd leave your distraught wife and injured son …?"

"I'll meet you there in less than three minutes." Ralph was already looking for the wagon's keys. He shut the laptop and hard disk and placed them under his desk. He locked the front door, got in the Volvo, and drove the three miles to pick up Jen and the two dogs.

In less than five minutes he arrived at Hidden Beach's parking lot, where Jen and the dogs were talking with a neighbor. Ralph waited in the car hoping to impress upon Jen his need to be elsewhere. It didn't work. In fact, it never worked. Jen went at her own speed. She laughed loudly with her fellow beach walker, and Ralph reminded himself as to why he loved her so. Her laugh was sunshine. And home-baked chocolate chip cookies. And a long hot shower after a day on the beach. Eventually, after what seemed like an hour, Jen meandered over to the car.

"Thanks for coming to get us."

"Enzo doesn't seem hurt."

The Shepherd immediately jumped into the back of the old wagon. But the Great Pyrenees didn't want to go home. She wanted to keep chasing seagulls. And there were fewer seagulls at home. Logically, she didn't want to get into the car.

"He's gimpy. It's his left shoulder. We need to call the vet as soon as we get home. Bean-butt, get in the car." The 120 pounds of white fur and love sauntered over to the side door. She didn't want to get in the back of the wagon. She wanted to get into the backseat.

"Okay, Princess. Get in." Ralph opened the door behind the driver's. Bean slowly got into the backseat of the car and shook off the sand and sea before falling onto the comfortable leather backseat.

"Can we stop at the market on the way home? I only need a few things."

"Sweetness, I got stuff to do."

"But it's the weekend. Do you really have to work?"

"This is really interesting stuff I'm working on. If we can get it to work, it'll change the world. It'll make us all more wise."

"Well, tell me about it then."

"I can't. Honey, you know the kind of Non-Disclosure Agreements I have to sign. I can't tell you much more than I just did." Ralph did feel bad about this, but it wasn't something he could change. This was how business was done in Silicon Valley.

"Yuck. I'm sick of having this discussion. Let's stop at the market, please?"

The slight guilt-ing won, and they stopped at the market. Ralph waited in the car with the dogs, hoping it would quicken Jen's pace. But it didn't. She even stopped twice on the way back to the car to exchange pleasantries with neighbors. Not for the first time, Ralph realized he was the consort to the Queen of the Beach of Santa Cruz.

When they finally got back home, ninety minutes had passed. The dogs ran into the backyard and barked at imaginary things. Jen asked for help putting the groceries away as she needed to call the vet. And Ralph needed to pee. The big white dog had obviously been enjoying some beach sushi, which she barfed on the kitchen floor. It looked like a few crabs. By the time he got the spew cleaned up, the groceries put away, and his wife off-the-ledge about a $35,000 shoulder surgery for the dog, much of the afternoon had gone. And he still needed to pee. When he finally thought about the tool project again, he was into early evening.

"Honey? Where did you move my computer?" Ralph asked this question about two dozen times a day. Jen liked things in their "right" place. She moved things often.

"Which one?"

This was a fair question. Ralph could see three computers in the living room alone.

"I put an old IBM Think Pad and hard drive under the desk before picking you up at the beach. It isn't there now ..."

"Wasn't that computer ten or twelve years old?"

"Yes, but it's a great computer when I need to be air-gapped from the internet."

"I haven't seen it in years. Are you certain it wasn't donated on the Goodwill trip we did over the holidays?"

"I used it just before I picked you up. It was for the project I'm working on."

"Are you certain you weren't using another computer or drive? There are dozens of those drives around the house."

"I'm positive. It was just there," Ralph said, pointing beneath the desk.

"But—well, did you notice if the back door was open when we got home? I think it was."

"You think someone might have walked in the house and stolen one of the oldest computers here? Walked past three or four iPhones, two MacBook Airs, a MacBook Pro, a couple of tablets, and a very expensive touch screen computer, so they could steal a $25 hard drive and a twelve year old PC with most of its communication modules removed?"

"I don't know. Maybe."

"Is anything else missing? Any of your jewelry? Aren't you the least bit concerned?"

"Well—I'll go check." Jen gave Ralph a very quizzical look and walked up the stairs.

Ralph did a quick inventory. His old convertible was in the garage, with its keys on the console. On the walls hung artwork that could fund a college career. Absolutely nothing was out of place. He walked upstairs and into their bedroom. Jen was getting changed.

"Anything missing?"

"No. Maybe you just misplaced it. Or maybe you were using one of the other computers and just thought you were using the IBM?" She was putting on some evening wear. He had forgotten they were going out to dinner that night.

"I don't think so." Ralph wanted to tell her about his hacking expedition, and thus she'd understand the seriousness of the situation, but was afraid she'd freak out. Ralph hated himself for suspecting Jen had moved the computer, putting it in the "right" place, and then forgot about it. But no, he was with her the entire time. He was certain she didn't move it.

Someone had been in the house.

ⅎⅎ

As Jen and Ralph walked into the restaurant later that night, Ralph couldn't help but notice that Eva was sitting at the bar between two very handsome men, and that she was wearing a big smile. She knew he was there, but did her best to ignore him completely.

Chapter 16

The founder of the start-up explained his technology to Ralph. He was looking for advice and perhaps some seed investment.

"As people move through a space within range of a WiFi signal, their bodies affect the radio frequencies, absorbing some waves and reflecting others in various directions. By analyzing the exact ways that a WiFi signal is altered when a human moves through the RF, we can 'see' where someone is within the room, identify a particular person by the way they walk, watch what someone might type on a keyboard, and even read a person's lips with startling accuracy—in some cases even if a router isn't in the same room as the person performing the actions."

"Holy privacy nightmare. For what purpose would someone want that?"

"Well, imagine the home router senses a person's entry into a room. It could communicate with other connected devices—lights, appliances, window shades—to customize the room to that person's predefined preferences."

"Yikes. I can only think about how it could be misused. Can I get a prototype to test?" Ralph often latched onto new hacking tools just by listening to entrepreneur's investment pitches.

"Sure. We can have one to you next week."

The prototype was delivered to Ralph. But within two weeks, the smart engineer had taken a $3M starting bonus and joined Google to lead another initiative. Ralph threw it in his art studio, with the dozens of other pieces of kit he had acquired via similar means. Someday he might have a use for it.

❧

Along with being an investor in smart entrepreneurs, Ralph had also been around that particular block once or twice himself. He'd been the CEO of three moderately successful start-ups. As a "silver-back" in the Valley, he often got requests for advice that wasn't exactly professional. But since there weren't many to provide life advice to Silicon Valley entrepreneurs, he wasn't reticent to assist when asked.

The entrepreneur's email asked, "How does one manage to date when you are a founder of a start-up? There aren't enough hours in the day. My former girlfriend and I dated for four years before she dumped me, saying I wasn't giving her enough attention. Is there a formula or something I should know about?"

Ralph wrote back:

"Hell, I don't know. I was single about 150 million years ago—or so it seems. In those days, I occasionally had the good fortune of bringing a very nice young lady to my home. Never on the first date mind you…. But occasionally, if the all of the gods smiled, on the second or third date. When a nice woman walked into my home, they often fixated on my antique birthing table that I left in the middle of the living room. Upon seeing the birthing table, she'd inevitably have one of three reactions:

"1) She'd run from the house screaming. Which is just as well, as she obviously had no adventure in her soul and would have bored me in time. After marriage, she would have nagged me into selling off my eclectic antiques and collection of classic convertibles to purchase a too-large, bland SUV—or worse, a minivan. She'd have demanded to live in a big boxy home in a safe neighborhood, without diversity or Indian take-out nearby. She'll refuse to move more than two miles from her mother, even when I got offered the job of my dreams in London. After ten or twelve years of marriage, we'd have moved to separate bedrooms, and it'd probably have been more fun. I'd have found myself working later and later at the office, just to avoid going home. In retirement, I'd have spent all of my time at the golf or sailing club ogling the twenty-something wait staff and telling all my friends what a stud I was in my youth.

"Or, 2) The young lady would have wickedly giggled and jumped on top of the birthing table and asked me to snap some nasty photos. While the moment would have been exciting and quite memorable, over time, I'd have learned those girls needed to be avoided as well, as the young lady would have inevitably jumped on any boy's table. Marriage would have been brief and/or frustrating, often tainted by questions of fidelity and mistrust. Over time, the marriage may have been mercifully terminated, or worse, I'd have settled into a maddening sense of apathy.

"Or, 3) The beautiful woman would smirk, and ask you to explain yourself and your unusual antique…. I'd explain to the bold young lady that I found this piece being sold when the local hospital modernized in the mid-

'80s, in lovely Great Barrington, MA, and I had needed a unique buffet in the dining room of my old Victorian home to house my serving platters, baskets, and extra flatware. She'd buy the story and think me slightly eccentric—and maybe a little strange, but in a good, charming way. She'd marry me two years later, and we'd live in Tokyo, Vancouver, London, and Nor Cal and strive to be happy ever after, even after she crashed my cherished antique Mercedes convertible.... But that's another story for another time.

"My birthing table is now in resident in my girlfriend's/wife's office. I guess what I am trying to tell you is that you need to find someone who will put up with your craziness, and you—equally importantly—are willing to put up with their craziness. Then life is manageable. And finally, that this decision—marriage—is the most important you'll make in your life. But it shouldn't really be that difficult of a decision—it'll feel right or it won't. Good luck."

"This guy is a fucking idiot," said the entrepreneur out loud when he read Ralph's email. He sent the email to his trash bin and reminded himself to avoid asking Ralph for advice in the future.

Chapter 17
2015

"Yes, please," said Ralph. This was pretty much the exact script used each and every time Ralph sought adventure.

At the end of the third day of negotiations with his soon-to-be Russian distributors, Ralph needed to get away from them. Badly. Don't take that the wrong way. Ralph really liked this team. They were smart and thoughtful. But as a group, they had spent fourteen hours together on day one, ten and half hours on day two, and four hours on day three, trying to cobble together a deal. And Ralph was certain he hadn't gotten that many hours of sleep in those same three days. Doing business eleven time zones away from the home office meant that you could work twenty-three hours a day and still not be caught up.

The Russian partner's negotiation style was to barrage Ralph with people, minutia, and moving targets. On the first day, Ralph met the department heads—and most of their deputies—of the Engineering, Performance, Finance, Accounting, Credit, Legal, Security, Product Management, and Project Management/Integration teams. Each team befuddled, obfuscated, and presented their ultra-specific challenges to the proposed deal.

Before Ralph arrived in Moscow, the original draft agreement was twelve pages long. On the last day, it was over four times longer. At the beginning of each meeting, the team leader would present their team's objections, ask Ralph to modify, and then demand to review it immediately. And the negotiation would begin again. The biggest challenge was that each of these departments had different objectives, and they occasionally clashed. And when they did, Ralph had to bring the two departments into the same conference room and act as a referee. Every single time a word was changed, by anyone, each of the department leads needed to review and approve. The document's iterations were fast and furious, but each department moved at different speeds. Inevitably someone was working from the wrong iteration, and the process would repeat. Ralph was begrudgingly capable of managing vast amounts of details, but it wasn't a natural or comfortable role for him.

After four hours on the third day, the Parties to the agreement finally declared themselves amenable to the deal. Ralph wasn't happy with the final product, but neither were his new partners. So went the imperfect "sausage-making" that was the resultant of any big deal.

After a few celebratory shots of vodka—it was Moscow and therefore the CEO, CFO, COO, and CTO all had bottles in their offices—Ralph shook hands, thanked them for their hard work, and Uber-ed back to his hotel. He decided he was probably too tired to watch a three-hour ballet at the Bolshoi—it would be terribly bad form to fall asleep in his chair—and hence he decided to check off a bucket-list item and visit a classic Russian steam room.

When Ralph asked the concierge about the prospect, the man frowned. Then he shook his head no. "Sir, I do not think it is advisable to visit a *banya* alone."

"Why? Is it unsafe?"

"*Nyet*, but …"

"Then I'd really like to try it."

After a very pregnant pause, hoping this silly American would reconsider, the concierge gave a huge Russian sigh. "Okay, but everyone visits a *banya* with a group of friends. Much vodka is consumed. They will not speak English. You may be very uncomfortable."

Ralph nodded. He was usually comfortable being uncomfortable.

"Are you certain this is what you want to do?"

"Yes, please," said Ralph.

A *banya* is a public sauna. Sometimes it also has a restaurant and spa. Ralph had never been to a *banya*, but had been intrigued for many years after reading countless spy novels—le Carré, Clancy, et. al.—that had the antagonist go to a *banya* in mid-plot and devise some unique way to foil the protagonist.

Residents of Moscow often called it the City of Rings. There were five roads that formed rings around the city. Muscovites describe almost every location by the location's ring. The innermost ring was the inner city. The Kremlin, a handful of senior government offices, and two or three grand five-star hotels occupied this prestigious locale. The Sandunovsky banya was also in this innermost ring. Built in the 1890s, the outside of this building was uninspired, as was much of the utilitarian architecture of Moscow. But the inside of the Sandunovsky was old and stately. The white marble with dark grey veins was considerably worn, slightly wavy with generations of people walking the same footpaths. Men to the left, and women to the right. The lockers where one deposited their clothing and personal effects weren't from the 1890s, but they weren't from the 1990s either.

Ralph quickly learned that the concierge was correct—they occasionally are. No one spoke English at the check-in, and no English language instructions were handy. He paid the 2300 rubles—about $30, the foreigner rate; locals pay 20% of that—for his towel and a rubber wristband with his locker key.

Ralph doesn't consider himself the brightest bulb on the string. But he has learned that mock confidence and mimicry can often be relied upon in times of doubt. So Ralph followed an older gentleman into the banya and did everything he did, a few seconds later. Disrobe, wrap the skinny thin towel around his waist, quick rinse under the lukewarm showerhead, nod at that guy—oh shit, he just scowled and said something sounding unpleasant—okay, not that, don't nod at anyone—and find a seat in the steam room with just enough space that one can lean back and man-spread.

Speaking of man-spreads, there was a certain awkwardness to the u-shaped, tiered amphitheater-style marble seating. Namely, as you were walking around the steam room—with only a few feet of real visibility—there was no other alternative than to glimpse each man's package. Their dangly bits. The twig and berries, as they say. And with a few hundred men in this facility, it was a bit much. Especially with the bravado in the room. Most of the Russian men reclined at a business class seat angle, proudly displaying their man parts.

If Ralph were telling this story, he'd also mention the smell. To be blunt, it smelled like a wet man who hadn't showered for a few days and lived on boiled cabbage and pork. The rank was pervasive and nearly overpowering. Which inevitably led to the question of hygiene. Yes, it was a question. But one Ralph decided best not to think upon too deeply.

After about ten minutes, the sweat started to really pour. The stinging eyes and, he was not above admitting, his own rank smell compelled him to action. Time for a rinse. But unlike the *onsen* of Japan—where there is a mid-step shower rinse, and the first step is a very thorough cleansing before the baths—the Russian men simply plopped into the communal pools. Ralph did his best not to think of the biology and, potentially, chemistry involved with this miasma. The main pool was probably 36 degrees Centigrade (95 degrees Fahrenheit). There were also smaller pools with varying temperatures. Ralph's favorite was the 10C pool (50F). But one can't really lounge in such a cold pool. So one kept moving.

After a few cycles of steam and then rinse, Ralph became curious about some of the adjoining rooms. Of course some were private VIP rooms, where only the invited may enter. Waiters bustled in and out of these rooms with bottles of vodka. But there also seemed to be rooms where something else was going on. And he wanted to know what.

After about the fifth steam-rinse cycle, Ralph wandered over to a door that men had been entering and then exiting about eight to ten minutes later—just a little pinker than when they walked in. Just then, a man summoned Ralph with a wave of his hand. Ralph hoped this was an employee of the steam room, but had no way of knowing, as the man was not wearing any clothes/badges that might traditionally signify he worked there. He wasn't even wearing the thin towel. Only a funny woolen hat. Otherwise he was buck-naked.

The man said something to Ralph in Russian, to which Ralph responded with an apology that he didn't speak Russian. The man smirked. Russians don't often smile, as this shows vulnerability. "Amerikan?" he asked. Ralph nodded affirmatively. Another smirk. Clearly this man was thinking he was about to enjoy whatever would happen next.

Ralph walked into the six by nine foot room and saw a low wooden slab. The man gestured for Ralph to lie down on this table, face down. It was only then that Ralph noticed the bundle of leafy twigs soaking in steamy water. The bundle of twigs was about a meter long and about half as thick. The white-grey twigs all had leaves, and the bundle sat in a near-boiling steamy bath of its own. After the visit, Ralph learned, via Google, that the twigs were white birch.

Ralph flattened down on the wood with a small gasp, as the wood was warmer than he might have thought, if he had thought about such things. The attendant removed the twig bundle from the soup and gave it a quick shake. He then whacked Ralph's backside with the leafy wet bundle. In retrospect, Ralph wasn't sure what was more surprising: the pain from the lashing, or the pain from the hot water.

"Is okay?"

"Da," Ralph said through clenched teeth.

Ralph immediately turned his head to the other side, both so the attendant wouldn't see him grimace and to ensure he wouldn't have to watch the all-too-close attendant's private man-package jump and jiggle as he put some strength into each uniquely placed whack. Ralph wondered if he was paying the price for Amerika's poor treatment of current-day Russia. "Take *this* for looking down upon Russia as a near-developed nation." *Whack*! "And this for paying $30 a barrel of oil when it costs us $29 to produce." *Whack*! "And try this for the ruble's falling value." *Whack!* "What do you think of *this* for the U.S. never acknowledging that we kicked your ass into space first?" *Whack!* "Take *this* for the fall of the USSR." *Whack!* "And why does Hollywood always portray Russians as gangsters?" Whack whack whack WHACK. The man gestured for Ralph to roll over on his back.

When Ralph finally extracted himself, he was pinker than pink. His body was covered in little scratches too. His skin itched. It wasn't the same as the Chinese and their loofa scrubs, but the rawness thereafter was similar. No one else seemed to mind. He decided he'd need only one more cycle, and then he'd make his way back to the hotel for a room service dinner.

As he was walking back to the steam room, he heard a familiar voice. But the voice was, interestingly, talking in Russian. He peeked into a private steam room, and there was McKenna. Not three meters away. The six men in the room with McKenna glared at Ralph for the interruption. But none glared more fiercely than McKenna himself. No acknowledgment whatsoever. Ralph decided to play the dumb tourist. He waved and said, "Sorry!" McKenna had a laser-tight focus and minutely shook his head. In Russian, he quickly made a joke about idiotic American tourists in Moscow and the men all laughed. Ralph went to the locker room, deciding to skip the last cycle.

As he attempted to brave the frigid temps, snow showers, and fierce wind while waiting for his Uber, Ralph thought, "What the hell is McKenna doing in Moscow? We were supposed to have dinner in London four nights ago. And he was a no-show. And when did he learn to speak Russian like a Russian?"

The A8 car arrived. As he slowly began to warm in the very comfortable leather cabin, his mind switched to another perplexing concern. How would he ever explain the redness over his entire body to his girlfriend/wife/boss, who he'd see in less than twenty-four hours? He could tell the truth, of course, but she'd never believe him. He was in trouble again. Yikes.

Chapter 18
2014

One of Ralph's many great passions was power tools. Yet, various governmental agencies that identified themselves with three-letter acronyms worked against Ralph. At least that's what he had convinced himself. In everyday life, Ralph hated everything related to conspiracy theories. But deep within his psyche, he was convinced there was something odd about his fortunes whenever he touched a power tool. Ralph's life skills were with the creation of business plans via succinct bullet points on a PowerPoint slide. Or maybe an especially well-reasoned pro-forma spreadsheet. But when any power tool touched his hands, bad things happened. Like the time Ralph took out an entire city block's electrical power in downtown Tokyo.

Ralph posted on Facebook, "Before this shows up on TMZ or becomes some viral YouTube video that you all share, when that local-yokel judge put that restraining order on me at the urging of my girlfriend/wife, and my use of all power tools was prohibited, there were a number of provisos and the like. I have some wiggle room. And just because I may be a little over my head with this one is no reason to snicker. Okay? My girlfriend/wife/boss will be home tomorrow evening and this will all be back together mostly and moderately cleaner than it is now. She loves surprises. Really. I honestly don't know what the big deal is....

"I promise I will never, ever attempt home improvement projects without my wife's consent so help me god. I promise I will never, ever attempt home improvement projects without my wife's consent so help me god. I promise I will never, ever attempt home improvement projects without my wife's consent so help me god.

"Unless she goes away for a weekend again ... then I am tackling the front yard.

"I promise I will never, ever attempt home improvement projects without my wife's consent so help me god. I promise I will never, ever attempt home improvement projects without my wife's consent so help me god. I promise I will never, ever attempt home improvement projects without my wife's consent so help me god.

"I think the ceiling looks great. The industrial look is trending.

"I promise I will never, ever attempt home improvement projects without my wife's consent so help me god. I promise I will never, ever attempt home improvement projects without my wife's consent so help me god. I promise I will never, ever attempt home improvement projects without my wife's consent so help me god.

"So I tore up her bathroom floor. I had some nice tile picked out. So it was orange and green, what's the big deal? The tile was on 75% off!

"I promise I will never, ever attempt home improvement projects without my wife's consent so help me god. I promise I will never, ever attempt home improvement projects without my wife's consent so help me god. I promise I will never, ever attempt home improvement projects without my wife's consent so help me god."

☙

"There's a light out in the Volvo!" Jen yelled while pulling out of the driveway. She reversed into the street and then stopped. "I've called them and they know you're coming. Don't dawdle or try to purchase anything beyond the headlight bulb. And you know the rest of the rules. I love you and will see you in a few days." Then she drove away. She was on her way to visit her parents 200 miles north.

Ralph had married a smart and beautiful Californian woman. He told everyone he had married way above his pay-grade, and no one ever even pretended to argue otherwise. Ralph had more than a few foibles. First among them all is probably his near-absolute mechanical incompetence. When he even contemplates changing a battery in a remote, watch or, heaven forbid, a car, there's inevitably smoke, and occasionally fires. Once there was a small-ish explosion. As has been documented elsewhere, various authorities have standing restraining orders disallowing Ralph from operating hand or power tools except in highly supervised environments—the organization Habitat for Humanity is still trying to collect on the damages that occurred the last time Ralph volunteered.

Ralph didn't like being mechanically incompetent and fought it hard. But the all-wise and kind Jen had literally met with the owner of every hardware and auto parts store in a sixty mile radius and convinced them that if they sold anything to Ralph she would 1) kick their ass; 2) bury their business; 3) hold them personally financially accountable—she showed them pictures of Ralph's previous misadventures, including the infamous Tokyo blackout. And it was well known in the community that Jen would follow through on her threats.

So Ralph needed either a note from Jen—validated with a real-time confirming phone call—or she needed to arrange the visit beforehand. Even when Ralph entered Home Depot, the greeter asked him for his note from Jen. In the instance of the pediddle, Ralph knew he'd visit the little auto parts store in Watsonville and the sales team would give him a not-so-kindhearted ribbing. What's worse, if he tried to visit any other auto parts store within an hour's drive, the sales teams wouldn't serve him. So he stuck out his chin and hoped for the best.

When he rolled into the parking lot, one of the senior sales guys was helping an older woman with some windshield wipers. Ralph had just been in the same spot about two weeks earlier, when his commuter car had needed new wipers. The salesperson waved and smirked at Ralph—or maybe that's just what Ralph imagined. Jen had forbidden Ralph from installing something as simple as wipers. It was terribly embarrassing, but such was the price to be paid for the Chinese maxim by which Ralph lived: "A happy wife is a happy life."

The salesperson behind the counter was new, very young, and acne-scarred. Ralph thought about testing the waters, but knew Jen's tentacles were long. Ralph smiled and said, "Hi, I'm Ralph and my wife Jen has called about getting your help with a new headlight for that old Volvo out there." He sheepishly pointed to their sturdy, sandy beach wagon.

"What year and model is your Volvo?"

"2001 XC70."

"Low beam or high?"

"Low."

"Got it. That's $36.95 plus tax. $40.09 total. You can just swipe your card and I'll go grab it."

Ralph swiped his debit card and keyed in his PIN.

"All set," the young man said, handing Ralph the package. "Do you need a receipt?"

"No, but I'm going to need a hand with installing this."

"What?" asked the pimply-faced man-child. He gave Ralph a look that could only be described as pitying.

Just as Ralph was about to respond, the senior salesperson walked back into the store.

"Nope, don't let him touch that. Sorry, Ralph." He took the package from Ralph's hands. "And this isn't the right one. The part he needs is in a box just below the register that says, 'Ralph/Volvo' on it. See it?"

"Yeah. But the one I sold him is the right one. I looked it up. It's the right one."

"I'm sure. But remember what we talked about last week? When I tell you to do something, I need you to just do it. No arguments, and no questions in front of our customers, okay? Now do me a favor. While I go install this on his car, please credit him his purchase. His wife has already paid for this." He was holding up the cardboard box.

"I don't get it. It's just a simple headlight lamp. It's like a two second job that any monkey could do."

"Brandon. Listen to me. We need to help Mr. Gibsen with the installation of his lamp. Now credit him back his purchase, okay?"

"Oh … he's *that* guy. Sorry, boss. I didn't realize. I was expecting someone who was … well. Yeah. Okay—sorry, sir. Can I have you swipe your card again please?"

Ralph mumbled, "I have this weird affect on electronics. Or anything mechanical, for that matter. It's not that I'm …" His voice faded away to a sigh.

Just then, the older woman with the new wipers backed into the cement pole protecting the front door of the store. It was a very slow speed crash.

"Oh, Mrs. Dominguez," the senior sales guy sighed. "Okay, Brandon, you install Ralph's lamp, and I'll deal with the senior citizen who will be worried about losing her license. Remember, *this* part," he said, emphasizing the box that was previously under the register with Ralph's name scrawled on it.

"Got it," Brandon said with confidence. Between dealing with poor Mrs. Dominguez or Ralph, he was certain he had the easier job.

Ralph stopped to make sure the blue-haired woman was okay—she was embarrassed more than anything else—then followed Brandon to the Volvo. The boy had already popped the hood and had the old bulb out.

"What's this thing?"

Brandon had extracted the new bulb from its non-branded packaging. He turned it over in his hand and compared it to the one he had just removed. The bulbs were similar, but there were some obvious differences.

Brandon looked at the packaging again. It was without any commercial or other markings. He then picked up the box that had Ralph's name and car scribbled on it. There was a Virginia postmark on the box. Ralph didn't think there were any auto part manufacturers in Virginia, but maybe it was just some distributor.

"Look at this."

Brandon showed Ralph a thin wire that hung free of the bulb. "The lamp has the right shape, it fits in the hole, and connector is right. But I don't understand this bit, or what this wire is. These aren't identical, for some reason."

The new lamp had a small but noticeable bulge where the wire hung down.

"Let me ask my boss, okay?"

Ralph nodded.

"Bossman, can you come check this …"

"Brandon! I am busy working with Mrs. Dominguez at the moment. Remember what we *just* talked about? Just do as you are told please."

Mrs. Dominguez was now leaning into the salesperson's shoulder, crying.

"What an ass," Brandon said under his breath. "I need to go back to school. All right. Look, it fits fine. Please turn your lights on and see if it works."

Ralph sat in the car, turned the ignition, and flicked on his lights. The reflection off Brandon's knees told the story. All was well with the new bulb.

Ralph shook Brandon's hand, thanked him, and bid goodbye.

On the drive home, Ralph couldn't help wondering about the new bulb. It was reminiscent of a piece of electronic gear that had been slipped into his bag when he was last in Beijing, visiting some senior government officials. That small puck-like device had the very same wire tail. And he was fairly certain it was a tracking device.

When Ralph got home, he checked his commuter, and even his old convertible. All three of the cars Ralph drove regularly had the same retrofitted front headlight lamp, with small, thin wires hanging from them.

Chapter 19
January 2017

"Ralph. What do I owe the honor of this call?"

"Happy holidays, McKenna. And how did you know it was me?"

"You mean Caller ID hasn't reached Silicon Valley yet? And you're supposed to be this hot-shot tech investor? We're talking about telephony that's been in every home for the last twenty-five years, you know."

"Yeah, well. I am what I am, I suppose."

"So quoted the great, spinach-fueled philosopher Popeye the sailor man. How's Olive?"

"Jen's good. And how about your children?"

"Ah, well, you know, they get older and have their own lives now. And, I ask again, Ralph, what do I owe the pleasure of this call?"

"Yes, well, hypothetically, does the Agency you used to work for ever use a person as an asset without their knowledge or acquiescence?"

"You know I haven't been in that industry in thirty or thirty-five years, right?"

"I said 'hypothetically,' didn't I?"

"Well, 'hypothetically' the industry doesn't do that, unless they have no choice. I've heard of the Agency using a student's computer as a mule to get something sensitive into a country undetected. Then they'll steal the student's computer in a café or at the airport. That sort of thing happens occasionally. Why do you ask?"

"Mule. An Ass. Yeah. No. Uhm, does that industry ever get an asset more deeply involved without their knowledge or consent?"

"Not really. Think about it. Control is the key to successful espionage. And if someone isn't controllable ... things can go bad really quickly. But now I'm curious— who are we talking about here? Is there something you need to tell me?"

"You're going to think I'm an idiot."

"I already do. If you weren't fucking rich and had the dream job and hadn't married up way beyond your sheer butt-ugliness, I'd have pegged you for an alcoholic Yellow Page advertisement salesman, or a driving instructor living in the basement of your mother's home."

"My father always told me I'd be lucky to get a job as a snowplow driver."

"Yeah, but you've always had a supernatural way of landing on your feet. Even when you don't understand how or why. You're a most lucky man. So tell me who you think might be being used as an asset."

"Possibly, it might be me."

"Ralph ... it'd be very easy to insult your intelligence right now. Too easy. But I have a feeling you have an interesting story, and I want to hear about it."

"Yeah. Well, I think I stumbled upon an attempt to change the way people learn. And not necessarily in a good way. And since I've made this discovery, things have gotten ... squirrelly."

"Come on, Ralph. Every fifteen minutes someone in Silicon Valley thinks they've found some new panacea to solve education for the planet. You lefties love that shit."

McKenna turned on his iPhone voice recording app.

"Yeah, I've been helping some smart folks on another attempt."

"And your progress?"

"Well, uhm, we've had a few significant break-throughs. It's with the Z-Prize team. The learning solution is a closed-feedback-loop system. The system knows when a learner has actually learned something new, but more importantly, *how* the learner has learned it, while cross-correlating the learned item with a big data set of beliefs and preferences."

"You remember I have a PhD in Education and another in Sociology, right? To me, this sounds like intellectual masturbation. This might be an interesting tech development for sure, but educators will never accept such solution."

"Said the taxi driver when I told him I had invested in a little company called Uber back in 2009."

"Okay, whatever. Get to the point. What do you think you've *stumbled upon?*"

"I found a small group of high net-worth folks that has secretly funded this effort, with the quid pro quo of having a back door built into the tool for their own purposes. And once I started asking about the purpose of this back door, my life got … very interesting."

"Did you practice that sentence? It is too succinct for you. Unpack it for me a bit. Who are 'the folks'? What could they do with a back door? And define interesting, please."

"Okay. The investors aren't names that most people will recognize. In fact, they're the sort that appear more comfortable just outside of the spotlight. They're traditional mid-western industrialists with their only common denominator being a strong political agenda that might be considered ultra-nationalist. They're all extremely wealthy, but apparently more concerned about their ability to influence their college football team's success rather than any geopolitical issue. Which makes it especially interesting as to why they'd be involved with this."

"Okay, I'll play along. You mentioned these industrialists had invested secretly. How are you certain the people you've found are the real investors behind this tool?"

"Well, let's just say I was at one of their monthly organizational meetings, to get an update of the development of this educational solution, and my mind started to wander. So I might have turned on a Pineapple to see if I was the only one who was bored."

"What's a Pineapple? And why did you have one at this meeting?"

"A Pineapple is a little bit of hardware hacking kit that, combined with some Wireshark software, can be used to see what people are doing when they surf the internet without using a security tool on WiFi."

"Didn't people notice this kit?"

"No. It's pretty small and basically sits in my backpack. You can buy it on the internet for about a hundred bucks."

"And why were you carrying this kit with you?"

"I always carry it with me. One of my portfolio companies helps people circumvent censorship of authoritarian governments. One of the side benefits of this app is it also protects and encrypts WiFi traffic. I show the traffic I see from the Pineapple to influencers so they see what's at risk when they don't use my app. I once showed Mark Zuckerberg pictures of his newborn little girl, which he'd taken on his iPhone. He doesn't understand privacy much, but as his little girl grows up, he certainly will. People tend to understand the need for privacy when dealing with family, health, and wealth."

"Some days you are a weird duck, Ralph. So you just *happened* to be hacking the WiFi at this meeting, and what did you find?"

"One of the algorithms I used is a search on note-takers from the meeting. I'm a little opportunistically lazy and sometimes people take better notes than I do. I like to focus on the big picture, hence I have learned to copy notes from others at the meeting. That way I'll know what tasks I've been given. So then I combined that with a similar search algorithm for my last name. That particular search found an email, which was a highly confidential update memo, to someone named Koch. But this update memo was different from the one I got via normal committee distribution. What made this particular email interesting was two specific things: one, the email said 'unequivocally' it was not to be shared with three members of the committee—my last name was included as one of the three."

"Being singled out for exclusion will always get your attention. But let me ask you something though. Didn't you question if you had any right to look at someone else's email? Aren't you the guy that's done the TED Talk on the importance of privacy?"

"Of course, but my intentions are benign. Yes, I was being lazy, which is the problem that many internet companies leverage when their users give up their privacy to use a search engine or a medical site. Do you think anyone would really use a site like WebMD if they knew their insurance company was buying that usage data to adjust their rates based on the user's search terms?"

"Get off your high horse, Ralph. You just admitted to criminal snooping."

"I am an imperfect being."

"You said it. Back on point. What did this illicitly obtained email say that has you convinced you may be an asset?"

"It said something to the effect that the 'back door was nearly complete and ready for beta-testing.' That the alpha testing had shown five nines of efficacy. And then the email stressed that this information was not to be shared beyond the project's 'investors.'"

"Five nines? What does that mean? And isn't it a normal thing for execs to not share information and progress beyond their investors?"

"99.999%—nearly perfect effectiveness. And sure, if this were a start-up Silicon Valley company, keeping secrets is completely appropriate. But this isn't a start-up. The investors and execs are doing this project pro-bono— of course in an effort to make the world a better place. That's the premise of these Z-Prize efforts. It would be hard to get that many smart people—that much firepower—in a room for that many months if some of them were somehow getting preferential treatment. These projects only exist because a few smart people give their time to make the world a better place."

"Again, back on point, you told me that things have gotten 'interesting' for you since this so-called discovery. Tell me exactly why you think you might be involved."

"Well, this is the crazy bit. It isn't just one thing. It is a bunch of little things. Like people showing up in my hotel room at 2 AM asking for my help. Like finding those tracking devices in my computer bag and cars. Like seeing you in the *banya* in Moscow about sixty days ago."

On his Wireshark software, Ralph imagined McKenna frowning and watched him turn off his voice recorder app.

"What the fuck are you talking about? The last time we last we saw each other was at your house in Cape Cod, with Peterson."

"And your Russian was perfect."

"Ralph, I'm playing this whole call back in my mind, and you know what? It sounds fucking ridiculous. Tell me the truth—have you been hitting the hooch?"

"I followed you when you left the *banya*, you know. Actually, *I* didn't follow you. My PD-100 Black Hornet nano-drone followed you."

McKenna laughed. "Just for a second—let me humor myself. How the hell do you know what a PD-100 is?"

"I put my business card in a bowl at the SOFIC convention last year in Tampa, and then about a week later I got the drone in the mail. They said I won it."

This was a little white lie. Ralph never dropped his business card in those bowls at booths at spy conventions or otherwise. The spam they created was fierce. And spam was something that Ralph tried to avoid. But when he got the pico-drone in the mail, the note did say he was a "winner."

"A PD-100 is a covert operations tool sold only to the U.S. government and our allies. It weighs only eighteen grams, can hover twelve feet above someone, following and recording their every action without notice, has a twelve-month waiting list, and retails for $250,000. And you're telling me you *won* one?"

"I've always been pretty lucky."

"Ralph, who do you really work for?"

"McKenna, I was hoping you might tell me."

The two fifty-year-olds were silent, each hoping the other might give something away. After sixty seconds, Ralph said, "I really need to figure out how to stop all this. Can you help?"

"You don't know who you work for?"

"Well, no. Do you know?"

McKenna hesitated, searching for Ralph's next hint. "Honest to God?"

"I fucking don't know who I work for. Or even if I work for anyone. Sometimes I think I'm being used as some kind of pawn, but I can't even be sure. I might just be crazy. And what's worse, I think my wife knows all about it."

"Have you spoken to anyone else about this? I mean, a professional?"

"No."

"I think it might be time to think about getting help."

"So you're not going to help me?"

"I can provide some good suggestions for someone you can talk to. I still teach at UMass. They've got some great professionals."

"I meant help with me finding out who I work for, and with stopping those folks from creating a tool of mass persuasion."

"How the hell could I help you with that? I'm a trusted consultant to a few Eastern European countries, helping them create educational policy. I stopped participating in that field of interest about thirty years ago."

"Then why do you know about the PD-100?"

"Because I like to read information about that field on the internet. Now please do us all a favor and check yourself into a psych facility for a few weeks. You sound miserable and you probably need the rest. I'll give you a call in a week or so. Bye."

From his Wireshark software kit, Ralph could tell that McKenna was still on the line.

"Does he who controls the curriculum control the world?" Ralph asked.

"Be careful, Ralph."
And the line went dead.

Chapter 20

"He's asking all the wrong questions." The two men were standing in the midst of the commuters in Waterloo station in London.

"You mean he's asking all the right questions, correct?"

"He's not that bright. He's lucky. But his questions are spurring his peers to ask better questions, and that's what we can't allow."

"Everyone always underestimated Ralph's mental acuity," McKenna said. "He claims he has the IQ of a blue crayon. At least that's what he's always telling people."

"Yes, he's always telling people he's an idiot. He's hoping people think he's just being self-deprecating. I just happen to believe him. He is an idiot."

McKenna acknowledged the insult, but thought that his senior-most handler might not know the half of it. McKenna had known Ralph for thirty some-odd years. And for some of those years, they were tight friends.

"He needs to disappear quietly. Can you have someone on your team arrange that?"

"He … he doesn't … well … do anything. What are we hoping to accomplish? Seems like we're going to add significant risk for very little reward."

"He's a pain in my ass. And he may inadvertently derail our efforts. I want him to inconspicuously disappear. Can your team do that, or are you too close to him?"

This quip, meant to lay down the gauntlet, was expected. This senior handler had infamously taken out his best man at his own wedding many years ago.

McKenna smiled at the jibe and looked down at his polished shoes. "I can take care of Ralph. But I want to …"

He didn't finish the sentence, because he was now standing alone.

Chapter 21
2002

While Ralph was in Asia, he sent a request to the Craigslist.com "Arts" forum for a few pictures in order to start a study of bellies for his next stone sculpture:

"No Porn PLEASE!

"I am an amateur (read: poorly-talented) stone sculptor. I'm looking for a few people to help me by providing pictures of their non-clothed bellies. I am looking for multiple photos (straight on, from each oblique and from the profile/sides) of the section between the rib cage and the pubis bone. Curvy bellies and distinct hip bones most welcome!"

Jen, Ralph's kind, lovely, and most-often-a-gamer girlfriend/wife, had finally put her foot down. Ralph got the distinct impression that Jen was not appreciative when people came to the house and he announced, "This is my wife's butt," he'd say while pointing at the 350-pound-piece of gray granite that he had carved to resemble her fine backside.

"Prior to taking the photos, PLEASE take a moment to cover all private parts."

No one did.

Either people who spend time on the "Arts" board were rule breakers, or they didn't really read the directions. Ralph often got photos that would make him blush. The weird part was, he received them for years thereafter, and over time they lessened only in photos, but the senders often told Ralph stories and offered advice. Some of the stories and advice were crazy, while others were funny or piqued Ralph's imagination. And this wasn't the only source of Ralph's near-constant correspondence. Ralph seemed to attract people with great regularity.

ↄↄ

The "101" building in Taipei is an amazing engineering feat. The world's second tallest building (101 is the number of floors), the elevator to the ninety-first floor takes only thirty seconds. The building has an elaborate counter-weight system that allows it to lessen the sway of the building in near-constant winds, typhoons, and earth tremors. On the ninety-first floor, you can view the counter-weight in action. The amazing thing is to watch this five-story, 660 metric-tonne ball suspended by thick wires swing as much as one point five meters (five feet) at any given moment, in any and every direction—all to reduce the building's sway by as much as forty percent.

Ralph rounded a corner and nearly knocked down Tom Warn, his old friend from the first time Ralph lived in Tokyo. Tall and ginger-haired, Tom had a big laugh. While not the most disciplined of teammates in his early career, Ralph had later learned that not all co-workers work the same way or with the same amount of effort.

"Ralph, what the hell are you doing here?"

"About to ask the same of you."

"Well, some of this and some of that."

"You look well."

"As do you."

Tom paused. "Hey, I'd love to chat, but I am meeting someone here in a minute or two, and I need to be alone. Is that cool?"

"Sure. No worries. Perhaps we can grab breakfast one of these days?"

"Not this trip. I'm out of the country tonight. But let's plan on getting together soon. And I want to hear all about your meeting Tommy. I heard he was in rare form and was thankful you stopped by."

"Tommy—the haircutter? You heard …"

"Yeah, well—there's my meet-up. Gotta go. Talk soon."

And Tom was gone. Ralph thought long and hard about how small a world it was that Tom had heard about Ralph's haircut.

Chapter 22

Ralph's wife Jen gave him a nasty cold prior to his departure for Seoul. Ralph's Korean hosts took it on themselves to give Ralph a homegrown cure. Mudfish gruel tastes almost as good as it sounds. Exactly like mud, old fish, and jalapenos. The cold was gone the next morning. Seriously.

Ralph and a small group of executives visited a top consumer electronic manufacturer. At the reception, they were asked to trade their dress shoes for slippers. The rationale—and one that Ralph agreed with in his own home—was that street shoes are dirty and may track in muck. But what still makes him laugh is that smoking was allowed throughout the office, even at the at the workers' desks. Smoking wasn't dirty?

On the executive (top) floor, the men's bathroom overlooked the city's landscape. The urinals were strategically placed up against the windows—so you could relieve yourself and enjoy a very attractive view, forty floors up. Ralph noticed that the company's foremost competitor's sky-rise building was directly where you'd imagine your urine falling if unencumbered by the urinal. Ralph asked the CEO he was visiting if this was intentional, and he assured Ralph with a twinkle in his eye that it was certainly not the case.

"And Ralph, Tommy in Taiwan says you should come visit him again soon. His girls—they miss you. They think you are very funny." The CEO laughed and shook Ralph's hand and walked off to his next meeting.

Chapter 23
2016

The flight was like a few hundred others. This particular one was from Boston to San Francisco. Five to six hours, depending on the winds.

Ralph had seat 1A. His seatmate in 1C, a small, well-turned-out Asian woman, was very proud of her new purse. Ralph didn't know the brand, but assumed it was expensive by the way she paraded it. Ralph hadn't said more than a half-dozen words to her during the flight. She was in deep-dark-blue power suit, the business attire of a corporate lawyer or high-priced consultant. Ralph was wearing a sun-bleached pair of orange shorts and a zippered sweatshirt with a start-up company's logo on the breast. Ralph sensed she was displeased to be sitting next to the unwashed masses.

Ralph probably wouldn't have remembered her at all had she not been found dead when the attendant shook her shoulder on final approach. That, and Ralph had noticed that she drank his diet ginger ale while he napped somewhere over the flyover states.

The expensive purse fell from her lap to the floor when Ralph and the attendant attempted to resuscitate her. Despite twenty minutes of hard-fought attempts, with no trained medical personnel on the flight, she did not resuscitate. Oddly, Ralph noticed that her mouth tasted of ginger ale and something metallic when her body reflexively spit up the last few things she had consumed during the flight.

Perhaps by design, Ralph did not notice that a person matching the description of McKenna's senior handler was the last person off the plane. And as he was barking into his phone, he appeared to be visibly upset.

PART TWO

Chapter 24

How strange is it to work in Silicon Valley in the latter half of the 2010s, Ralph thought. The previous day he had a few important meetings and wore a button-down dress shirt and blazer. Not much focused on most details, he didn't notice that one of the shirtsleeves had a monogram. His young female co-worker asked why he needed a shirt with a monogram.

"Is it because you spend time in a golf club where the ownership of the shirt might be confused among the other members?"

Then she asked how old the shirt was. Ralph was absolutely certain the shirt was older than her.

ↄ

The Consumer Electronic Show in Las Vegas is typically a few days after New Year's. It is a three- or four-day convention of 180,000 technology wonks desperately trying to impress each other.

Ralph had attended this show (and its precursor) for more than twenty-five years. In that time, he had learned a few things. There were a few must-have items, including: PowerBars, blister Band-Aids, a current Uber App, and at least fifty one-dollar bills (tipping, but not for strippers—they apparently didn't accept anything less than a $5 bill).

Ralph had his assistant working as many hours as he did, because as was often the case, meetings scheduled months in advance were often changed ad hoc due to traffic, hangovers, and hookers that wouldn't leave wealthy executives rooms. (For requests to reschedule meetings, Ralph had heard all of these excuses and more.) Ralph attended CES each year to support his portfolio companies and learn about what people thought was "hot" this year. Because every super-geek on the planet attended, the event was a perfect opportunity to schedule a few dozen meetings and avoid traveling to the four corners of the planet.

After the first day of the show, Ralph had thirty-seven new business cards in his pocket. He was starving, parched, and grumpy. At the beginning of the day, he had had eleven meetings on his calendar, and he was trying to recollect if he had met with thirteen or fourteen different teams during the day—with only one of the meetings in its original time slot.

With about 20,000 other grumpy executives, Ralph was in scrum to take the monorail to his hotel—he was cheap, so he was staying at the Excalibur at the south end of the Vegas strip. Only five hundred souls could fit on each train, and hence the LV Convention Center stop had a few hundred rent-a-cops trying to wrangle people into some sort of orderly flow. As people were from all parts of the world, the normal proxemics did not apply. It was a free for all.

Ralph's head was down, trying to remember his yoga teacher's stress relieving techniques. He was actively imagining himself swimming in a lake.

Okay. He was floating on a cloud. Good. Heart rate dropping.

He was sitting in a hot spa. Nice. Stress flowing from his body.

He was having his scrotum tickled.

Wait—he was really having his scrotum tickled.

Ralph gasped, jumped, and opened his eyes all at the same moment. And he realized he was face-to-face with Eva.

"Well hello, Ralph. What are you doing here? Are you following me?"

Ralph was never quick when surprised. "Ah … hello, Huawei."

"Did you forget my name? I am very hurt. But the last time in Israel you said such mean things to me. You so mean. Maybe I should just ignore you."

"Eva, what are you doing here?"

"I am here with my company for CES. We have a very big booth here. And you have not yet visited us to say hello. What are you doing here?"

"I am also here with one of my portfolio companies."

"Ralph, do you notice anything new?"

Standing too close, Eva was rubbing her breasts on Ralph's arm and chest.

"Ah, no." The last time Ralph had seen her, about two months earlier, she was very long and lean. Almost miraculously, she had become curvaceous.

"Oh, you are very mean to me always. I have added 20cm to my breasts and 15cm to my hips, because you said that I looked like a little boy. It was very painful, what I did for you. Just so you like me."

Being packed into a very tight scrum and only moving a few feet every few minutes in this monster queue, Ralph was fairly certain that his chest, upper arms, and back had experienced each and every one of those 20 new centimeters, as she made a great show of her new assets.

"Look, your boss made some dramatic threats." Ralph leaned close to avoid being overheard.

"Oh Ralph, I knew you liked me." Eva wrapped her long arms around his neck and with a fierce hold, kissed him.

"Hey, stop," Ralph said, without as much conviction as he had hoped to convey. He tried to push her away, but ended up inadvertently pushing her away via her breasts. Her shirt popped a once-latched button.

"Save that for later, Ralphy. Don't get too fresh. Too many people here." Eva giggled, trying her best to be coy. "I must say 'thank you.' My new 'body' is all due to your outburst in Israel. But next time my boss is sitting next to you, please say, 'I only want to sleep with a woman who is covered in Tiffany diamonds,' okay? It might work. Please remember, I like Tiffany diamonds. When we get engaged, you buy me a nice Tiffany diamond ring and earrings. More than five carat, okay?"

"I am happily married," Ralph blurted.

"No problem. We take care of her for you. Bad car accident or VX gas in hairspray, like we did for Kim Jong-nam."

"What the fuck Eva? Some of the things you say are beyond incredible. And by the way, my wife will kick your skinny ass."

"Oh, I know she is someone with a big team, but I am also a part of a big team, the biggest team."

"My wife doesn't have a 'team.'"

"Sure, sure. You pretend not to be involved. You can also pretend your wife is not a senior leader of another team. Sure, sure. You keep your silly cover story if it makes you feel more safe."

"Hold on. This is crazy. Are you telling me my wife is somehow involved?"

"You play such games. Sometimes I think you might just be as stupid as you try to pretend. But now that we are reacquainted, we must talk about the EdTech project. My team needs full access to the code and all of the research. All of it. And we need you to provide that access. What is your price for this access? From our last discussion, we know you do not scare easily. But maybe you would let my government invest one billion dollars in your tiny venture fund. Would that be sufficient? We would not need to see any returns. We might not even care about the principle, okay? We might be willing to turn it all over to you. Does that get your enthusiasm?"

"I don't know what you are talking about. There are a dozen projects going on in the EdTech industry at any given time."

"Ralph, you are only working on one of those projects. The Z-Prize is the only one we need. And for now we only need your password to the Basecamp and Dropbox accounts. Once we have verified we have your access, we'll make a billion dollar investment in your fund. The Cayman Island's investment vehicle will be a series of shell organizations that you will own outright. It is that simple. Plus, as a bonus, you'll have me."

"Eva, is this some sort of crazy prank? I mean, what the hell is really going on?"

"No Ralph, this is the most serious offer you will ever receive." Her bad Chinese accent faded dramatically.

Ralph looked up just as McKenna's bulk pushed his way into Ralph and Eva's path.

"Ralph, is this your hooker? She's hot."

"Fuck you, old man. Get lost."

"Nice that I don't have to introduce you two." Ralph was certain they would know each other but didn't know there was no love between them. "Do you guys work on the same team?"

Ralph felt a prick in his thigh. Then a burning sensation. "What the heck was that?" He grabbed his thigh. He immediately felt lightheaded and was unsure of his ability to continue to stand.

"What did you just hit him with?" McKenna threateningly asked Eva.

"Just a love potion. You really need to get out of here, old man. I don't know who you are working for today, but this is my asset now."

"An asset doesn't need a stick. What you just did is a federal crime, and I am not leaving."

Eyes with daggers were exchanged. Ralph nervously giggled and tried not to drool.

"Who is this, Ralph?" asked Eva, nodding to McKenna.

"McKenna is my old college friend. He was in the CIA once, but claims he isn't now. But I think he still works as a spy of some sort."

"Interesting." Eva smiled.

McKenna was looking around for options. There were very few, with the crushing queue. He looked closely at Ralph's eyes and frowned.

"This sucks," Ralph said too loudly. Many people turned to look at him.

"What sucks?" McKenna asked much quieter.

"All of it. This fucking never-ending queue for the train. This hot woman giving me an injection and an erection. My wife may be a spy. I am thinking that you both may want to hurt me. It all sucks," Ralph said three times louder than he needed.

McKenna loudly whispered apologies to the people in close proximity. "We're all very drunk. So sorry." He forced a laugh. The people in the scrum went from smiles of understanding to wariness as Ralph rambled without filter.

"She keeps rubbing her breasts on me, which feels really good. But they're each holding a tight grip on my arms," Ralph told a few people, trying to draw them into conversation. They did their best to stay away. "Not her breasts," Ralph clarified, "them." He nodded to Eva and McKenna.

"What did you stick him with?" McKenna asked Eva. "And was it intravenous?"

"It is a concoction of Nembutal, Methedrine, and ataraxics. Which allows for non-intravenous admin. I've got about fifteen minutes before he passes out."

"Well, I guess that means we're now working together, because this scrum will be longer than fifteen minutes. Agreed?"

"No. He is mine."

The queue was all encompassing. They couldn't have escaped if they had to. Both Eva and McKenna were trying to exert their will on Ralph, each to their preferred direction.

Whispered threats were uttered between combatants.

"Back off, old man. We'll take you out."

"I'll squish you like a bug."

Yet neither could pull Ralph away. And Ralph was drawn towards the queue heading to the train. The scrum was exceedingly tight.

"I need to sleep soon," Ralph muttered to no one in particular.

Eva quickly realized they were at a stalemate. "Okay, we work together."

"I am very scared of her." Ralph was exaggerating his stare at Eva. "And turned on. And scared of what Jen would do to me. I love Jen so much." Ralph was nearly yelling.

Eva and McKenna spoke over each other, trying to get Ralph's attention. Ralph was now singing, "All you need is love. Love, love, love. Love is all you need."

"Stop. We are accomplishing nothing. You ask a question and I ask a follow up. Then I ask a question and you ask the follow up. And we start with a baseline question to ensure he isn't faking. Agreed?" McKenna demanded. They were still ten minutes from the front of the line. Although the scrum was body-to-body, people were reading the situation and giving them as much space as they could.

Eva agreed. "Ralph, can you shut up and answer a few questions for us?"

"You have the longest legs of any Chinese woman I have ever met. And an amazing ass. It is perfect. Did you really get your boobs done for me?" Ralph slurred.

"That isn't very nice talk, Ralph," cautioned Eva.

"Shut up, Ralph. Do you remember when we were at college? Who was Doctor Lawson's wife?" McKenna asked.

Ralph started giggling like a schoolboy with a secret. "She was a naughty woman. Remember the Polaroids she gave us?"

"I remember. Now a follow up question. Did you sleep with her?"

"Of course I did. I mean everyone did, right? She was a swinger." Ralph paused. "But I didn't really. I got the chance, but I got scared. And I said no. We talked for about two hours, but I didn't touch her. I wanted to be cool like everyone else on the debate team, but I couldn't do it. I lied." Telling his failures, Ralph felt terribly sad.

"I'd say the serum is working. Do you agree?"

Eva nodded her agreement.

"Who do you work for Ralph?" asked Eva.

"My wife Jen."

McKenna and Eva nodded at each other. "And who does Jen work for?" asked McKenna in turn.

Ralph giggled. "Enzo and Beanbutt."

"Who are they—the Italians? AISE?" Eva asked McKenna.

"They aren't Italians. He's from Germany and she's from the Pyrenees," Ralph corrected.

"Fuck. Stop. He's talking about his dogs."

"Although we aren't sure which side of the Pyrenees she's from. Could be Spanish or French, right?"

The plan for structured questions and follow-ups had already flown out of the window, and McKenna and Eva were each trying to get the wandering mind of Ralph to focus on their immediate question of importance.

"Who gives you your instructions? What is your wife's role? Is she your handler?" asked Eva.

"What is the efficacy of the EdTech project? Can it be directed to large groups?" asked McKenna.

"Do you work with the Qataris? Emiratis? Do you work for the Germans, Russians, or the Chinese? Do you take direction from the CIA? Or Military Intelligence?"

"Is there a way to stop the EdTech project? Have they chosen between fMRI and the BBCI? Can the technology be thwarted or overcome?"

"I have to pee," Ralph said seriously. "And go to bed soon. I am very, very tired."

Within moments, Ralph became incoherent. Then he slumped over. McKenna and Eva ended up carrying him, which was no small feat. Ralph woke in what he thought was a nice hotel room. It seemed to be dawn.

McKenna and Eva were sitting together, speaking quietly.

"Huawei leads China's Cyber efforts, right? Is there any difference between the government and the company?" asked McKenna.

"China knows its own companies represent the most realistic opportunity to ensure the internet has a decidedly Chinese presence. China now leads the world in e-commerce, accounting for forty to fifty percent of global sales, and has four of the top ten internet companies in the world by market capitalization. China's internet strategy, as promoted in its latest Five Year Plan, embraces this vector," Eva explained in a neutral accent.

"But 'cyber' in Chinese, as I understand it, is more of a military or national security effort, correct?" asked McKenna.

Ralph listened carefully, trying to clear his mind. He didn't move, as he wanted to learn if these two were on the same team or otherwise.

"China's 'cyber' efforts include defensive and offensive capabilities with international targets, including a wide range of actors, including so-called human rights, democracy, and independence movements outside China. These digital actions also target foreign governments and Fortune 500 companies equally. We even have such tools as reported in the Western media as 'The Great Cannon,' which can redirect website requests of internet users into denial-of-service attacks, or even launch software executables that we control."

"So why does the Chinese government have this much interest in this EdTech tool?"

"Because it is a rule-changer. Huawei hasn't actually sold any telecommunication or internet equipment to developing countries in the last fifteen years. We basically give it away with the intent of owning and controlling all of the world's digital traffic. If we owned the EdTech tool, we could do the same with people's thoughts and actions. We understand that it isn't a science-fiction 'mind-control' tool, but it *is* an iterative, controllable methodology to ensure that the owner could exert influence—and know that the influence is believed or learned—on the entire digital world. And to know when that influence was modified or diminished over time. Its potential uses are limitless."

"It isn't much different than the Middle East king who only allows his subjects to see one version of world events."

"The difference is that the king's people would also know who believed the king's version of events, and who didn't. Those that didn't would be targeted for re-education or more draconian actions."

"I understand. Can I have a few days to consider your offer?"

"Of course. But if you don't work for us, we will assume you are working against us. Understood?"

McKenna grunted his acknowledgment. "Let's get out of here before he wakes. We both probably have things we need to do. Are you're certain he won't remember anything about the last twelve hours?"

"We are fairly certain—there is a ninety-seven percent amnesiatic effect to the cocktail stick I gave him. We have offered him a very large sum of money for his cooperation. I'll touch base with you both in the next few days—for your answers. In the meantime, stay out of my way and out of contact with this buffoon. Agreed?"

"Agreed."

Ralph heard them tidying up, and then heard one of them leave when a heavy door slammed. He didn't think he was in his hotel room, but couldn't be certain.

Ralph didn't move, but felt someone in very close proximity. He felt a warm breath on his exposed cheek, and a quick peck of a kiss.

"I hope I won't have to kill you. You are the most interesting person I have met in this in line of work."

Just as she finished the sentence, Ralph's phone buzzed on the nightstand. She picked it up and handed it to a very fuzzy Ralph.

"It's Jen. Tell her I said hello, will you? Maybe then she'll kill you before I have to," Eva said. Then she walked out of the hotel room, not nearly as quietly as Ralph hoped.

"Good morning, Sweetness!" Ralph's voice was raw and gravelly.

Chapter 25
2014

Sometimes things got a little weird for Ralph. But as the great philosopher/adventurer Hunter S. Thompson once said, "When the going gets weird, the weird turn pro."

The previous night, Ralph got a call asking him to fly to a small country on the Arabian Peninsula and have a lunch meeting with someone. As he was already in the geographic neighborhood, Ralph agreed. It was actually a huge inconvenience, as he would need to reschedule a bunch of meetings, but he was nothing if not opportunistic. When Ralph spoke to that person's personal secretary, asking for an address, the woman, who spoke with a very clipped British accent, simply said, "The Palace." When Ralph asked if "The Palace" had any specific address, which he could give his taxi driver, the personal secretary scoffed and said, "Sir, everyone in this country knows where The Palace is located."

When he arrived at The Palace—the taxi, a 1984 Ford Crown Victoria, had no meter and the driver demanded $150 USD for the fifteen-minute ride—a greeter (the protocol officer) looked Ralph up and down and asked if he had a tie, and socks. Ralph replied that he had neither. The officer was not impressed.

"You simply cannot meet his Majesty without a tie and socks."

"Will his Majesty be wearing a tie and socks?"

The officer was taken aback at such a question. "Well no, sir. He wears the country's traditional dishdasha. And he is His Majesty."

"I am from the sacred land of Santa Cruz. And my wife and I are leaders in the region of Aptos. We find wearing socks and ties to be against the laws of nature. Please allow me the courtesy to wear clothes of my culture."

"Oh, I see. Of course, sir. Thank you for explaining your region's cultural mores to me. I'll be sure to explain this to his Majesty and his staff."

After the meeting with His Majesty was over, the same protocol officer met Ralph, who was looking to get a taxi back to the airport.

"I trust that your meeting was productive, Mr. Ralph?"

"It was very interesting, thank you."

"And when will you be traveling back to your land of Santa Cruz?"

"Next week, after a quick stop in São Paulo," Ralph humble-bragged.

"Very good, sir. And if I may be so bold, sir. Please give my sincerest regards to the waitress Louisa at Manuel's. Their *pollo mole* is the best I have ever tasted."

Ralph smiled—he'd been caught out. "I'll be sure to do so. It is good mole. Many thanks."

Chapter 26
Shanghai 2016

"Are you here to kill all my family? Or just intimidate the fuck out of me? And please, Ralph, please tell me how you found us?"

Eva—or as he had just learned, Lei-Han—was still visibly shaking.

♋

About a week earlier, Ralph and one of his Augmented Reality portfolio companies had been invited to meet with the Secretary of Hangzhou, a ten-million-soul metropolitan city south of Shanghai. The secretary was the political arm of the two-person government leadership team that managed the capital of the Zhejiang province. The mayor was the administrator, but the secretary was the more significant player in the Communist Party.

Hangzhou's secretary was tired of being overshadowed by the success of Shanghai and its massive start-up achievements. In an attempt to leapfrog the competing cities, he and the mayor had decided the resort city needed to import Silicon Valley entrepreneurs and their new technology. This would be the first province in China to allow, recruit, and encourage Westerners to build companies in China. Hence, one of the smallest investors in Ralph's AR portfolio company, a twenty-nine year old with a terrifically rich father, had given Ralph a call.

"Ralph, it's Will Sheng. If you show up in Hangzhou and give a fifteen-minute presentation with a demo of the Augmented Reality platform, I think the city will grant our company between ten and fifteen million RMB (about $1.4-2.1 million U.S. dollars) to start a branch office in Hangzhou. And then with an officially registered office in this city, within forty-five days I'll raise another ten to twelve million U.S. dollars at whatever valuation you think makes sense."

Ralph made a trip to Hangzhou and made the pitch to a team of three academics, two VCs, and the secretary of the city. The pitch went very well. Many cigarettes were smoked. The audience was respectful and excited. Ralph brought along two trusted Chinese-speaking associates, and at the end of the Q&A session, which lasted another sixty minutes, the secretary announced in Chinese that the award was a non-recourse grant of fifteen million RMB to the AR start-up. Ralph's team had huge smiles. Warm handshakes abounded. More cigarettes were smoked. There was a bounce in everyone's steps. The secretary promised that the grant money would be in the account as soon as the company was officially registered and a bank account was created.

Then Will spoke up. "My father would like to invite everyone to a celebration lunch at my family's office."

Will's dad was a developer, and had the tallest building in Hangzhou. A few new Maserati SUVs were waiting out front of the City Government's office. To avoid the appearance of favoritism, the secretary decided to forego the lunch. But everyone else piled into the SUVs and, to minimize the traffic, a police team escorted them.

The office building's lobby was the same as ten thousand others. Only the private elevator to the owner's floor gave notice of the opulence to come. Ralph stepped out of the elevator onto golden-pink stone floors that were arranged in the shapes of clouds at sunrise. An assistant ushered them into a greeting room, where they were served chrysanthemum tea. Ralph's normally gregarious teammates were dumbstruck. Will's father finally emerged and name cards were exchanged. More flowery tea was served, this time with fresh fruit. The tea and fruit servers were all stunning women—it was almost as if they had stepped away from a skincare television advertisement to serve tea.

Will and Will's father, Mr. Wen, doted on Ralph. Wen's English skills were less than adequate, but Ralph was certain the wealthy man understood every word the English speakers said. Soon a trio of press photographers arrived, and unobtrusively took everyone's not-quite-candid photos. A group photo was staged, and then everyone was again ushered into the lunchroom. The round table could seat forty or fifty, hence the twenty-person group took up only a semicircular portion of the table. Ralph was seated between Will and his father. The wait staff brought large plates of food, placing them on the ever-revolving center section. And then Eva walked into the room.

"Ralph, I'd like you to meet my most-beautiful daughter, Lei-Han. I apologize—her clothes are never modest enough, and she is always running late for important meetings."

As she introduced herself in flawless American-accented English, there was absolute panic in her eyes. "Hi, I'm Lei-Han Wen. Nice to meet you, Ralph. And congratulations on your company's grant award."

"Lei-Han works for Huawei in their Los Angeles office," Will said, "but she is vacationing with us here in her hometown for the next few days. My mother, father, and I are very excited to have her home. We never see enough of her."

Like hell she works for Huawei, thought Ralph, maintaining his most-polite smile. *Apparently I've seen more of her in the last few months than her family*, his thoughts went on. *And if her old man thinks she's dressed immodestly today, he should have seen her in Vegas about two months ago when she was wearing that very shear, very form-fitting dress with the plunging neckline that stopped just above her pubic bone*. Ralph tried to clear his mind of that image, but was having the damndest time doing so.

"And look, she is slightly blushing. Perhaps she has a small crush on you?" her father asked with a chuckle.

"Very nice to meet you … is it Leng Hein?" Ralph extended his hand.

"Lei-Han." The panic had not left her eyes, and she was not subtle about shaking her head in a negative manner. She grasped Ralph's hand with a vice grip, and attempted to tap a message on his palm with her middle finger. The handshake extended longer than customary, but no one seemed to notice, except Will, who slightly raised an eyebrow.

"Will, please let Lei-Han sit between you and Ralph," Wen said.

"I think she likes him. Look at how nervous she is," the younger brother teased. "And he would be a great catch. But I'm afraid he's married, Lei-Han. At thirty-four, you need to find a husband soon or you'll become 'day-old Christmas cake.'"

She punched Will and he winced in pain.

"Damn Sis, have you been working out?"

There was much talk around the table, in Mandarin, about when the company would IPO, how much it would be valued at, and what each person would do with their newly-earned wealth. Ralph hated these discussions with his every fiber, as there was some very heavy lifting between here and there, but because the words were in Chinese, he could pretend he didn't understand. He focused on the boiled bullfrog that was placed in front of him.

"Would you like some wine?" asked the prettiest of the lean and tall wait staff.

"Ralph doesn't drink alcohol," Lei-Han scolded. She gave Ralph a hard look for his perceived ogling of the pretty server.

"Sis, how do you know Ralph doesn't drink?" Will asked. "Have you met before?"

Eva/Lei-Han hid her wince well. "You forget I work in L.A., and know Californians generally don't drink at lunch."

"It's true. Or at least not anymore. How long have you worked in the U.S.?" Ralph asked. "Your accent is perfect."

"About seven years. But I also went to school in the U.S."

"Oh, which school?" Ralph knew he'd be able to use this information, and it'd probably be the truth.

"I went to Cal."

"Berkeley?"

"No, she went to Cal Poly," bragged Will. "I didn't get into Cal Poly, I went to USC." Will wanted equal time in the spotlight.

"University of Spoiled Children," Lei-Han teased. "And that was only because of Daddy's donation."

Will rolled his eyes. "Whatever."

"Although," Ralph said, "I do know a woman who is your twin—your doppelgänger. Her name is Eva, and she also works for Huawei." He wanted to see Eva/Lei-Han sweat, even just a bit.

"That's hilarious," Will laughed. "When Lei-Han was a child, she asked to change her name to Eva. That's so funny." He stared hard between Eva and Ralph.

Now Eva/Lei-Han's eyes turned to Ralph. He saw pleading in them. "Yes, I always thought if I became a movie, or maybe a pop star, one of my names would be Eva—and the other would be Jen. I do love those names." She gave an empty laugh.

Ralph's smile disappeared. "Well, now that I get a better look at you, I can tell you're not Eva. You're much more attractive than she is. She always wears a threatening scowl, and has a permanent crease between her eyebrows."

Will laughed. "She's always wearing that menacing scowl! And look at her wrinkle, just between her eyebrows," he said, pointing at his sister. "Maybe it is her!"

"That's not true," Lei-Han/Eva said. Then, when a few around the table tried to hide their laughter, she realized she was wearing the same scowl she had just disavowed. She smoothed the skin between her eyebrows and blushed. A few people at the table laughed gently at her mild discomfort.

The subject quickly turned back to how soon the company would IPO and how wealthy they'd all soon be.

The lunch was spicy, especially the Beggar's Chicken. The sea cucumber was rubbery and had a peculiar metallic taste. As usual, Ralph was getting sweaty with any spicy food. He decided he needed to wipe his brow and excused himself.

When he asked for directions to the men's room, the server who had offered Ralph wine decided to guide him. Eva shot him a look of daggers.

"It is just here, Ralfu," the server said, pointing to a door just outside the dining room. "I'll wait for you."

Ralph did his business, washed his face, and tried to rinse his mouth from the taste of the sea cucumber. When he opened the restroom door, the pretty server was still there. She leaned in close enough her lips touched Ralph's neck and whispered, "Eva humbly requests to talk to you before you make your move. Please? When we get back into the room, please ask her father about the special chrysanthemum tea. He'll offer to have Will or Lei-Han show you the tearoom on the building's roof. Say 'yes' to his suggestion please. Please?"

She brushed her breasts against his arm. Ralph nodded. When he returned to the table, more food was revolving around the very large table. Ralph grabbed pieces of watermelon and listened carefully to the discussion. By this point in the lunch, the crowd had tired of talking in Ralph's native language. While he didn't speak Mandarin well, he understood enough. One of Ralph's teammates was telling a story of Ralph's wealth, and he reminded himself to show no acknowledgement that he understood. People stared at him, and he pretended not to notice. He did see that Lei-Han was busy trying to catch the eye of the server who had escorted Ralph to the "little skier's room."

In Mandarin, Will's father asked if Ralph had enjoyed lunch, and if he wanted anything else. Ralph had to pretend he didn't understand, until Will translated.

"Thank you for your wonderful hospitality. I am very full. I especially enjoyed the Beggar's Chicken and sea cucumber. But my favorite thing thus far has been that tea. It is wonderful. So fruity. Might I have another glass of that exceptional tea?"

Eve's father beamed. "Of course." In Mandarin he told Will and Lei-Han to take Ralph to the teahouse, and be sure to explain about the Hangzhou mini-chrysanthemum tea. The pretty server ran ahead to turn on the teahouse's air conditioner, and to boil some fresh spring water.

When the elevator came, only Ralph, Will, and Eva got in. "We'll be back in about an hour okay, Dad?" The father nodded and turned back to his lunch audience, immediately resuming the discussion of whether two simultaneous IPOs could be done for the Chinese branch as well as the U.S. parent company.

When they left the elevator, Ralph was in awe of this rooftop teahouse. An oasis on top of a forty-story office building, it was constructed of bamboo of all sizes.

Will flashed a sly smile. "Do you guys want to get high? I brought a doobie."

"I'm cool." Ralph partook on occasion, but the thought of a Chinese prison was an adequate deterrent.

"Me too," said Lei-Han/Eva. Will wandered off to one end of the building's roof, well beyond shouting distance.

"Are you here to kill all my family, or just intimidate the fuck out of me?" Eva was visibly shaking. "And please, please tell me how you found us."

"Nice to see you too, Eva."

"If you and your team kill my family, this'll be a suicide mission for you. You'll never make it out of China alive." The wrinkle line between her brows was red and pulsing.

"Eva, sometimes you can be pretty dramatic. I am an entrepreneur and small investor, not a killer, and I did not come here to threaten you or your family. I know your brother. One of the companies I've invested in presented a plan to open a local office to the regional government, and Will invited me to meet your father for lunch. I had no idea you were somehow connected to all this."

She gave him a look of frightened disbelief. "Fuck you, Ralph. People like you and me, our craft has one unwritten cardinal rule: we don't involve our families. And you are standing in my family's home. And I am frightened, not for my life—you can take it—but please, please leave my family alone. They know nothing about my real work. You will accomplish nothing by hurting them."

Ralph paused. "Look, let's make a deal. I'm as surprised to see you as you are to see me. I promise not to harm or do any future harm to your family, if you promise to honestly answer a few questions for me. Deal?"

Eva checked to make sure her brother was still fully engaged in his smoke. "How can I possibly trust you?"

"I don't know. But what choice do either of us have right now? I need your honest answers. So, we'll have a trade: You'll get my commitment not to bring harm to your family, and in return you provide me with some straight talk. Unfiltered truth. Deal?"

This time Eva gave Ralph a hard stare. He knew Eva was not a person who easily gave her trust.

"Ralph, who do you work for? Really?"

"That was the first question I was going to ask you."

"Fuck you. I'll kill you and your team with my bare hands if I have to."

"I'm serious. I think I'm being used as a pawn in your trade, but I have no idea by whom. Or why."

"You can't be serious?"

Ralph looked down. If he couldn't convince her, he'd gain nothing. "I'm not a great entrepreneur, and I'm probably a shitty investor. I'm certainly not the smartest guy at lunch today. People do things for me and I end up looking smart. I appear to be a successful entrepreneur and investor, but I'm certain someone else, or a large number of someones, are influencing these events."

"Okay, suppose I believe you. How does your wife and McKenna fit into this scenario?"

"Those were to be my next two questions to you."

"Shit, Ralph. You can't possibly be this clueless."

"Ah, yeah, I can. Because I am, in fact, clueless."

"I don't believe you."

"Well, you're probably trained not to believe me. But I have no training, and I'm trying to figure out how and why I fit into this mess. And at this point, I don't care how big a fool I appear to you. Some people think I am a spy. But I am actually an idiot, and I am just trying to make sense of all this."

"How did you find me? How did you find us?"

"I didn't. Your brother found me. He invited me, as he wanted to get more involved."

"The project you're working on here, is it part of the Z-Prize project? And what is its effectiveness of the Z-Prize tool?"

"Hold on. How do you know about that? And aren't I supposed to be asking you the questions?"

"Right," she said with resignation. "We have no idea who you—or for that matter, your wife—are working for. Our files for you are plentiful, as you travel often and meet with people we're interested in. Your wife's file is thin, but we're certain she's in the game. Up until very recently, we assumed she was your handler. But after tapping your Amazon Echo and Apple Siri devices, we now believe she works for someone else. Initially, we thought she was to keep tabs on you. But we now believe that isn't her entire job, as her signature or mode of operation is more of a handler's handler. She is farther up in the food chain, we believe. McKenna is most certainly a hired gun—mostly in the 'ambiguous' sides of our business. His skill sets are in ferreting out information when no information is forthcoming. He's working for the highest bidder. And we believe that to be those secretly controlling the Z-Prize project."

"Are they connected?"

"That was going to be our next question to you, Ralph."

"Who do you work for?"

Eva again looked up to locate her brother, who was still enjoying his doobie. "I work for the Huawei corporation. But corporations in China have two sets of bosses. I work for the set that isn't concerned with profits and losses."

"Is my wife safe?"

"I don't know. But she works quietly, behind the scenes, and most often those people are the most safe in our industry."

"How do I find out who I work for? How do I communicate with them?"

"Have you asked your wife this question? If I were you, that's the first person I'd ask. My guess is that you probably work for her."

"I just can't imagine that. Don't get me wrong—she's certainly bright enough. But she isn't interested at all in what I do day-to-day. I invite her to my meetings and my business trips, but most often she begs off. She enjoys walking the dogs on the beach, not learning about new esoteric technologies."

"Maybe you're right. But have you asked yourself why you haven't asked her? Is it because you're afraid of the answer?"

"It just seems far-fetched. I think she'd just think I was crazy."

"Any more than any of this?"

"No, I suppose not."

"So ask her. What I will tell you is that there are many organizations trying to learn who you and Jen work for. And this industry doesn't like unanswered questions."

"I asked McKenna. He tried to convince me I was crazy."

"Sure, if he's not working with your team, he'd obfuscate."

"Why are people interested in the Z-Prize education tool?"

"Bluntly—same answer. No one likes unanswered questions, and there is a huge amount of chatter around the tool. People in my country are worried it'll be turned into a massive weapon. As silly as it sounds, a weapon of mass persuasion."

"That does sound silly."

"But from what I have learned, it might just work. It might work well. And we'd never know it was being used on us. For example, worldwide politics has been less predictable recently. Can you explain it?"

"Are you thinking our orange president is using the tool on his own populace?"

"Stranger things have happened, Ralph. It explains a few things."

"I just…. No. it can't be …" Ralph was flummoxed.

"For what it's worth, we don't think the tool is fully operational. So the Trump/Clinton election may just be a fluke. A flaw in the notion of the democratic process. But I don't care if you're a Republican, Democrat, or an independent—there's some strange stuff happening."

"We can agree on that. So what do we do next?"

"Well, I'm fairly certain you're not going to give me the Z-Prize plans and algorithms on a thumb drive. Moving forward, we'll all try to answer some of those unanswered questions."

"But—" Ralph was interrupted abruptly.

"Listen to me. My brother is wrapping up his kit, and he'll soon be joining us. He's a keen observer for a stoner, and I'm certain he's noticed from early on that we're somehow connected. In order to quench his curiosity, you're going to need to be absolutely genuine ..." And then Eva kissed Ralph and wrapped her long leg around his waist. She moved his hand to her ass. Ralph found it very difficult not to be genuine.

"What? Yo, Sis! I knew you guys knew each other! Wow. There was some weird-assed tension when you walked into the room and saw Ralph. Too funny. Making out with the old, rich white guys. Nice," Will teased.

Lei-Han looked properly embarrassed and attempted to straighten her skirt. Ralph was dumbfounded and didn't move.

"Ralph, she's my older sister and stuff. Can I ask you to take your hand off her ass?"

Ralph slowly realized where his hand still was, and then quickly put his hand in his pocket. Lei-Han possessively rearranged Ralph's hair and straightened his pants, which had somehow taken a quarter turn.

"Ah, sorry," Ralph sputtered.

"I'm actually kind of psyched. She's like thirty-four and we've never met any of her boyfriends. This is great that she's found someone. We were worried she was like 'day-old Christmas cake,' you know? Sis, just so that you know, I also have a gweilo girlfriend in the U.S. We'll make a promise to each other not to tell Mom or Dad, okay?" Will was most excited to share his secret.

"I'm not thirty-four," Eva snapped. "I'm twenty-eight."

"Yeah, sure, Sis. I just had my twenty-ninth birthday and you were born five years before me," he laughed. "Girls are funny. More worried about their age than when they get caught shoving their tongues down some old guy's throat. Sorry Ralph, that's twice I've called you old. I don't know how old you are, but you sure look old."

"I'm only fifty," Ralph said weakly.

"Only!" The siblings laughed at his expense. The elevator came and they met up with everyone else, just as post-lunch cigarettes were being finished.

The threesome stood in the lobby, waiting for the fancy SUV to arrive. When it rolled up, Will opened the door and suggested that Ralph should probably not kiss Lei-Han goodbye, as their father's people were sure to be watching them. Then he got in.

Turning to Ralph, Lei-Han said, "Against all of my training, I think I believe you."

He nodded his appreciation.

"That doesn't mean I will help you."

He nodded his understanding.

"And let's not even pretend we can be friends."

Ralph thought back to the kiss and decided this was a very good thing.

"But that was a genuine kiss. And a good one—from an old man. Thanks."

As he shut the door of the car, he blushed like a fourteen-year-old boy.

❧

As soon as the car joined the traffic, Will's phone received a new SMS from his dad. It read, "How does Lei-Han know Ralph? Do you know? Can you find out? She looks flushed like a just-picked flower. He may have made inappropriate advances on Lei-Han."

Will chuckled, leaned over to show his sister the note, and they jointly decided to not head back into the office and face their father's further questions.

❧

When Ralph got back to the hotel lobby, the manager made a great show of announcing that Ralph had been awarded an upgraded room, a suite. Ralph wasn't sure why, but in the elevator he heard—in broken English and basic Mandarin—that the upgrade was due to the secretary of the city, apparently as a thank you. It sounded pleasant, until it was accompanied by some snickering. Ralph questioned the manager about his suitcase and few belongings in his old room. He was assured his kit would be found in his new room.

When the manager opened the door to the suite, Ralph was pleasantly surprised. There was a living room with a few comfy chairs and a large screen TV. The room also had a small kitchenette, dining table, and karaoke machine. As the manager walked him down the hallway, they passed a large closet room, and a deluxe bathroom with a fountain shower and six foot deep bathtub. The real surprise was when they got to the bedroom. On the bed were three young, barely-dressed women. Only the manager was unsurprised. Ralph let out a sigh. The women were not happy that Ralph was a gweilo. They collectively let out a disappointed moan. And the manager snickered, again. Then he let himself out of the room.

Ralph used a phone and called his Chinese right-hand.

"Koh, here is the situation." Ralph explained the scene. "What do I do?"

"Well Ralph, I hate to tell you this, because you're such a nice guy, but you're going to need to take one for the team …"

"What? Not going to happen."

"Just kidding, Boss. I know Jen would kill you in your sleep. I'll be there soon to save you. I can handle all three. In the meantime, it'd be seen as an insult if you sent them away. Turn on the Karaoke machine and show them your best dance moves."

Twenty minutes later, just as Ralph was demonstrating his dance moves to Taylor Swift's video "Shake it Off," Koh entered the room.

❧

Later, in a Huawei van in front of the hotel, Eva watched a recorded version of Ralph demonstrating his dance moves, via close circuit TV that had been previously installed in the room and laughed. "Oh, you are such a good boy, Ralph."

Chapter 27
2016

Talking with several start-ups each week meant that Ralph picked up quickly on the current hot concept in Silicon Valley. Each week, month, season could be different. Ralph had met with three disparate companies in three different fields, and each presenter had used the term "gamifying" to describe a process to goad users into long-term, positive engagement. Much like every other trend in Silicon Valley, these verbal trends started when a group of VCs announced they were making an investment based on VC buzz terms—in this instance, "Gamification."

The following week, Ralph met with representatives of the German government, including the Minister of Labor, who interestingly also had the title/responsibility for refugees/migration. Germany, like many countries in the EU, and Japan for that matter, had a macroeconomic challenge, in that their country's population was aging out. In 2015, the average age in Germany was 46.1 years old. In 2016, the average age was expected to be 46.8. If this trend continued, this vector of the citizen's average age would bankrupt the country, as too few working-age citizens would be available to pay taxes to the support the government's long-term commitments.

The solution that Ralph initially proposed, and was later accepted and improved upon, was "gamifying" the German immigration process. Germany needed elder care, health care, and tech workers for it aging population and tax needs. One of Ralph's portfolio companies provided its users with a privacy/security platform that allowed unfettered access to the internet, even of areas with censorship. Since this company's app solved the censorship challenge throughout the world, they were a popular app in the various smartphones' app stores, particularly in areas where censorship was prevalent. This was especially the case in MENA—Middle East and Northern Africa—where about 50% of the citizens used the app at least once a month. The use of the app was "free," that is, advertising supported, hence Germany became an advertiser. Or more accurately, Germany's Labor Ministry became an advertiser. They bought all of the advertising in countries where immigrants—or refugees—congregated before pushing off to safer environs. And instead of utilizing standard advertising, the Labor Ministry built a launch platform for advising immigrants/refugees on the process of immigrating to Germany. And as a complement to detailing the process, the government awarded points for potential immigrants who took online courses to learn skills that Germany needed. There were multiple courses on elder and health care, there were computer-networking courses, there were cultural courses, and of course there were courses on the German language. As students/refugees progressed, they could also earn certificates. And as potential immigrants, they could earn points as they hit each milestone to increase their priority placement for immigrating legally into the country. The platform would track the points each applicant earns, and those with the most points rise to the top of the list.

Today, potential refugees and immigrants have a place on the internet to learn what skills earn their families a spot at the top of the list to legally immigrate. And the Germans also inform the travelers about the hardships of ill-advised migration. In the first six months of operation, more than thirteen million people signed up on the German platform. It was a quiet but well-celebrated success within the government. Until it wasn't.

Astroturfing is the practice of masking the sponsors or organization behind a message—e.g., political, advertising, religious, or public relations—to make it appear as though it originates from and is supported by grassroots participants. As the German government's platform grew, so did the resentment of its success. And the vile organizations that had the most to lose began to set up mirror sites with significantly different content. Their goals were to create chaos and distrust. And their techniques, while not as sophisticated, were winning a small portion of the battle.

This is why Ralph got a call to revisit the Deutschland Labor Minister. In Berlin, he walked into a room with the minister's assistant, and was surprised with the large size of the room and the staff present. There were fifty people in suits. As usual, Ralph was wearing a pair of khakis, a zippered sweatshirt with his company's logo at the breast, and slip-on sneakers with no socks.

"Herr Gibsen. Willkommen in Deutschland."

"Danke, Hendrik." That was about the extent of Ralph's German language skills.

Ralph was suddenly conscious that he was wearing the wrong costume. "Sorry about my lack of tie or suit."

"I am not sure we'd recognize you in a suit, Ralph," the minister teased. "Do you even own one?" He and some of his team had visited Ralph in Silicon Valley, and at that time Ralph had worn shorts and a T-shirt. The minister's team wore suits.

"I do own a few, but I admit the last time I had one tailored was probably twenty years ago."

Most of the people in the room spoke perfect English, albeit begrudgingly.

"Let's get down to business, shall we?" The room was suddenly silent. "We'll first review our progress to date and then explore challenges and options for the future."

For the first twenty minutes, the presentation was positive and congratulatory in nature. But the last slide—on the sentiment of target migrant—was worrisome. In the last sixty days, the sentiment for the program had turned from 96% positive to 55% positive.

"So much of our efforts are at risk. In the last few months, there have had more than a dozen platforms that mimic our content that have come to the internet and dilute our message. What's worse is that these platforms sow the seeds of distrust and confusion. They mimic our sponsors, our online classes, our gamification. But upon completion, the fake platforms convince the potential migrants that the points are meaningless or, worse, a ploy to keep people from traveling. And for whatever reason, these fake platforms are making better progress—almost as if they were more persuasive with our target audience than our own. And yet the content is identical, only the conclusions are different."

"So how are these rogue platforms becoming known to the target audience?" Ralph asked.

"They are apparently advertising on your company's anti-censorship's app. Are they outspending us? Is that part of the problem? Is that something we can fix?"

"Not really. I looked at the numbers before this meeting, and someone is spending some money, but they aren't out-spending you."

"Then what else can it be?" asked a frustrated bureaucrat. He was angry and looking for someone to blame.

"Well, I think part of the problem might be the message. As you are undoubtedly aware, in this part of the world, the populace is susceptible to the possibility of malintent."

With some open disdain, the same bureaucrat shot back, "We are aware that the MENA region manufactures conspiracy theories better than any other product or service in the region."

Ralph tried not to acknowledge the same. "So from a messaging and content perspective, the alternative narrative seems to be gaining traction."

The bureaucrat had obviously decided he was to be the bad cop in this discussion. "So what is your company's response? What actions are you taking?"

"We aren't taking any actions. Each month the app we make is used by 600 million people who want to circumvent their government's censorship of the internet. We provide an unfettered internet. We do not produce your content or messaging. We have no expertise in the same." Ralph wanted to clearly delineate roles.

The minister jumped in. "But Ralph, some of the genesis for this effort is yours. And as I have shared with you, some of my own peers in this government do not support working with your company." Ralph knew that some members of the German government were steadfastly against working with an anti-censorship company. Especially since the German government spent a huge amount of resources attempting to block historically sensitive content. "For better or for worse, you are entangled with our project and we need your help."

The meeting went on for nine hours, with a few heated moments and a great deal of frustration. Ralph contributed as best he could, but felt out of his depth. As they were wrapping up by recording action items and deliverables, the minister asked Ralph to join him privately in his office. Ralph had no other meetings planned, and was hoping the minister wouldn't ask him to dinner. He was spent.

"Ralph, may I be indelicate?"

"Of course, JT." Ralph didn't want to appear too familiar, but he had been asked to use the minister's name when they last met.

"In your profession, you work with any number of companies and projects. Could one of these other projects be impeding our progress?"

Ralph was unprepared for this question. "My immediate response is 'no,' but maybe I should ask for more specifics."

"Well, I need to ask specifically if there is any chance that the Z-Prize EdTech project is being tested or used to influence our immigrants?"

Ralph paused, carefully considering his words. "JT, I am not even sure how you know of this tiny little research project. But this experiment isn't even out of the lab. As far as I know, it hasn't ever been used on humans."

JT stared at Ralph, trying to determine his conviction. "Why is there significant chatter in the Intelligence Community on this project? Really, Ralph, what is going on?"

"I'm not sure. In fact, you aren't the first to ask me about this."

"There is the English idiom about smoke and fire. There sure seems to be plenty of smoke. Do you need help from us? If you … gave us access to the Dropbox accounts, my team could quickly determine if it was a real threat."

The minister's smile was tight.

"I can't do that. I have responsibility to the team and the mission of the project."

The minister looked deeply hurt. He paused and gave Ralph a dramatic look. "Ralph, we have enjoyed working with you. But if you cannot share this with us, then we need to view the project—and you—as a threat. My bureaucrats aren't very sophisticated. They see non-Germans as either friends or enemies. And your lack of willingness to share is going to be viewed as hostile."

"I am not hostile."

"But your new president is not helpful."

"But you realize, of course, that this project has nothing to do with politics or the Intelligence Community, correct?"

"And how about you? Are you a member of the IC?"

"I am not."

"Are you certain of that fact? Absolutely certain? Because I am not certain. And if you become a person that is deemed hostile to Germany, I am not at all sure I can protect the projects of your other portfolio companies that you have ongoing with our government. Is that fully understood?"

Ralph nodded. Then he was dismissed when the minister turned away to take a call. On the way out of the office, Ralph was only certain about one thing: how uncertain his life had become.

Chapter 28
Summer 2017

After wrapping up a few potential partnership meetings, Ralph was in Beijing's airport. He had been on the road in Southeast Asia for about ten days and was looking forward to getting home. The summer's humidity was wearing him down. He was sitting in a Starbucks and thinking about braving the customs and security lines when he got a WhatsApp message.

"We need to come to agreement on your proposal. Prefer to do it face to face. Can you fly to Qatar today?" messaged Mohammed.

Ralph desperately wanted to say "fuck no." But the deal was important and might make the world incrementally better. "Sure," he responded. "But let's meet in London because it's fucking hot in Qatar. Cool?"

"Can't fly to London today. Let's meet in Doha at my hotel tomorrow morning."

"Let me try to change my flight. More soon." Ralph immediately got on the phone to call his assistant, but as soon as he dialed he realized it was 6 PM on a Friday night back home.

"Mika I am sorry to bother you."

"Fuck. I almost didn't pick up. Someday I am going to leave you, Ralph. I am heading out to dinner with my boyfriend. And every time you start a conversation by saying you're sorry, I know I'm in for a couple hours of work."

"Yeah, sorry about that."

"Oh, shit. Two 'sorrys' before you've even asked me for the favor. I need to cancel my date, don't I?"

"Maybe just postpone for an hour or so? Sorry."

"Does Jen know you aren't coming home? She's going to be pissed."

"Not yet. I'll deal with that in a few. Let me tell her, okay?"

"Right, 'sorry.' I just texted her. I only sent the fireworks and shit emojis. She just sent back the dead man walking emoji. Wouldn't want to be you, sleeping on the couch for the next few weeks…."

"Yeah. Okay, you know the drill. I'm at the Beijing airport and need to fly to Doha instead of SFO. Need to get there preferably before 10 AM. Can you do this for me?"

"What airline? Which hotel? Do you need a car to pick you up at the airport? How many nights? Which of your appointments do I need to reschedule next Monday?"

"Don't care, but check to see if you can find one where I can bring my laptop onto the flight. The new president's people have limited the use of electronics onboard for some of those flights. Mohammed's hotel—I think he owns the JW Marriott, right? Please check to see if they have any non-smoking rooms. Yes to the car. Make sure it's an Audi because Mohammed's brother owns the dealership in Qatar. I think only two nights, so get me a direct to SFO on Monday afternoon—or is two nights a Sunday afternoon flight? Can you call me back in ten minutes to confirm?" Ralph rattled all this off in thirteen seconds. If there were an Olympic competition in rearranging flights and packing for a ten-day business trip, Mika and Ralph would be on the podium.

"It would be a Monday flight home. All of your morning appointments would need to be postponed, right?"

"Yeah, just those before 1 PM. I think the rest I can handle, either in the Uber en route to the office or once I'm there. Can you bring a clean towel for me on Monday? Oh fuck, Jen just sent *me* the dead man walking emoji. What did she have planned for us this weekend?"

"You've got a houseful of guests, and you had promised to BBQ. I've got a clean towel for you under my desk, and China Airlines has one B class seat available in two hours. It gets you into Doha on time. The JW hotel just sent me a text informing us your room and car would be waiting. Mohammed's assistant Rose is awesome. Can I send her flowers?"

"Yes, and send flowers to Jen. A big bunch of hydrangeas. Call Sid's BBQ place in Santa Cruz and order a delivery of twelve 'three meat specials,' all with coleslaw—no baked beans. Jen loves their coleslaw. I think I was supposed to BBQ on Saturday night. But double check that please. Then buy yourself and your questionable boyfriend a nice bottle of wine at dinner tonight. Californian, not French. And not more than a hundred bucks. Cool?"

Within two hours, Ralph had apologized profusely to Jen and was "wheels up" and heading towards the Middle East. Qatar was the naughty neighbor amongst the many Arabian tribes, and Ralph's meeting may help save face for a few nation-state neighbors in their most recent discussions. It was worth the effort.

The eleven-hour flight was uneventful. Ralph spent much of the flight time reading a novel a friend had recommended. When they landed, the heat was glimmering off the concrete runway. Ralph was one of the first off the plane, and was greeted at the end of the air bridge by a woman holding a sign.

"Mr. Ralph. Nice to see you."

Ralph nodded, but as always felt awkward when greeting a woman in a full burka. There were no eyes to acknowledge. He wasn't sure where he should look when speaking to her.

"How are you? How was your flight? Did you check any bags?"

"My flight was fine. No bags checked. Just what I have here." They were walking in the opposite direction from all of the other passengers.

"Great. Have you checked your messages yet?"

"Not yet. What's going on?" Ralph and his black-clothed friend were now heading toward the far end of the terminal. Ralph knew most of the world's airports well and didn't think there were any public exits where they were heading. Ralph wiped a sheen of sweat off his brow.

"Slight change of plans. Mohammed is sorry for the inconvenience. After you spoke about the cool, dry air in London, Mohammed decided to fly there immediately to cool down. He has arranged alternative transportation and hotel for you."

Ralph was in a daze from his long-flight. He shook his head to clear the cobwebs. "Another flight?"

"We are terribly sorry, yes. Mohammed and I apologize again. But you'll be able to completely relax on this flight, I promise." They had arrived at the end of the terminal and she used an electronic key to open a set of doors to the outside. The 45 degree Centigrade/122 degree Fahrenheit degree windblast was a shock to Ralph's system. They were joined by a suited man in dark wrap-around sunglasses who carried Ralph's bags down the stairs to the tarmac. There was a big Audi Q7 at the base of the stairs. Ralph was quickly guided to and ensconced into the backseat. The small woman sat next to the driver. "It'll just be a moment."

Maybe Ralph should have been freaking out, asking too many questions and making everyone else nervous. But he had learned to shut up and listen in such situations. There were no threatening signs. Everyone was being friendly. He could demand answers, but instead he grabbed a bottle of water that was in the center armrest and enjoyed its refreshment. The big Audi rocketed down the taxiway. They accelerated around a Qatar Airlines A380. Ralph estimated the big SUV was going about 120 mph (200 kph).

There were several planes in the near distance. In moments, they had pulled up next to a white Boeing 757 with only minimal markings. In a flash, the driver was outside and holding Ralph's door open. Ralph made sure that he was being invited to get out of the car, rather than forced to leave the car. After a few dozen heartbeats, he got out of the big Audi. They were just next to the stairs to the plane. He opened the door for the woman in the front seat, and motioned for her to join him. He saw her nod her appreciation. The driver was extracting his bags from the back. The woman started to climb the stairs and looked back after three or four to make sure Ralph was joining her.

At the top of the stairs, they entered the plane and were greeted with a polite nod from the flight attendant. The plane's interior looked like a well-appointed modern living room, all in light Scandinavian woods and beige leather. Thankfully, the AC was blowing fiercely. As soon as they had crossed the threshold, Ralph's escort disappeared deep into the plane, the driver handed him his bags, and the attendant closed the airplane's doors, nearly on the back of the retreating driver. And only moments thereafter, Ralph heard the pilot spooling the big engines. The attendant took Ralph's bags, motioning for him to take a seat. There were about a dozen to choose from. He took one of the seats near the window and buckled himself in. The attendant double-checked that his seatbelt was secure. She smiled as she handed him a cold bottle of water, and then she disappeared. Ralph hadn't been in his chair for thirty seconds when the plane began moving. Sixty seconds later, the plane was lining up for the main runway. A small woman appeared and took the seat next to Ralph. It was Rose, Mohammed's assistant.

"You look surprised to see me, Mr. Ralph."

"Were you behind the burka?"

"OMG! Didn't you realize it was me? I'm so sorry. I, well, I forget that sometimes Westerners can't immediately tell who we are. No wonder you were quiet ... I probably scared the bejesus out of you." She was mortified.

Ralph laughed. They had met a dozen or more times. She was educated in Boston and had shared many stories about going to college in Beantown. She and Ralph were ardent Red Sox fans.

"Well, yeah. I probably should have asked what was going on."

"We're going to London to meet with Mohammed."

"Okay. And is there anyone else on the plane?"

"Just staff and you."

"This huge plane and it is only for us?"

"It's for you. I'm here just to escort you. Once we're at 8000 meters, I'll show you around. But this is a nice plane. It has a master suite where you can sleep, a lovely spa area where you can get a massage and haircut, and a chef who can cook you anything you want."

"Sounds like heaven."

Rose smiled. "I often take this plane with Mohammed's guests. His plane is even nicer."

"I'm surprised—I could have taken a commercial airline. It feels wasteful to be here with only a few of us."

"Enjoy it. The last flight I was on was with a pop star that was to sing at Mohammed's daughter's birthday party. She found the disco Karaoke machine and we sang and danced for the entire ten-hour trip. But I have even a better surprise for you. I recorded last night's Red Sox-Yankee game. We can watch it and I'll get the chef to steam us some beer dogs. What do you think?"

Ralph knew he probably shouldn't share this episode of his life on Facebook, as it was too unbelievable, even for Ralph. But he had a big smile, and felt some of the pressure of his world scrub off his shoulders. "Let's first find Taylor Swift's video of 'Shake it Off.' A little dancing would be good for my soul. Then let's watch the Mighty Red Sox kick those puny Yankee asses."

For the decorum of the culture, the attendants all joined with Rose and Ralph as they flew and danced for the first ninety minutes of the flight to London. Everyone laughed and cheered when it was Ralph's turn. Being well practiced by now, his dance moves accurately mimicked Taylor Swift's in her video for "Shake it Off." Later, the beer dogs were cooked perfectly, and the Red Sox beat up on the lowly Yankees.

Often, Ralph was the luckiest guy he knew.

⤬

At Heathrow, on his way out of the country via a U.S. commercial carrier, Ralph was pulled aside at immigration. He was led away from security and into an office.

His bags were confiscated and emptied of their contents. This was always embarrassing, as he hoarded snack foods in his computer bag. He also had every available connector cable for a presentation machine. Hence his bag always got extra scrutiny.

"My name is Mr. Smyth," the middle-aged, frumpy bureaucrat in a bad suit droned. "Might you be kind enough as to answer a few questions for us?"

"Sure, Mr. Smyth."

"What was the purpose of your eighteen-hour visit to the United Kingdom?"

"Business." Ralph believed that less detail was always better than more detail.

"Yes, and could I ask you to be a bit more specific?"

"I had a business meeting in London with a potential customer."

"A tad bit more please."

"My company wants to complete a business agreement with another company and I met with the leadership of that company in order to detail the business arrangements we might or might not pursue together."

"Mr. Gibsen, if I might cut to the chase. You flew into LHR on a Qatari royal family-owned airplane. Not just an airplane, but a 757 airplane that seats 200 on a normal day. You were the only person to disembark and proceed through customs and immigration. You traveled from LHR via Wheely, an Uber-like competitor owned and operated by the FSB in Moscow. You had one two-hour meeting on the top floor of the Intercontinental Mayfair with a person of great international interest. Prior to Qatar, you were seen in Hangzhou in the presence of an agent of the Chinese Military. There was even an intimate moment caught on camera. We'll show you the telephoto images, if you'd like. I am told the young agent is quite the looker. And yet, you don't—how shall I put this nicely—typically command such attention from the opposite sex with your squidgy middle-and-aging façade. When a member of the IC from one of the FVEY members has such an interesting last seventy-two hours, we typically expect the agent to report into MI5 as a professional courtesy. But somehow you choose to ignore this courtesy and, amazingly, do not show up on any of our records."

The official paused to let Ralph jump in. Ralph didn't.

"What are we to make of such a scenario, Mr. Gibsen?"

"I'm not sure what to tell you. All of what you said is perhaps true—except for the part about me being a part of the Intelligence Community. I am a small investor following up in some business opportunities. Unless you know something I don't?"

"Mr. Gibsen, all I know is that my team tells me that while you were meeting Abdulla and his team, there were six teams from various friendly and unfriendly countries watching you. And that is just the ones my team saw. There may have been more."

"Perhaps they were following Abdulla?"

"No one needs to follow Abdulla—he is speaking at Parliament tomorrow, for God's sake. The man's publicist telegraphs his every meeting, his every move—except yours. You flew in from Qatar on his private plane. Tell me what was discussed at this meeting."

"I cannot, as it is protected under our NDA. But I assure you, it was only business. A deal for us to provide legal and forthright services to his media company that we hope to close in the next few weeks. And if it were disclosed, I think you and most of the free world would approve."

"We'd like to be the judge of that." The man again paused to see if Ralph had anything to add. Ralph didn't. "What can you tell us about Mohammed, and/or Eva?"

"Not much." Ralph explained why he was on Mohammed's plane. He didn't mention his Taylor Swift dance moves. "And Eva? She's a strange woman I've met a few times at trade shows. She kissed me. I didn't kiss her back. Honestly." Ralph wasn't exactly certain that was totally honest. He might have inadvertently returned her kiss. But he was certain he didn't mean to.

Mr. Smyth wasn't impressed with Ralph's explanations. "What else can you give us?"

"Nothing. I am a small investor and I travel extensively to help the companies I invest in. The companies I support tend to be those that are attempting to make the world a better place."

Mr. Smyth released an exasperated sigh. The pause was too long. "It is public knowledge that you are a key member of the team working on the EdTech Z-Prize. Have either Mohammed or Eva attempted to lever you for information regarding this project?"

Ralph was slightly taken aback with the question. He did his best to avoid looking like the question threw him. "No, of course not. The Z-Prize project is a 'do-good' project where no one can directly benefit. If we are successful, all humans will benefit because we've dramatically improved the process of learning."

"And what else can be done with that tool, Mr. Gibsen? Why is there terrific amounts of chatter about this project?"

"News to me. I'm surprised that anyone has heard about it. We meet every few weeks, and half the time we can't get a quorum for decisions. With that said, the decision making is transparent, as we publish a quarterly review of our progress." Ralph paused. "Are you sure you're barking up the right tree?"

Mr. Smyth was unimpressed. "Is that your counsel? I do not know who you report to, but I hope they are disappointed with you."

Ralph shrugged. "I'm not sure what to tell you."

"Then you are dismissed, Mr. Gibsen. But be assured, you've made no friends here today. Your unwillingness to help has been carefully noted and will be the topic of intense diplomatic discussions. Watch yourself."

And with no further acknowledgement, Mr. Smyth left Ralph to find his way back to the immigration and security section of the airport on his own.

Chapter 29
1990

Inevitably, a long business trip eats a weekend. Patpong is a very sketchy entertainment neighborhood in Bangkok. It is sketchy enough the guidebooks tell visitors to stay away. Whorehouses, peep shows, and illicit gambling are features. Being single and in their thirties, Ralph and his colleague Tom Warn were drawn to this neighborhood like mosquitoes to a picnic.

The guidebooks also say that visitors should NEVER be lured into a second-story establishment. These are beyond the purview of the local police force, and bad things would inevitably ensue. Tom and Ralph, being rather large guys in their prime of life, felt in need of an adventure. And thus to a second-story establishment they were lured.

The strip show wasn't much of a strip show. The small and lean tout walked them up the stairs to a completely empty club. The guy wore a polyester Hawaiian shirt, with pit stains that were at least a generation old. He assured them there was no cover charge, and that plenty more guests would be arriving soon. There were two women dancers in the club. They were completely disrobed, and older than both businessmen by at least a decade. And they never bothered to look up at the men. They were too preoccupied with the task of shoving ping-pong balls into their vaginas.

After ten minutes of watching the ping-pong balls fly from the women's vaginas into a bucket fifteen feet away, Tom and Ralph received warm beers.

"Excuse me, can we get cold beers?"

The tout looked at them and shook his head. "Those are cold."

Undoubtedly, the beers were slightly cooler than the sweltering room. Ralph was fairly certain that the most recent basic cleaning of the bar was done under Japanese occupation. "Do you have any beers that might be colder than these?"

"No."

"Could you send us a few bottles of ice water?"

"No. Only beers."

Ralph and Tom shook their heads, chalking it up to the adventure. After another twenty minutes, they decided to visit a 7-11 convenience store they had passed a few doors down Silom Road. They told the tout they were leaving. The tout then harangued the two women to visit upon Tom and Ralph. The women were decidedly bored, with no interest in the two large foreigners. The women were also, upon closer inspection, not one but *two* decades older than the business travelers.

"We need to go."

The women were now gyrating in front of Ralph and Tom. All four looked wildly uncomfortable.

"You want to fuck these girls?" asked the tout.

"No," both gentlemen responded, perhaps a bit too quickly and aggressively.

"You want other girls?"

"No, just our bill please."

"Prettier girls?"

"No. We really have to go."

"You want boys? We have some young boys for you?"

"Ah, no. Just our check please."

"Okay, no problem."

The tout laid a slip of paper on the table and disappeared.

Tom and Ralph took turns looking at the paper, each unable to understand the few markings that were on the check. They decided they'd leave the Baht equivalent of about ten dollars, and go find a cold bottle of water or three. Ten bucks seemed sufficient, since that was the going rate for beers at the Grand Hyatt.

As they were heading for the door, the tout intercepted them. He was waving the Baht and speaking Thai in what was decidedly an angry tone.

"You not pay enough!"

The naked women also began yelling in Thai at Tom and Ralph.

Ralph, attempting to play the peacemaker, asked how much they owed.

"More. Beer and entertainment."

Ralph had only exchanged about U.S. $100 into Thai Baht when he entered the country. He brought out another bill and handed it to the tout. Then he tried to get around the small man and two small women, who were now blocking the doorway.

"More, more, more!" the three chanted.

"Their anger certainly seems disproportionate to the situation," Ralph told Tom.

"Quite."

"Tell us exactly how much we owe you, please," Ralph told the tout.

"More."

"How much more?"

"How much you have?"

"No." Ralph and Tom were slowly losing their patience. "How much do the two beers cost?"

The two women were now in a frenzy, barking incomprehensible Thai at the two awkward foreigners.

Ralph pulled out another bill and handed it to the tout. The money instantly disappeared, much like its predecessors. "We've now paid approximately forty dollars for the two beers. I think that is enough."

"No, not enough!" yelled the tout.

All three of the Thai were now screaming. The tension was crazy.

"Then how much?"

"More, more, more!" they chanted.

Tom grabbed Ralph and whispered in his ear. "Let's just go. This is their scam. We've paid them more than a fair price. Let's just leave."

Ralph agreed and tried to walk around the three. As did Tom. But the three gave no ground. One of the woman pretended Ralph had stepped on her foot and started wailing.

"You hurt her!" shouted the tout. "Now pay doctor's fee."

"I didn't touch her. She's faking."

The Thai man poked Ralph in the chest with his index finger. "You hurt her."

"I have never touched her." Ralph reached for another bill and it disappeared again, this time snatched by the woman with the "hurt" toes.

"More, more, more!"

Tom, being six-four and fit, decided to end this scene by pushing his way through. "We're leaving. Thank you."

Using his forearm, he tried moving the small man out of his way.

The Thai man stood his ground remarkably well. He was now bellowing. "You must pay more!"

The two naked women were now in a rage, swinging their fists at both men's chests. The punches didn't hurt much, but did make the situation even more odd.

"More, more, more!" they chanted, breasts flopping every which way.

Ralph tried his loud voice. "We have paid you! We are now leaving! MOVE!"

That only served to ratchet up the noise and the tension.

"More, more, more!" The volume rose even louder.

Tom's forearm was still pushing the chest of the Thai man, who may have weighed less than half of Ralph. Yet the tout was still pounding his index finger into Ralph's chest. And the two older women were screaming and hitting both Ralph and Tom.

Ralph lost his cool. With a growl, he bear-hugged the two naked women and stopped the whirlwind of punches. He picked them off of their feet and, as gently as he could with all their squirming and kicking, moved them out of the way.

Both Tom and Ralph would remember, in great detail, the click of the hammer being pulled back. The huge handgun the small man brandished was also disproportionate to the situation.

Years later, they would relate the story to friends, and each time the pregnant pause would lengthen after the introduction of the weapon.

In the end, the adventure boys spent about $150 for each beer. They didn't have enough Baht. They had to come forth with additional currencies. The tout was a human calculator when it came to various currencies. And he didn't discriminate. He took Japanese Yen, Indian Rupees, Hong Kong and Singapore dollars, and U.S. greenbacks.

On the way out the door, the women lined up and thanked Tom and Ralph for their kind patronage.

"Come back soon!" said one.

"And bring some friends!" called the other.

Chapter 30
2017

The early flight from Paris was booked tight. As they were getting ready to proceed, Ralph's seatmate asked for a favor: to switch chairs in order for her daughter to sit next to her. As the daughter's seat was one behind his own, Ralph smiled and kindly moved to his new seat.

His new seatmate was an older Asian woman. She had already plugged in her headphones and was watching an episode of *The Big Bang Theory*. She was one of those people who quietly spoke, laughed, and gasped at the sitcom. As Ralph was guilty of being someone who sung along with his headphones on, he decided to simply smile at the woman's outbursts and watch his own movie.

Just after the breakfast service, about an hour and a half into the flight, the Asian woman sitting next to Ralph caught his attention by waving her hand in front of his face. Ralph pulled off his headphones.

"I was a contemporary of your mother's, you know."

"Excuse me?" Ralph wasn't sure he had heard correctly.

"Are you really going to turn away the love of my daughter and a billion dollars for your silly principles?"

Ralph waited for his brain to process what he had just heard. "Stop. First, tell me who you are. Then tell me how you knew my mother. Then tell me this discussion isn't somehow related to Eva."

"Your mother was a woman that we all greatly respected. A worthy and genuine adversary."

"My mother was the executive director of a YMCA. She taught children to swim and dance."

"She did? That's nice. She also taught a great many agents to survive and thrive in this little game we play."

"I don't believe you. Who are you?"

"That's not very important. But I am—for all intents and purposes—Eva's mother. And your soon-to-be mother-in-law and handler. You may call me Millie."

"Millie, is it? Can I tell you how frustrating this is? This whole thing? I'm not the person you think I am. I'm the guy who must check the front of his pants and shoes to ensure I haven't peed all over myself each time I urinate. I am an idiot. I am not now, nor have I ever been what you think I am. I cannot be any clearer about that."

"You are very convincing. So much so, I actually looked at the front of your pants. But no, you are not 100% convincing. You are working with someone to attempt to hurt the PRC. Which at this time makes you an idiot and the enemy. We have offered you an attractive alternative. One billion dollars. And my daughter. You will either work with us, or the punishment will be swift and severe."

"No."

She paused. "I could kill you here."

"But you wouldn't achieve anything. Your big, scary talk is a bluff. Easily played. And as an FYI, you aren't bettering your position with threats or inducements. No. I will not help you. And without my help, you have no other access to the EdTech tool."

Ralph pulled on his eyeshades, and started the seat toward its lay-flat position.

"Sit up or ignore me at your peril, you fat ugly man."

"No."

She rapped him hard in the head with her knuckles.

"Ow," Ralph whelped.

"Madam. What is going on?" the male flight attendant was in business class and had apparently seen Millie rap Ralph.

Ralph sat up and pulled off his eyeshades.

"Nothing is going on. Mind your own business. Go back to your station," Millie barked.

"Lady, I'm about to get the captain and tell him what I saw. If I do, you'll spend the next nine hours in cuffs. Now, why did you hit him?"

Millie looked stunned. She stared at her lap.

Ralph motioned to the attendant, asking him to come down the other aisle as to allow them to talk privately.

"I think she might be senile—or having a senile moment. She keeps talking garbage about me being a spy. And I think she may have had an accident. It smells of urine. Doesn't it?"

The flight attendant crunched his nose. He decided he didn't really want to smell anything. "I'm going to get the captain and let him decide what should be done."

"Well, I feel bad. She's ancient, and probably scared out of her wits. Let's leave the captain out of this unless she does anything else, okay? That way we get out of this flight without arrests and delays. Cool?"

Ralph and the attendant stared at Millie. She didn't acknowledge them, and continued to stare at her lap.

"Madam, this gentleman has given you a reprieve. He is a nicer man than I am. But if you so much as look at him funny over the next nine hours, I will restrain you, and you will be arrested for assault when we arrive at our destination. Is that clear?"

After a pause, Millie nodded quickly, still not looking up.

"Do you need a translator to understand my advice to you? I need you to say, 'I understand.'"

"I understand," she said.

"Sir, will you follow me? I am going to move your seat."

"That's not really necessary. She's just a little old senile lady who has peed herself."

Millie glared.

"I must insist. I do not want to spend the flight wondering if she will behave. Please gather your personal effects and follow me."

This felt like an order, not a request. Ralph followed, but with caution.

The flight attendant pointed to a seat, next to which sat McKenna. Hiding his own smirk, the attendant was trying hard to read Ralph's emotions.

"I don't know which of us has worse luck with women." McKenna had been married and divorced more than a handful of times. "But that woman I just saved you from is one of the cruelest bitches I've ever met. She once skinned a friend of mine alive because he wouldn't share some data she needed. She is a bad mamba jamba."

Ralph was perplexed. "What the fuck are you doing here? And are you going to gaslight me and tell me I'm making all this shit up?"

"Oh, 'Nice to see you too, McKenna. Thanks for saving my bacon, like you did all those years ago on Plum Island.' Where is the love, Ralph?"

"Not feeling it today."

McKenna paused. "I can understand that."

"Let me repeat myself. Are you going to tell me once again that I'm making all this up?"

"I am not certain what 'this' is. But after our last call, I did speak with a few people and have learned that the EdTech project you are working on in Silicon Valley is a hot button for the Intelligence Community. Many people are trying to figure out if the tool can be or has been weaponized."

"That doesn't make much sense to me. The tool is years away from being able to be used with any efficacy. And just because it can capture the moment something is learned, there is no research to date on it being able to change a belief."

"Ralph, fake news changed a U.S. election. You don't think this, in the wrong person's hands, could be used for mal-intent?"

Ralph looked into his lap.

"As you know better than most, countering violent extremism with soft propaganda is fairly effective. What if your portfolio company was using the tool for CVE or refugee issues? Could it be used to make a difference?"

"Probably not in its current form, but yes, yes it could."

"Okay then. Your next question is going to be, 'Who do I work for?' Truth is, I've talked with dozens of people, and no one claims you work for them. But just as interesting, no one—including the Chinese team a few rows back—claims that you *don't* work for them."

Ralph took that in and shook his head. "I'm not cut out for this shit."

"Well, for better or worse, I'd say you're in it. Tits deep."

Ralph cringed.

"Did my non-PC comment offend you? Holy shit. You need to man up. Put on your big-girl pants. You've stepped in deep and now you need to make some big decisions. Luckily, I can keep it simple for you. One, you can start a bidding war for the information. I think if I handled the negotiations—for a small percentage of ownership—we could make a few tens of millions of dollars if we sell this."

"The Chinese have already offered me a billion."

"Fuck me."

"Yeah."

"Or, two, you can try and stop it from becoming a weapon."

"Is it me, or did you purposely just change the pronouns for the two options? '*We* sell it' and '*You* find a way to stop it.' What's up with that, partner?"

"The only way you can afford my daily rate is if we decide to sell the technology. Otherwise, you're on your own."

"Come on. I am modestly well-off."

"Dude, you are as rich as they come. But my nation-state clients write me a $10 million retainer check just to get my attention. Wet work is two mil a day. But I'll give you a hell of a discount if you want me to take out the old Chinese bitch a few rows back. Maybe 50% off?"

"You're right. I can't afford you."

"Cheap bastard."

"Thanks. Is my wife involved in all this? The Chinese grandmother told me my mother was …"

"I don't know. I checked on your wife. There's much smoke there, but I couldn't find a fire. As for your mom, I think she was involved in the IC, but that's just a hunch. I found no corroborating evidence for either of them. Hell, I'm not certain *you* are involved. But people think you are. So, welcome."

"Thanks. What do I do next?"

"Because you apparently won't even consider selling this technology, you need to find a way to either make sure it can't be weaponized or stop it all together."

"Technology is amoral. If you build a tool, it can be used for good or evil. Hence, I think I need to stop the development outright."

"Probably. I don't think there's a way to write software that has a conscience, is there?"

"I have a few friends exploring the idea of using AI to determine truth, but the best we can hope for is at least another decade of research and heavy lifting."

"Yeah, then you'll need to stop it. How are you going to do that?"

"No idea. But unless you tell me otherwise, I'm going to assume you and I are on the same team. Let me pass a few ideas and we can bat them around. Cool?"

"That's fine. But let me just remind you, I work for whoever pays me. At this moment, for this project, I can help you. But that can and probably will change. Understood?"

Ralph nodded. He wanted to believe McKenna, but wasn't sure he should.

Chapter 31

The dog's nose juggled Ralph's gonads, and then sat down on Ralph's foot and smiled. Ralph was standing in the TSA Fast Track Lane line, passing through security at San Francisco International Airport.

Ralph had an enormous amount of pride in his ability to get through airports quickly. Insomuch, he was wearing baggy cotton shorts, a lightweight cotton sweater, loafers, and had kept everything out of his pockets. Ralph called this outfit his "flying uniform." His staple. Ralph refused to check bags—it might slow him down—and his carry-ons were already on the conveyor in the X-ray machine.

The dog's handler looked carefully at Ralph. Then back at his canine, who was still sitting on Ralph's foot. Then again at Ralph.

Ralph would have kept walking, but he would first have to get the large dog off his foot.

"Sir, do you have anything in your pockets?"

"No, they're empty."

"Would you mind stepping aside please?" The TSA dog handler was staring at his dog, and had his hand to his earpiece.

When the handler pulled the canine off Ralph's foot, the smiling dog again jabbed him in the crotch.

"And now through the metal detector please."

As Ralph momentarily prepared for his very short walk through the electronic threshold, the dog again tried to sit on his feet.

Ralph noticed that all TSA staff members and many fellow travelers now had their eyes solely on him. His computer and overhead bags were being additionally scrutinized for bomb residue. The entire TSA area had become very quiet. He walked through the metal detector with not a single chirp.

The TSA chief officer, a towering man who wore his buzz cut hair "high and tight," as they say, left his desk and intercepted Ralph before he could take two steps past the detector.

The brute of a man asked Ralph, "Might I ask you to walk through the Millimeter Wave Scanner once for us, sir?"

It really wasn't much of a question. Ralph complied with a nod. The officer made a show of unsnapping the leather guard on his handgun holster, and then grabbed Ralph by his right shoulder, guiding him back through the metal detector. This time, with Ralph and the TSA officer linked, the alarm went active with great force. Ralph and the dog both winced with the high-volume alarm. Instantly the dog lifted its upper lip, growling fiercely and lunging hard against his handler's leash.

The roided officer whipped Ralph around and frog-marched him back through the scanner and into the nearest interview room. The alarms screamed. All eyes were on the commotion. Ralph was now sweating profusely. He tried to wipe some of the sweat from his brow, but the officer interpreted the action as potential flight. The dog was now in a frenzy.

"Get that fucking dog in here with us, now! Make another move and I'll taser your very large ass."

Within moments, Ralph's hands were in plastic restraints, his clothes were forcibly removed from his body, and he was being bent over to be cavity searched. The dog was led back in, and was growling fiercely. The handler was struggling to keep the dog at bay.

As he manhandled Ralph, the officer shouted, "Shut the fucking dog up, now!"

A slender, diminutive older woman in a gray wool suit opened the door, took a moment's look at the mayhem, and softly said, "Please stop, Officer Higgins."

Both the dog and the officer froze. Silence.

Ralph looked up with tears brimming in his eyes. He was frightened and trying desperately to pull his boxers up from his ankles.

"Take your hands off Mr. Gibsen, Officer Higgins. You are relieved of this incident. Please move now."

"But ..." The officer looked like he'd been hit with a brick. He released Ralph with a reflexive shove. Feet entangled in his underwear, Ralph landed on his large ass. The officer was out of the room in short order. Ralph managed to hike his boxers.

As the dog handler reached to help Ralph stand up, the dog leapt directly into Ralph lap. The large dog whined, wiggled, and lapped at Ralph's chin and cheeks.

"What's going on?" the officer in charge asked. And soon everyone was laughing, as the dog had bowled Ralph over from his chair, trying to lick away his tears.

The handler said, "Betsy, heel," and tried to pull her away from Ralph. The dog continued her quest, her tail happily dancing.

"Mr. Samuels, is this normal behavior from this dog?"

"No, Ma'am. I've had the privilege to manage Betsy for the last three years, and I've never seen anything like this. Strangely, she hasn't once given me her alert."

"That is very strange. Please take Betsy to the staging area and give her a re-test. Report back to me immediately. Mr. Gibsen, please put on your clothes. I'll be back in five minutes to talk to you again."

Ralph composed himself, mopping his frightened tears and dog saliva. He sat trying to figure out what the hell was going on. He wondered if the dog had smelt his wife's homemade chocolate chip cookies that he had attempted to sneak into his computer bag. He was in shock and vowed to never again bring homemade cookies on another business trip.

After exactly five minutes, the woman, who introduced herself as Director Smith, returned with the dog handler and Betsy. Betsy aggressively strained at her leash. The handler gave her enough slack, and she sat on Ralph's shoe-less foot. Betsy wedged her snout under Ralph's left hand so that his palm rested on her head.

"Mr. Gibsen, how long have you been a Global Entry member, and how many times have you traveled through this airport's security perimeter in the last twelve months?"

"Ah, two years or maybe three, and maybe about twenty times ..."

"No, it has been thirty-nine times in the last twelve months. And how many times have you seen this handler and his dog?"

"Maybe a dozen times. Betsy is a beauty. Is she a Lab mix?"

Hearing her name, Betsy snuggled closer to Ralph.

"What is your profession and why do you fly often?"

"I am a very small venture investor, and I fly because my portfolio companies' customers aren't always in Silicon Valley. I help where I can."

"Are you a member of any government organizations that you can or perhaps cannot tell us about?"

"Well, I have a new and really small role with the Naval Postgraduate School in Monterey."

"And you didn't think to tell us the code phrase at any point in the last twenty-five minutes?"

"I … don't know any code phrases. I'm new to the role, and I sit on the appropriations committee of the Foundation …"

"I do not expect you to tell me the truth if you are on a mission, but you work with the preeminent spy school in the developed world, and you've seemingly wasted my resources by not following protocol."

"Really, I don't know anything about code phrases. I'm just a small entrepreneur."

"Fine, you are not required to tell me anything. As my granddaughter says, *whatever*, Mr. Gibsen. But before I let you go, I have two questions."

"Please, of course."

"Why is Betsy fawning over you? Are you transporting something you shouldn't? And in relation to my second question, even after at least a half-dozen warnings by my team over the last thirty-six months, why must you continue to bring those homemade cookies with you when you fly?"

"My wife makes the best chocolate chip cookies, with oats and walnuts. They are really delicious. They make me happy. Would you like to try one?" Ralph reached into his bag and handed a cookie to the director, and then one to the handler. Ralph licked his fingers after passing the cookies out, as did Betsy. "My cookies are the only item I'm carrying that maybe I shouldn't."

The director took a bite. "MMMmmm. Yes, they are delicious. Please don't carry them anymore nonetheless. And what about Betsy?" Betsy now had two paws on Ralph's thigh. She was hopeful she'd also be offered a cookie.

"I really don't know. Maybe it's the cookies, or the fact that I have a few big friendly dogs at my home. But maybe it's just because most dogs like me. They always have. And I don't really know why."

Later on the plane, as Ralph was looking to find his computer charger, he found a small tracking device in his bag. It was the size of a pants button, with a small wire tail. Ralph had emptied the bag the previous evening, trying to find a way to lighten the load. The only possible time it could have been added to his bag was during the TSA inspection.

Unless.... "No," he thought. "It couldn't have been my lovely, cookie-baking wife."

Chapter 32

Lest anyone think Ralph was a near perfect business-making machine, he wasn't. Not by a long shot. He often woke to find one of his portfolio companies in disarray. On this morning, Ralph had found that his Augmented Reality platform and printer company had some terrible news based on a recommendation Ralph had made. Emails and instant messages were flying.

A distributor of the company's product, for whom Ralph had worked for many years, had filed for bankruptcy late on a Friday afternoon. They owed Ralph's portfolio company more than $2.5M, and there was a strong likelihood the portfolio company would never see the money. The money wasn't enormous, but the loss would trigger a cavalcade of lenders calling their notes. People were freaking out. They feared—rightly so—that this could end the company.

"Hey! Okay! Hold on. First …" Prior to Ralph's outburst, there were a dozen voices competing for attention on the conference call. "We breathe."

The voices on the call were silent for ten seconds. Then they started to creep back into crescendo mode.

"Stop." As chairman of the Board of Directors, at least in title, Ralph was the most senior. "Everyone needs to take three extra-large breaths with me. Please breath in—count to ten—and then breathe out." Ralph took his time.

"Okay, it would be easy for us to discuss our fears or frustrations. But that's not very productive. Let's start by defining our end goals, and then reverse-engineering how we achieve them. Rob, you start."

The CEO of the firm calmly shared his primary goal: finding a way to keep the lenders focused on not calling their notes, and bringing the company's products to retailers in the holiday season.

"Do we all think this is the right goal?" Ralph asked.

There were slight modifications to the goal, and one attempt to take the team into a discussion of blame, but Ralph steered everyone back. When people agreed on the goal, Ralph asked them for concrete steps that could be taken to achieve it.

The CEO started. "I'd like to see if Apple retail, Target, and BestBuy would allow us to ship directly to them, without the use of a distributor. We've been paying 30% to this distributor mostly because this is the way these large retailers have done this process for years. But it'd be just as easy for us to ship directly to these stores and act as our own distributor. Then we could push the savings to our lenders, and make up the $2M in maybe a single quarter."

The ideas came fast and furious, and many were really good. Soon the team had six action items, with defined owners of those action items and expected timelines. No one spoke about "what ifs" or who was to blame for their rotten luck. The team had purpose.

Only after the all-day meeting was over, and Ralph was driving home alone, did Ralph allow himself to think that his company had just been the victim of a deliberate attack.

Chapter 33

On an outbound flight to Beijing, a few hours after the productive meeting on how to deal with the distributor's bankruptcy, Ralph started the same process for what was happening at the EdTech project. He wrote into his Evernote account:

- Goal: Stealthily, bust-up the tool as a weapon:

1. Locate the source of the funding and find a way to stop the funding (without resorting to violence);

2. Expose the bad guys and try to get them to never contemplate this effort (or something similar) again;

3. Extract his friends and colleagues from any potential harm, especially Jen;

   a. Who are my friends? McKenna? Eric? Eva? Could Ned help? Where was Tom Warn and Peterson? Mrs. Miyagi? She told us thirty years ago to "stay in touch." Need to arrange a trip to Tokyo in order to try to find some help;

4. Potentially bring in state-actors/known enemies to do some of the grunt work (the Huck Finn approach)—if I must, give away something small while not giving the whole thing away—erode the project's (and possibly my) credibility at every opportunity—<u>without</u> making myself a martyr;

5. If one of my store-bought hackers learns the whole story of what I'm trying to do, there would be a significant risk that they'd make their own play for the Chinese billion dollar payoff. Would McKenna? Eva?

6. Break up the tasks, including creating tasks that were not important or necessary to the effort. Back doors are only effective if they aren't known. But the existence of a back door is practically a certainty (via intercepted emails from a few chosen committee members). Back doors can be welded shut, or just as easily exposed, but the hacker who is asked to execute the task often understands that the back door signifies considerable value or opportunity, and hence hackers could be bought to close back doors, but just as often, they'd close one and build two more for themselves, often just to satisfy their own curiosity;

7. The preliminary records of the efficacy of the tool were spread amongst at least twenty committee members. Changing the preliminary results might be impossible. But changing the future results—as the tests became more complex—might be possible;

8. Spread FUD—fear, uncertainty, and doubt—about the hardware (possibly affecting children's

brains) and make certain the software has a few politically charged aspects that will reflect the United States' newfound fascist worries. Today, all politics and all education are local decisions;

9. Do the above with stealth;

10. Don't fuck it all up. And don't get caught.

೧

Meetings with the EdTech working committee were every week. Meetings with the steering committee were infrequent—once a quarter, at best. Ralph didn't typically attend all the working meetings, but he needed to get as much data as possible. He prioritized the EdTech meetings over his normal work and travel load. He stayed behind after the meetings ended. He took the engineers out to lunch. He asked many questions. He didn't learn much more than he already knew, but was becoming certain that Mr. Roger Phillips was the lead suspect—mostly through body language and the reverence displayed to him.

Ralph set out to research Mr. Phillips' life and wealth, deploying a series of cloaking technologies. In a perfect world, he'd build a full dossier while also installing a key-logger software on his computers and cell phones, creating a minute tracking mechanism on his every whereabouts via an IoT and vehicle hack. In Ralph's imperfect world, he found his target had done a commendable job protecting information about his personal life and wealth management choices.

It was only by a fluke that Ralph learned about a good-sized yacht the Phillips family owned and kept in Santa Cruz harbor. One of Ralph's portfolio companies was celebrating a big new customer with a dinner at one of the harbor restaurants. Ralph had gotten to the dinner earlier than planned, and decided to take a quick stroll and admire the sailboats. He was lost in thought and nearly walked into Roger, who was standing at the trunk of his Mercedes Maybach S550 and loading his cart with a cooler. They nodded, both men trying to place where they knew each other, without wanting to show they didn't immediately place the other. Both caught on after a few beats, but the awkwardness remained. Roger mumbled something about his "niece," using his body to shield Ralph from a twenty-something woman accompanying him.

"Have a great weekend," Ralph wished as he walked past. He also noted Roger's car license plate.

The very next day, a wealth manager from one of the largest New York banks was taking Ralph to lunch, attempting to earn his business. The man was doing his best to talk about internal rates of returns and the great parties they threw for their clients. The banker's younger co-worker was also making efforts to slyly name drop Silicon Valley's "Who's Who," all apparently clients. The name dropping gave Ralph an idea.

"I'm mostly interested in having a full-service relationship with my bank." Both bankers nodded knowingly and greedily. "For example, I was with Roger yesterday in the Santa Cruz harbor, and he told me your wealth management team managed his family's affairs and possessions, like his yacht, crew, and Santa Cruz property. Jen and I have a couple of properties, so that's of interest to me."

"Roger Phillips?" The two bankers looked confused.

Ralph nodded encouragingly.

"Ah, Mr. Phillips isn't with our bank, but that service we can also provide," said the young banker, hoping to salvage something. He continued pitching until Ralph interrupted.

"Really? He's not with you guys? Hunhh. I must have misremembered what he said."

The lunch meeting ended as many do, with promises to stay in touch and consider this and that. Neither party expected anything from the meeting, but both parties were going through the motions. When Ralph got back to his office, he pulled out his digital Rolodex and started dialing wealth managers. Ralph prioritized the largest first.

On his call to the Union Bank of Switzerland, he used the same basic script he had at lunch, and his hopeful wealth manager contact didn't deny that Roger was a client.

"Can I meet with his logistic team this week?" Ralph cut to the chase.

"I can arrange something, sure. Not sure his exact team will be available, but we have some of the best people in the world at our firm."

"Oh, ah, no. Roger said that his team was incredibly adept and not to accept anyone else. There was a detail-oriented woman named—was it Robin?"

"No, his management team is led by Jane."

"Yes, Jane! That's it. Can I meet with her?"

"She's hugely busy with managing Roger's life and a few other Silicon Valley luminaries. But please excuse the lack of my normal delicacy—how much money are you thinking to let us manage for you?"

Ralph tried not to laugh. This banker had the delicacy of the Death Star. "Probably a few million, to trial for six months or so."

"Mr. Gibsen, Jane doesn't leave the office for less than $50 million. But we can have someone else …"

"All right, if she's as good as everyone says, I'll consider moving $25 million to UBS management." Ralph crossed his fingers, hoping his bluff wouldn't be called out.

"Wonderful. I notice that Jane just happens to have a slot free at 10 AM tomorrow morning. We'll both be at your offices, then. Ta ta."

❧

When the UBS bankers arrived the following morning, just after saying good morning and introductions, the partner handed Ralph a massive folder of legal documents.

Ralph immediately went on the offensive. "Who the hell is going to help with this pile?"

The wealth manager realized he may have played his card to soon. "Oh, I am sure your personal accountant and lawyer can assist, but ..."

Ralph scoffed, making the wealth manager the bad guy. He turned away from the relationship banker and spoke directly to the logistics specialist. "Jane, see, this is what I hate about bankers." Ralph noticed the banker get red-faced. Jane was seemingly thrilled with the role reversal. "You ask them to help ease the load, and they hand you a month's worth of busy work."

"Come on, Mr. Gibsen, you know the drill, we have compliance, and lawyers, and boat-ton of procedures ..."

Ralph interrupted the flustered banker. "I've already turned you off." He smiled and turned to Jane. "Jane is going to tell me how she will make my life easier."

Jane smiled. Ralph could tell she didn't always like her business partner, and was relishing the newfound attention. She took the thick folder away from Ralph. "Well, our priority is making your life easier, so that you can focus on what is important to you."

"That's what I have been trying to find."

"Not only can we make some of the busy work disappear, we can show you unique and safe ways to minimize your expenditures. For example, we buy health and life insurance with such volume in our bank that we can add you to our policies, with a significant discount to what you would pay otherwise."

"Okay, but Roger was alluding to some magic you made happen with his yacht, his Maybach, and a few of his properties. Tell me about what you can do for me. For example, I have a few collectible cars."

"Well, we all have some bad habits," said the partner with his utmost bonhomie, clearly trying to get back in Ralph's good graces.

Jane pushed on. "Beyond the basics of scheduling maintenance appointments, paying assorted invoices, and acquiring the best insurance, our ultimate goal is to ensure your investments are able to be enjoyed by you and your family at a moment's notice."

The partner interrupted Jane, trying to push for the close. "We even have some unique, very clever and 'safe' mechanisms that we use with Mr. Phillips, like moving all his investments—the boats, the many cars, his wife's artwork, and he has a plane or two—to a Montana tax residency. This gives him favorable tax treatment and significant savings when he sells these investments later in life."

"His yacht is registered in Montana?" Ralph gave his most skeptical shrug of the shoulders. "And that hasn't got him into any trouble? I did some reading on this—don't the investments have to spend six months and one day in the State of Montana? I'm going to guess that ship hasn't been anywhere near Montana in its existence. To haul that 150-foot yacht to Montana and back would be hundreds of thousands of dollars, right?"

"You should see what we have in the Isle of Mann for Mr. Phillips's family—it is complex, especially bringing cash into the states, sometimes in suitcases, but it allows him great flexibility for his international investments. And you do a great deal of investments internationally, correct Mr. Gibsen?"

"Mr. Phillips's tolerance for risk on those sorts of things exceeds our bank's guidance." Jane was already back-peddling.

"All right. Look, this discussion shouldn't be about Mr. Phillips. UBS can mold our services to your needs and comforts …"

The meeting lasted another ninety minutes, but Ralph had gained plenty to work with. He now had several new avenues to slow Roger down.

Chapter 34

Ralph needed a quick trim. He had noticed a newly opened salon just around the corner from his hotel. Haircuts in China were pretty-easy affairs. For a low-maintenance guy like Ralph, not much language needed to be exchanged. *Hold your index finger a half-inch from your thumb when on the sides and back of your head*, he thought, *and hold them about two inches apart on the top. Not much can go wrong.*

The Asian haircut typically starts with a fifteen-minute neck, shoulder, and a head rub. It is Ralph's favorite part. And this young woman was especially gifted. Ralph has the big shoulders and neck of a swimmer. He likes his massages on the firm side. And this 50 KG woman was a velvet-touch brute. Ralph dramatically pouted when she mimed that the rub had concluded and he needed to walk to the shampoo station. The enterprising manager saw her cue, and via WeChat as an interpreter, offered a two-hour, full-body oil massage for 500 RMB. The salon apparently had a few massage rooms upstairs. The haircut would be thrown in for free. Ralph knew that he needed to negotiate, but quickly settled on 400 RMB.

"No happy ending, okay?" Ralph typed into WeChat to the manager.

She responded with, "Okay, no sexy sexy," proud of her limited spoken English.

Ralph checked his wallet, and saw he didn't have enough cash. "Could you take this card?" He offered up his Visa.

"No problem." The manager barely looked up.

"But this is an international card. Are you certain?" Ralph typed into WeChat.

"No problem," she answered.

Ralph was probably paying too much, but he had no plans for this late Saturday afternoon, and massage/haircut was as pleasant a diversion as could be hoped for on a lengthy business trip.

The massage was not without a few awkward moments, including the attempts of the manager and two more women to check out Ralph's nether regions when he rolled over from prone to supine. The masseuse also attempted a few "fly-bys," as Maverick would have called them, but Ralph was quick with the "no sexy sexy." The masseuse giggled each time. In all, he enjoyed two solid hours of pampering.

Back downstairs, he got a shampoo, haircut, shampoo, haircut, shampoo. On the way out, he bowed and thanked everyone. There were many smiles. A photo of the manager, her haircutters, and masseuses was suggested and performed, including a copy on Ralph's phone. When Ralph looked at picture, he decided he'd erase it as soon as he walked out the door. Jen would undoubtedly require an explanation of why he was standing with a dozen young pretty women in short skirts and low-cut blouses. It would be easier to just make the picture go away.

Ralph handed his credit card to the manager. The purchase didn't go through. They tried again, and again still.

The mag stripe, the chip, and the RFID chip; nothing worked. They asked for another card. Over the next fifteen minutes, they tried all of Ralph's cards, on several different card readers. Nothing worked. The mood in the salon got tense.

"Can you pay via WeChat or AliPay?" they asked via WeChat.

"No. I don't have access to those methods of payment."

"How will you pay then?"

"I asked you when I got here if you could take my credit card. You said you could." Ralph was now feeling uncomfortable. His card had been swiped many times, and hence he was concerned it would set off alarms with the credit card companies, or perhaps he'd find that they had completed each request for payment and he'd owe thousands and thousands of RMB. Either way would be a major bother.

"Look, this isn't fun anymore. I'll give you the 323 RMB I have in my possession. That's all I have. And I'll walk back to my hotel to get you the remaining hundred. Okay? I'll return in less than an hour."

"No, you are a cheater! You will not come back. You a bad man. We call the police," the manager threatened. The other twelve salon people closed in around him.

One of Ralph's portfolio companies—the one that helped internet users circumvent censorship—was not well loved by Chinese authorities. The thought of spending hours with the authorities over less than the equivalent of $12 was spiking his anxiety. As was the sheer numbers of salon workers who had joined the fray. Stress builds from group thought, Ralph realized for the hundredth time this year.

He tried his best to sweet talk his way to having someone go with him to get the money from his hotel, and then paying the manager when he came back in less than an hour. But they were absolutely not willing to let him leave without paying his bill. Abruptly, Ralph put the 323 RMB on the counter and made a run for the door. The crowd shouted and hands were laid on him.

"This is crazy," Ralph said too loudly to no one but himself.

When she walked in the door, she was laughing like a Bond villain. "Ralph, how come every time I see you it appears like an all out riot is only a moment away?"

The cacophony of the salon workers died to complete silence. She was north of six feet tall, without her heels, and had an immediate presence that when she walked into a room—any room—all discussion stopped. Everyone was staring at her. The salon hadn't been this quiet since Ralph had walked in as the first "white ghost" to grace the establishment.

"Hello, Eva."

"Hi, Ralph. I like your hair. They did a good job. So cute."

The crowd of salon workers again exploded. Eva raised her hand, and again there was quiet.

"These people believe you owe them some money."

"I do. Do you want me to tell you the story?"

"No. I've been sitting in the van for the last hour listening to all this."

"What …" Ralph was so flustered he couldn't put even a few words together.

"Darling, which one of these bimbos was your masseuse? If she attempted to spill your seed, I will kill her slowly. I am a merciless and vindictive mistress."

"Nnn … no."

Eva switched to Chinese. She quickly learned who was in charge, and asked everyone else to leave the room.

The salon workers were shocked by the request, but they obeyed. Quietly. Eva continued, and Ralph only caught a bit of the exchange.

"Ralph, it seems you do not have sufficient funds to pay this establishment for services rendered. You are shy by exactly sixty-seven yuan. They want to call the police."

Ralph started to laugh. "I met your mother last week."

"Yes, she told me. She also met McKenna. She didn't have a great first impression of either of you. Are you now working together?"

"No, McKenna works for people that have more money than me."

"Yes, he does."

"Is that really your mother?"

"No, my mother was a sweet and gentle woman who passed away a few years ago. You would have liked her. And you've already met my father and brother. Any more questions about my family?"

"Not right now. Can I borrow sixty-seven yuan to get out of this mess?"

"Hmmmm. This'll be fun. Negotiating with the famous Silicon Valley businessman Ralph Gibsen. Yes, I will trade you sixty-seven yuan for the Dropbox password for the EdTech project. Deal?"

Ralph shook his head.

"How about the password to the old IBM I stole from your home office?"

"No. I need that back."

"No? Hmmm. How about an engagement ring? From Tiffany's?"

Ralph looked down and ran his fingers through his newly cut hair.

"All right, my final offer. You will be my gigolo for the next two nights. I'll pay you sixty-seven RMB for your presence in my bed. The police or me? And remember, I am just a girl under all this … tough exterior with a gentle, loving soul underneath…. Be kind."

"I've got another idea."

"You didn't say no. My heart soars."

"Seriously, Eva. A beautiful woman like you eats guys like me for lunch. I have a better idea for us."

"And a compliment! From this moment forward, my heart will never be still."

"Can you be serious for just a few minutes? I think I have the beginnings of a plan to trash the evil fuckers who are trying to misuse the EdTech project. And I think there's a role in it for you."

"That doesn't sound nearly as good as you ravaging me on a beach in San Tropez while I am wearing nothing but my new engagement ring from Tiffany's. Nor does it sound as good as an offer for the passcode to the project. But still, it is intriguing. So I will pay your massive debt and you'll take me to a very nice restaurant and tell me of your plan. Agreed?"

"Dinner, really?"

"You must wear a suit and tie. And hold my hand."

"No suit. No tie. Sports jacket, button down shirt, and long pants. That's my best offer."

"But you must have the hotel staff iron your shirt. It has been in your suitcase too long, and it is all wrinkled. And why don't you have any socks in your suitcase?"

"How do you know that?"

"Never mind. Now let's get in my car. I'll drop you at the hotel, and you'll be ready in sixty minutes. Then you can tell me how lovely I look, and then tell me how we are going to trash those evil fuckers." Eva flicked a few thousand yuan on the counter and took two steps toward the door. She stopped and turned. "Before we go, which one is she?"

Ralph picked Eva up like she was a bride going over the threshold. She kissed his cheek and they both started to laugh.

∽

At dinner, Ralph and his ironed shirt and sport coat explained his plan. He showed her the photo, and Eva committed to helping as best she could.

Chapter 35

During a "U.S. Infrastructure Vulnerabilities" presentation at the Naval Postgraduate School in Monterey, California, Ralph and the fifty attendees learned that the single most-troubling challenge in protecting the world's key infrastructure from cyber terrorists was the Programmable Logic Controllers (PLC) from the German conglomerate Siemens. The Siemens PCS7 Controller had been designed in the late 1970s, and since its launch had been sold in the hundreds of millions.

As cyber terrorists hadn't existed when this PLC was designed, the engineers who built it had hard-coded a backdoor into the device. This backdoor made the lives of these engineers easier. When the inevitable maintenance call came, the engineers had a way to expedite a fix without requiring the end-user to know their password. Over the last forty years, hundreds of millions of these controllers have been deployed in everything from kitchen coffee makers, medical devices, factory equipment, and nuclear power plants. And for the modern day hacker, the easiest entry point in the world was the Siemens' PCS7 PLC.

This backdoor wasn't closeable without the entire replacement of the controller. And even in some critical infrastructure—like power grids, dams, and control systems for data centers—the PCS7 hadn't been replaced because of the snowball effect around the costs of replacing the module. The controller couldn't be swapped out, because the machine language firmware running between the PLC and the product's hardware was non-upgradable. Hence, the controller module couldn't be simply or inexpensively replaced. Most often, the entire system needed to be replaced. In the average nuclear power plant or factory floor, this might cost in the hundreds of millions of dollars.

On almost every MRI machine on the planet, the PCS7 controller coordinated the movement of the imagery machine's sensors. The EdTech tool used an MRI machine. The hard-coded backdoor of the PCS7 allowed Ralph the ability to access and add a bit of code to overdrive or underdrive the sensor module chipset on the tool's tester. Now the readings of the sensor could be manipulated. To that bit of code, he added a random number generator, and wrote additional code to manipulate each test result to be multiplied by 1.0R (where R is the random number). This would create inconsistencies and make the new results suspect.

When the test tool was left unattended, Ralph used a simple USB tool called PoisonTap to install the code modifications. The process took less than sixty seconds.

❧

Tracing back his entire career to find someone who could help him with his potential involvement in the spy business, the only person Ralph thought of was his old mentor, Ned Hollingsworth. Ned was the first person to suggest selling his company to the Japanese firm. And the training program at the Japanese firm was how he met Mrs. Miyagi. Ralph had remained friends with Ned over the years, but had been lax with keeping in touch. As he reflected, he had much less contact than he should have, for such an influential person in his life. Ned's daughter Tori had friended Ralph on Facebook, so he reached out to her first.

"Hey Tori. Hope all is well. I want to reconnect with your dad. What's the best way?" he queried via Facebook.

"It is about time, Ralph. He thinks of you as his son he never had, and you've reached out to him maybe once every five years for the last thirty."

"You're right. I'm a bad friend. I'm sorry."

"Tell him, not me, shithead."

"I'm really sorry, Tori."

"Me too."

Tori gave Ralph Ned's contact details. Ned had taught at a Boston college for fifty years, and had now retired to Cape Cod, within a few miles of Ralph's vacation home.

"Hello, Ralph."

"Ah Ned, it's Ralph Gibsen."

"I know that. Don't they have caller ID in Silicon Valley? How can you be this famous venture capitalist and you don't know anything about caller ID?"

"Ah, yeah. Ned, I called because I wanted to apologize …"

"For not marrying my daughter?"

"What? No. But you told me I couldn't touch her, remember?"

"You were a bit of a letch, Ralph. I mean, as a young man. Chased too many skirts. Then again, so did I at that age. Never mind. You couldn't possibly be any worse than the guy she ended up with. What a looooser."

"I'm sorry. Not for Tori, as for not keeping in touch as well as I should have."

"Yeah, I'm sad about that. But, hey, did that thing work out?"

"What thing?"

"You know, the folks you sold your company to? Always wanted to ask you about that, but figured … I'd better not. At least not until you retired."

"Well, funny enough, that's why I was calling you."

"Really? Are you done? Those guys, they seemed shadowy. I figured that was why I didn't hear from you for many years. That they might have—what do they call it—recruited you into their world."

"Are *you* a part of that world?"

"Ah, well. No, I was cleared for 'Top Secret' security with MITRE for many years, but I didn't bother to renew that after I left MITRE. Are *you* part of that world?"

"Well, that's kind of why I'm calling—and to catch up with you, of course."

"Okay, how can I help? And don't think I didn't notice you didn't answer my question."

"Sharp as ever, Ned. What do you know about the people you introduced me to?"

"They were a part of MITRE. But not the team I worked with. The team I worked with was on the policy side of things. The guys that came to talk with you were mostly unknown to me, but someone said they were on the pointy-end of the spear, as they say."

"How did it come to pass that you introduced them to me?"

"I remember this pretty well. They already knew all about you, apparently. I assumed that your mother was somehow involved, or that friend of yours."

"My mother?" Ralph remembered that Ned had met his mom on a half-dozen occasions, when Ralph was earning some success on the debate team. "She was pretty cool, but she wasn't involved with the spy community, to my knowledge. She managed a YMCA and later started a post-grad school for physical fitness and pain relief."

"Well, there were rumors. And what about your friend—was it McGuire?"

"McKenna. I've talked to him. But he isn't much help. He left the sanctioned spy world for the unsanctioned. He's basically a freelancer."

"He was a good student. But there was always a whiff of something raw about him. I remember when we had a faculty meeting and we were awarding the grad school awards, one of my colleagues suggested that we create a new award for McGuire: 'Most Likely to Run a Small Third-World Country.' I never had anything but positive experiences with him, but I always feared getting caught alone in the elevator together."

"I consider him a friend. But he lives a complex life. And I'm never sure where I stand with him. Do you by chance have contacts to check who he works with?"

"Not anymore, Ralph. Most of my friends are long retired. Where do you stand? I hope you're one of the good guys."

"Me too."

Ralph told Ned of his situation. He was happy his mentor didn't belittle his story. In the end, Ned asked good questions and offered to try to reestablish a few of his MITRE contacts who could potentially help Ralph learn more about his situation. Ned didn't hold out much hope, as his contacts were older than he was. But he'd make an effort. Ralph felt he needed people on his side, and he was hugely grateful that Ned was.

Chapter 36

Ralph got off at the Warabi train station, and tried to walk the same route he had thirty years earlier, to the little hot spring onsen where he had first met Mrs. Miyagi. The road was familiar, but the storefronts were almost universally new. The health club where he first met Tom and Hiromi was still in its spot, but had certainly been updated, maybe more than once. He walked past, determined to find the facility where he had been trained those many years before. When he rounded the corner just past the yakitori shop where he had befriended the yakuza, he saw that the onsen was no longer standing. In its place was a sprawling apartment complex that looked no more than a few years old. Ralph stood looking at the complex for more than a few minutes, wondering what he should do next.

The yakitori shop was locked, but his old health club was open. Ralph walked in and inquired about a membership. He was given a tour and quickly realized his rusty Japanese language skills weren't up to the task. He walked past the public baths where thirty years earlier he had first joined the community by disrobing and entering the spa, amongst the pointing and giggling of much older women. It was a traumatic moment in Ralph's life, but a moment he drew upon every so often when he needed to do something brave. He smiled as he thought about the times he recollected, *If I can walk into a spa naked, with seventy-year-old grandmothers and the small world of Warabi speculating openly about the size of my whatnot, then I can do this....*

There was only one other place to look in Warabi, and that place caused Ralph to pause. On the east side of the station was an enormous family home and dojo for the art and practice of Kendo sword fighting. It was also the home of Hiromi, Ralph's Japanese girlfriend from his first expat stay. He had loved only a few women in his life, and Hiromi had been one. The relationship had ended awkwardly, when Ralph wanted to explore the world and Hiromi had *giri,* or obligations, to her family's business. When he had first met her, she was his aerobics teacher at the same health club he had just visited. Ralph had spoken no Japanese at the time, but the first words he learned were *migi* and *hidari*, which were 'right' and 'left,' and perhaps the most necessary words in an aerobics class.

Hiromi was one of the most naturally attractive women Ralph had ever met. She never wore makeup, and outside of her collection of neon-colored leotards, she often wore the most mundane clothes big money could buy. Hiromi's family was well off, and their fortune had survived many generations. And not only had Ralph fallen in love with the group's only heir, he had also loved Hiromi's grandmother, the matriarch of the family.

While many in the family cast a wary eye at Hiromi's *gaijin* (hairy barbarian) boyfriend, *Oba-chan* (grandmother-child) doted on him unconditionally. She would sneak him treats, pat his ass, laugh at his awkward Japanese stories, and always demand that she sat at his left, so that she could be the one to serve his meal. Oba-chan had a bad habit of teaching him the absolute worst phrase for any given situation. One day, when Ralph was tasked with providing driving directions in the left-hand front seat to Hiromi's oh-too-serious father, she taught him "*san-no hashi.*" Depending on emphasis, the phrase could mean either: 1) the third bridge; 2) three sets of chopsticks; or 3) the third whorehouse. Of course, Oba-chan took great amusement in teaching Ralph the wrong emphasis, which caused Hiromi's father a bright red face, and unstoppable giggles from both Oba-chan and Hiromi.

When Ralph left Tokyo for the first time, the stoic Japanese goodbye celebration was awkward, as Oba-chan kept sobbing loudly. She stood only 4'8" but pulled Ralph's head to her bosom and cried. Ralph was surprised that he also cried at this dear show of affection. Nearly thirty years later, one of Ralph's favorite pictures of himself was of him gazing lovingly at Oba-chan as Hiromi hugged him from behind.

When Ralph got to the gate of Hiromi's home, he noticed nothing had changed. The property looked as it did in the sixth century when it was first constructed.

Ralph rang the bell at the gate. He waited and counted his first thirty breaths. The home was huge, and Ralph was arriving unannounced. He knew that the person answering the gate might have a long walk. He thought hard about walking away. This encounter could only be awkward. But he couldn't move. It wasn't quite ten minutes before he heard someone slide open the door.

"Ralph-san?" Her eyes didn't betray her surprise.

"Hiromi?" He instantly knew it was her. She had aged very well. And she was genuinely surprised to see him, as one might expect after nearly thirty years.

"*On a gashi masu*—ah, *ito-ne*—follow me," she said over her shoulder, as she ran through the small pebble garden from the outer gate to the inner gate's garden. She started talking excitedly in Japanese. Ralph only caught a little bit of it—something about trouble and something broken. There might have even been a swear word. Ralph quickened his pace, not sure what to expect as he rounded the corner. A brown-haired toddler was dragging a large koi from the small pond, and Hiromi was attempting to wrench the old noble fish from the young boy's grasp.

Hiromi rambled off another sixty seconds of Japanese, bouncing between the toddler and Ralph.

"*Watashi wa nihongo ga heta desu*," Ralph said with a sad smile.

"Those were the very first words you ever spoke to me, Ralph. Your accent has improved. But your confidence is somehow lessened."

"Oba-chan, you speak English?" The toddler seemed surprised.

The three took a moment to study the situation, and each other.

Ralph spoke. "He called you Oba-chan?"

Hiromi laughed. It sounded beautiful to Ralph's ears. "That's because I am his grandmother, Ralph." She shook her head, laughing. But her laugh was tinged with heavy undertones.

"We can't be old enough to have grandchildren, can we?" Ralph asked. "You certainly don't look old enough." He felt anxious and bewildered.

She smiled at him. There was sadness but gratitude in the smile. "You have almost always been kind."

Ralph didn't really want to think about that comment. *Almost always.* The memory of the instance of his most unkind moment replayed in his mind.

The koi was wrestled from the three-year-old's hands and gently placed back in the pond. Hiromi gently scolded Henri-chan. Henri-chan looked crushed, as he obviously cherished his Oba-chan.

"Ralph, please meet Henri. Henri, please meet Ralph-san."

Ralph went to a knee to shake the young man's hand. It was all very formal.

"Ralph-san, please sit down. Do you have some time? Would you like some tea?"

Ralph sat at the garden table. "If it is no trouble, *o-cha ona gashi masu.*"

She smiled. "Uhm, Henri-chan, do you want to go with me to get some tea?"

Henri was in the process of climbing into Ralph's lap with a book. "Would you read this to me?" It was an English translation of *The Story of Ferdinand.*

Hiromi glanced and then giggled at his chosen book. "*Omoshiroi to tekisetsuna.*"

Henri said, "Oba-chan says this is a good book to read to me."

"Well thank you for your translation services, Henri. I love this book."

"Me too."

"Why do you like this book?"

"Because my Oba-chan says that Ferdinand is just like me."

That's exactly what my mother said to me, thought Ralph. Ralph read the book to Henri. Henri asked good questions, much more thoughtful questions than what someone would expect of his age.

About fifteen minutes later, Hiromi re-joined the boys with some tea and cookies. The cook followed Hiromi out with a few additional items.

"Nakamoto-san?" Ralph asked.

Nakamoto-san bowed deeply and smiled. Ralph stood with Henri in his arms and bowed as well. Then he put Henri down and took the woman's hand in both of his.

"It is lovely to see you." She was Hiromi's mother's confidant.

Nakamoto-san was flustered with the attention. Pushing gently for Ralph to sit. Henri was also pawing Ralph, trying to get back in his lap.

"You may remember that Nakamoto-san's family has been a part of our family for more than seven generations. I would not know how to survive without her." Hiromi repeated herself in Japanese in order for Nakamoto-san to more fully understand. Nakamoto-san was embarrassed at these open affections. She hurried off to her kitchen to make something to return the favor. On her way, she tried to persuade Henri to go with her, and even after she bribed him with his favorite treat, he didn't want to leave Ralph and Hiromi.

"Ralph-san, I have been following your career from afar. Congratulations on being such a successful businessman."

"Hiromi, I am still an idiot. The very same idiot. Albeit older. And yet, you look ageless."

"There are advantages to being the head of a personal care company." Hiromi's family had started Japan's largest skin care company in 1872. Today the company was the fourth largest such company in the world.

There was an awkward pause. "I need to first apologize to you, Hiromi. I should have been in touch."

"Ralph, do you mind terribly if we leave our past in the past? I just want to enjoy these moments with you."

Ralph smiled. He didn't want to re-live the past with Hiromi either, but that's what he had come to do. For the moment, he decided to get caught up. "Tell me about your family. Your grandson is *kawai-ii desu-ne*."

Henri had climbed back on Ralph's knee and was quietly reading his book. Ralph jiggled him to get a quick smile. "I Google your name occasionally, and the media doesn't reveal much about your personal life."

"We pay dearly for that particular privilege." She looked weary. "Sometimes I think I would have been much happier if I had run off with you to see the world. But I had the *giri* of my family and its business, so I stayed." She smiled with some sadness.

Giri was the very Japanese concept of "burden of obligation." Much of Japanese society was dictated by these evolving family and community obligations. The Japanese concept of *hara-kiri* (sword through the stomach) was the releasing of these same obligations.

She continued slowly and Ralph sipped his tea and listened. "When you left, my Oba-chan urged me to leave with you. But I would have missed her too much. She lived another twenty-five wonderful years. When my parents both passed about five years ago, Oba-chan lasted only a few months. She was heartbroken."

"That was when grandfather moved to Sydney. I've never met my grandfather," Henri confided.

"Yes Henri, thank you for your help with my story." Hiromi grabbed his cheek. "My husband left me about five years ago, to move full-time to Australia. It was the right thing to do. As you'll remember, divorce is a social embarrassment. So he moved away. We had grown apart after having our children."

Both Ralph and Hiromi were looking at Henri. He continued to pretend to read his book.

"I have two children, a boy and a girl. They both live near you, in San Francisco. My son is a fashion designer, and has a wonderful partner named David. They live in the Marina district, and have a few small dogs they adore. My daughter is an artist and spends much of her time traveling, putting her watercolors in galleries. She's Henri's mother. And I took over the family business about five years ago. I learned I'm okay at my job. I don't necessarily love the work, but it's what I must do."

Ralph put his hand on top of Hiromi's, and Henri mimicked them. They had a small chuckle. Ralph removed his hand.

"And because I follow you on Facebook, Twitter, Instagram, Line, VK, and LinkedIn, I know much of what you are up to almost every day. But tell me anyways. Give Henri and I your life story, Ralph."

"My life, it's not very exciting really. The social media stuff is just a highlight reel."

For the next few minutes, Ralph told his nomadic story, emphasizing his relationship with his mom and his marriage. He did not mention that he and Jen had lived in Tokyo, some ten years after he had left Hiromi.

"I'm sad I never met your mother. I know how influential she was to you. And if it is not inappropriate to ask, why did you and Jen never have children? When you lived here, you told everyone who would listen that you wanted fourteen children. It scared my mother even more than you being a *gaijin*."

They laughed.

"The truth of Jen and me being childless is kind of sad. Simply, we kind-of-forgot that we were growing older. When we were young, our lives were busy. Growing businesses, travel, and living in foreign cities. I remember looking at my wife one morning after five or six years of marriage and asking if she wanted children. We agreed it was time to try. But we married later in life, when she was thirty-seven and I was thirty-six. And our attempts at bearing children failed. And then Jen had, uh, female plumbing issues for a year or two, and we had to focus on her wellness. And then we were forty-five years old. We attempted to foster and adopt children, but the powers-that-be denied us because of my nomadic lifestyle. And thereafter we decided we were best to focus on big goofy dogs that were in need of our love."

"And now you flood Facebook with pictures of your furry children."

"Guilty as charged."

There was a lengthy pause. Henri wandered off. He was now bored of grownup talk. Catching the koi was much more fun. Nakamoto-san came out of the kitchen with a hot pot of tea, placed it on the table, and quickly disappeared.

"Why are you here, Ralph-san? I love spending time with you, but I can't help but wonder why you are here. Is one of your small companies looking for a partnership with one of my companies?"

"No, Hiromi-san. It's kind of embarrassing, but it has nothing to do with your business."

"You are the only friend I have who has not asked me for some sort of a business favor. And I was hoping you might want to run my business. My father followed your career earnestly and asked me many times to reach out to you, to see if you'd be interested."

"Well, that's interesting. I'm not sure your father said more than ten words to me in the two years we were to-gether."

"He was always afraid you'd take me away."

"I'm certain I'd not be the best person to help run your business, Hiromi. Instead, I'm hoping you might help me remember some aspects about when I first came to Warabi."

"Thirty years ago? My memory is good, but nowhere near good enough, I'm afraid. Do you mind if we invite Nakamoto-san to join us? She's still the neighborhood gossip. She'll remember more than me."

"That's a great idea."

Nakamoto-san was invited and joined them soon thereafter. Ralph explained what he was hoping to remember. Nakamoto-san had a keen memory, and remembered the blind woman who ran the onsen. She thought she was a witch, and that her last-name was Sato. She also remembered the witch's son, who Ralph and Hiromi knew from the health club. Sato-san was the former newspaper editor and squash and lunch partner/confidant to Ralph and Tom Warn. Sato-san had never mentioned that Ralph had met his mother at her facility.

"Strange," Ralph thought out loud.

Hiromi ran inside and grabbed an iPad and did a quick search on the *Nihon Keizai Shinbun* editor Sato to learn if he was still alive. They found a laudatory obituary of only two years earlier. Sato-san had died, childless, at the age of eighty-nine, in Warabi. His childhood home was in the general area of the onsen, according to the newspaper obit and Nakamoto-san. Nakamoto-san asked Hiromi a question in Japanese that Ralph couldn't translate.

"Didn't Tom live with Sato for some time?" Ralph asked. Tom had gotten in trouble with his landlord—perhaps due to the landlord's attractive daughter—and needed to move out at short-notice.

No one remembered. But Ralph was certain that there was a connection there.

"Is it all right if Nakamoto-san makes a call to one of her friends who lives on the west side of the station?"

"Of course."

Henri soon joined Hiromi and Ralph, asking if Ralph could take him for ice cream at Ueno Park.

"Why do you ask such things, Henri?" demanded his shocked grandmother. "That's not very polite, and Ralph is a very busy person, he cannot …"

"It's a great idea," Ralph agreed. "Let's go as soon as we hear back from Nakamoto-san."

"But Henri, where did you get this idea? It is so random."

Henri explained. "The picture in your bedroom. It is you and your Oba-chan being handed ice cream by Ralph in Ueno Park. Your smiles are the happiest smiles I know."

Hiromi reddened. "But how do you know it is Ralph handing us those ice creams? All you can see is a tall man's back …"

"Because you have the same smile today as you do in the picture. And it is my favorite picture of you, grandmother."

Nakamoto-san came with news, which saved Hiromi further embarrassment. It seems that Sato-san was hugely rumor-worthy, as he had never married, and rarely socialized. He had left the newspaper at the height of his career, under some suspicion. There were unsupported rumors that he was dismissed because of large expense account irregularities, and an even more outrageous rumor that his office and home were used to help train international spies. Ralph learned two other interesting tidbits: 1) when they demoed the onsen to replace it with a new apartment complex, there were many underground tunnels and a large cache of weapons—some modern, some from World War II, and some from a time when Japan was much less industrious—found in an underground bunker; and 2) A very tall ginger man named Tom Warn owned the apartment complex.

After Nakamoto-san had conveyed what she had learned and gone back to her beloved kitchen, Hiromi asked, "Should I try to stop my curiosity about his sub-ject, Ralph? It is strange, and just by knocking on my gates, you've given Nakamoto-san enough new material for gossip for many years." She laughed. "But I feel there is something that has you concerned."

"It's probably best that you not get involved, Hiromi. I don't want to sound dramatic, but I don't know much about what I'm involved in, and it probably isn't good."

"My company has great resources. I offer them at your pleasure," she said solemnly. "You don't have to answer this if you cannot, but are you a spy?"

Ralph looked down at his feet, unsure of what to say. At that moment, Henri re-joined them from some great adventure.

"Can Ralph take us to Ueno for some ice cream, Oba-chan?" begged Henri.

Ralph still had more questions than answers, but he took Henri and Hiromi to Ueno Park for ice cream.

In Tokyo, he'd made a new ice-cream-eating friend, and re-established a few friendships he'd appreciate for the rest of his life.

Chapter 37

Ralph did two entire loops of the London's Heathrow Airport T5 Arrival area. No one was waiting for him. Damn. And strange. Jen had said … hold on. The mini-cab driver's sign read "JENANDRA."

Ralph did a triple-take, and then asked if he was the correct driver. Jen didn't like using Uber. She always booked their transport when they traveled together. In this instance, Jen was flying into London from San Francisco, and Ralph from Tel Aviv. Because Ralph was terribly frugal, they had arranged to swap homes with an acquaintance of Jen's. The London family was staying in the Gibsen's Cape Cod vacation home, and Ralph and Jen were in the Brits' Kensington flat. As Ralph spent as much as 180 days a year in a hotel, he loved these home swaps. It made him feel like he was a local living in a foreign city with his lovely wife.

Jen's flight was running ten minutes late, according to the messaging boards. Ralph was anxious. Holding his ridiculous sign, their driver was bored but zen-calm. *I'd be a terrible limo driver*, Ralph thought to himself.

It flew through Ralph's tiny mind that such a sign would be great spy-craft. *No one would suspect. Damn— I'm terribly antsy.* It was Ralph's great pride to be the "fastest" through any given airport. Today's effort wasn't his personal best for LHR, but it was in the upper third cohort. *Got through LHR from the plane to Arrivals via immigration and customs in fifteen minutes and forty-five seconds.* He knew every shortcut, Fastpass line, and never checked baggage, even for a three-week trip. *Let's see how long it takes her.*

His phone buzzed. It was a SMS from a startup founder looking for an introduction to a business leader Ralph knew. Ralph typed out the intro in thirty-five seconds.

Nothing from Jen yet. And the message boards had her plane landing three minutes ago. Typically, they both sent an SMS when they landed.

His phone buzzed again. It was the CEO saying thanks for the intro to Ralph's portfolio company. And then he asked for an introduction to another friend. Ralph banged out this new introduction in another forty seconds. Nothing from Jen. Ralph surfed LinkedIn for a few minutes— he'd lost track of where the person worked, as the average tenure at a Silicon Valley company was less than eighteen months.

After the messaging sign said the plane's bags were being delivered, he was annoyed with himself. Ralph could get through LHR in fifteen minutes, but Jen was going to need at least twice that.

His phone buzzed. Finally, it was Jen. "On my way. LU"

He typed, "Let's go. Hustle! We've got adventures to track down. LU2." He then erased that and told himself to relax. He re-typed and sent: "Coolio. I'm here with the driver. LU2."

Ralph suggested the driver sit down, as the man was looking even more bored and put out. Ralph took the silly sign and waited at the rail, holding it diligently. He surfed *Time Out London* to see if there were any good shows or events. Ralph saw a classic car event, and wondered if he had built up enough "GF points" to have earned an afternoon spent ogling old British cars. *Probably not*, he thought to himself. But maybe some consignment clothes shopping on Portobello Road or in Chelsea might earn him enough …

His phone buzzed again. A friend was touching base, wishing he and Jen a fabulous break.

Ralph's mind wandered. Jen was often unreachable for hours. She'd say she was on a hike with the dogs, but her whereabouts were often unknown. At one point, Ralph bought a tracker for the willful Great Pyrenees puppy, as he was trying to teach her to walk the beach without a leash. The breed did not always come back in an appropriate time frame when called. Jen often said that the puppy was willful—like her father. "That apple doesn't fall far from the tree." Even after Ralph spent hours setting up the tracker, the expensive device was somehow lost within days of the purchase. When Ralph asked Jen if he should buy another, she admitted it kind of creeped her out. She'd prefer not having something like that in their lives. So the dog only got a few minutes off-leash each day.

Jen also moved at a different speed than Ralph. She was deliberate in her every action and liked to know as much as she could about any given situation. Ralph was more like the Alexander Pope quotation, "Fools rush in where angels fear to tread…." (He was the fool, not the angel.) Ralph had to remind himself that he had to adapt to her, not her to him, and he had adopted a series of actions to confront his anxiousness when he deemed Jen was moving too slowly.

Jen had no social media presence whatsoever. Yet each morning over coffee she'd stand behind Ralph while he checked his Facebook and Instagram feeds. She'd often ask him to comment or "like" a friend's update on her behalf, but she could never be persuaded to join social media herself, no matter the amount of peer pressure.

Jen was also enormously private and sensitive with her phone and email/messaging apps. She received dozens of messages per hour. Ralph knew this because she refused to switch her phone to silent mode, even during sleeping hours. Ralph called her the "queen" of the local beach, and he assumed most of these messages were about her social activities like book clubs, hikes, and coffee dates.

As he started to question Jen's involvement, he thought about hiring a PI to investigate her activities, or a hacker to infiltrate her messaging. But he could never bring himself to do so. It just felt wrong. He also feared the awkward potential confrontation thereafter. And he couldn't ask McKenna or Eva to do so, for the potential discomfiture therein. Ralph viewed himself as a person who trusted his wife and friends. If he learned somehow that his trust had been misspent, he'd be devastated. In nearly eighteen years of marriage, Ralph had also never questioned his wife's fidelity. *It's probably better to not know*, he thought.

Ralph knew his wife's standards, ethics, and morals were not identical to his own. He wanted to celebrate that fact. Questioning where exactly those boundaries lay seemed a significant break of trust.

Jen was loved by so many—it was undeniably fun to be in her company. She loved to laugh, and to make people laugh. She was genuinely without judgment. Her friendships spanned generations, cultures, and social and political categories. When she invited her friends to the house, Ralph was always surprised at the diversity of the group.

And Ralph wasn't always as comfortable with her friends. Some seemed to feed off her abundant energy like leeches. Some had prejudices or beliefs that Ralph couldn't accept. Some lived lives of vast value inconsistencies, or made their livelihood disingenuously. But Ralph kept these thoughts to himself. After all, he suspected her love of the "misfit toys" she surrounded herself with explained why she had chosen him—another misfit toy—as a life partner.

Ralph fully realized he was not a typical model husband. He worked too many hours, and could often be grumpy. He wasn't handy around the home. He wasn't always tidy. He failed miserably with most details in life. His travel often took him away from home more than 180 nights per year. And his books and artwork littered their house. He'd typically be in the middle of four or five novels, three print magazines, and two or more art projects. And that was just on the living room coffee table.

Ralph had significant misgivings about his questioning Jen's chosen lifestyle. In the end, if Jen were really an international spy master—or whatever she else had chosen to be—Ralph would have been curious to learn more, but wouldn't want to know if it put their relationship at risk. It was that simple.

The messaging sign at Arrivals now showed that all bags had been delivered on Jen's flight. So that meant she'd probably heading through immigration. Ralph messaged her with "Use Fastpass—it's on the far right of the immigration hall. Your B class ticket will allow you to do so. Quicker. And then grab bags (should be first off belt and set aside) and head through green 'Nothing to Declare' aisle at customs. LU"

The driver was sound asleep on a chair reserved for elders and those with disabilities. Ralph noticed people were giving him a very wide berth. A little girl and her sibling were pointing and laughing as they passed by. He wasn't going anywhere anytime soon.

Ralph walked over to Nero's coffee and got a drip coffee for himself, and a mocha latte with skinny milk, just a little foam, and some whipped cream for Jen. He expected her at any moment. It had been thirty minutes from when her plane had reached its gate. He drank his coffee.

At forty-five minutes, he looked over at the driver and noticed the man was still asleep. He needed to use the loo, but couldn't get the driver to notice he wanted to switch-off at the greeting rail. Ralph's coffee was now empty, and Jen's was getting tepid. He sent her an SMS, "All OK?"

Sixty minutes and Ralph could still see a bag or two coming through Arrivals with an SFO tag. But at seventy-five minutes, there were no more SFO travelers coming through the doors. At ninety minutes, the message board no longer had the San Francisco flight on its long list of arrivals.

The driver approached Ralph with a weary look. He asked if he could get paid and leave. He had other appointments that day. Ralph apologized profusely and asked for ten minutes. The driver looked at his watch and begrudgingly agreed.

Ralph punched out another SMS to Jen. "You there?" No response.

The driver checked his watch every thirty seconds. He could wait no longer. Ralph paid him forty-five pounds and the man was gone in a flash.

Ralph had an ultra-premier status on the airline that Jen was on. He dialed the secret number and was connected in the first ring.

"Thank you for calling, Mr. Gibsen. How can I assist you?"

"Ah, hello. Uhm, yes, this is Ralph Gibsen. How did you know it was me calling?"

"We have your cell phone on records and use caller ID, I am sure."

"Oh. Okay, look, my wife is supposed to be on an earlier flight from SFO to LHR. Flight UA901. She's flying on my miles in B class, and the flight landed about ninety minutes ago. She hasn't come through to Arrivals. I've gotten an SMS from her, but nothing since. Is there any way if you can tell if she's been detained somehow?"

"No, sir. I wouldn't be able to tell. If you have her booking confirmation code, I can tell you if she rebooked the flight. But that's all I can tell from my systems."

Ralph gave her the confirmation code. The agent took a moment and confirmed that Jen was on the flight.

"Well, maybe she's stuck in immigration or customs? Is there anyone I can call to find out?"

"I'm afraid not."

Ralph thanked the agent and went to find a bathroom. Then he ran two laps around the Arrivals area to ensure Jen hadn't slipped out while he was relieving himself. He checked his phone constantly. He dialed her number. The ring tone had changed to the UK ring tone. His mood leapt. She was in the UK! But then the line dropped. *Too strange*, he thought. He ran one more lap around the Arrivals area and returned to the rail with his sign.

People-watching at the Arrivals area of Heathrow airport is an amazing activity. Emotions are on display for all to see. Anxiousness, love, yearning, fear, joy, annoyance, remembrance, relief—Ralph saw them all in thirty-second glimpses.

At 120 minutes late, Ralph was starting to panic.

He called his assistant in Silicon Valley. "Mika, sorry it's late. I've got a weird situation. Can you check my calendar? Jen was supposed to arrive two plus hours ago and she's not here."

"Who is this?" Mika had answered Ralph calls for four years. She knew who it was, but she wanted Ralph to be extra aware that he was calling past midnight on a school night.

"Mika, it's Ralph. I'm slightly freaking out. I'm at Heathrow to pick up Jen, and she's two-plus hours later than she should be."

"Good morning, Ralph." Mika cleared her throat of sleepiness. "Hold on. I don't sleep with my computer by my bedside."

"Yeah, sorry. Uhhhm, I hope I made a calendaring mistake with time zones or something when I booked her flight with frequent flyer miles."

"You shouldn't book flights. I should. You don't have … well, it's the truth."

"Yes, I lack detail orientation. We agree. Thanks. Can you …"

"I'm online. Your calendar says she was on flight UA901. She should have landed more than two hours ago. You didn't make any mistakes with your calendar. Are you sure she was on the flight?"

"The UA agent I called just confirmed she was scheduled, and did not reschedule the flight. She claimed she didn't have any more information than that. Can you check with your airport mafia to see if you can find her? I'm genuinely worried."

"Unnaturally so. What's going on? This isn't like you. You never stress out—ever. The last time you woke me in the middle of the night, you needed me to check on the extraction clause we have on our Director's umbrella insurance policy, after you spent nine hours naked in the interrogation room in Shenzhen. And to be blunt, you sound significantly more stressed now than you did that day."

"It's my wife! And my life has gotten a little more wacky than usual recently."

Mika waited for Ralph to further explain. When Ralph offered nothing more, she said, "Okay, let me call a few of my friends in the network."

Mika's friends worked in the travel industry, and she had found numerous deeply secret ways to bend the industry to her needs. The network spoke Russian exclusively, and Ralph hadn't given it much thought until this moment.

They rang off. Ralph did one more lap. The roving security guards were now eyeing Ralph suspiciously.

Ralph stopped at the information desk. The clerks were particularly unhelpful, as they wanted to sell pre-paid hotel rooms and taxi trips. But they told anecdotes of people taking as long as four hours to get through to Arrivals.

It was now two and half hours after the plane had landed. There was a permanent sheen on Ralph forehead. He'd wipe away the layer of nervous sweat with his palm, but it would reappear in seconds. The roving guards were now walking past Ralph with regularity. Ralph made certain to look them in the eye and nod.

At three hours late, Ralph called and SMSed one more time. This time the call went right to voice mail, and the SMS was just one of ten that Ralph wasn't entirely sure had been delivered. He decided he needed some protein in order to think correctly. As he was standing in line at Nero's for a grilled chicken and Comté Toastee, Ralph looked across the lobby and saw long blonde hair under a baseball cap. Jen rarely wore a baseball cap. But the blonde hair falling out of the cap looked like hers, and the woman had Jen's build. She was being aggressively shepherded by two large men that Hollywood would describe as "muscle in uniforms."

Is that Jen? Ralph wondered. He left the line and ran. Only ten or twelve steps into his sprint, Ralph was tackled by one of the roving security guards. His computer bag and roll-on bag scattered fifteen feet away in opposite directions. A weapon was drawn from another guard's belt. Fortunately, Ralph relaxed. His face was pushed into the granite flooring and his arms were secured behind his back. The guard on top of him was feeling around his waist for anything untoward.

"You are being detained for suspicious behavior, do you understand me?" the guard yelled into Ralph's ear.

"Yes. May I explain please?"

"In a moment. Please do not make trouble for yourself. My partner has both a handgun and a Taser pointed at your chest. He is trained extensively to use these tools. I am going to pick you up now. Do not attempt to escape. I am taking you to a holding and interrogation area."

Ralph noticed there were now six officers surrounding him. He said carefully, "I acknowledge. Please also pick up and bring my bags."

"Is there something unsafe in your bags?"

"No. There is nothing unsafe. I just don't want them to be left behind."

The guards formed a barrier around Ralph. Every eye in the building followed their march to an unmarked door. The heavy door opened automatically with a click and a hiss, and all crowded into a room meant for half the number of bodies that now occupied it.

Ralph was forcefully placed in a seat, and the guard who had tackled him took the seat opposite. A few officers left the room to return to their rounds.

"You understand you are being detained for suspicious behavior, do you understand this? We'd like your consent to look at the contents of your person and bags. Do we have your consent?"

Ralph paused. "Yes," he said slowly, and then added, "I'd like the opportunity to tell you why I am here."

"Would you empty your pockets onto this tray and allow us to frisk you?"

Ralph nodded.

"The detained nodded his acknowledgment. Sir, you are now being made aware that you are being recorded on CCTV devices. Please acknowledge this fact."

Ralph nodded affirmatively.

Officers began disassembling Ralph's luggage. He placed his wallet, phone, and passport on the tray. The items were the entirety of what was in his pockets. Ralph was asked to stand and place his hands on the wall. He was thoroughly frisked, and swabs were used on Ralph's person and his luggage for various residues. As the officers emptied his bags, there were a few raised eyebrows and one long whistle. The items of interest to the officers were also placed on the tray, including several passports. The officer apparently in charge occasionally adjusted his ear bud to listen and seemingly take instruction. He turned over all the items on the tray, and looked to a high-definition camera above the table. He nodded. Ralph was pushed down into his chair. The officer that frisked him shook his head to the officers in the room.

"Please remove your shoes and belt and track jacket."

Ralph did so awkwardly from a seated position.

The officer that had taken the swabs walked in and also shook his head.

"May we have the passwords to your phone and computer?"

"No. My electronic devices contain significant material that is sensitive to my livelihood as an investor. As this information may be deemed proprietary and material to the U.S. Securities and Exchange Commission, I'd be legally negligent to allow this information to be passed to anyone." Ralph had practiced that statement, he just didn't imagine he'd need to use it in the UK.

After visiting the Middle East, Ralph was actually carrying a burner phone, but his MacBook contained Prezi presentations about ultra-high resolution imaging satellites, countering violent extremism programs, and another of government censorship mitigation that would cause too many further questions. Over the years, Ralph's lawyers had taught him that any digital information could be legally protected, at least until the court's decision said otherwise.

"We can simply plug it into our world-class equipment and download everything. We break passwords every day. Only, our equipment often plays havoc with your disk drive and scrambles everything when we give it back. You're gonna lose all your pictures and important documents unless you give us the passwords."

Ralph waited two beats. "That's a very obvious bluff. I can believe that works often, but unfortunately not with me. One, this MacBook doesn't have a disk drive. It uses an SSD. Two, the laptop is using OTP encryption. If it was using ASC or PGP, you could probably bust it open with enough big iron and a couple ten thousand pounds worth of processor time. But One-Time Pad encryption—no chance of busting it open. If you try, it would crush your monthly budget. And three, if or when you decrypted my devices, you'd find they were burners and only have a few legitimate business presentations on them, all of which would make sense if you first were to Google my name."

The lead officer listened carefully and picked up one of Ralph's passports—the one that he carried in his pocket. A few airline ticket stubs fell out. The latest Tel Aviv ticket was the first examined.

"Theodore Ralph Gibsen. Is there a special phrase you should be whispering in my ear at this point?"

"I am not a member of the Intelligence Community."

The MI5 officer took a beat or two. "That's close enough. And what took you this long to say that particular phrase?"

"Can we start again? My name is Ralph. I am a Silicon Valley investor in great start-up founders. I arrived at this airport about four hours ago, and I am waiting for my wife. She was on flight UA901, which arrived about three hours ago. I thought I saw her being escorted between doors in the Arrivals lobby, and was rushing to see if it was her, when I was tackled by you. I have been entirely cooperative within all reasonable expectations. What is your name please?"

Stone-faced, the officers all stared at Ralph. At least sixty seconds passed. Ralph was about to continue when the lead officer held up his index finger. "Stop. Give us a moment or two." He nodded toward the others.

The officers all filed out of the room. Ralph was alone with his stuff. After ten minutes, Ralph picked up his phone to see if Jen had messaged.

"Put that down. Please do not touch anything." Ralph locked the phone as he did so. An officer had entered the room when Ralph was looking at his phone. The junior-most officer apparently had been told to stand in the room with Ralph while the rest of his team figured out what to do with him.

"I apologize for the confusion I've caused." Ralph attempted to get the officer into a discussion, but the officer ignored him.

Another ten or fifteen minutes passed. "Can I just check my phone to see if my wife has arrived? Or can you check on your records or cameras please? She's going to be terribly upset with me if she shows up and I'm not there to greet her as promised."

Ralph was answered with silence. After another ten minutes, the door opened and the same officers filed in. They were joined by a man in a suit.

This man stood to the side. His stare was intense. The lead officer looked at the man in the suit and then proceeded. "Mr. Gibsen, I am going to give you a series of facts, and when I am finished, you are going to confirm those facts and then help us link those facts together into a cohesive story. Is that clear?"

Ralph nodded.

"The detained has nodded affirmatively."

The lead officer took a deep breath and looked at his notepad for assistance. "You arrived at Heathrow this morning at 8:02 AM via BA012 from Tel Aviv. You used the Fastpass lanes per your privilege as a first-class passenger. As you did not check any bags, you passed through customs in the Nothing to Declare aisle. Sixteen minutes later you checked your watch and went to the BA Club World reception in the Arrivals area, where you took a shower and had a cup of coffee and a bit of powdered scrambled eggs. Approximately at 9:15 AM, you left the BA lounge and found a mini-cab driver with a sign that said 'JENANDRA.' You engaged the driver in conversation, telling him you were waiting for your wife. Your wife never appeared and the driver was paid and left the airport at 10:50 AM. A few minutes thereafter, you placed a series of calls, including two on encrypted channels. The one we can see was to the United Airlines Services line."

The man looked up, took a breath, and then continued.

"At 11:45 AM you approached the information desk in Arrivals. They reported you were belligerent and sweating. At 12:22 PM you ordered a chicken Toastee at Neros. Seventy-two seconds later you ran quickly, trailing your baggage, towards the northeastern section of the Arrivals lobby. You've been visiting with us in this secure section of the building for approximately 125 minutes.

"In your possession, we have found an iPhone 7 Plus that is password protected, three U.S. passports with greater than 600 stamps from approximately eighty countries. You have four credit cards in your name, and two in your business name, including one that is for China use only. You have a California driver license, a membership card for AAA, a health insurance card, a Costco card, and two London and one Santa Cruz California bookshops' frequent buyer's club cards—Foyles and Waterstones, and Bookshop Santa Cruz. You also have approximately 200 pounds Sterling.

"In your computer backpack, you have some increasingly interesting kit. We found a Mac laptop that is password protected. We found a Samsung Android phone that is also password protected. We found a Raspberry Pi computer that appears to be a key logger, another—called a 'PoisonTap'—that appears to be a network penetration tester, and one that we have no idea what it is."

"Please do not plug that into your network. That VXer was the dude that did Cobian RAT," Ralph pleaded.

"There is a 'Stingray/Pineapple' WiFi/4G measurement cloning and hacking tool, and something charmingly called a Bash Bunny, which apparently can wreak absolute fucking havoc on any USB port it is plugged into."

"For the love of God, please do not plug that into your network-enabled computers."

"Enough interruptions, Mr. Gibsen. I'll be finished in just a few minutes. Then you can speak on your own behalf.

"You have about twenty connectors to every computer port ever created. You have a bit of kit that Nigel wants very much to confiscate—a PD100 micro-drone. Eighteen grams and worth about 200 thousand quid—the price I paid for my flat in London twelve years ago. A miniature Augmented Reality printer. You've got more than forty-five different currencies in your bag, in individual envelopes. And my favorite is that you have an assortment of snack foods that looks like someone gave 100 pounds to a seven-year-old in Marks & Spencer and told them to have at it.

"Beyond that you have a roll-on bag with an assortment of dirty clothes. You have not booked any hotels in the UK, haven't booked a car, and haven't placed a call to anyone in the UK using a public telephone network. There is a home registered in your name on the tax records that appears to have a long-term renter in place.

"After examining your remarkably suspicious kit, and when asking if you had a special phrase to give us, you gave us an old phrase that is approximately correct for someone working in the Intelligence Communities who did not want to confirm they were working in the field. Typically, I'd hand you off to the MI6 and let them deal with you. But they do not have more than a cursory few notes of record of you and do not have your remit. This is likely a diplomatic row you've created, but that is not of our concern today. When we purposely left you alone with your kit, you used two- or three-factor authentication to check your SMS messages, which are transmitted over public telecommunication networks that you'd be aware we would have access to. Which brings us to this conclusion: you are either a horrible spook or some idiot wasting our time by trying to get our attention. Which is it? And have we presented these facts correctly?"

Ralph paused. "Two things you have said are incorrect. One, I flew business class on BA012 from Tel Aviv. Not first class. And I have four passports. Your team may have missed one in my bag. It's hidden in the padding for the laptop. I keep it there in case the location I'm visiting confiscates my more obvious passports."

Before the statement was complete, the officers were scrambling to find the wayward passport. It was where Ralph specified. The officers started to further disassemble the backpack computer case.

"Stop, please." The lead officer requested of his team. "Mr. Gibsen, you've been honest in telling us about the passport and flight—and in the case of the flight, I'd be lying if I told you it wasn't to test your accuracy. Is there anything else on your body or bags that we should be aware of?"

"I wouldn't be surprised if there was an assorted tracking device or three in my bags. Over the years, I've found several in my bags as I travel. I repeat, I am not in the Intelligence Community, but my investment activities give some governments reason to examine my life."

"Those investment activities would be?"

Ralph spent ten minutes explaining some of the projects he was working on. He talked about the companies and the potential partners, including GCHQ and imaging pico-satellites, and Sir Alistair Harris's Stabilization Group and countering violent extremism work. "I try to only invest in founders who want to make the world a better place, yet even a few of my not-for-profit projects can be used to help efficiently educate the world or, in perverse instances, be terribly misused to be instruments of human control."

The officers looked skeptical and uncomfortable.

Ralph asked, "Would any of us outlaw the use of a kitchen knife because it could be misused to hurt another human?"

There was thoughtful silence.

"And sometimes governments are interested in me because I also have a pro-bono role with the Naval Postgraduate School (NPS), helping them prioritize research investments."

"What exactly is that school?" asked the junior-most officer.

"Predominately a research and teaching school for U.S. and U.S. allies," Ralph replied.

"A spook school," declared the lead officer. Another thoughtful pause. "And is that why you have all of this espionage kit?"

"No, this is not for the NPS. But in the digital security world, we need to know what we are fighting. I bring this 'kit' with me to show potential partners what they are up against. For example, if I can show you the pictures and email on your phone, could I possibly convince you to use my solution that would prevent someone else from doing the same to you?"

"And the reason you carry four current passports?"

"I travel to a few places where the governments disallow visits if there's an enemy's stamp in your passport. For example, I cannot use the same passport to travel to Israel and the United Arab Emirates. I utilize four passports to ensure I can travel as freely as a U.S. citizen can reasonably expect."

"And one more time, what exactly are you doing in this terminal today?"

"I am, anxiously, waiting for my wife to arrive on flight UA901. Would there be any way you could check if she's arrived and get a message to her?"

"Is there any reason that she would not want to see you today?"

Ralph was puzzled. "No. She sent me an SMS as she landed. No."

"Right. We are going to let you cool here for a few more hours while we do a few more bits of research about the companies and organizations with which you are involved. We are also going to do a strip and body cavity search because while I want to believe you, we are paid not to. If everything checks out as you say, we may help you look for your wife."

Finally, a carrot, Ralph thought.

Ralph went through the process of a detailed search. It was a terribly humiliating thing to be so vulnerable. He was asked to strip naked and squat and cough over a mirrored surface before someone inserted their finger into his rectum. There was an endoscope inserted into his ears and nasal cavities. The cold sweat pouring off Ralph's body was freely dripping to the linoleum floor. He agreed to let a female officer wipe his forehead with gauze—only after did he realize the action was not done for his comfort but to analyze the chemical out-gassings. After twenty more minutes of poking and prodding, Ralph was sat on a plastic chair and left alone in the cold room, without clothes or any of his personal effects.

Two hours passed slowly.

Ralph was trying to stretch to reduce some of the stress that had built up in his back and shoulders, when the lead officer came into the room.

"Fucking yanks. Don't tell me naked yoga is going to be the next new thing."

"Have you found my wife? May I have my clothes back?"

"You are assuming everything checked out as you said."

"Because it does."

"Maybe. But there has been a new development."

Ralph didn't speak. After thirty seconds he asked, "Is my wife okay?"

"This recent development has little to do with your wife. While we were checking your new passport, we noticed that your credit score among the three U.S. credit rating agencies had dropped from approximately 800 points to 400 points—within the last three hours. Why would that happen?"

"I don't know a reason that this might happen."

"I think that's the first lie you've told me."

Ralph thought about this. "Maybe. The process for trashing someone's credit is remarkably easy. The credit rating agencies use unsophisticated algorithms that measure things that are easy for a hacker to manipulate. And because the U.S. is highly focused on litigation, the agencies' algorithms tend to reduce credit scores the moment they smell something funky, without even a modicum of human intervention. Perhaps someone wants me to have a terribly miserable day. By chance, were you alerted to my presence in the Arrivals hall by an anonymous source?"

The officer was stone-faced, but quickly looked at the camera over Ralph's shoulder. After a few more beats, he stared intently at Ralph's eyes and asked, "Who would want to target someone like you?"

"Could be—well, could be any number of people. Or, more likely, organizations. I'd suspect I'd start with the countries of the Middle East and Northern Africa. Then maybe China, and possibly my own country, or even the UK. Then there are a few competitors that'd take pleasure in my discomfort." Ralph had a policy to never offer more than what was asked. He feared he may have broken his own rule.

The lead officer paused. "Yes, we were alerted anonymously to look out for an agitated man in the Arrivals Hall this morning." He paused again. "I have more questions than answers in my discussion with you, Mr. Gibsen. And I think if we sat here another four hours, that wouldn't change much. But I do not think you are a threat to the public. We are going to let you go, for the moment, with all of your kit—except your phones and your laptop. I am also going to hold your passports for further study. Officer Gilligan will collect your contact details. We were not able to track down anything useful about your wife. I'd personally like you to leave the airport for at least the next twenty-four hours. We'll call you when we decide what to do with you next."

After providing all his contact details to the officer, he asked for a receipt for the gear he was leaving behind, and contact details for the MI5. He was denied both. Then he was escorted to the taxi queue, and put in a cab heading for the Intercontinental Hotel Mayfair.

❦

On the trip into central London, Ralph tried to figure out how he'd contact his wife. He decided he'd need to pick up a cheap prepaid Smartphone as soon as possible. When he got to the hotel, his worst fears transpired: his credit cards had all been put on hold, and he was unable to check in. As Ralph was a frequent guest of the hotel, the manager offered to allow him to utilize the Business Center and see if he could straighten things out.

When Ralph attempted to log in to his business Gmail account, he learned that Google had flagged and quarantined his address due to suspicious activities. When he logged into his personal email account, he saw that all his credit cards had been shut down, due to suspicion of money laundering. Ralph also saw that his cellular service provider and his home's utilities in the U.S. had also been suspended. Worse yet, he saw a note from his bank saying that his accounts were frozen. The bank was calling due his three mortgages with immediate effect. He was unable to login to Skype, WeChat, WhatsApp, or Line. There wasn't a single note from Jen.

Ralph did an immediate inventory of his situation. He had somehow lost his wife. He had 140 pounds Sterling in his pocket. He had no means to communicate or get any of the information he needed. He was without immediate and perhaps long-term shelter. Running to the U.S. Embassy might cause more problems than they could possibly solve. Some person or organization was coming at him hard, and had inflicted significant damage. And he didn't know how to deal with it. Yet his most pressing need was to ensure his wife was not in harm's way.

The phone in the Business Center required a code in order to make long distance calls. The firewall and antivirus package on the hotel's computer wouldn't allow him to download any messaging apps. Ralph wracked his brain trying to think of how he could get in touch with Jen or his assistant Mika. He realized that his personal Gmail account might be compromised next. He began copying phone numbers of people who could be able to help, and which he didn't know by heart. After just the fourth number, his personal account was shut down, and he could no longer access his contacts list.

"FUUUUUUUUCK!"

Ralph's outburst brought the manager to the small room. "Ah, any luck, Mr. Gibsen?"

"None."

"Well that is unfortunate. But I may have found a small bit of good news for you, sir. I have looked at our frequent stay program, and you have spent well over 100 nights with us at the Intercontinental hotel platform over the last twenty years. You've never once redeemed your free nights. So the good news is that I can offer you eight nights in our standard deluxe room for free, or four nights in a small suite. I'd just need your passport in order to check you into the hotel, and we could have your bags up to your room this instant."

"That's great news. Well done. I've got only one problem: my passports are being held for the evening by MI5 at London Heathrow airport."

The manager looked dumbfounded. "But sir, in this age of assorted threats on our fair city, the authorities have instructed us that there can be no exceptions. I can only allow you to join us at this hotel if you have a passport."

Ralph frowned. The British loved their rules and bureaucracies. He wasn't going to be able to persuade his way into a room at this hotel. At least not this evening. He changed tracks: "MI5 will be contacting me here within the next forty-eight to seventy-two hours, as I gave them this hotel as the address where I'll be staying. I'll need you to personally explain to these folks my whereabouts and hold these messages for me—as well as potentially other messages from my wife, Sheik Mohammed, and Sir Alistair Harris. They were all expecting to call on me over the next few evenings."

This wasn't entirely true, but it was a way for Ralph to remind the manager of the high-flying partners with whom he had visited the hotel in the previous sixty days.

The manager nodded his understanding of the gravitas.

"I'm also expecting a few packages to be delivered for me, from MI5, MI6, GCHQ, and potentially others. I'll need you to personally put them into your office's safe—*not* the hotel's safe—for my retrieval. You will be held personally responsible for their safekeeping." Ralph hoped that packages would be delivered, but had no way of knowing. "And finally, I need your team to hold my bags for the next few hours."

"Mr. Gibsen, you've been a very good customer to us here. But I am anxious to submit to your requests. It all seems … involved."

"I assumed you realized, these weren't really requests."

The manager was stunned, but quickly recovered. Ralph was bluffing, but needed this bluff to work. Moments passed. Ralph could almost hear the manager mentally adding up the value of his more than 100 nights' stay.

"Of course, sir." The hotel manager stuck his head out of the Business Centre and caught the attention of the bell desk. In just a few moments, Ralph had a receipt for his bags and was leaving the hotel.

By then Ralph was famished. And he didn't do his best thinking on an empty stomach. While he needed to conserve cash, he also needed protein and carbohydrates. And he needed help. He headed to a little café called L'Artise Muscle, which was behind the hotel in the heart of Mayfair.

The lone waitress, Monique, smiled broadly and gave him a kiss on each cheek. She announced Ralph had joined them, and the chef/owner came out and did the same. Ralph didn't need to order, as the chef had served Ralph dozens of times. The bread and butter were delicious. The moules divine. And the cassoulet without comparison. Ralph's mood had gone from dire to bearable. He complimented the waitress and the chef. They beamed with pride. After a moment, Monique asked after his well-being.

"How are you, Monsieur Ralph?"

"*Comme ci comme ça.*"

The waitress didn't like that answer. The chef asked if he was having problems with a woman. Ralph raised his eyebrows, and everyone nodded knowingly. The waitress had her hand on his shoulder.

"You know, we met many, many years ago."

Ralph couldn't remember where or when they had met. He cocked his head like a puppy who doesn't understand.

"Do you remember the man who first brought you here, maybe twenty years ago?"

Ralph thought back. He shook his head no.

"It was Mr. Tom Warn. Do you by chance stay in touch with him? He was here a few weeks ago, and asked if we had seen you recently."

"Wow. I haven't done a good job of staying in touch with him. We worked together in Japan maybe twenty-five years ago and I saw him in Taipei recently. Did he by chance say where he was?"

"He travels a lot, like you. I have his number, and I shall give it to you. We were lovers for a time, but alas, he broke my heart. Never fall in love with a ginger-haired man."

"I'll try not to."

They both laughed. She walked away to find her phone. When she came back, after seeing to a few more customers, she gave Ralph a slip of paper.

"May I ask a weird question, Monique?"

"Of course."

"Any idea where I can get a prepaid Android phone?"

"There is a Carphone Warehouse on Regent."

"Yeah, well, but, I'm in an interesting situation. I'm going need a local smartphone, where they don't need identification. My passport was …"

Monique started laughing. "Every time I see you, you have these ridiculous circumstances—most *clandestin*. Flying off to Isbequestan or Timbuktu. You are a either a poorly-talented spy, or just *un corniaud*?"

"More the knucklehead than the spy, I think," Ralph said.

"Use my phone and call Tom, as he plays such games."

She handed him her phone. Tom's contact information was on the screen. Ralph touched the screen and the phone dialed. Monique wandered off to take drink orders from new customers.

The phone rang and then changed ringtones. Tom was not in the UK.

"Mmm. *Bonjour, mon amourexe*."

"Easy cowboy." Ralph laughed.

"Monique?"

"I'm almost as good looking in a skirt, but sadly I am not Monique."

"Ralph Gibsen? What are you doing on my girlfriend's phone? That woman broke my heart. Must I kick your ass?"

"Hi, Tom. It is Ralph. How are you?"

"I'm well. And I am delighted that Monique passed you my message."

"It's been a long time. Are you well?"

"I just told you I was. What's going on? You sound uncharacteristically distracted."

"Well, I'm fine. No, that's not entirely true. I am in a spot of bother, as the Brits would say. By the way, where are you?"

"Not in the UK. But can I help you with your spot of bother?"

"Maybe. Monique says you might know where I can get a smartphone without a passport or a credit card."

"I love you, Ralph."

"What?"

"I have never known what's going to come out of your mouth. The world can get terribly dull and predictable. People like you are never predictable."

"Yeah, well...."

"Okay. I am surmising you are without phone and passport and credit cards. This is an interesting story already."

"We haven't spoken in what, five or six years?"

"Except for a brief hello in Taipei at the 101 Building, it may have been ten or twelve years..."

"Still in telecom?"

"Kind of. You? Investing, right?"

"Uh, right. This is going to sound weird, but I need to give it to you straight. Today, I work with startups that attempt to make the world a better place. Sadly, that often means I upset powerful people who like the world as it is. And today, I seemed to have upset someone who is lashing out hard. My wife is somehow missing. While waiting for her at the airport, my passports, phones, and computer were temporarily confiscated by MI5. Someone there has recently had his finger or perhaps fingers up my bung hole. My credit cards and various email and other accounts have been targeted for attack and are currently inoperable. I've got 140 Pounds Sterling to my name. Oh, and the banks are repossessing my homes with immediate effect. And did I mention I need to find my wife?"

"Oh—wow. That's kind of a bad day."

"Other than that, I am well-fed and healthy. And good news for you—I think Monique misses you."

Tom laughed. And then, upon the absurd reflection, so did Ralph.

"I am terribly excited about all this. Because, now I get to return the many favors you've bestowed on me these many years."

"I don't remember any favors, Tom."

"Well, that's because you don't keep track of things you do for people with a ledger. I remember three instances where you made my life significantly better."

"Hmmmn? No."

"Yes. In 1988, when I was working for you at Sony. One day I walked into the office after lunch and I was terribly high. I was having women troubles. Morita-san walked into our section and asked me a bunch of questions. I stumbled and fumbled. Later that day, he asked you whether I was pulling my weight. You covered and vouched for me. If anyone else was my supervisor, I would have been fired and my career would have gone in a different direction."

Ralph laughed. "We all had women trouble in those days—we were in our mid-twenties. Plus, I really needed your help on that big project."

"Then when you left Tokyo, I was in a bit of a cash crunch. More women trouble. You lent me a significant amount of money, and I've never really paid you back."

"It wasn't that much money."

"Today, it's not much. But then, as a percentage of our annual income, it was huge. And thirdly, about ten years ago, I needed a crash pad. I was in a 'bit of bother' myself at the time, but I didn't share the details with you. You offered up your Cape Cod home, as you were on the other coast. I spent much of three months there."

"Wow, you do owe me big time," Ralph said jokingly. "I absolve you of all your perceived debts if you help me get an Android phone with data service."

"No deal, too easy. I want to save your bacon, Ralph. Appreciate it if you'd let me do so."

"Since I am kind of flustered, I'm just going to be grateful for any and all of your help."

"Flustered? Just because some burley man had his fist up your butt? In the old days, we would have called that an interesting weekend."

Ralph laughed. "Times have changed—but I don't remember ever enjoying that."

"So where are you staying?"

"I was booked at the Mayfair Intercontinental, but they need a passport for me to redeem my frequent stay credit."

"Lovely hotel, but too high profile for you. And they always follow the rules, as they are preferred by our Middle Eastern friends. I want you to go to Number 5 Maddox Street. It's a little boutique hotel without a sign on the street, and it doesn't follow every rule. I'll have my assistant get you a place there. They are like serviced apartments. You'll need a Mac, and iPhone, a credit card, and some cash. Do you need a temporary passport for any reason?"

"You can do that? Will I need to go to the embassy?"

"Yes, Ralph, I can do that. And no, do not go near the embassy for any reason, okay?"

"All right. I'll probably only need a passport for the acquisition of the cell phone and to check into the hotel."

"I'll take care of those things for you."

"Thank—"

Tom interrupted before Ralph could fully express his gratitude. "All right, I have to get working on this. I'll touch base in a few days, okay? And two things. One, leave the wad of cash you have with Monique, and kiss her on the cheek for me. There'll be cash in the apartment when you get there. And two, before you bring your bags anywhere near the hotel, make sure you go through them with a fine-tooth comb. Or better yet, let someone on my team do so. There will be at least three tracking devices in your luggage. There may also be one or more in your shoes and belt, so run to the men's room and do a quick check. Got it?"

"My luggage is at the bell desk at the Intercontinental."

"Perfect, let me send you a car. Ask Monique to take you out the back way—the car will meet you at the Mews Hotel. Do you know where that is from where you are?"

"Yeah, it's only a block from here. I used to stay there all the time."

"Of course you did, you cheap bastard. Rich as the Queen and he stays at a hotel that charges a hundred quid a night. Sheesh."

Ralph didn't take offense. Men of his generation often insulted each other to show affection.

"I'm going to be presumptuous, if I may, Tom. I assume you can do the aforementioned because you have the means. Might you have the means to take an expeditious look around for my wife?"

"People in our line of work always have the means, Ralph."

Ralph paused to let that sink in. "Well, perfect. Can we spend a minute or two on this topic?"

"Sure. And my team is already working on finding Jen."

"Oh great. Ah, awkwardly, with all the recent changes, I don't know much about my network. I found a major—

let's call it problem—and I need to report it to someone up the chain."

"Really? I don't know if I can help with that. I wish I could. Really. This is going to sound weird, but I always assumed *you* were the top of the chain."

"Well, I'm sure I must have a boss."

"Interesting, but above my pay grade. Hey, I've got to run. Let's talk in a few hours. Kiss Monique on the cheek for me and leave her all your cash. My guy will meet you at the Mews Hotel in fifteen minutes. He'll also give you a quick scan and grab your bags from the Intercontinental. Be safe. Talk soon."

"Thanks," Ralph said, but he could tell that Tom had already rung off. "I think." Ralph waved at Monique to get her attention.

"Thanks for the use of your phone. That was awesome to reconnect. If it isn't too much to ask, I need another favor or two."

She nodded, but with a hint of apprehension.

"I need to kiss your cheek—for Tom."

She smiled deeply and extended her cheek. Ralph took his time. She smelled of clean linen and caramelized onions.

"Oh my, Ralph. Your wife is a lucky one."

"You are very sweet, Monique. This is for my bill." He handed her the entire wad of cash. This act made him feel enormously vulnerable, as he would be without any monetary resources. But he had decided to trust Tom.

She smiled, peeled off two twenties, left them on the table, and tucked the remaining cash into her pocket. "I love you yanks. Tipping is *tres charmant*."

"And finally, I need to have you walk me out the back door please."

She laughed. "You are going to need more than that, Ralph. There is an undercover gendarme who has been watching you carefully. I saw him follow you here. Thus, I will capture his attention." She unbuttoned her shirt by two buttons and pulled up her skirt, to ensure the hem was slightly higher than mid-thigh. "And I will go wipe off the tables on the sidewalk. When my skirt flips up to expose my lace panties, you will stand up and walk past Guy in the kitchen. He will not acknowledge your presence. Be quick. At the sink, take a left, and then a quick right. You'll see the door. It unlocks by spinning the dial counter-clockwise. It'll lock when it closes. *Bon chance mon ami.*" And she was grabbing a rag to bus the sidewalk tables.

In thirty seconds, the wind had whipped her skirt, and more than half of the world seemed captivated by nothing else. Ralph slipped out the back without notice.

He walked quickly to the Mews Hotel. At the entrance was a big black S-class Mercedes with dark windows. As Ralph got within ten meters of the autobahn cruiser, the driver got out of the car and held open the door.

"Good afternoon, Mr. Gibsen. Mr. Warn sends his regards. My name is Sam, and I am going to help you for the next few hours."

"Hi, Sam. And thanks."

"This car is especially equipped to notice if you have any active surveillance. I can tell you we see nothing on my equipment. But as you are aware, today's best gear isn't active—it is passive, waiting for the right frequency to light it up. We are almost certain that your clothing has passive tracking and perhaps listening material. So we need you to disrobe and get into the black tracksuit and slippers that are sitting in the bag next to you. Everything off please."

Ralph hesitated. "Ah, well …"

Sam quickly interjected, "Mr. Gibsen, I've worked for fifteen years with Mr. Warn. He speaks highly of your craft and he trusts you implicitly. Now, so do I. What I am doing for you now could cause me a great deal of trouble. I know you are feeling vulnerable at this moment, but realize we are on the same team, and I will protect you to the best of my abilities. I need you to trust me please."

"Okay." Ralph pulled off all his clothes and shoes and stuffed them into the bag that had previously held the black tracksuit and slip-ons. At the bottom of the bag, Ralph found a black knit beanie cap, a pollution mask, and a pair of large sunglasses that slipped over his eyeglasses. He didn't have a mirror, but was sure he wouldn't recognize himself in this get up.

In a few minutes, they pulled up to Number 5 Maddox Street. Sam said, "I am going to check you in for the next two weeks, paid in advance. We can extend if need be. Please do not leave the car until I open the door for you as the car has a Faraday grid built into everything but the trunk. You have been off the grid for the last few minutes. This means MI5 will be trying to figure out where you went. After you get into your room, do not use any communication equipment. Only use the iPhone and laptop that will be delivered to you in the next few minutes, is that clear?"

"Yes. Can you ask Tom if he can re-route the T-Mobile Master Switching Center for my phone number to this new phone you'll deliver? I'd be grateful in case my wife calls or messages. Tom used to be a master of the MSC."

"I can assure you that he has not lost his touch. He will do as you have asked, if he can. But you'll need to stay off email or any of your social media—or they will learn we have subverted their systems."

"Understood."

"Over the next ninety minutes, we will have delivered six or eight packages to your apartment. Only open the door or go out on the deck wearing your beanie, mask, and sunglasses. Do not sign for anything but via an 'X' on the delivery notice. Hang the 'Do Not Disturb' sign on your door. When I get back to the car, I will drive your old clothes to the Intercontinental and check you into that hotel using your name. MI5 can and will find you—but arranged and paid for by a frequent MENA guest. I'll bring your luggage up to the room from the bell desk. I'll hang a 'Do not Disturb' on that room's door as well and forward that hotel phone to your new iPhone. A computer bag and a carry-on are all that you have left at the bell desk, correct?"

"Correct. But won't I need my clothes and kit here?"

"You are not going anywhere until we get you clear of this. New kit and clothes are what will be delivered to you over the next ninety minutes. In addition, each night at 7 PM we'll bring you dinner, and groceries for the next day's breakfast and lunch."

"Wow, all right."

"You can use the internet only with your VPN to try to fix your credit card, email, messaging app accounts, and assorted banking challenges. But for the next few days, please do with new accounts only, even if you get the old ones restored. Clear?"

"Yes."

"There is a solicitor's phone number and contact details in the envelope, as well as my direct line. If you get into trouble at any time, dial the conference call number—it is the only number that's been programmed into your soon-to-be-delivered iPhone. The solicitor also wants to help you make headway on restoring your life. Call her directly as soon as the phone is delivered. It is our assumption that MI5 has been trying to ring you since you lost their tail with lovely Monique and your tracking went off-line. Be prepared to have a strong cover story when they reach you. You've done this a million times, I am sure. I am only giving you reminders of solid craft work."

Ralph sat stone-faced, deep in concentration. His mind was racing, but in his professional life he often needed to play the part of the smartest guy in the room, even when he wasn't. He decided this was definitely one of those times. "Right. Anything else?"

"If we are lucky, this will be cleared up in twelve hours or less. If we aren't, we devise new plans."

"Yes." Ralph wished he was as confident as the façade he was giving Sam.

"When I come get you after checking you in, I think you ought to bend your knees, round your shoulders, and stoop like you're eighty-years-old. That's your cover, by the way. Eccentric old gentleman wanting to hide from his squabbling family. There are CCTV cameras over every inch of London, so sell them on your walk to you room, okay?"

"Roger that."

"I'll be back in a flash."

Sam left and was back in under 120 seconds. He opened the door, and Ralph exited the car. Ralph took his time getting to the building, walking stooped and slowly. Once inside, he looked around for the elevator. There wasn't one. Ralph slowly walked up the stairs to the penthouse apartment, which took up the entire fourth floor. It was a spectacular apartment. Not only comfortable but elegant, with great art on the walls and a library with overstuffed chairs. The kitchen had every tool that Ralph could imagine.

"Out of curiosity, what does this apartment cost Mr. Warn?"

"About three grand?"

"A week?"

"A night."

"Ah. Well. That's nice." Ralph was wondering if he needed to pay Tom back at some time, and why he couldn't go to the Mews Hotel at a hundred quid a night.

Sam handed Ralph a bulky envelope. "The cash and passport are only for emergencies, which, if we're lucky, you won't need. Your wife is our highest priority. We'll find her soon. Call if you need anything." And then Sam was gone.

❧

Ralph walked through the apartment, exploring each room. It was basically a three-bedroom, two-bath flat, with a dining room and library. He opened the envelope. There was a passport, a credit card, and three wads of cash. Pounds, Euros, and greenbacks. Ralph did a quick look at the credit card and passport—they used the same name: Scott Stiffler. There was also a Post-it note stuck to the MasterCard, specifying a PIN of 4321. The wads of cash were in bundles of 20,000. He sat down and took a deep breath. He was in over his head, but at least he now had options.

Over the next ninety minutes, Ralph's doorbell rang eight times. The first delivery was an iPhone and Mac-Book. As soon as they were activated, Ralph called his new solicitor. She was impressively efficient—she had already gathered Jen's flight details and Social Security number. Ralph knew she was in a conference room, as she was heard delegating tasks to her many minions. Then the solicitor requested Ralph's Social Security number, bank information, and email account details. He provided, and then she rang off.

While Ralph was on the phone, someone else was trying to get through. The caller ID was the Intercontinental Hotel. As soon as he got off the phone with the solicitor, it rang again.

"Ralph speaking."

"Mr. Gibsen. Where are you right now?"

"Who is this please?"

"This is the officer you spent six hours with this morning."

"You've not given me your name. Would you like to do so now, or would you like me to give you one instead?"

"That's not really your concern at this moment."

"Then I'll call you Nigel."

"My name is not Nigel. You may call me Officer."

"That's kind of rude. What is your real name please? If you won't tell me, then it is going to be Nigel." Now that Ralph was not under this man's direct control, he wanted him to be uncomfortable. Uncomfortable people often make mistakes.

"That's none of your bloody business. Where are you now?"

"Nigel, that language isn't appreciated. It is entirely unprofessional. Are you recording this call? Will your boss appreciate that outburst?"

"Listen you smarmy twat—"

Ralph hung up on Nigel.

The phone rang six more times before Ralph decided to answer it again.

"Hi Nigel. Going to play nice or call me a twat again?"

"If you hang up on me again, I'll string you up—"

Ralph hung up.

Nigel waited about ten minutes before he called again. "Hi Nigel."

"Mr. Gibsen. Please do not push your luck."

"Nigel, what is your real name?"

"I am not prepared to give you that."

"You want my cooperation, yet you don't want to offer me any. Does that ever work for you in the real world?"

Nigel hesitated. "You need to understand I am 100% in control."

Ralph hung up again.

This time when the phone rang Ralph said, "No one is 100% in control, Nigel. I can work with you, or I can work against you. Your choice. What is your real name? I'm sitting in front of my new computer and I am going to Google it to ensure we are telling each other the truth."

"How did you get a computer? And how did you get a room without a passport?"

"What's your real name, Nigel?"

Nigel again hesitated. "Your games are going to get you into a world of hurt."

"Is this a threat, Nigel?"

Silence.

"If you aren't there, I am going to hang up again, Nigel."

"This is bollocks."

"Maybe to you, Nigel, but I am not playing games. I have cooperated entirely thus far. I am establishing that if you require my further cooperation, then I'd like the same cooperation from you."

"That's not how this works."

Ralph was silent.

"Did that muppet hang up again?" Nigel asked his team.

"No I think he's still on the line," said someone else who was also on the line. More silence.

"My name is Officer Nigel Vorly."

"Nigel? Really? How did I guess that? Thanks for sharing, Nigel. I am at the Mayfair Intercontinental Hotel. Didn't you call me here?"

"The hotel is not allowing us to get to your room. We want to see you. Right now."

"That's not going to happen. I've had some guy on your team put his finger or maybe it was fingers up my butt, and I am taking a long bath. That's uncomfortable stuff you guys are peddling. And apparently you'll need a warrant to break into my room without my permission."

"You disappeared from our surveillance for seventeen minutes after your lunch. How did you do that?"

"Have you looked for my wife? Do you know if she's safe?"

Silence. "We do not know where she is." More silence. "We think she is in country, but we did not see her in the Arrivals area via CCTV recordings when she was supposed to be there."

"I didn't realize I was under your surveillance. When I left Heathrow, I went to the hotel. I was unable to check in because you have my passports and my credit cards are not working. Thereafter, I went to have lunch at a favorite Mayfair restaurant and saw a friend. He secured me a room. As I am his guest, apparently, the hotel did not need my passport. I have no idea when those seventeen missing minutes occurred, but perhaps you can tell me more about your broken surveillance when you deliver my passports and kit back to me?"

Silence.

"How did you get a computer and connectivity?"

"If you would have listened to me as to what I do for a living, you would have known I help small tech companies get bigger. Over the years, I have helped Apple. They sent me a laptop and iPhone for my use when I asked. When will I get my passports and kit back please?"

"When we damn well want to give them back."

"That's not entirely true, now is it, Nigel?"

Silence.

"I have employed a solicitor and she tells me that you can hold my passports and kit for twenty-four hours. Unless, of course, you arrest me using Section 41 of the Terrorism Act. Then you can hold them until the trial. But that will put an enormous amount of scrutiny on the incident. My solicitor has already taken my statement and is preparing a press briefing. She has a request within your organizations for the CCTV footage, which is in the public domain. Unless, of course, you make that arrest. Apparently, she's a personal friend of your Prime Minister. And she says that the Prime Minister of the UK is trying desperately to recruit entrepreneurs and Venture Capitalists like myself to come to London and sprinkle our pixie dust. She believes if this is a Terrorism Act arrest, the PM will take an instant interest in the case, as it may have a chilling effect on efforts to bring growth to the UK. But, hey—what do I know? Didn't you call me a 'muppet' earlier?"

"I did not."

"We both know this is a recorded call, and I'm guessing it's discoverable, so let's not try to bluff and bluster, okay?"

A heartbeat or two. "I apologize for calling you a muppet."

"Apology accepted."

"When can we see you?"

"I'm willing to meet when you're ready to give me back my kit. I think that'll be tomorrow morning, about 10AM, correct?"

Silence. "We really would like to see you now." Nigel was trying very hard to be polite.

"Sorry, but I'm currently indisposed because my anus hurts due to your rough treatment. Funny, that would be the most probable headline in the tabloids in the morning, wouldn't it? I'll have to call my solicitor with the press briefing headline immediately after we bid goodnight to each other, Nigel." Ralph knew he was playing a dangerous game of chicken, but sometimes that's the game one was forced to play.

"We expect to see you at the Arrivals area of Terminal 5 at 10 AM sharp."

"Ah, well, that'd be a problem, as I have run out of cash and my credit cards all have been put on hold. As I do not have a passport, I cannot exchange currencies. Getting to you will therefore be difficult. Might I tempt you with breakfast here at the hotel instead? My treat? I promise to share much of what I've learned, after you have given me my kit, of course."

Silence. "Please hold."

Ralph waited for about three minutes. The on-hold music was stress inducing.

"Mr. Gibsen. That was my boss's boss on the phone for me. Apparently, your solicitor was able to reach her in very short order. We will be providing your computer, two phones, and four passports to you as soon as you desire. We could agree to breakfast at your hotel tomorrow morning at 10 AM, if you are in no hurry. As we are government employees pursuing an official investigation, we cannot allow you to pay for our breakfast." The officer was sounding like a scolded puppy.

"Cool, I shall see you tomorrow. I do want to apologize. I feel like I treated you without the respect you deserve. But you didn't leave me much wiggle room but to act as I did."

"You've been a right-bastard."

"If the shoe was on the other foot, would you have done anything differently?"

"Hell, yes. I would have known the consequences of messing about with this security force. But then again, you seem to have friends in high places, so maybe I would have done the same as you. Someday, I'd love to get the straight story from you, especially how you convinced that waitress to provide such a complete distraction."

"As soon as I learn the fulsome story, I'll give it to you."

Ralph politely asked one last time about any further information they might have on Jen. They said they didn't, and then they rang off.

He was wiped out but couldn't sleep because of worry. At 9:35 PM, Ralph's phone buzzed. He picked it up and saw a SMS from Jen.

"Landed. Wahoo! On the runway safely. LU and see you soon!"

He immediately called the conference call number Sam had provided. Sam and the solicitor answered within moments. Ralph told them about the SMS. As they discussed Ralph's conversation with Nigel and the logistics of getting Jen from the airport, Ralph also looked at United's website. There were no United flights from the West Coast of the U.S. that arrived within four hours of Jen's SMS. Sam must have been doing the same thing, as he mentioned the same within another ninety seconds.

"Let's leave that discussion for another time," Ralph responded. "How can we get Jen here without bringing the entire MI5 to my door until tomorrow?"

Sam said he could handle it—three of his cars were converging on the airport to provide diversion to anyone following her, two of which would take Jen's bags to the Intercontinental, and the other would bring Jen to Maddox Street, after a license plate switch or two. Ralph's job was to convince Jen that the car and hotel switch wasn't inappropriate.

Ralph called Jen's phone. "Sweetness! Welcome to lovely London."

"Hi, honey. Are you and the driver here?"

"Not yet. But the line for immigration and waiting for your bags will take you at least an hour, I'm sure."

"Maybe I can do it faster than that. What's your best time?"

"Maybe. But the driver won't be there for a few minutes. Take your time."

"What?"

"Small mixup. Probably my fault. But we thought you were coming in twelve hours ago."

"I did. And then I had to meet some clients, and got delayed. Didn't you get my SMS?"

"I don't think I did."

"Oh shit. I am sorry. Anyway I have arranged for a driver to pick me up."

"Well, I think I met that guy twelve hours ago. He's long gone. And now I've arranged a guy named Sam to come get you. He's about fifteen minutes out. You'll not have to wait much at all, okay?"

"All right. Thanks, I think. I'll meet Sam at the T5 Arrivals area. Ah, you sound stressed, is everything okay?"

"I've had a rough day. Let Sam get you and then we can talk about it here, okay? We've moved hotels, and there's something with the cars—you'll need to change cars for some reason. Just go with it, all right?"

"Oooookay. But just give me a few details, I can prepare myself."

Ralph paused. "I think we … might be under attack for something I'm doing at work. Someone seems to want to shut us down. Let's talk more when you get here."

"You're so dramatic, Ralph. You make me laugh."

"Well, it'll be interesting to see if your credit cards and other stuff work."

"What? That's crazy. Did you call the accountant?"

"We've got someone working it. But for now, please follow Sam's directions."

"All right, this is weird. But tell me how you know Sam."

"He's a friend of a friend. He's made my life bearable today."

"Okay. Talk to you soon. I love you."

"Love you, too."

Ralph smiled, but then he remembered something. He missed a SMS. But she hadn't gotten his? If he didn't trust his wife, this would be something that'd require more thought. But for now, he was just glad she was safe.

∽

When Jen got to the Maddox Street hotel, Ralph hugged her fiercely. She was abundantly tired, and she crumpled onto the comfy couch before even looking around the apartment. Ralph noticed that her left cheek had a slight abrasion, which she had tried to conceal with foundation. She was asleep in an instant.

❧

The next morning, after sleeping well, Ralph walked to the Intercontinental for breakfast with Nigel. Sam followed discreetly behind. Jen had woken moments before Ralph left, and decided she needed to shower and get ready. She had planned to spend the rest of the morning calling the banks, but fortunately the solicitor had nearly everything restored before they were awake.

The breakfast with Nigel was uneventful. He walked into the hotel lobby, handed Ralph his passports, phones, and computer, thanked him for the offer of breakfast, and excused himself. He needed to get back to work. Sam took the passports and phones and laptop from Ralph, and threw them in his car's Faraday cage. He promised to get them cleaned and returned to Ralph later that afternoon.

The solicitor continued to work her magic, and by noon the following day, Ralph and Jen's lives were back to normal. Almost as if nothing had happened.

Jen made a few apologetic comments about her change of plans at the airport, but was terribly excited to be back in London, and in such a lovely place Ralph was quickly swept up in her verve and enthusiasm. And soon life resumed.

Chapter 38

"You seem to be a little down. Everything okay?" Peterson asked. Peterson and Ralph enjoyed coffee together every few weeks. They shared stories, most often stories about their own lives. Silicon Valley can be lonely, as often people outside Silicon Valley can't relate to the speed, audaciousness and sometime sheer stupidity of the lifestyle. Peterson had just taken a new female friend on a trip. They flew to South Africa, bought a small six-seater Cessna, and travelled north taking six months and adding 850 hours to the plane's engine. They arrived in Southern France, got bored and ventured back to the Central Coast of California. Ralph was envious of the adventure, but loved that Peterson was re-energized.

"I've missed you man." Ralph paused. "And a few things have gotten a little weird."

"I've missed you, too. And I am assuming what you are talking about is more weird than normal weird, or you wouldn't have mentioned it, right?"

"Yeah. It is significantly weirder than you spending $70,000 to acquire an oven in France to learn how to make real baguettes."

"That's not really that weird, is it?"

"Not to you or I, but the rest of the world might raise an eyebrow."

"I guess I am okay with that. Then, on 'our' scale of one to ten, with buying a humidifying bread oven being, say, a 'two,' and Putin buying a U.S. election being a 'nine,' where are you?"

"Yeah. Fair question. I think I'm at a solid 'seven,' or maybe even a 'light-eight.'"

"That's got my attention. You tend to be pretty conservative with your scores. I'm now sitting forward to listen carefully. Tell me of your weirdness Ralph."

And because he had practiced the explanation of his situation in his head a few times, Ralph spoke for ten minutes without interruption or fear of judgment. He explained the Z-Prize EdTech program and the intercepted communications. He described the opportunity for the tech's misuse. He relayed his concerns with the EdTech investors, McKenna, Eva, his mom, and even his wife. He talked about his first series of actions to stop the misuse of the project, and the ensuing couple of days of hell in London. He outlined his need to find his "network" and drive to a solution.

Peterson listened carefully. He asked a few clarifying questions, mostly about the potential for the misuse of the tech. Then he asked, "How many bosses do you have in your professional life right now?"

"Hundreds it seems. Everyone is my boss. My investors, the startup founders where I help out, the not-for profit project teams. My wife. They are all my bosses."

"And how many of them, do you think, would think they're your boss?"

Ralph paused. "They'd probably view me as a partner."

"Exactly, you view them as your bosses because you subscribe to the notion that they are all internal customers—hence your bosses. But to them, I think they'd view you as *their* boss—maybe not their only boss—and they are appreciative as the recipients of your service."

"I might be confused."

"No, you are not confused. I've just explained that you and I are the bosses you're probably looking for."

"Oh. No. Well, yeah, maybe."

"I stand ready to help, by the way. Give me a few days to think about it."

"Cool, thanks."

"Now let's talk about where we are going to source the coarse ground wheat for the new baguettes."

Chapter 39

A week after the Heathrow fiasco, Jen and Ralph were back in Northern California at a grocery store picking up something for dinner. When they saw their smartphones blowing up with text messages, they knew something had happened.

Ralph's mother had passed away.

Ralph doesn't remember much of that evening, other than the feeling of gratefulness as hundreds of people were sending their love and support.

༄

A few weeks later, at Bubsy's life celebration, Ralph stood in front of hundreds of friends and strangers, telling the story of the old fish talking to the two young fish.

"The old fish asks, 'Isn't the water glorious today?' The young fish look at each other like the older fish had lost his mind. 'What is that guy talking about?' they ask each other quietly. 'And what the hell is water?'"

Bubsy always loved that story. She felt she appreciated and often understood her surroundings better than many. The three or four hundred souls that had over-filled the Unitarian Universalist Church on Cape Cod all shook their heads knowingly and wiped away their tears. More than a handful had heard this story before.

In the receiving line, Ralph was a teary mess, but pleased to meet many of his mother's friends. Everyone was kind and loving in their memories. Ralph was moved that so many had been positively affected by his mother, even when the connection wasn't entirely obvious. People had traveled from all over the world. And three things genuinely surprised him: 1) how often people told him that they were willing to help in any way his family needed—it was a constant theme; 2) Tommy the Taiwanese hairstylist sobbed for the entire ninety minutes of the remembrance; and 3) just how far everyone else stayed proximately away from McKenna and his girlfriend. Only Peterson spent time with the shunned couple.

Chapter 40

"Guilliam, pick up the damn phone!" Ralph yelled.

The phone had gone to the answering machine, but Ralph was certain his brother was screening his calls.

"Dammit, pick up the damn phone you troglodyte." Ralph loved his little brother, but they lived at two different speeds.

"Speak." Gil had a huge IQ and a nearly eidetic memory. He also didn't suffer fools. And if he had been born within the last twenty years, might have been diagnosed on the spectrum of Asperger's.

"You're ugly and your mother dresses you funny." Ralph was one of those guys who didn't often say "I love you" to other men—he did so by insulting them and knowing that the recipient knew the appropriate translation.

"According to most, we look remarkably alike, and our mother dressed us both, and I inherited most of my clothes from my older brother. What exactly does that say about you?"

Ralph could not win an argument with his little brother. He moved the discussion along. "Crazy thought. Do you think our mother could have been a trainer of spies?"

"Sure. She had very strong passion and ideals. She had great intellect, and loved to teach. She had access to an enormous number of diverse students." Gil paused for three beats. "Yes, that would make sense."

"What?"

"Ralph, how many people do you know who have a minimum of ten visiting guests every day, and on holidays like Thanksgiving and Christmas, twice or three times that amount?"

"Bubsy was popular. She was the social queen. She dispensed advice and wisdom to those who asked. She did crafts or a bit of writing with the local hoi polloi. But a spy?"

"And sometimes the international hoi polloi. You know she used your Barn for maybe a dozen group meetings a week? Can't say I every gave this much thought, but I am not the least bit surprised."

"Hold on. How can you say that? This was our mother. She surrounded herself with unique people. We used to call these gatherings 'the land of misfit toys,' remember?"

"And who suspects the misfits? No one. And who better to lead these folks. People like Bubsy."

Ralph thought about this for a few moments.

"Ralph, I am busy with a nine-year-old Chinese girl who is kicking my ass in Go. She has a 192 IQ. Do you need me for this discussion, or can you now figure it out on your own?"

"A Chinese girl? What?"

"On the computer. We play games to stretch her intellect and problem-solving skills."

"Who is we?"

"I don't know. People like myself on the internet that ask for help. You realize I am different than many humans, right? And the internet is a great way for people like me to hang out with others that have similar psyches. I am drawn to people like myself."

"Okay, I get it. One last question. If I wanted to connect with Bubsy's old spy boss, how would you suggest I do that?"

"Can you imagine *Bubsy* having a boss? That's a funny thought."

"Okay, you're probably right. She was probably the leader. So then how do I connect with the person who got her job?"

Gil sighed. "Sometimes, things that are frightfully obvious … you just miss. It shocks me. Let me ask you a significant question: What if *you* are now in charge?"

"But …"

"Think about it, older brother. I love you too, even when you're an idiot." And Gil rang off.

It took a few moments to sink in. But after the third or fourth time being told he was the person in charge, Ralph began to seriously contemplate the possibility. He was surprised that it wasn't an entirely uncomfortable proposition, but he'd need to adapt quickly. And at that moment, he mentally committed to playing this hand with his "new team" to the best of his ability.

Chapter 41

Ralph was on a series of flights. He knew it was obnoxious, but he needed to move fast. As he walked by a group of Chinese businessmen at the Istanbul airport, he said, "Tell Eva to call me ASAP."

They looked at him like he might be crazy.

On one of his flights, he sat next to a woman of Asian ancestry. "I humbly apologize, but I need Eva to call me right away."

"Who is Eva?" she responded. The woman slid as far away from Ralph as she possibly could.

The flight attendant had a pin that signified she spoke Chinese. Ralph asked as kindly as he could, "Would you kindly tell Eva to call me when we land?"

After landing, Ralph turned on his phone on the runway, and it immediately rang.

"Holy shit, Ralph. Size six. I've offered you my contact details a dozen times. What's so damn important that you decided to use the intercom at the airport to get me to call you?"

"What's size six?"

"My ring finger, in case you've decided to buy me a Tiffany diamond ring. You can finally see me naked."

"Oh."

"Back to business, Ralph. Stop visualizing me naked. That's creepy. What's going on?"

"I am thinking about conducting an auction for the stuff we've been talking about—I have a starting bid of one billion dollars and highest bidder wins all."

"What? Can you even do that?"

"Do I need to repeat myself?"

"No, I guess I'm just surprised."

"Okay. Can you pass this to your bosses please?"

"Ralph, you realize my bosses aren't going to like the auction format. It may upset …" She paused. "Oh."

"Yes."

"Got it. I think. Okay, I'll report exactly what you told me. You are 'thinking' about conducting an auction."

"Exactly."

"I'll be in touch. In the meantime, I'll need access to the most recent results."

"Agreed."

"And I'll SMS you my contact details. Do me a favor, don't do that again, okay? You scared quite a few people today."

Ralph rang off. He was threatening to sell something he didn't own. Something sure to make people take notice. And if he had learned anything in his career, it was that bluffing confidence often worked.

☙❧

"Hey McKenna. It's Ralph."

"Yes. I see that. What do I owe the pleasure of this call?"

"Not a social call. I need to tell you that I'm in the process of considering an auction for the data to build the EdTech tool."

"But I thought …"

"Yes, I know."

"But it'll cause …"

"Yes, I know."

McKenna took twenty seconds before speaking. "You've decided to wear your big boy pants today. You understand that this a highly risky proposition."

"Yes."

"And as an auction, if they can't win, they'll do everything they can to destroy it."

"Yes."

"And you."

"Tell your minders. Please."

And for once in his life, Ralph was the first to ring-off.

⸎

"Hey Peterson, I need a favor. I think I've found a way you can help me. I need to make it known that I have a really hot start-up that'll change the way digital advertising works. Can you hit up Google and Facebook Ventures? Tell them you heard that I'm taking offers for investment. Selling 20-33% of the new company for the highest bid."

"Interesting. Who is going to hypothetically run this company?"

"Hoping I could convince you to run it."

"Well, I could be a co-founder."

"But you understand…."

"Of course, I understand. Neither of us really wants to work that hard. But we'll need to make it look like we want it. Maybe need to rush to convert one of my farm's buildings into an office."

"I was thinking about selling a story to investors that we got frustrated with the lack of consistency with the fMRI approach, and have decided to use the brain interface approach via the iris. And our customer focus is the consumer for advertising—not education and kids. What do you think?"

"I think we'll create a bidding war."

"You'll need to tell Facebook and Google that we need harsh Non-Disclosure Agreements and everything we talk about is of the utmost secrecy."

"That'll mean that everyone in the Valley will know about it in milliseconds."

"And if we refuse to talk about it to the insider press—specifically Ina and Kara—then we'll get maximum coverage. Feeding frenzy."

"I'll put together a few slides and call a few people."

"Perfect."

"You realize this may damage your reputation, when found out."

"When it is found out, you need to promise you'll blame me for the debacle, okay?" Ralph asked.

"We'll see."

"No seriously."

"So you've decided we are to be the men that you were looking for. Brilliant. I'm in."

တ

"Ned, can you convince a few hundred people to throw some shade on this EdTech idea—specifically the lack of consistency?"

"Sure. I've got a few speeches coming up."

"And I want to make you a board member of a new start-up company. Except it isn't a real company."

"Make sure I get some stock options."

"Sure, plenty of stock options for a company that won't do anything, fine. The story you need to convey is the tool still lacks specificity. Hence, Timmy Junior might be looking at Sally Junior's bra strap and he registers a new memory. The tool today can't tell the difference between the bra strap and a differential equation in Algebra."

"Is that really the case?"

"I'm certain it's something that can be solved, but at this time, it's fuzzy. Spread some fear, uncertainty and doubt that it won't work."

"Wow. You're stepping up to take your mom's role. Good for you."

"I'm uncertain of everything Ned, and I mean everything. But someone has got to do something."

"Well self-actualized. Stay safe out there."

∽

The religious singing started when they arrived at Ben Gurion Airport, outside Tel Aviv. As Ralph deplaned onto the stairs to the tarmac, he was met by a person holding a sign with his name. All the plane's other occupants were pushed onto a bus, and Ralph was encouraged to a black car. The man holding the sign didn't respond to Ralph's questions, but pointed to the car. The sign holder opened the rear passenger door, but Ralph had opened the front passenger door and was sliding the passenger's seat back. He nodded to the driver to get his approval and the driver nodded back. Ralph sat down and the driver asked for his passport.

"Can I ask what this is about?"

The man handed the passport back to Ralph. "Just going to drop you off with the rest of the passengers in thirty seconds. I wanted to inform you that the State of Israel is interested in participating in the auction you are conducting."

"Good to know."

"You'll send us the prospectus?"

"Yes. To where?"

He handed Ralph a card with an innocuous Gmail address. "You know your maternal grandmother was Jewish? She was adopted by a Christian Missionary, but it'd be appropriate if you gave that fact some consideration."

"Okay."

"And if we think the auction will be won by one of our neighbors, we'll do our best to destroy the technology and all those who created it."

"I understand. This is just business. I suggest you bid aggressively."

"Mr. Gibsen, you don't have the reputation of being a person that ignores their values."

"Well, if Israel wins the auction, then you will use the tool appropriately, correct?"

"Speaking unofficially, it is my opinion that governments are not the most thoughtful and responsible entities. Any government can have an orange president."

"Your point is well taken. Perhaps then I give it to the world?"

"Then it has little value."

"There are many options."

"Governments dislike too many options. Makes for awkward solutions."

They reached the terminal just ahead of the bus with the other passengers. "Go in peace, Ralph."

"And to you." Ralph joined the rest of the plane's passengers in the immigration queue. Then he stopped and ran back to the Mossad agent. "Hey! Stop!"

The agent rolled down his window as Ralph jogged the few steps to the car.

"Was Peterson an agent of yours?" Ralph asked.

The man's face broke just enough for Ralph to know it was so. "I do not know anyone by that name."

Ralph paused, thinking fast. "If your government wants to participate, you'll first need to make it right with Peterson. Before you'll get to bid. Understood?"

The man considered playing dumb. But he looked carefully at Ralph's face. In the end, he nodded minutely, and then drove away.

♂♀

"Hey Ralph, there are a few gentlemen in the lobby to meet with you." Ralph's assistant Mika looked apologetic and slightly confused.

"I thought we blocked out this morning. I need to work on the Board of Directors presentation."

"We did. They just showed up. They have no appointment, but they are scaring the receptionist because they are carrying handguns in their jackets."

"What? Let's call the police, right now."

"Okay. What about Michele at the front desk?"

"I'll go get her. You call the police. Send a priority Slack message to keep our team away from the lobby and first floor—tell them it's a potential emergency."

Ralph ran down the stairs. There were six imposing men in business attire and none of them were sitting. They were trying to wander around. Michele the receptionist was trying to keep them corralled. Two of them looked like they were standing guard at the front doors.

"Michele, Mika needs you upstairs right now." She seemed relieved to be asked to leave.

"They have no appointment and won't sign in. Hence, no Non-Disclosure Agreement," she said, opening the electronic door to go upstairs.

"Shall we move to a conference room?" Ralph asked with a weary smile. He was trying his best to keep them from wandering. Without an electronic card they wouldn't get far, but Ralph didn't want them making surveillance of the office and its layout.

"Our men will stand guard," the most imposing man said, mustering great authority.

"They'll join us in the conference room, or we'll do this meeting in this lobby."

"Unacceptable. We have information that we must convey in secrecy."

Ralph sat down in the lobby and pointed his Smartphone at the man who was pretending to be the leader. He took the man's picture.

"What are you doing?" The man was aghast. Others covered their faces as Ralph pointed his Smartphone's camera at each. He noticed the youngest member nod slightly at the blustering man.

"Please stop taking our pictures. We are important diplomats and you...."

Ralph kept taking pictures.

"Yes, we agree to move to your conference room. All of us."

They all moved in the direction Ralph pointed. Ralph opened the door of the conference room and shepherded everyone in. One of the men asked to use the men's toilet. Ralph suggested that he could, but that Ralph would need to join him. The man involuntarily looked at the youngest member of the team. The man declined the accompaniment and sat down.

"What part of the Gulf are you from?" Ralph asked.

The men all adjusted their chairs. And shifted their suit jackets. Everyone looked uncomfortable. Things were not going to plan.

Ralph stood, introduced himself, and handed his card to the youngest member of the delegation. He offered to shake his hand. He offered no business cards to any other member of the delegation. But the big-bluster man was trying to get Ralph to shake his hand.

"We are a team of businessmen from Kingdom of Saudi Arabia's Ford dealerships."

Ralph started to laugh. One of the men slid a business card across the table.

"You are treating us very rudely. We are important members of the international community and you must treat us with respect."

"Really? Respect is earned, not demanded in this culture—more so in Silicon Valley." Ralph appeared to study his phone. "What is your name?"

"It, it is not important," the blustering man stammered.

"I know who you are. I am looking at your Facebook account. How is it that a member of the Saudi military forces has access to Facebook? Isn't that illegal in the KSA?"

"That is not my account!"

Members of the delegation were obviously caught off guard, and three conversations started as each decided to quickly cover their own asses.

Ralph stared at the youngest and nodded. "I trust you are all using my product to break the censorship of your government." This statement caused bedlam. Voices raised and the word "sedition" was tossed about.

The youngest man held up his hand. Silence was immediate.

Ralph stared at the young Saudi and asked, "Can we speak privately?"

There was more outrage and dissent. And then silence when the young man nodded his assent.

The blustering one switched to Arabic, "Your Majesty, we cannot protect you if you are alone with this camel fucker."

"Why does everyone call me a camel fucker? I've never even seen one of these majestic beasts up close. And last time I was in your country, some people decided I needed a cavity search. Was it your finger up my asshole the last time I was there?" Ralph said in English.

Silence.

"May my team wait in your lobby?" the young prince asked.

"I'd greatly prefer they wait in their armored Denalis. I'll open the shades of this conference room. They'll be able to see that you'll remain safe."

The man nodded, and the men begrudgingly filed out of the conference room and then the building. A single police car arrived as they were getting into their black SUVs.

Ralph asked, "Do you need to go flash your diplomatic credentials at those cops?"

"No, a few of them are lesser royalty and have diplomatic passports as well. They'll be fine."

"Shall we start over? My name is Ralph." He held out his hand.

The young prince stood and shook it with a firm grip. "You can call me Al."

"How can I help you, Al?"

"Can I first apologize? That last bit was awkward and not my proudest moment. And the body cavity search— that's terribly awkward."

"Okay, whatever. No big deal, I guess." Ralph paused, and the prince shifted uncomfortably. "Did you go to school in Boston?"

"Best five years of my life." The prince smiled as he said it.

"Red Sox fan?"

"Pfffft. Of course. And I know you are as well, as I follow your Twitter feed."

"We look good for a long push into October."

"Dude, don't jinx us," Al said with conviction. "The kid Beninitendi has got such a sweet swing."

"Yeah, wicked." Ralph paused. "Can I ask a personal question?" The blinds were open and four more police cars had joined the originals. They were giving the Saudi team a major inspection over the handguns in their possession.

"Sure."

"It can't be easy living like you do. Guards, handguns, armored cars. Ever wished for something else?"

"I went to school at Harvard and London School of Economics. Most of my family has the same upbringing. I didn't want to go back to the Saudi Arabia after Boston and London. If I wasn't born into the family, I'd probably be working for you here."

"I think you'd be working with me, not for me. We can make it happen, you know."

The prince smiled. Moments of reflection passed.

"What are we doing here?" Ralph asked.

"We have heard you are auctioning off a new weapon. We want to make sure you know of our interest."

"Okay, noted."

"So, what is it?"

"What is what?"

"The weapon, what does it do?"

"It isn't really a weapon. It's really a sophisticated tool for making education more efficient. But a few people think it could be used as a weapon of mass persuasion."

"Can it?"

"I have no idea. I don't build weapons."

"Don't you come as part of the deal?"

"Hell no."

"Well, who's going to run this program?"

"Someone from the winning team. But not me, or anyone from any of my teams."

"Then it has very limited value to my country."

"Then don't bid."

"But there will be other bidders."

"Of course."

"How much would it cost us to hire you and a team?"

"I don't build weapons."

"There has got to be a number that would make you spend a few years with us. You'd live like a royal."

"Not interested. Thanks."

The prince paused. "Can we also buy that facial recognition tool you used on General El Kuwaiti?"

Ralph laughed. "I was totally bluffing. That app probably exists but it's next door at Facebook, not here."

"How did you know he had a Facebook account?"

"Everyone has a Facebook account."

"I'd probably have a lot to learn here working 'with' you."

"Come join us then."

"I've got responsibilities to my family and country. I need to transition our country's petroleum blessings to support the next few generations of Saudis."

"Why just the Saudis, and not the entire region?"

"That's the question I asked my parents when I was young. It is the only time I saw my father act irrationally. We'd need to get everyone else in the Gulf to submit to our rule, and that's not possible at this time."

"Respect is earned, not demanded."

"You are a dreamer, Ralph. What is it going to cost us to win the auction?"

"The Chinese have a 'stalking horse' offer at two billion dollars. But my guess is that the U.S., Germans, and Israelis will push the final number up to three to five times that amount. And I am not committing to sell it if I don't think the value is sufficient. I may start a company or something with it if I don't get the right deal."

"That's a significant amount of oil."

"Especially if Tesla moves the auto market and oil consumption decreases by two to three points. Then the price per barrel moves from near $60 a barrel to—what? $10 a barrel?"

"That'll never happen."

"You hope that won't happen. But if I was in your role, I'd forego bidding on this tool and spend as much money on building an entrepreneurial class of Gulf citizens as I could. But, then again, I am an idiot. I'm probably wrong."

Al paused. "I always love coming to the U.S. You are aggressively changing our world, and yet, first to admit you have no idea what you are doing."

"Sometimes the world works best that way, as none of us sees their world the same way as another."

"Please send us what you can for my team to examine. We'll need four months to study the proposal before we can bid."

"I'm planning to give everyone four days to bid."

"That's impossible. Our experts won't be able to drop what they are doing and make an educated offer in that time frame."

"Maybe you shouldn't be bidders then?"

"But we can't let this fall into someone else's hands. It could be used to take away our power."

"You'll figure it out."

"Ralph, give us two months—only two months?"

"This isn't really a negotiation, Al. The smart move is for you to tell your family that the money could be best used elsewhere to build the long-term viability of your region. You could be the change your region needs."

"You ask for far too much change. We can't." And Al closed down.

"Change is the only way I know to progress."

Al's eyes got hard and he looked out to his team. The police were putting handcuffed Saudi personnel into cop cars. It was obvious that there were quite a few flustered and curious humans in the melee.

"Can you tell the police to let my people go?"

"I'm just a businessman. They won't listen to me."

"But you control …?"

"No, I don't control the police. And if I were you, I'd hang in our office until they leave—or you'll also get to experience the backseat of a police car."

"But how will I get to my hotel?"

"I can get you an Uber? Maybe even a Tesla."

⟡

Ralph put the second part of the grand plan into motion. He contacted Eva's email and asked her to put her portion of their plan in motion. Then he called to make sure she got it. Ralph was surprised that she didn't flirt or even question his call. She just said "Yes" and rung off. He did the same with McKenna.

Over three weeks, Peterson and Ralph had acquired and experimented with a small robocaller. Robocallers were universally hated, but remarkably effective, which was why they were gaining in usage. In the more conservative "fly-over" states, 35% of the people robocalled listened to the entire message. And the credibility score of the content of these robocalls in these particular states was generally two to three times higher than the national average. After a few thousand outbound tests, and some creative tweaks, Peterson and Ralph had a script and hired a voice-over artist with rather few questions about who was paying his day rate fee. The voice-over artist sounded much like a certain orange president.

They had agreed to a series of recordings to target both red state voters and those on the fence. The caller-ID was programmed to say, "President Trump Reports." The computer server was set up in Ukraine and the downlink was in a small exchange in Montana. The server that made these outbound messages could accomplish 4,000 simultaneous calls per minute. Allowing for robodialling between the hours of 8 AM and 8 PM over three time zones, the call volume was about 3.6 million per day. After twelve days, the robocaller was dismantled and its hard-drive was thrown in the incinerator. The robocaller had completed more than 40M calls and had gotten 13M with positive feedback, i.e., people requesting more information be sent to them via email.

The script was straightforward and used the maxim of "the best lies carry a strong element of truth." The script told of an elite cabal of wealthy coastal liberal scientists pouring billions of dollars into an education-oriented, mind-warping machine that would ensure that every child grew up hating Christ, Ronald Reagan, and guns. These newly minted flag burners would believe the Clinton-cabal-nonsense as their absolute truth. The only way to stop this potential menace was to fight tooth and nail against computer controlled education reform by these blue-blooded socialists. With more than 13M positive responses, the robocall's content had been dutifully reported as fact by Breitbart, InfoWars, and all-pervasive Fox News.

Even Snopes was reporting the story as "Investigating Veracity Ongoing."

Ralph had also hired a few millennial graphic artists. They created some witty memes and peppered them on Facebook to traditional red state voters. These silly memes featured a lap-top carrying Hillary Clinton and her husband as they led thousands of wholesome children over a cliff. Others invoked a picture of a very white Jesus with a caption balloon saying that "no good Christian ever learned anything of value from a computer," and one that had a picture of an AK-47 that said, "liberals would stop at nothing to take good American's guns away, even using mind-warping computer programs as so-called educational tools."

Some of the memes were posted by fictitious right-wing groups Ralph invented and disseminated via Facebook's self-serve ad network using credit cards bought at drug stores using cash. Ralph invested about $5000 on this method on each of the three memes. And in a week's time, they had snowballed to more than 400M unique shares on all major social platforms. By the end of the first week, even *the Washington Post* and CNN were asking difficult questions to the Z-Prize team. Some government officials from both Germany and the UK had put forth initial legislation banning this new form of educational robo-learning.

But after only three weeks, the news and social media cycles had all but forgotten this once-threatening menace.

❧

Eva came through. Her team denigrated the credibility of some of the tool team's membership. The fur flew. Questionable tax returns, numerous pictures of meetings between competitors that shouldn't have happened, cross-dressing conservatives, self-professed vegans enjoying steaks. The Reddit and Twitter-fueled scandals caused significant embarrassment, but little real damage. The photo of Roger Phillips fondling his topless "niece" on his boat in Santa Cruz harbor was front and center in the Silicon Valley news media for a few days. There was talk of divorce lawyers and criminal investigations. But, after a few weeks, the scandalous news had blown by.

∽

McKenna's efforts focused on creating FUD—fear, uncertainty, and doubt—around the medical effects of computer-generated learning. McKenna found a researcher's decade-old research paper on the potential for a negative impact on a youth's evolving brain when staring into a computer screen for greater than six hours per day. McKenna anonymously paid the down-and-out researcher $2,500 to modify, enhance and re-submit his paper to scholarly journals as an update to his earlier work. McKenna supplied the new "data."

The fabricated data showed possibilities of long-term CTE brain damage, potential for brain cancer and, worse yet for the targeted audience, propensity for sexual deviancy. The major conservative news outlets covered the topic with verve. The talk radio folks had a field day. The internet was aghast with its repulsion. Apple, Samsung, Lenovo, Dell, and HP all vehemently denied the truth of this "study." They sent their experts to point out the flaws in the professor's analysis, and in turn delivered more convincing "real" data. But the news was complex, and hence didn't hold for more than two cable news cycles.

❧

Hiromi's team used its considerable influence with the editors of the women-oriented press corps. They raised further questions about machines potentially teaching children, and the ethics and values the machines might instill. The editors were respectful and gave her deference, but their commitment lacked conviction, as this wasn't seen as appropriate fare for their younger audiences.

❧

Ralph had a Z-Prize steering council meeting. He openly vented at the new efficacy data the tool was producing. The data was much less convincing, he said, now that it has gotten into further real world scenarios.

Ralph knew, of course, that this was mostly due to the random variance he had hacked into the results. But he appeared to be deeply disappointed, and pushed for the project to be paused and re-evaluated. He enumerated the public's resistance to the project. He loudly proclaimed that the controls for the tool's misuse were lacking or ineffectual.

Almost to a person, the committee voted to proceed—against Ralph's vehemence and best arguments. In no uncertain terms, tarnished members of the team fought for this imperfect project and voted to proceed.

Phillips, particularly, looked decidedly pleased that he was able to keep Ralph and his dissenting arguments at bay.

❧

"No backdoors were found." All three freelance contractors came back with the same reports. The information from Amir was either inaccurate or someone had gone to great trouble to ensure they weren't found. Sir Al Harris also sent him a sad-faced emoji via Skype and said, "Pen-tested the hell out of the thing, no holes. Stay well."

೧

Ned used his influence in front of some important educational and governmental audiences to draw negative attention to the tool and its potential misuse. In reviews of his talks, Ned was either ignored or blamed for being too old to understand the opportunity of the tool.

೧

With the assistance of some engineers in India, Tom Warn developed a Summer 2016 video of Putin advocating the use of the tool on the American public, especially in swing states. "The "deepfake" video's creators had built a recurrent neural network that captured hundreds of Putin's past speeches, copying his facial expressions and mouth movements for each unique sound. They then hired a Russian voice actor to mimic Putin for a scripted discussion with his aides. The engineers then morphed the actor's scripted voice onto the neural network and the program morphed a B-roll video of Putin's face into the exact movements of the script. The effect was photo-realistic and indistinguishable from the real thing.

Warn then released the video to Reddit, and within twenty-four hours the cable news stations had all given it coverage. The talking-head pundits all commented that the Russians didn't deny that the conversation might have taken place, but Putin joked that if Russia had used the tool, then they'd probably do so again today to convince everyone today that the new president was not "bought and paid-for" by the Russian government.

Within three news cycles, the story faded like many others.

cる

Ralph's appointment cancelled at the last minute. The CEO of the target partner based in NYC only wanted to talk with Ralph's portfolio company's CEO. Ralph thought that was asinine, but since he now had two hours free, he pulled out his Museum App on his iPhone and looked for the nearest fine arts museum. The Frick Museum was just up the road on East 70th on the Upper East Side of Manhattan. Prior to jumping in an Uber, Ralph bought a $4.95 chocolate chip cookie and reminded himself why he had always disliked this dirty, smug city.

Ralph was wandering the museum grounds when he felt someone touch his shoulder.

"We've paid your people. When will we get the product?" asked the young man with the heavy Russian accent and the beat up knapsack on his shoulder.

"What?"

"We've paid your people. When will we get the product?"

"I heard your question, I just have no idea what you're talking about. Who are you and which one of my companies sold you a product?"

"It doesn't matter who I am. We paid you, now we need the product."

"The accent doesn't sound real to me. I work with quite a few Russians."

"If you are trying to swindle us, we will make your family's life miserable."

"Let's try again, who are you? Which of my little start-up companies sold you something?"

"I am a representative of the Russian government and we bought the mind control formula from you."

Ralph started to laugh. "I think you are mistaken. Who did you pay?"

"Your people."

"I don't have people. Just myself. Who did you pay?"

"Just yourself?"

"Yes, and I have not received payment, from anyone … yet."

"But there are many bidders, yes?"

"Only one right now."

"A few million, yes?"

"Two billion."

"Oh. Shit."

"Your accent seems to have disappeared."

"So then you're not going to give it to me."

"Nope."

"Does it really control people's minds?"

"No, it doesn't."

"It doesn't?"

"Nope—it just knows if someone has learned something. And it keeps trying to teach until the target person does learn."

"My kids need that."

"That's what it was designed for. Do you really work for the Russians?"

The man paused and shrugged his shoulders. "They paid for my grad school after my parents immigrated here thirty years ago. I occasionally get asked to run favors. My uncle had some role in the FSB many years ago."

"Yeah. Okay. Are we done?"

"Yeah. What do I tell my people?"

"Tell them to bid more than two billion dollars if they want the tech."

"But it doesn't seem to do much beyond what a good teacher can do."

"Yeah, maybe. Maybe just a bit more efficiently."

"Okay. You must be a really good spy, because you are a really shitty salesman."

"Thanks."

"All right, I am outta here." The young man turned and left without even enjoying the art or architecture.

"Take care," Ralph called after him.

Ralph spent the next two hours learning about how Frick picked the art he bought, and how he built the house specifically to showcase the art. It was fascinating.

∽

In the end, there wasn't really much of an auction. Ralph sent a twenty-page PowerPoint presentation with the basics of the technology to those that had expressed interest. He shared the preliminary results and the most recent results. He postulated on the use cases for the technology, focusing advertising and education. The price tag of the technology via an auction process caused each nation to really think about the value of the tool. Most countries decided it wasn't of much value. Money could be deployed elsewhere. Some universities were given a small research grant to learn how to detect and counter any future tool usage.

The largest private equity investors are herd-like. Once one was skeptical, they all backed away. The mark of a great communicator is someone who can lead an audience (in this case investors) to the trough and then away from it—without them being aware they were being led. Peterson did just that.

The Z-Prize team became ultra-concerned about the potential misuse of the tool. They allowed Ralph to create significant fail-safe algorithms that would prevent the tool to be used for large groups. The team members were under no illusions that the tech wouldn't be reverse-engineered or modified sometime in the future, but for now they felt safe it would only be used for the intended purposes.

Epilogue

It was 2:30 AM in Central Moscow, and Ralph was dancing to some deep techno on a reinforced table at a club called Mendeleev. He'd just finished three or four flaming shots of Sambuca, his drink of choice as it burned off all of the alcohol. His Russian internet security partners were enjoying watching the Westerner loosen up. While Ralph was dancing on the table, someone looking to get his attention grabbed his left back pocket and ripped his pants. Ralph was having too much fun to notice. His plaid cotton Nordstrom boxers exposed, someone else pulled some more, and soon Ralph had a pocket-sized tear from his derrière to his calf. He never stopped dancing—until the bouncer threw him out of the bar for being indecent. He landed on the sidewalk and stayed there to collect himself.

Eva sat on the ground next to him. "I can't believe what a goofy dancer you are. You're going to need to take lessons before our wedding dance."

"What are you doing here?" Ralph asked between bursts of laughter.

McKenna sat on the other side of Ralph. "Dude, I think you stole some of my best dance moves."

"No way. I've spent a lifetime working on those." Ralph paused. "What are you guys doing here?"

"Aren't you happy to see us?" Eva asked.

Ralph checked his emotions. He was happy, excited, anxious, and scared. "Sure, but what are you doing here?"

"We're just here for a little celebration. Mission accomplished. Or maybe mission almost accomplished," McKenna joked.

"What? Are you kidding? Nothing I did worked. Every single thing I did backfired or was totally without the desired effect. I failed miserably." Ralph was suddenly sober.

"Well, you are a complete unadulterated chowdahead, that is a certainty," McKenna said.

"But even though you haven't yet bedded the leading lady—that's me by the way—you did earn the desired outcome. The tool is no longer going to be used as a weapon."

"But none of my efforts worked. I completely fucked up. Sure, the tool has become less-hyped. And maybe if we're all lucky it won't be used as a weapon for a year or two, but ..."

"That's all that most of us in this field hope for," McKenna interrupted. "You built a team. You had a plan. You executed the plan." He paused. "Hey look—we got some champagne. We should go watch the sun rise over the Moscow River." They pulled Ralph up off the curb. "Plus, that'll hopefully keep your large ass off the tables."

The evening culminated at 5:30 AM, after they finished the third bottle of cheap champagne on the bank of the Moscow River, just as the sun's first light gleamed off the golden domes of the Kremlin's many cathedrals.

❧

Ralph would never know if the efforts of his ad-hoc team had any real effect. About three months after he put his plan into action, the EdTech funder—Bill Koch—died in his sleep. The story was big news for a day or two, and then it wasn't.

And during this same time period, Roger Phillips, completely distracted with his wife's divorce proceedings, voluntarily inserted himself into a sex addict's rehab facility.

The media continued to grow concerned with the possibility of Artificial Intelligence taking over the world. A North Korean dictator kept trying to provoke anyone that would pay attention. Some starlet released another sex tape. The world moved on.

❧

"Ralph, stop telling people you may be a spy," Jen said for the umpteenth time. "It's embarrassing."

Ralph smiled. Sometimes, he thought, when a conspiracy theory is especially well received, it's only because the theory explains a complicated situation with relative ease. It's often easier for people to believe a powerful cabal of Go players are controlling their fate. But the truth is most often that the Go players are no smarter and no more in control of their environments than anyone else. And hence, complicated situations are only a result of an extremely complex environment and the will and whim of the participants.

"Well..." He thought carefully before asking, "Aren't *you* a spy?"

She snickered. "Of course I am. Now go help me make a drop to my top secret team." She stared, stone-faced.

"Uhm, what?"

"Take out the trash!" She laughed and handed him the kitchen trash bag.

"Yes, dear."

Ralph took the trash to the curb just as the garbage truck was arriving. When he turned to go inside, Ralph caught a glimpse of the driver's chunky gold sunglasses. He did a double take and thought, *Tommy?*

The End

Acknowledgments

This is absolutely a book of fiction. None of it is real. Nonetheless, some of my friends and family may see small portions of themselves in a few of the characters. Thanks for you being you.

Huge love to my lovely and fun GF/wife/boss Jen [damn, I meant to say Rhonda].

Big thanks to Editors: Randy Rosenthal and Leya Booth. Publisher: Steven Booth. Muses: Peterson Conway VIII, Brian Frazer, Bill Glasser, Scott Stiffler, Christopher Moore, Lisa Lutz, Carl Hiaasen, Neal Stephenson, Harlan Coben, Susie Bright, and Shelly King. Supporters, including Peter Loge, Jordy Berson, Vika Vendolina, Tanya Carecia, Raz Zia, Tim Martin, Eric Koh, Bobby Machinsky, Tobey, Teri and Aggie Fitch, Pat Peyton, Nancy Newson, Ted Hollingworth, Greg Payne, Greg Post, Gil Brent Vachon, David Rogers, Heidi Rogers-Wayman and Luke Wayman, Francis Corpuz, Nina Simon, Michael Gilligan, Marc Douthit, Brett Dewey and Gregoire Senthilles.

The teams at my portfolio companies teach me something new every day. Thank you. And to the woman in seat 3D for the yoga practice discussion, thanks. Seat 1C, sorry that you died after drinking my ginger ale.

Special thanks for all the inspiration and encouragement from my Mom, Bubsy.

Ralph and the Toll Guy Tragedy

At the end of the meeting, Ralph's host gave him a wearable device to evaluate for potential investment. As an angel investor in numerous start-ups, Ralph had worn more than a few entrepreneur's dreams on his wrist. This smartwatch had an integrated EKG and a defibrillator, in the unlikely event one's heart rate got irregular. The same Vietnamese entrepreneur also had watches in the prototype stage that monitored the bloodstream for various deficiencies, and injected hormones or other medicines when needed. This new tech, in the CEO's eyes, would make the world a better place.

To be polite, Ralph put the watch on his wrist as he exited the meeting room. Ralph thanked the start-up team and promised to follow up. The meeting room's attendees all stood at the lobby, waiting for the elevator. Seemingly at random intervals, someone would say something, and everyone would bow. Ralph hated this particular Asian custom. Due to his impostor syndrome issues, it made Ralph even more anxious and uncomfortable. Everyone had better things to do than wait for the elevator. The elevator took six minutes to arrive and Ralph had bowed seventeen times. When the elevator door opened, it was packed tighter than traffic on Highway 1 on a long holiday weekend. Ralph bowed deeply to his hosts, went for the emergency exit door next to the elevator, and headed down the stairs. His hosts were aghast and hollered, but Ralph just pushed onwards.

Ralph tried to remember what floor he was on. Was it seven or seventeen? Or seventy? He wasn't in Shanghai, Shenzhen or Beijing, so he was almost positive it wasn't seventy, but who knew? At least he was moving.

At the next landing, he learned it was twenty-seven. He was now on the twenty-sixth floor and was walking through what looked like someone's apartment. Awkwardly, at least for Ralph, the woman was watching a variety show on her mobile phone with the volume turned up loud while cooking some sort of greasy soup on a single gas burner. She looked surprised when Ralph passed, but immediately put her head back down to finish her show. Ralph noticed that each of this modern skyscraper's stairs was unique; each a non-uniform height. It took some concerted thought not to trip and tumble.

At each landing, Ralph walked into another family's makeshift home. Most were neat and clean, but a few were so crowded that people moved chairs so Ralph could pass by. One "home" had nine sets bunk beds in a space that might comfortably fit four cuddling people.

It took the pear-shaped Ralph about ten minutes to navigate the stairs and crowded landings. He laughed to himself when imagining the stories over dinner that would be told about the huge foreign man--Ralph was 6'4", 250 pounds with mocha-colored skin--traipsing through so many homes. When he arrived at the second story landing there was a man with a fist full of small currency. He held up his hand like he was expecting a toll. Ralph popped the smart watch into his hand.

"Be careful with this. I think it's a prototype," Ralph said in English.

The Vietnamese man quickly tucked the fancy blue-banded watch deep into his pocket and in-tone alone admonished Ralph in Vietnamese for disturbing his tenants. When Ralph finally stepped onto the ground floor lobby, he noticed that Eva had her back to him, her eyes glued to the elevator's doors.

Ralph decided he'd surprise her. As a covert agent for the Chinese government, one that often followed him around the globe at the direction of her bosses after he had somehow persuaded her to work off-script with him to solve a worldwide threat, she was always surprising him by showing up in the most-unexpected places. His turn. He smiled in anticipation. He poked her playfully under her rib cage on her right side. He planned to say in Mandarin, "Put your hands in the air," but he got out no more than two syllables before his world tilted and blurred and he was on the granite floor. His gonads stung, bile was at the back of his throat, there was blood pouring from his nose, and he was looking up the very short skirt of a tall, leggy, blue-black-haired beauty.

"Sweetie, you're not the first man to want to look up my skirt, I can assure you. But there are easier and much safer ways for you, okay?"

Ralph tried to sit up, but his once solid world was suddenly viscous, and he fell back and whacked his head.

"Has no one ever given you a self-defense course, Ralph?"

Ralph tried to shake his head no, but that only sent his world into a faster spin. Ralph's entire covert experience was one single foray a few months prior when he identified and then begrudgingly attempted to stop a dastardly plan to over-take the world.

Soon, two of Eva's teammates had lifted Ralph to his feet and were attempting to steady him and find something to mop the blood from his face.

"Who the fuck takes the stairs, Ralph? This is Asia—you probably saw fifty things you shouldn't have seen in that stairwell. You're also probably going to need a bunch of needles to ensure you don't catch anything."

"There were dozens of families living in that stairwell, Eva. Why?"

"Because people are poor, and they need a place to live. And no business tenant would ever think to take the stairs. Ever. So an entrepreneur, who doubles as the foreman of the cleaning staff, probably gets a few bucks for making the space available to those families. If the entrepreneur is smart, they probably kickback most of what they collect to the building's supervisor. That's often how these things work."

"No one's the wiser?"

"Until some knucklehead bursts down the stairwell because he can't stand a few moments of discomfort waiting with a bunch of suits for an elevator," she said, clearly annoyed.

"You're mad at me for that?"

"No, well, yes." Eva shook her head. "Hanging out with you gets my head all scrambled. You never follow the rules. All of these people will now need to find new places to live for the next few weeks. It'll be a huge pain in the ass. Jesus, Ralph, you're making me into someone who actually gives a shit."

Ralph smiled apologetically. "Should we go out and kill something? Maybe a nice chicken or pork for dinner?"

"Don't make fun of me, Ralph. I'll hurt you some more. I'm in no mood for your feeble charm. I'm grumpy—and horny. I haven't been with a man since I've been tasked with following you around these last three months, and it's starting to make me slightly crazy."

"Well, I can't really help you with that." Early on in their weird friendship, Ralph had been the recipient of Eva's professional seduction attempts. As a fifty-four year old, he had the maturity of a scared, seventeen-year-old virgin. And, in his twenty years of marriage to Jen, he had only fantasized about straying. In truth, he was more scared of Eva than turned on. "Maybe you can visit one of those spas where you can get a massage and a happy ending?"

"Ralph!" she said angrily. "Do I look like the kind of woman who needs to pay to get laid?"

"No of course not." Ralph was momentarily at a loss for words, as Eva was looking authentically offended. "I was only trying to be helpful. I'm really sorry, Eva, if I've offended you." He reached out and gave her shoulder an affectionate rub.

She leaned forward and gave him a kiss that lingered just a little too long. He pulled away with a jerk. She smiled. He blushed. "Don't you find me just a little attractive, Ralph?" He laughed nervously. "You did seem to find a few extra moments to stare at my legs while you were on the floor just a few minutes ago."

"Eva, come on. You know I think you're gorgeous. You're stunning. Really, really beautiful. Any man, or woman for that matter, would be thrilled to be with you, but you know I'm married to Jen. And I take that commitment seriously. If I wasn't...." But Ralph decided it best not to finish that sentence.

This time it was Eva's moment to blush. "You know Jen is not within eight thousand miles, and as I check your hotel room every night for sensors while you're asleep, I know we'd never be found out. Aren't you even slightly curious to find out if I'm a tiger or a pussy cat?"

"Wait—you come into my room when I'm asleep?"

"Just to make sure you're safe. Really. By the way, give me the stupid watch you just got from those fools looking for your investment. I need you never to wear that thing." She started to push Ralph out the lobby and toward her Mercedes Sprinter van.

Ralph was still disturbed by the thought of Eva in his hotel room each night. "I gave the watch to the 'toll guy' on the first-floor landing."

"What is a 'toll guy'?"

"The guy on the first floor who was renting space to all the people in the stairwell."

She nodded to one of her crew who was holding Ralph steady, and he shot back into the lobby and up the stairwell. Ralph didn't realize how wobbly he still was. The extra hands had been a steadying factor. Ralph attempted to climb into the van, but found it was still locked.

Just then, Eva's crew member came running toward them at full tilt. He was yelling in Mandarin. The van door flew open and Ralph found himself pushed to the floor. Eva was atop him and the helper jumped on top of her. The van accelerated more aggressively than Ralph would have imagined. He was in great discomfort, on the floor of the van with two people on top of him, and with some significant lateral G-forces as the vehicle weaved through traffic. Ralph flinched twice when two bullets pounded into the roof of the van. Ralph's discomfort increased dramatically when he realized that warm liquids were pouring over him and sloshing to the floor. But he shut his mouth and let the professionals do their job. In this melee he hoped he would feel Eva move or say she was okay. After less than three minutes, he felt the van scrub and hop the curb into a driveway. They came to a violent stop and he heard a heavy gate close. The liquid that was sloshing around the van while they were moving settled into the lowest spots on the van's floor, only a few inches from his head. Ralph knew some of the warm liquid was blood, as the color was brown red. He also smelt urine and burnt flesh.

After an impossibly long ten more seconds, he felt Eva move on top of him. Ralph let out an involuntary gasp of relief. But she was swearing in Mandarin. In moments, it became clear that a crew member had taken a bullet and was missing most of the left side of his frontal lobe. In his charred left hand was the watch that Ralph had worn only four minutes earlier, and it was barbecued almost to the point of being unrecognizable. Only the melted blue rubber wristband was the telltale.

"Okay, listen and follow my instructions carefully, Ralph. There's a penthouse apartment on the top floor of this building. Get upstairs quick. Lock yourself in. Don't open the door for anyone, not even me. I need you to find a way to stop the bleeding from your nose. Use a bag of ice on the bridge of your nose and some toilet paper up your nostrils. As soon as the flow stops, get into the shower. Throw your clothes and computer bag into the black garbage bag and send everything down the chute to the left of the toilet. Turn the shower water up hot. As hot as you can stand it for no less than 30 minutes. There are a few liters of rubbing alcohol and Listerine in the shower. Pour both all over yourself. Soak your hands and wrists in it. Then more hot water. Scrub hard—the explosive residue from the watch won't come off easily. There might be some fresh clothes or maybe just a robe for you to wear. Put them on and wait for us. Do not try to contact anyone. Sit tight. Can you do that for me?"

Ralph had a million questions, but he saw she had moved deftly into her most-professional mode, so he acknowledged his fears to himself, nodded his agreement, and started running up the stairs. The penthouse was at the top of four flights and the door was locked but had a fingerprint reader. Ralph was gobsmacked when his finger opened the lock. He replayed every instruction that Eva had spoken in his mind repeatedly and used great discipline to follow them without deviance.

After more than an hour, and without once looking out a curtained window, he heard the front door's lock release, and he girded himself for a fight.

Eva walked into the apartment in a white cotton bathrobe, similar to the one Ralph was wearing. She ducked easily when the floor lamp Ralph threw at the apartment's intruder sailed over her head.

"Oh shit, I'm so sorry, Eva," he blurted out before the lamp had fully landed on the floor. He had half a roll of toilet paper up his nose to staunch the earlier bleeding. He sounded like he had the worst head cold imaginable.

She stepped over the busted floor lamp with a pronounced limp. Ralph could only now see the very thick bandage wrapped around most of her calf. She reopened the door to tell the newly installed guards with machine guns that they were all okay.

"We save your life and you throw a floor lamp at me?"

"Sorry, I was scared."

"Yeah, I get it."

"Are you okay?"

She stopped and looked at Ralph for a few moments before speaking. "I always forget you weren't trained for any of this. It must seem surreal." She spoke slowly and with compassion.

"Are you okay?"

"What is most interesting to me is that I've spoken with two dozen of my people in the last ninety minutes, and you're the first to ask me if I am okay." She paused. Just as he was about to ask again she said, "Yes, I am okay. Not great. I just lost a friend and coworker today. Shen was a good man. His wife and child will never know what happened to him. He just won't come home to his family ever again. That's terribly sad, but part of the life we have chosen. A small piece of shrapnel entered and exited my calf. I hope the scars are small. I really like my calves. They are one of the few parts of me that our plastic surgeons never needed to modify. The shooter has been dealt with and you are safe. So I'd call myself okay. How about you?"

"I'm fucking scared out of my mind. But I am okay too. Thank you. Thank you for everything."

"That's something else I am not accustomed to. Someone saying thank you. You are welcome."

"What can you tell me? What just happened?"

"Well, Ralph, what we know right now isn't much. But your silly walk down the stairs probably saved your life. The 'toll collector' who was given your watch suffered what looks like a major heart attack and the watch burned into his skin. That's what Shen was yelling when he ran to the van. You were supposed to die when the defibrillator kicked on in the crowded elevator with many witnesses. But when they lost track of you, they got scared and turned the watch into a small electrical incendiary device. They also had a sniper on the roof to follow the watch's GPS in case the defibrillator failed. That's how they had such an accurate shot, even after we passed seven hundred meters down the road. The sniper was using an AI-controlled weapon with smart bullets. We should be able to find the purchaser of this weapon in the next few hours. Do you want to hear more details, including the gory bits?"

"No. I don't. But I think I have to. I think I need to listen to it all."

"I agree. You need to know in order to make good judgements in the future. My team apprehended and inflicted a non-trivial amount of pain to loosen the lips of the shooter with the expensive weapon. We did the same to the CEO who gave you the watch. Both claimed they were paid large sums of money wired from Middle Eastern banks to play their roles. We confirmed this to be true. Neither of them knew much at all about you or your wife. They knew nothing about the people that hired them. In other words, you were and probably still are a target of a professional hit. Someone wants you taken out. And they'll take enormous international risks to do so. And just so that I scare you a little more, the CEO and shooter didn't die peacefully."

Ralph studied Eva's expression while trying to hold back the bile from reaching his mouth. "I don't approve of those methods, but I appreciate that you've made us safe for the moment."

"Speaking of which, we need to move from this location very soon. We should have new clothes and a few more helping hands within the next fifteen minutes. While this apartment building is secure, and thus far, we've not picked up any potentially threatening chatter from listening to the Vietnamese police radios, we don't want to give your pursuers an easy target. Understood?"

"Yes. I am kind of freaking out, but what can I do to help?"

"You need to think about who and why someone wants you dead. We've double-checked all the players from our last adventure and all of those folks are still licking their wounds. With all the heat we brought to them, and with the surveillance we left behind to keep tabs, we don't think there is anyone who would make this kind of play. It's got to be someone else. With that said, there is one certain someone who has fallen off our radar. Have you heard from McKenna recently?"

"No. Not since that drunken night on the Moscow river." Eva and McKenna had found Ralph a private taxi that would take him back to the Westin. "That was the drunken evening of dancing on the bar with my big hairy ass hanging out of my shredded pants." Ralph smiled and looked down at his current lack of pants. "How about you? He works in your world, not mine."

"I spent another thirty minutes with him, after we paid that Uber driver about 300 dollars to take you back to your hotel. You were a mess." It was her turn to gently rub her bandaged calf. "We made out and fooled around a little bit after you were gone," she said smiling, as if embarrassed by her disclosure.

"You what?!?" Ralph's mouth was agape. "McKenna? Ew."

She laughed heartily. "So good to know you are truly jealous." She adjusted her robe to show another half inch of her long legs. "Both of you aren't much to look at, but in truth, he's an amazing kisser."

"Ew. Gross. Ew. Okay, whatever, but seriously, is that the last time you've communicated with him?"

She smiled. "Jealous, much?"

"Hell yes. I know I have no right to be, but McKenna? You can do so much better than that."

"That's pretty similar to what he said about you when he saw me flirting with you."

"He's a dirty dog." Ralph sulked for a few moments. McKenna had been a friend through thick or thin in college, but his time with various covert agencies had made him less empathetic than Ralph had expected on their last adventure. "But we wouldn't have gotten out of that last one without his help."

"True." Eva got pensive. "But yes, that was the last time we spoke. Whatever happened with the guy that McKenna was working for? The guy working for Roger Phillips of the Z-Prize? Didn't he try to knock you off via a ginger ale on a cross-country flight?"

"Yeah, not sure where he went. He should probably be on the list."

"A list? You think we need a list for the people who want you dead? You're an angel investor, Ralph, not a hit man."

"Six months ago I wouldn't have thought of a single name that might want to do me harm, but since delving slightly into your world, I think there is probably a list."

"All right, I'll find you some paper and you can start your list. My team will investigate."

"Eva?" Ralph paused. "I cannot stop you from following me. But why are you and your team helping me? I desperately don't want to appear to be ungracious, especially after you've just saved my life today, but I'm not ever going to be a member of 'your team.' You understand that, right?"

Ralph had met Eva only six months ago in Israel, and within a few minutes, she had already threatened to kill him. She was publicly an employee of Huawei and, insomuch, also a member of the Intelligence Community for China. After a few harrowing adventures, she and Ralph had agreed to work together to thwart a group who wanted to take over the world by building a weapon of mass persuasion. Ralph wasn't sure where Eva's alliances were, and he wanted to make sure his were well understood.

"I've been wondering when you were going to ask me this question." She made an exaggerated shrug of her shoulders and quickly peered into the four corners of this great room. "Let's just say my bosses have assigned me to you for the foreseeable future. My team believes you aren't a threat to them, and you should be slightly in our debt for services and safety rendered. You tend to stumble into places and situations we want to learn more about so, as you know, I am tasked to play nice, observe carefully, and give you the space you need to progress."

Ralph was certain this room was actively being surveyed. "So you'll protect me when I need it, but only if I'm giving you opportunities to see what I'm seeing, correct?"

"I think that's correct. But it's not like you could stop us from following you. Ninety-five percent of the time you don't even know we're around."

"And how many other people on the globe have this kind of relationship with the government of China?"

"I really wouldn't know."

"Guess for me, please."

"As far as I know, no one. Just you. They purposely don't tell us much. I've asked around to people I trust. No one I've spoken to has ever heard of this type of deal."

"And what if I decide not to play nice?"

Eva looked down, tucked her legs under herself, and pulled her robe back over her legs. "I honestly don't know. My bosses would probably want me to make great threats about that possibility, but I don't think threats motivate you." She rolled her eyes and smiled.

"I've not invested any of the money your bosses somehow put into my VC fund. I'm not entirely sure how your team coerced my lawyers into giving your bosses the necessary paperwork to make that enormous investment. It just sort of showed up one day in Clam Pie VC's bank accounts."

"Obviously my team thinks you will make fine investments and returns for them."

"And if I don't? Or if I don't acknowledge the strings that may or may not be assumed to be attached?"

"I don't think my bosses believe you'd be motivated by those so-called strings attached via those investment funds. You're already a wealthy man. So maybe, if you aren't motivated by threats, or money, or by my shapely figure—damn you—then maybe you'd be motivated by more altruistic causes. And just to be clear, my people aren't afraid of that particular motivator as much as you might think."

"Okay. That helps. You know I don't. …"

A quick knock and the front door swung open. In a second and a few tenths, Eva had vaulted on top of Ralph and had a gun pointed at the door. One of Eva's team announced in Mandarin some code words and Eva lowered her weapon. The team walked in carrying some bags.

"Where did you have the gun?" Ralph was flummoxed. "You can't hide a gun and a holster under that tiny terrycloth robe. It's not possible."

"Delighted you noticed. But the weapon was between the cushions in the couch we've been sitting on. Now go with him and put on those clothes. He's also going to add some coloring to your 'old man's' gray hair. We need to get out of here."

Ralph and Eva split into different rooms to get ready. Within five minutes, a brown-haired Ralph met a blond-wigged Eva in the penthouse's lobby.

"Wow. You look different."

"That's the point, Ralph. We need to get out the country without being noticed. We've both got tiny shims in our shoes, so we'll walk differently. We'll be okay, as my team will keep us safe until we get to the airport."

They were walking downstairs when Ralph tripped on an uneven step. His mini-stumble sent him into one of Eva's team. The man scowled at Ralph's inadvertent bump. His expression changed almost immediately to a forced smile. The misstep happened so quickly, Ralph was certain he and the man were the only ones to notice.

In a new big BMW sedan, with doors that felt like they weighed three times more than they should, Ralph was placed in the backseat next to a wiry older man in a bad suit. Eva was up front next to the driver, the same man who had given Ralph the forced smile. They left the safe house, with three identical BMWs following them. Within sixty seconds, the four cars had each gone in different routes. The driver was trying his best to coax the heavy car to dance through a number of crowded intersections. After a tense ten minutes, the driver told his passengers that they were away safely, with no tails, and would be at the airport in thirty minutes.

Everyone had been very quiet. When Ralph spoke, the car's tension seemed to increase. "Eva? That list we spoke of?"

"Sorry. I forgot to get you some paper. Maybe there will be some on the plane."

"I don't think we're going to need the list. I think there can only be one organization that could have the wherewithal for this attempt on our lives."

"Don't keep us in suspense. Who?"

"Yours."

The silence was thick. For twenty seconds, no one moved. No one breathed.

"That's bullshit, Ralph, and your accusation is really inappropriate and hurtful." She didn't look over her shoulder at him. Her eyes were only focused on the driver. "You owe us an apology, you asshole. How many times do we have to save your pitiful life?"

"Eva, I'm so very sorry, but I'm fucking certain of it."

"Stop the car!" yelled a furious Eva.

The driver, going over 150 KPH, hit the brakes hard. In a fluid movement, he pulled a weapon from his shoulder holster and fired. So did Eva. The two weapons sounded like thunder had struck in the armored car.

Ralph wasn't a fast man but undid his seatbelt and used the negative momentum of the heavy braking to propel himself into the lap of the wiry man. The driver's bullet had lodged itself into the polycarbonate window about four inches from where Ralph's head had been three seconds prior. Eva's bullet had misshapen the driver's head with a decidedly Picasso influence. She had one hand on her weapon and the other on the steering wheel. The car was traveling only on momentum and, due to his weight, had dramatically slowed.

The wiry man was pinned beneath Ralph's lumberjack-like girth. He didn't move. His palms were facing Eva's weapon. He said in Mandarin, "I am not a threat, Niece."

"Get off him, Ralph."

Ralph slid off and buckled his seat belt.

The wiry man said in English, "Thank you, Ralph." He switched to Mandarin. "I can drive once we get this scum into the trunk. I can move the body alone, but it'd probably be faster if we all did so. If I were you, Niece, I'd keep the gun trained on me while this old water buffalo and I wrestle the body into the trunk. Is it a plan?"

"Uncle, we will follow your plan. And be aware, the old water buffalo speaks passable Mandarin." Eva used the honorific "uncle" not to convey a familial relationship, but to tell Ralph that she trusted the wiry man.

It was Ralph's turn to roll his eyes. At 20 KPH, she applied the handbrake and the car came to a standstill in the breakdown lane. "Now. We move now."

The three doors opened at her command. Within twenty seconds, with Ralph carrying the legs, the body was in the truck. Eva never pointed her weapon away from the wiry man's chest. Soon the man with the bad suit was driving to the airport.

"How did you know?" Eva asked.

Ralph paused, then spoke slowly. "I wasn't sure I knew until I made the accusation. There are only two countries in the world that have developed the granularity in GPS to get under one-meter resolution. China and the US. Plain-old GPS has three-meter resolution. That smart gun was fired at over 700 meters and took out Shen's hand as it covered his head. The watch was in Shen's hand. And the U.S. and its intel teams still aren't welcome in Vietnam. Hence the U.S. wouldn't have been able to make these kinds of logistical arrangements in Vietnam. Yet the Chinese move around this country freely. And in addition, the email invite to meet the entrepreneur smartwatch maker came only three days ago, from a ZTE server IP address. Being a geek, I check that sort of thing to ensure I'm not wasting my time. And since the IP address came from a ZTE box, and most developed countries, including the U.S., won't use ZTE servers due to known surveillance concerns, the only logical player was your own team. Huawei would most certainly use ZTE servers, just to obfuscate the originator. Your team was the only real option. And when I made the accusation, the man now in the trunk was straining to keep his breathing even."

"Fuck." It was obvious Eva was silently trying to punch holes in Ralph's theory. "The next question is even more difficult. If you're correct, then are we the rogue element, or are they?"

"Either way, I'm not feeling great about our next move." He looked at Eva with vulnerability. "I'm significantly frightened."

"I understand. Professionals are, after all, trying to kill you."

"Can... I stay with you?"

Eva smiled. "Ralph you old romantic. You have no idea how long I've wanted to hear you say those words, but I've got to get to my superiors to figure this out. And if my superiors are the ones trying to kill you, then it doesn't really make sense for me to bring you along, now does it? I'm heading to Beijing when we get to the airport. And I'm going to say something you might not like: Get on a plane, and don't tell us where you're going."

Ralph started to laugh. A very nervous laugh. "Ahh, well, I don't know if that makes sense, Eva. Weren't you supposed to be protecting me? If so, then I should stay with you. At least until we figure out what's going on." He couldn't believe he actually said those words. He hated to be dependent on anyone. Especially Eva.

"Sorry, Ralph, but you're not thinking right. I think it's best if we split up. For now. I'll send you an email when I learn more from my side. Until then, I need you to act as if nothing happened."

Ralph contemplated the possibility of being able to act normally when he knew that highly sophisticated people were trying to kill him with heart-attack-inducing watches and smart bullets. He quickly calculated that his chances were slim.

They pulled up to International departures. Ralph jumped out quickly. He had no bags. His passport and wallet were his only possessions. He leaned against the passenger door, keeping his head down. Eva rolled down her window. Ralph leaned in and kissed her forehead. "Thanks for saving my life... again. Stay safe."

She nodded. "You too. I'll be in touch just as soon as I can. Get yourself on a flight within forty-five minutes. Then I'll catch my own. Okay?"

"Okay. And then, if I'm in trouble, how will I find you again?"

"I'll find you, Ralph. I always do."

Her facial expression was a mix of determination and sadness. She wouldn't look at him, again staring only at the driver. Her gun hadn't moved an iota. Ralph took his cue and ran. After going through the revolving doors, he turned back. They were already gone.

Made in the USA
Middletown, DE
26 March 2020